Chef Yasmina

AND THE
POTATO PANIC

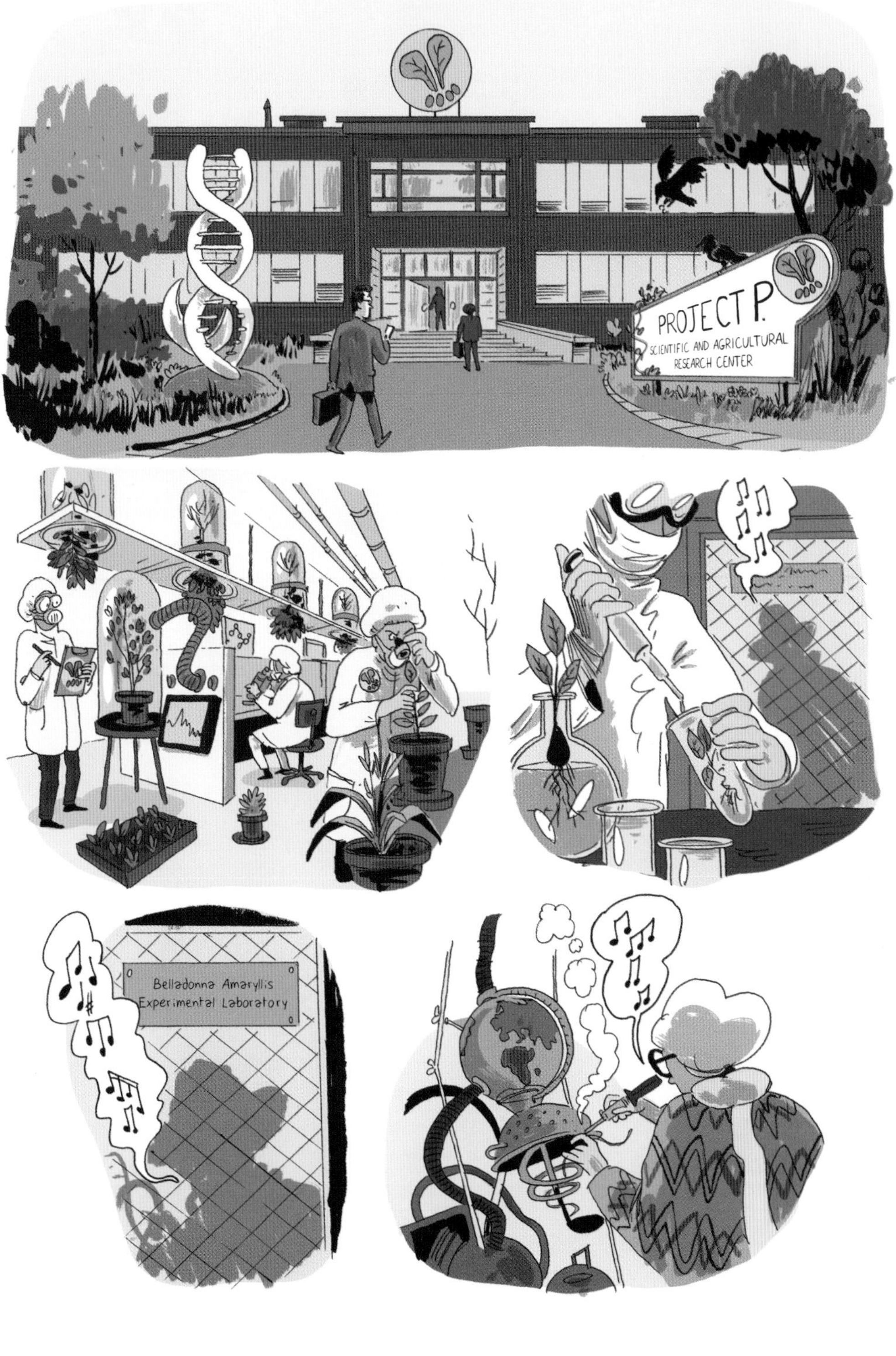
PROJECT P.
SCIENTIFIC AND AGRICULTURAL RESEARCH CENTER
Belladonna Amaryllis Experimental Laboratory

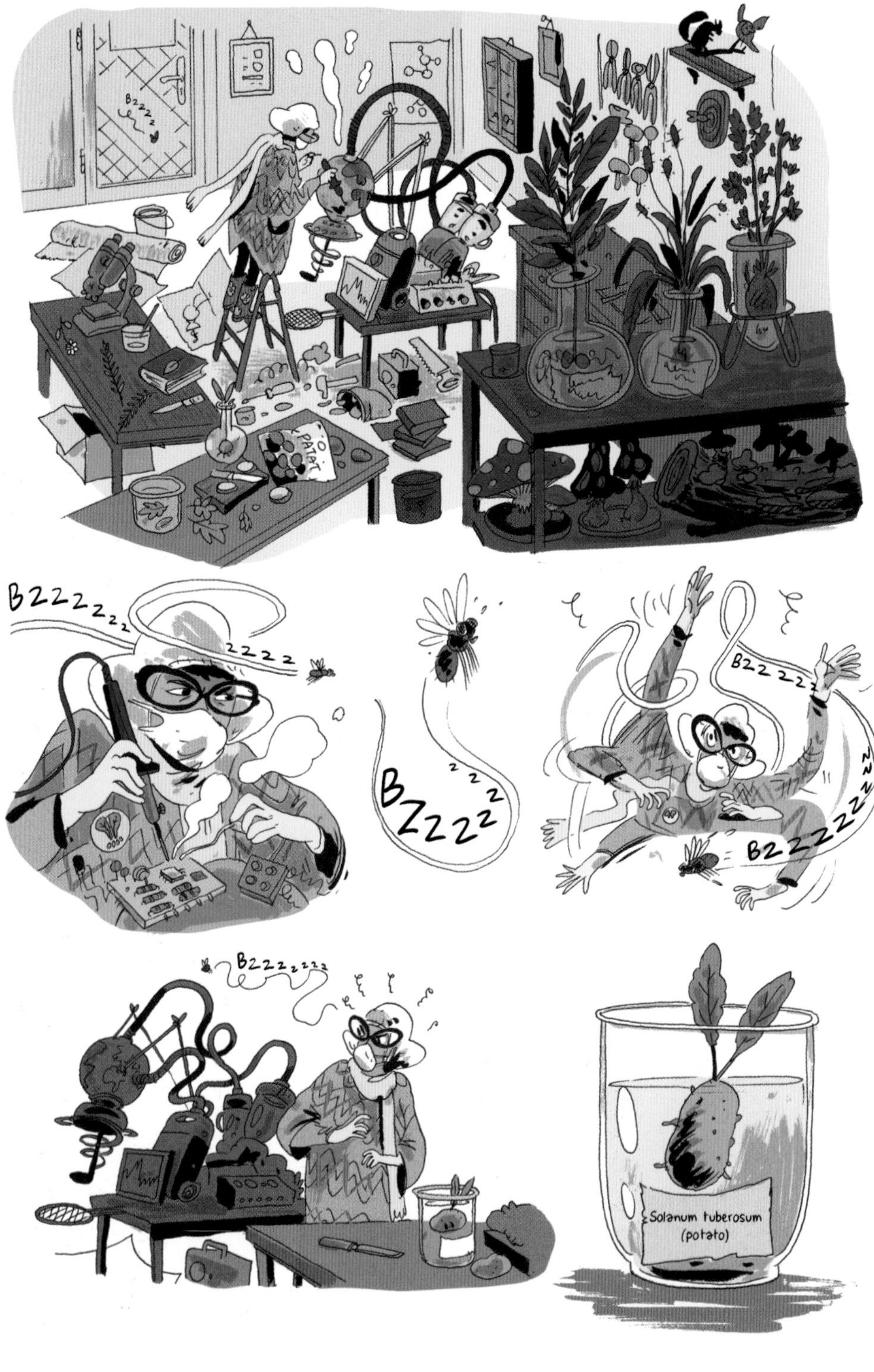
PATAT
BZZZZzzz
zzzz
BZZZZZ
BZZZZZZ
BZZZZZZZZZ
Bzzzzzzz
Solanum tuberosum
(potato)

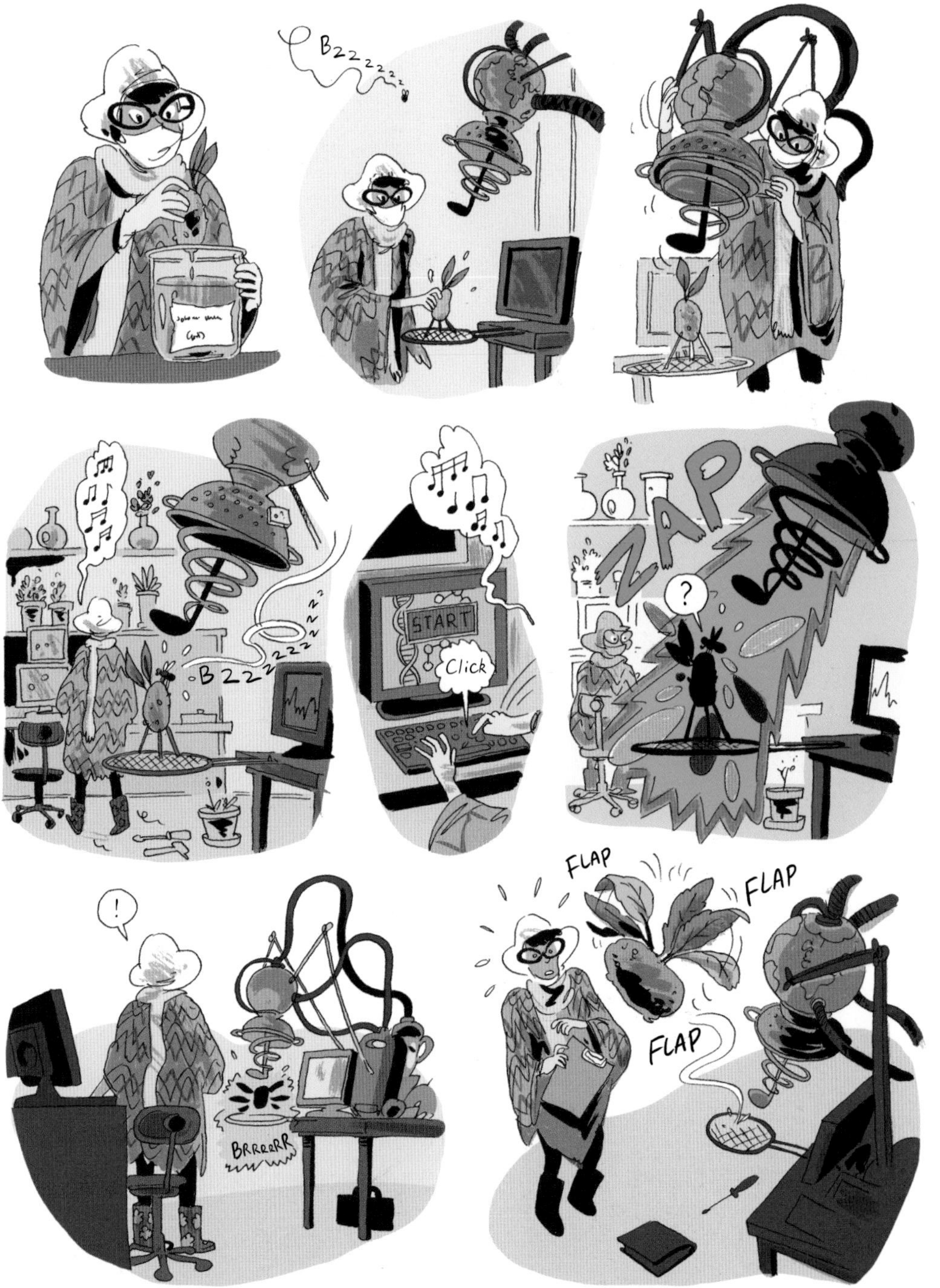

Bzzzzzzz
Bzzzzzzzz
START
Click
ZAP
?
!
BRRRRRR
FLAP
FLAP
FLAP

Chef Yasmina

AND THE
POTATO PANIC

WAUTER MANNAERT

First Second
New York

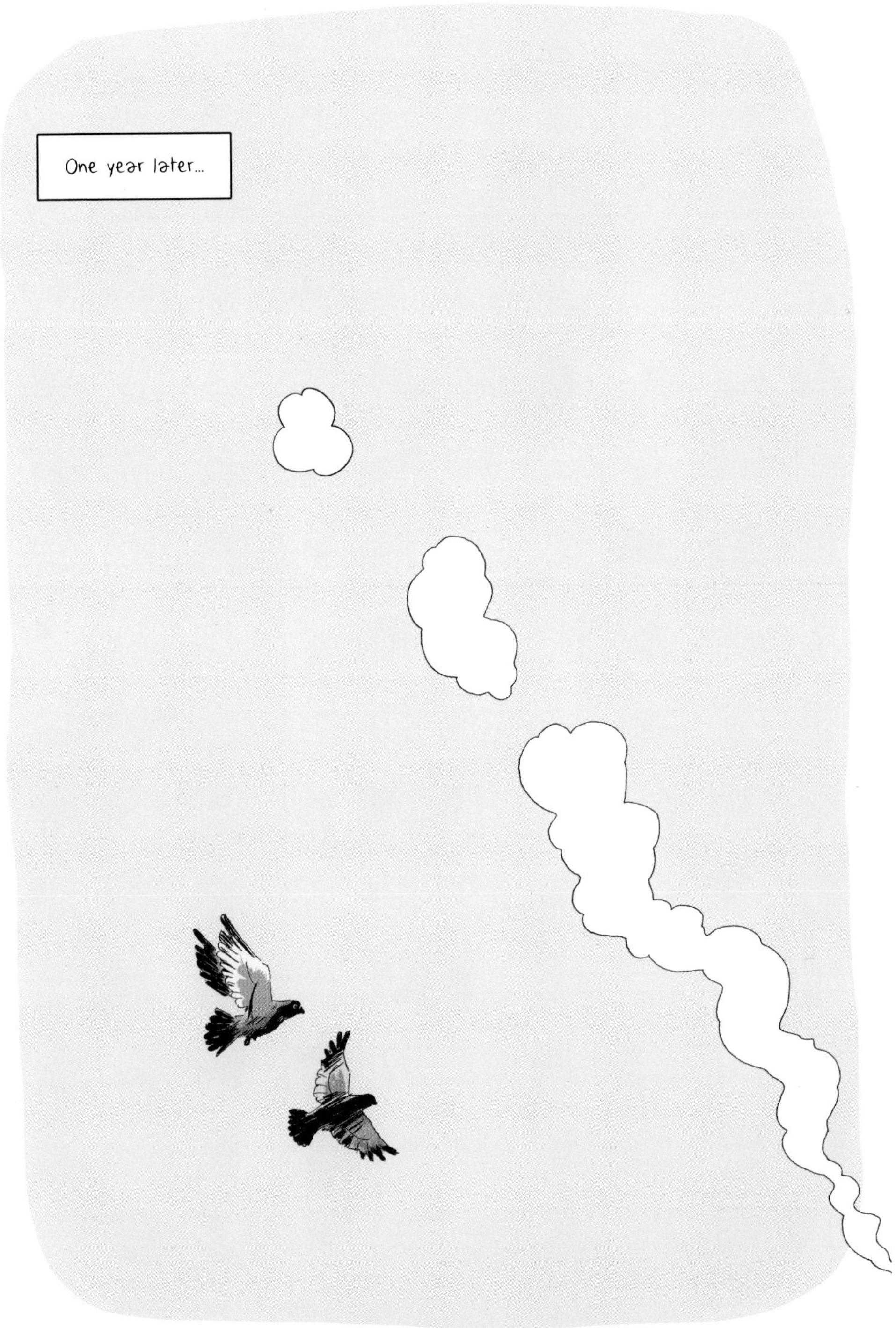
One year later...

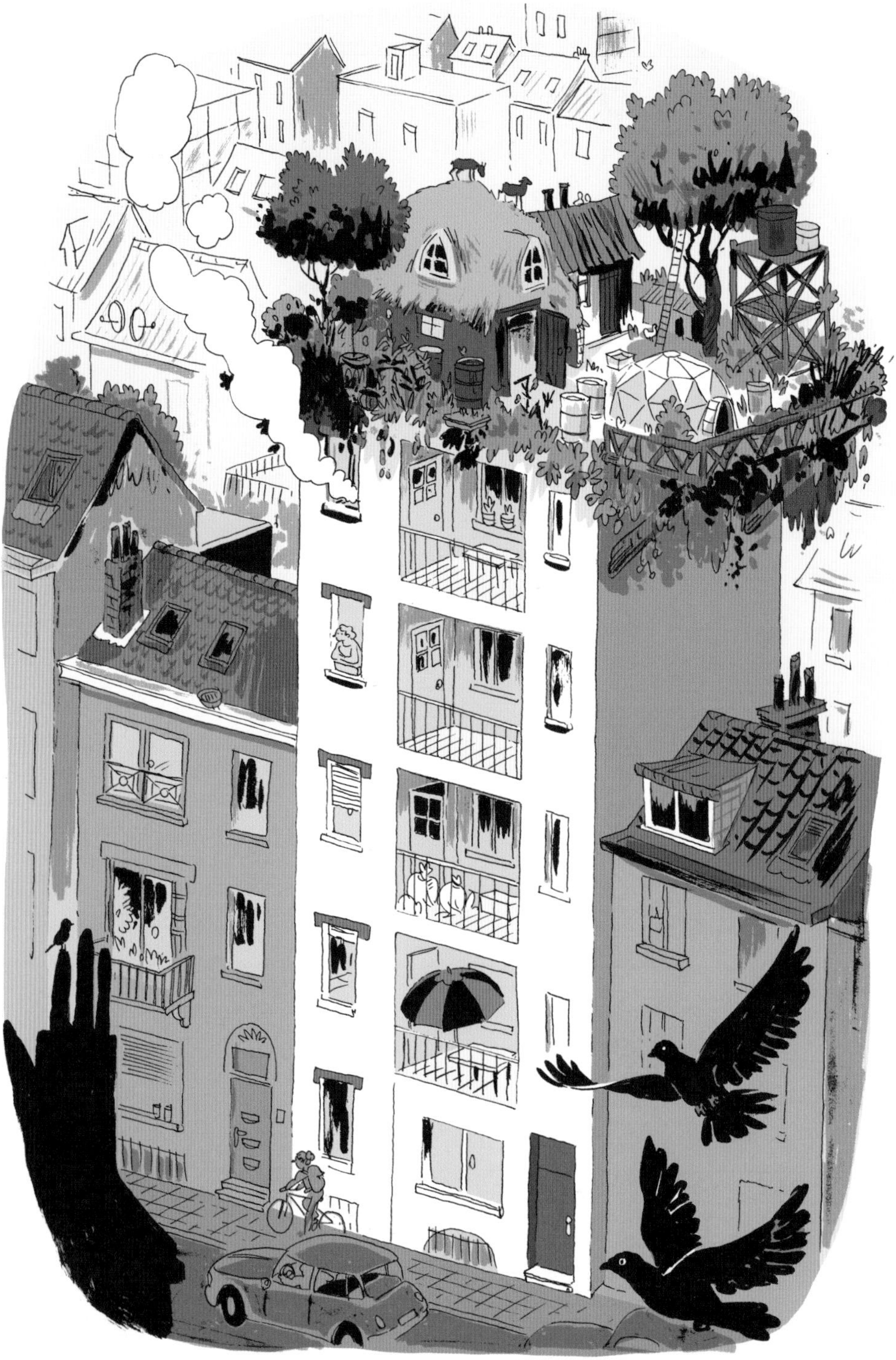

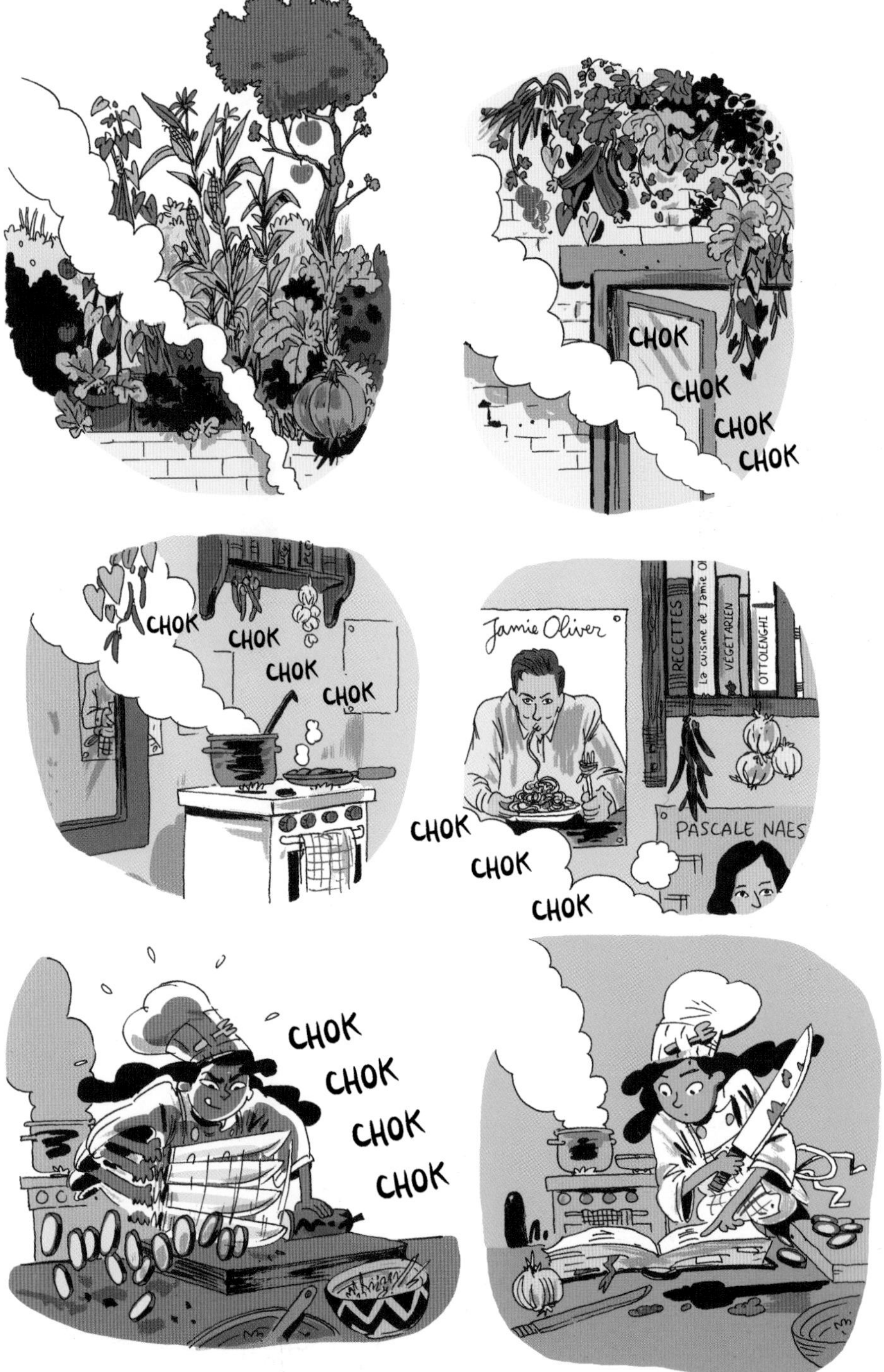
CHOK
CHOK
CHOK
CHOK
CHOK
CHOK
CHOK
CHOK
Jamie Oliver
RECETTES
La cuisine de Jamie Oliver
VÉGÉTARIEN
OTTOLENGHI
CHOK
CHOK
CHOK
PASCALE NAES
CHOK
CHOK
CHOK
CHOK

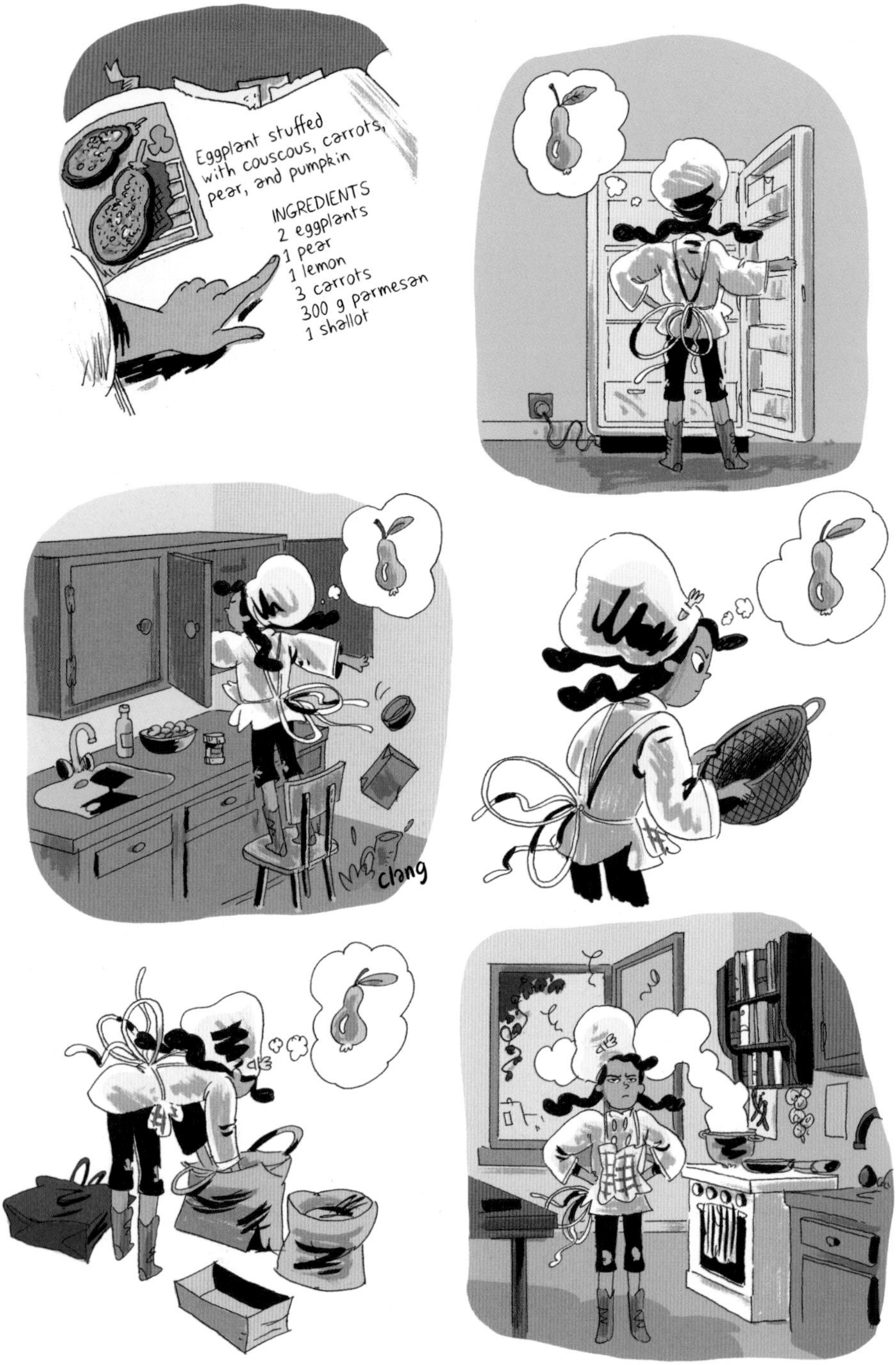
Eggplant stuffed with couscous, carrots, pear, and pumpkin
INGREDIENTS
2 eggplants
1 pear
1 lemon
3 carrots
300 g parmesan
1 shallot
clang

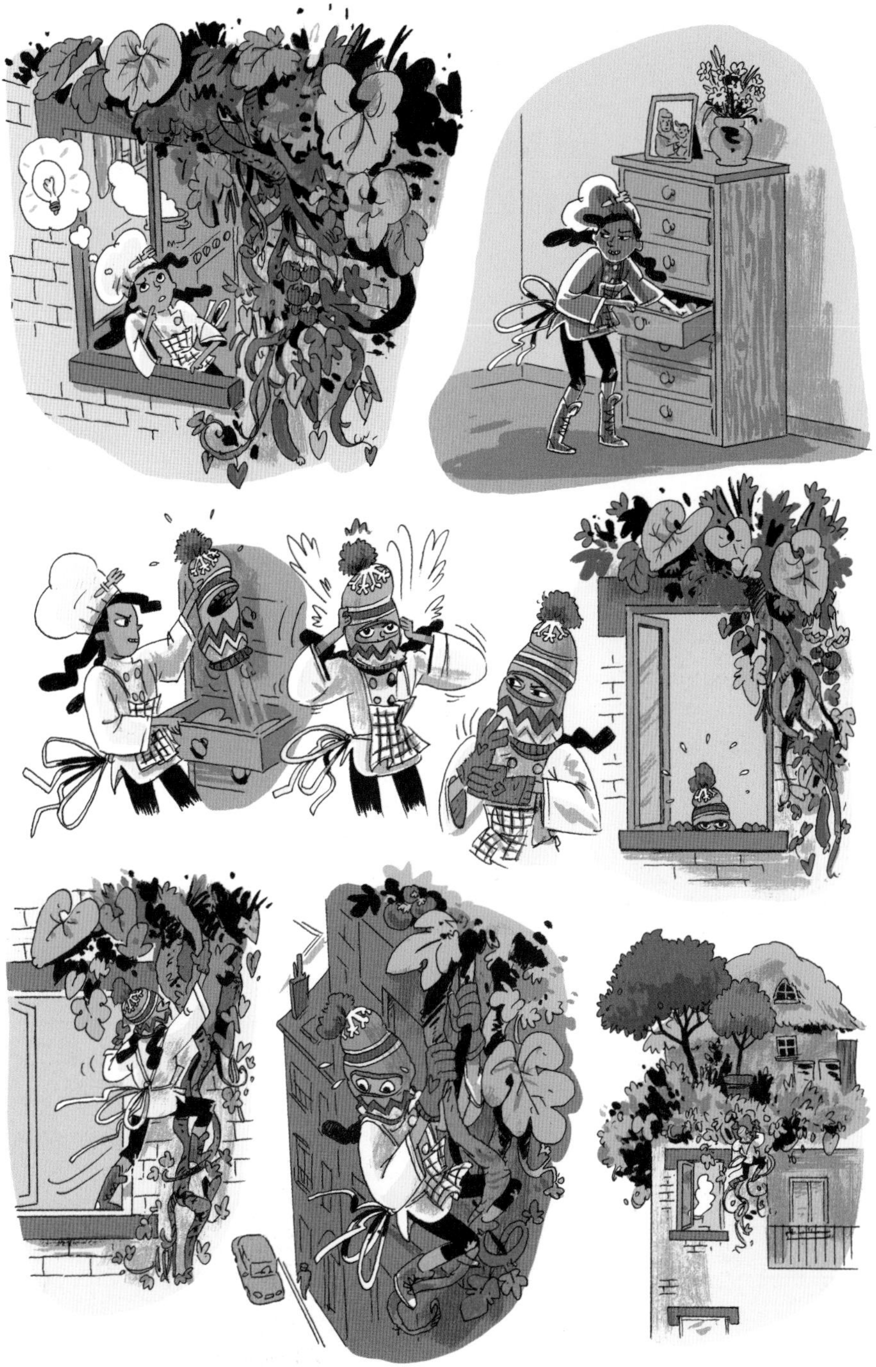

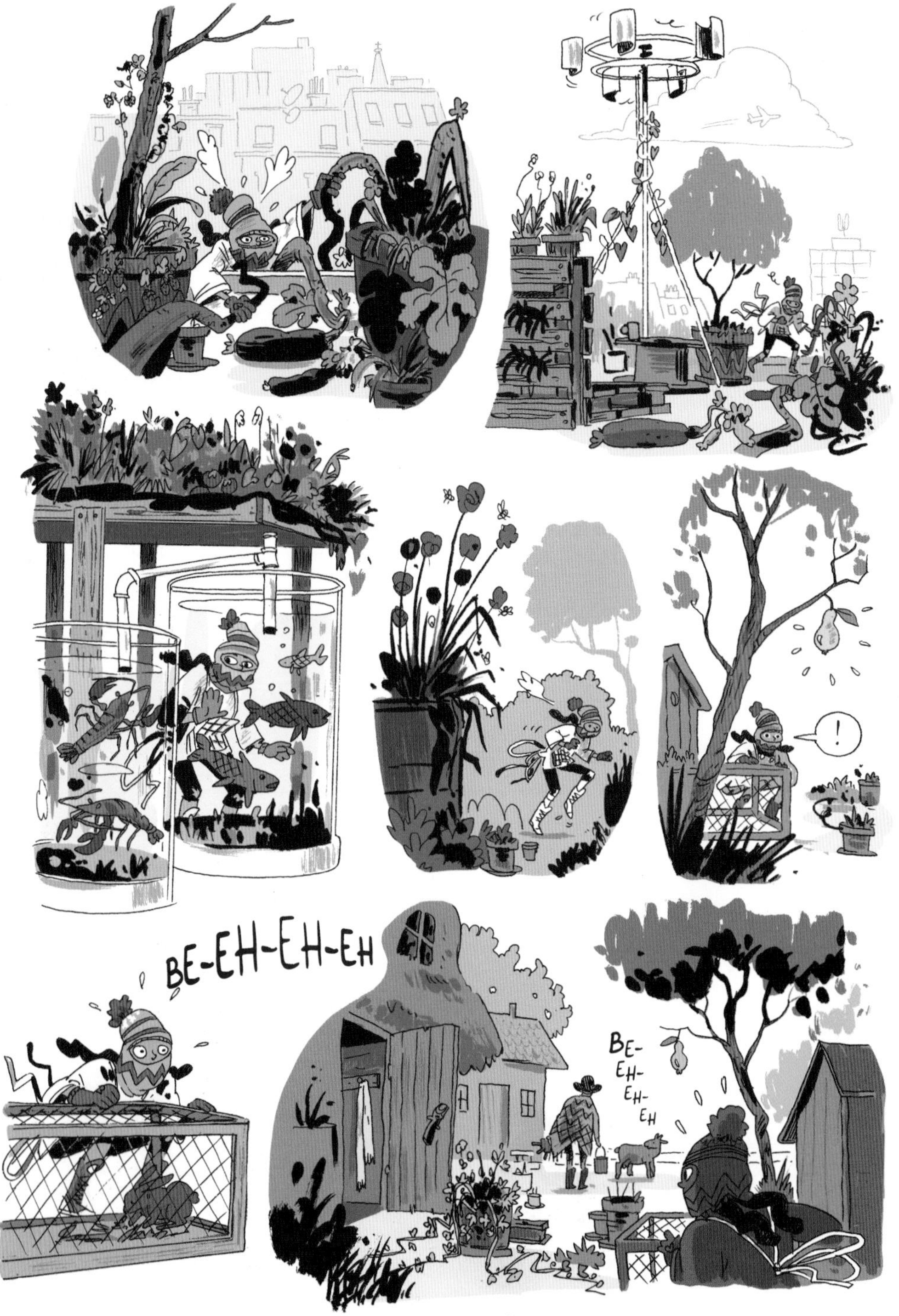
!
BE-EH-EH-EH
BE-EH-EH-EH

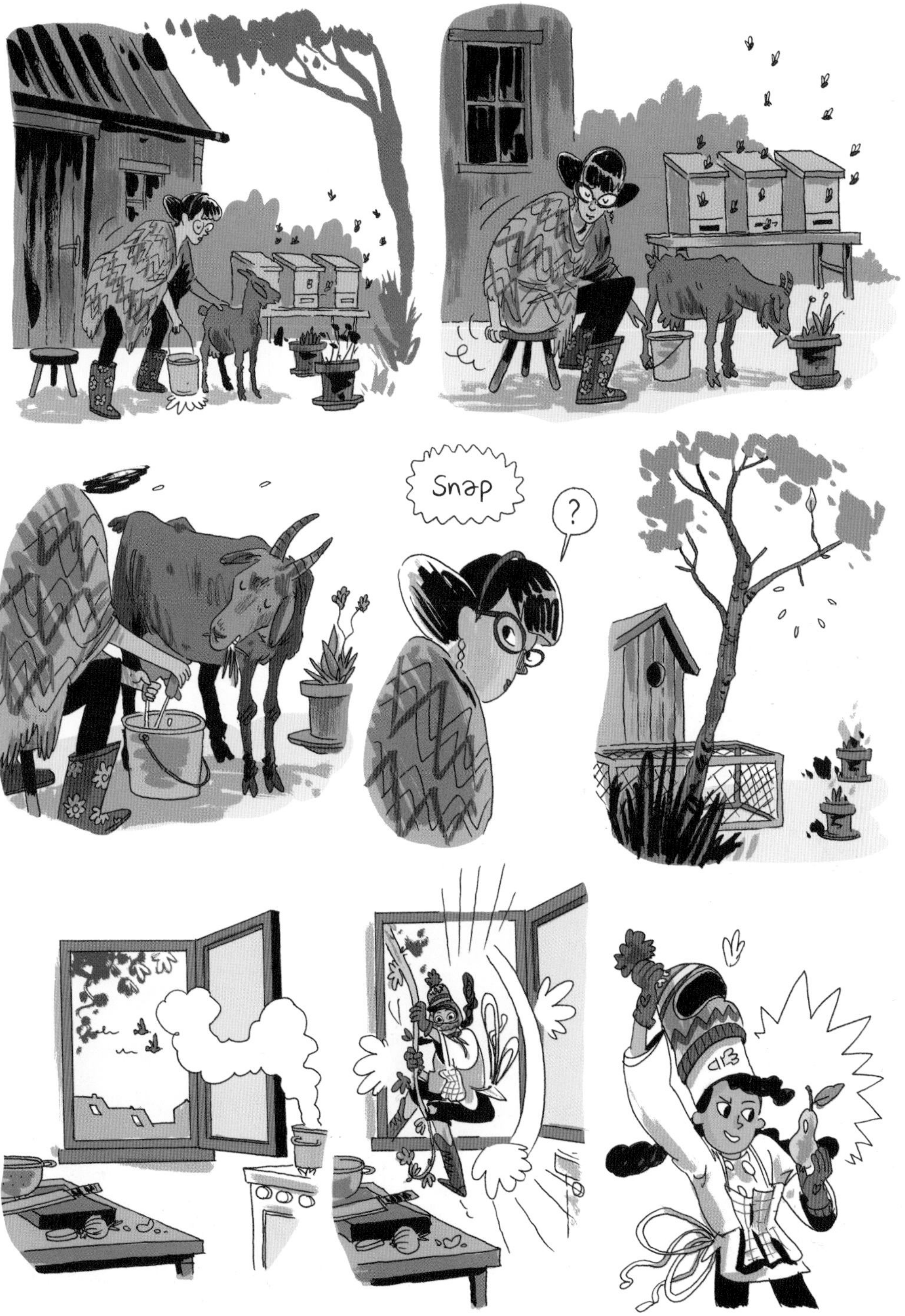
Snap
?

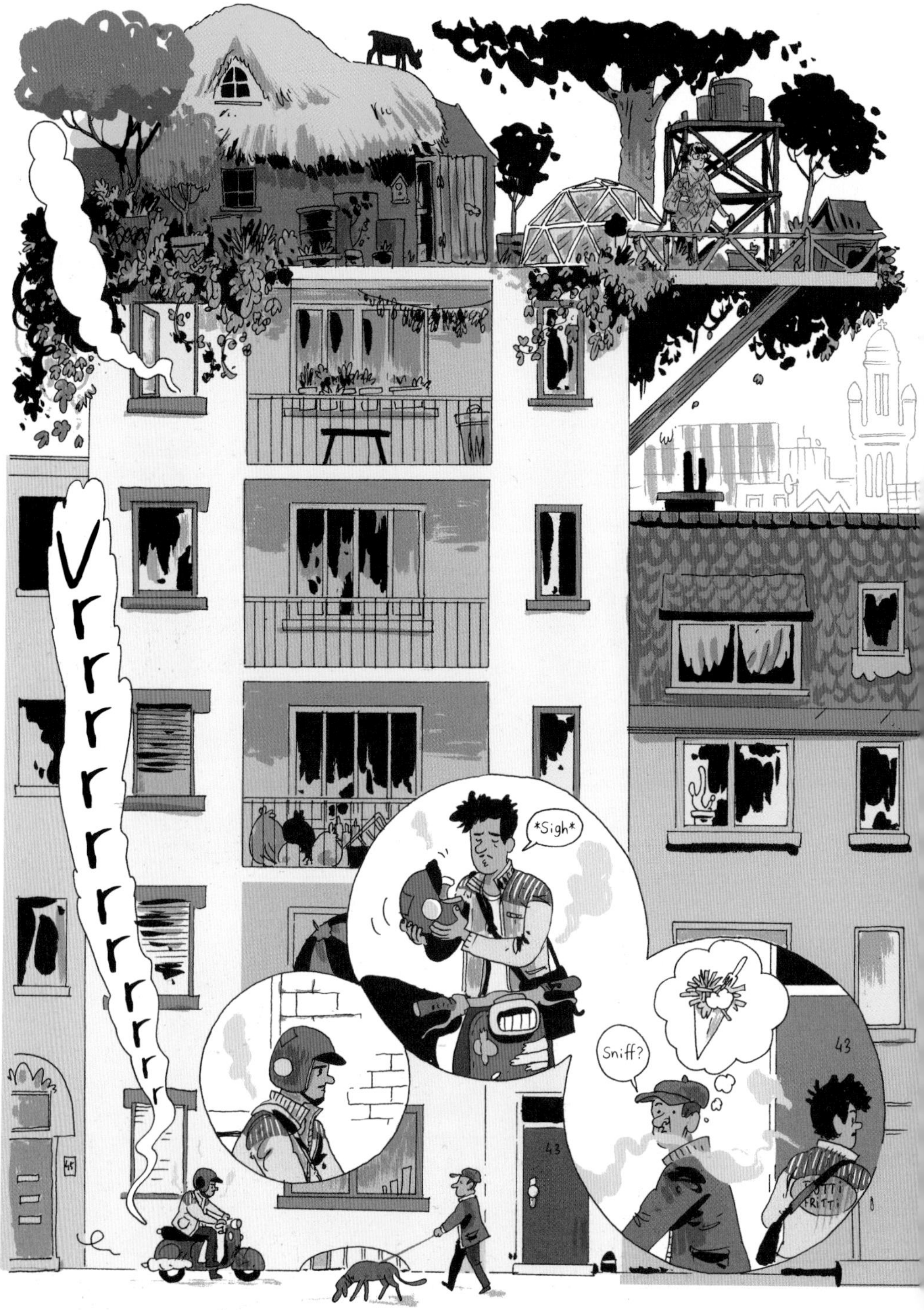
Vrrrrrrrrrrrr
Sigh
Sniff?
43
45
TUTTI FRITTI

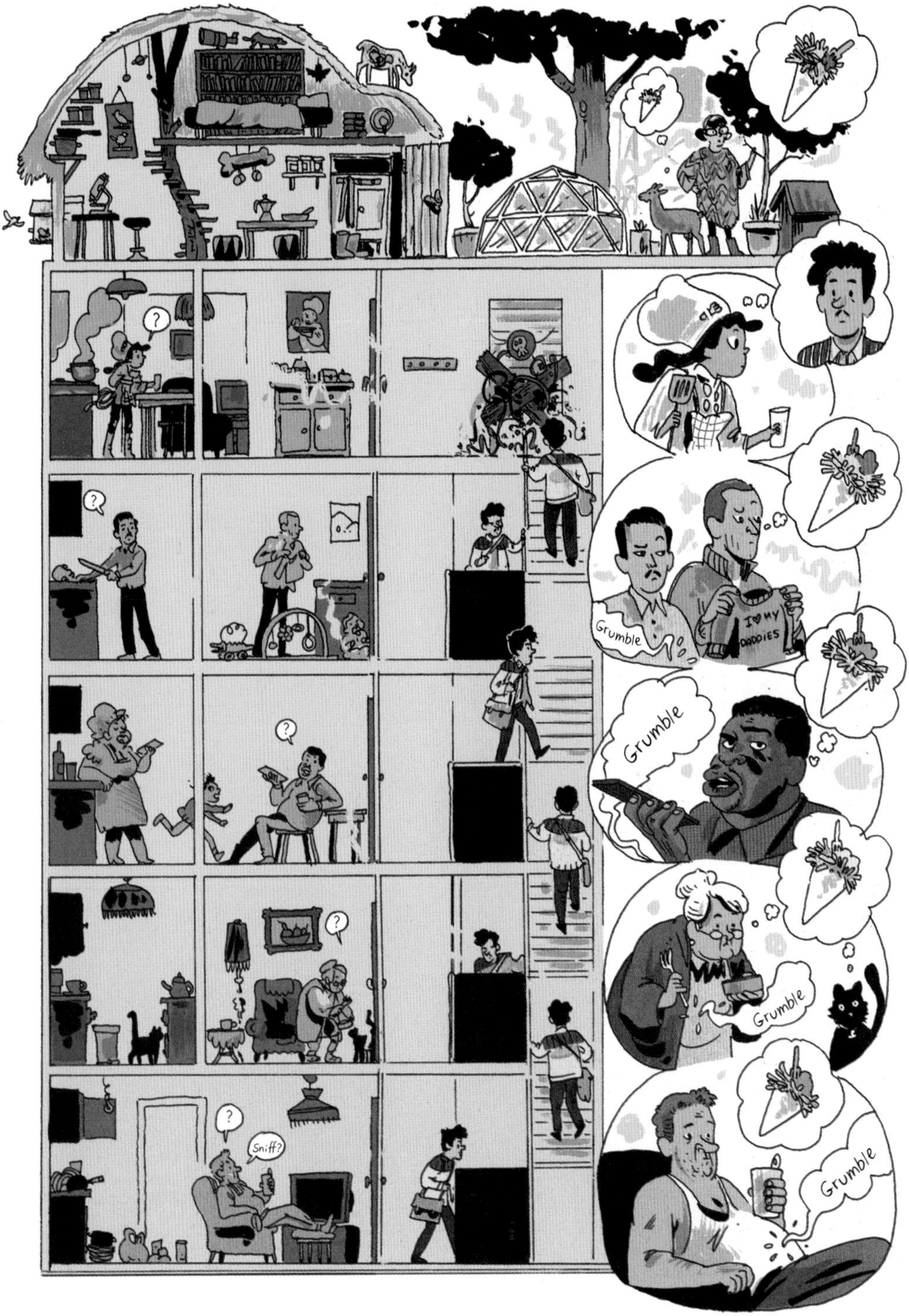
?
?
?
?
?
Sniff?
Grumble
I ♥ MY DADDIES
Grumble
Grumble
Grumble

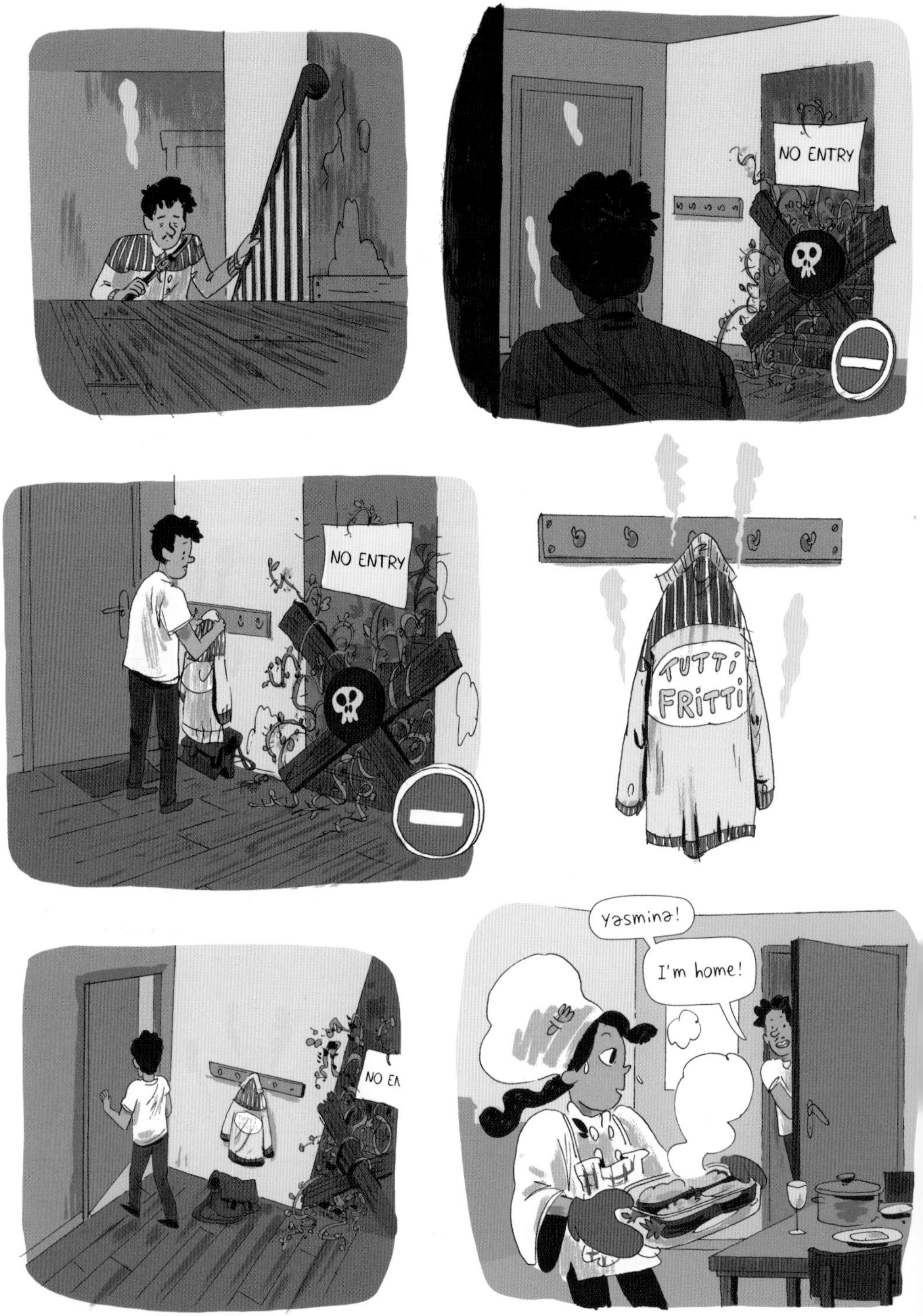
NO ENTRY
NO ENTRY
TUTTI FRITTI
Yasmina!
I'm home!

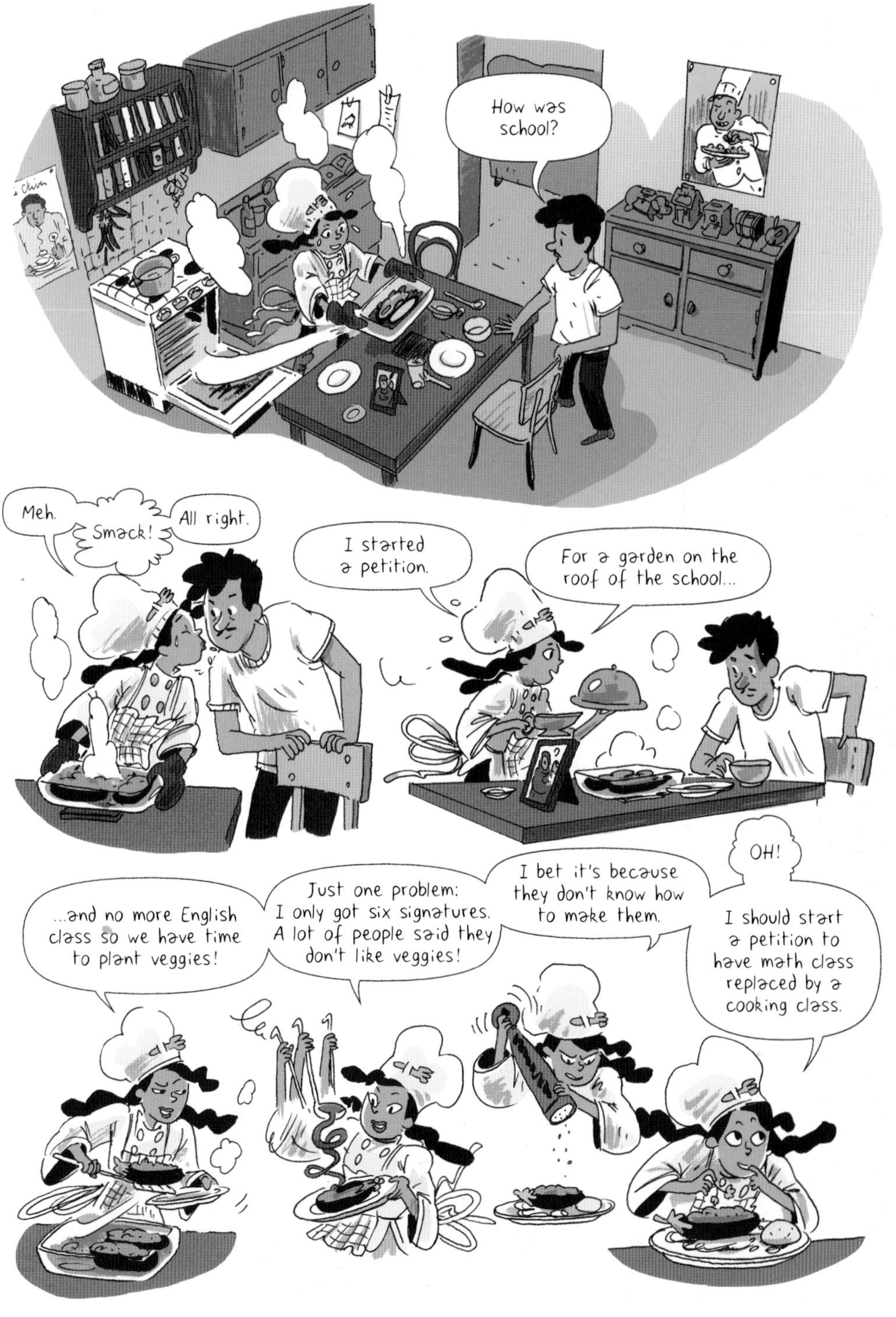
How was school?
Meh.
Smack!
All right.
I started a petition.
For a garden on the roof of the school...
...and no more English class so we have time to plant veggies!
Just one problem: I only got six signatures. A lot of people said they don't like veggies!
I bet it's because they don't know how to make them.
OH!
I should start a petition to have math class replaced by a cooking class.

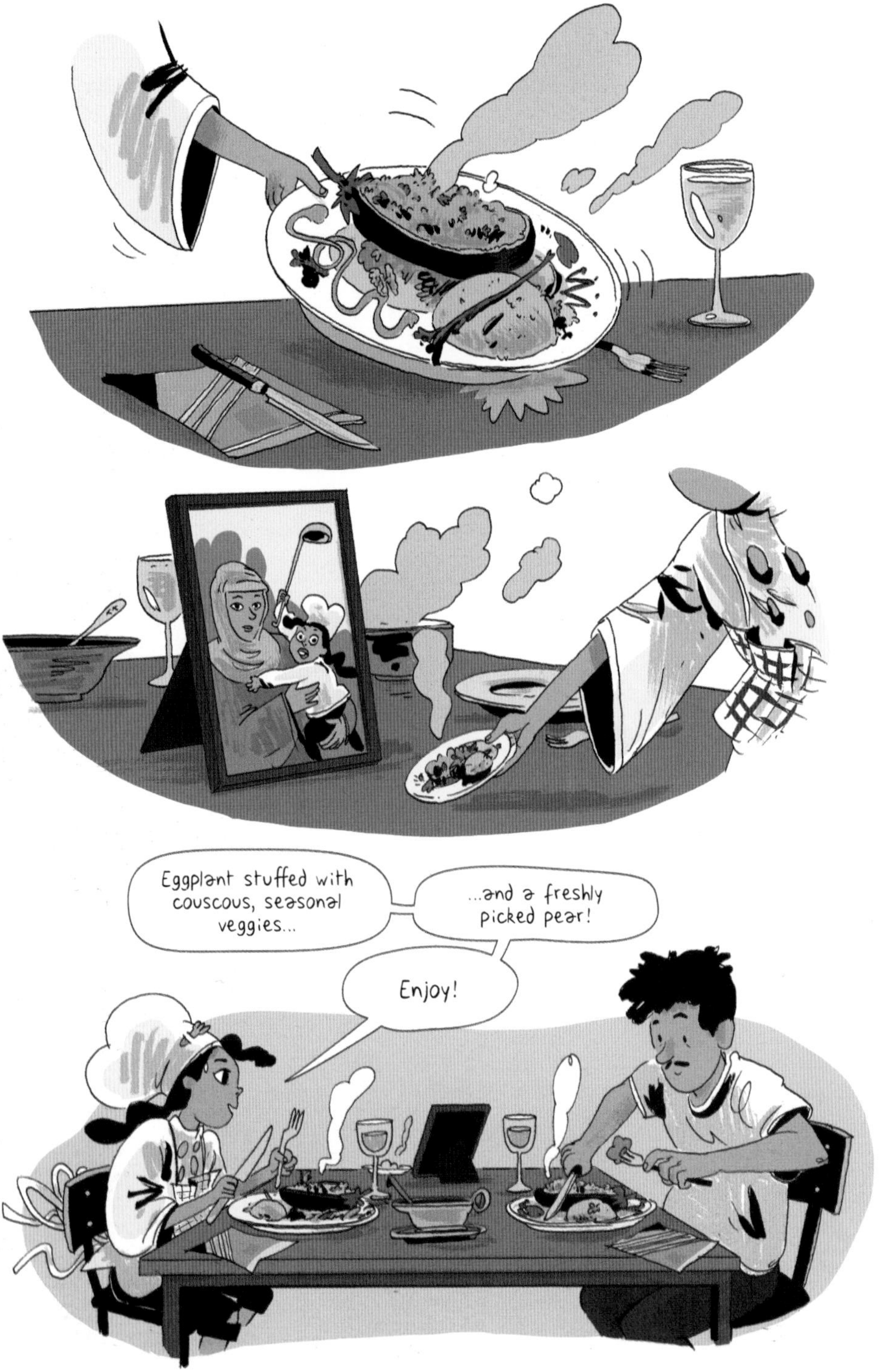
Eggplant stuffed with couscous, seasonal veggies...
...and a freshly picked pear!
Enjoy!

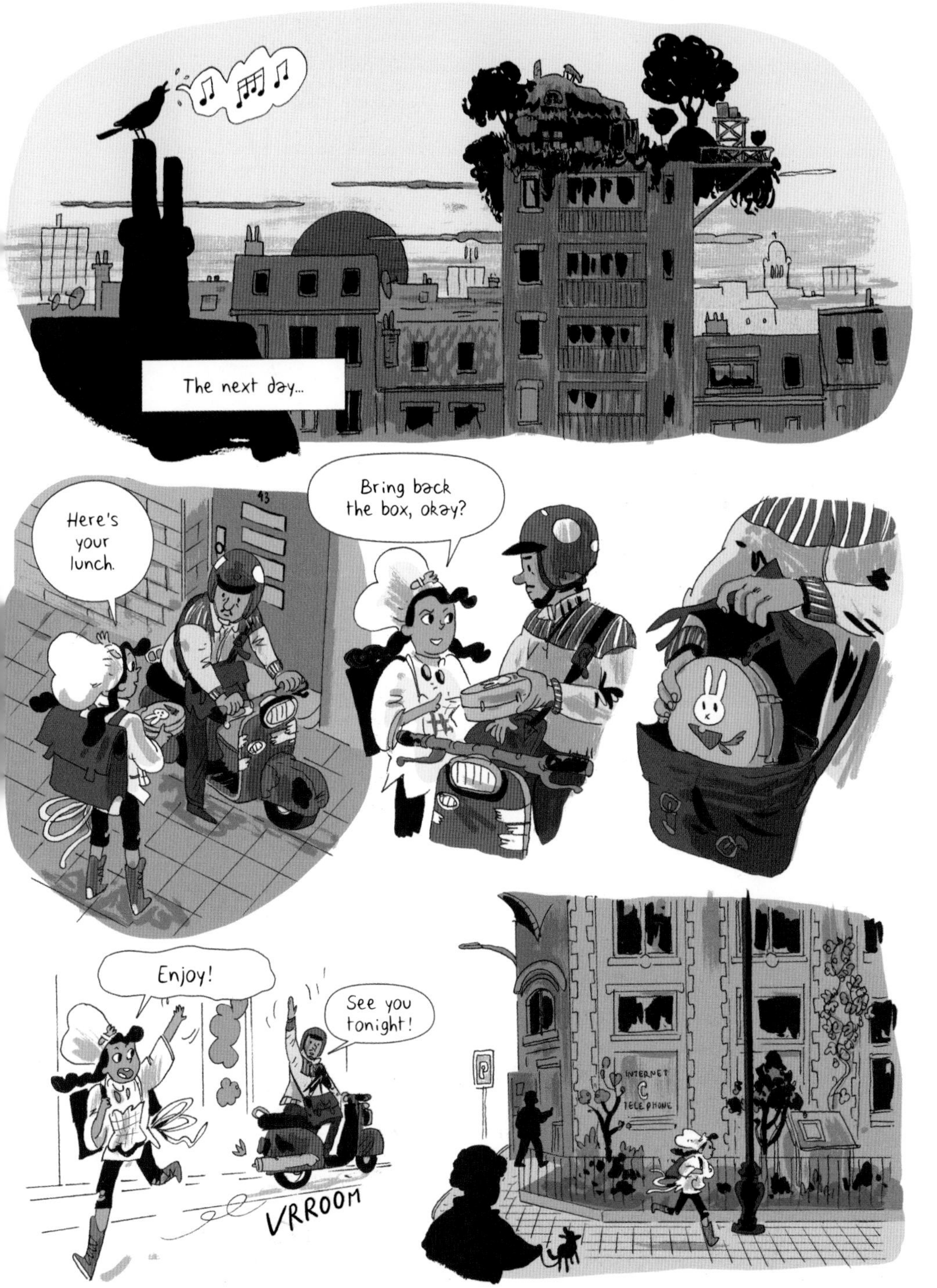
The next day...
Here's your lunch.
Bring back the box, okay?
Enjoy!
See you tonight!
VRROOM
INTERNET
TELEPHONE

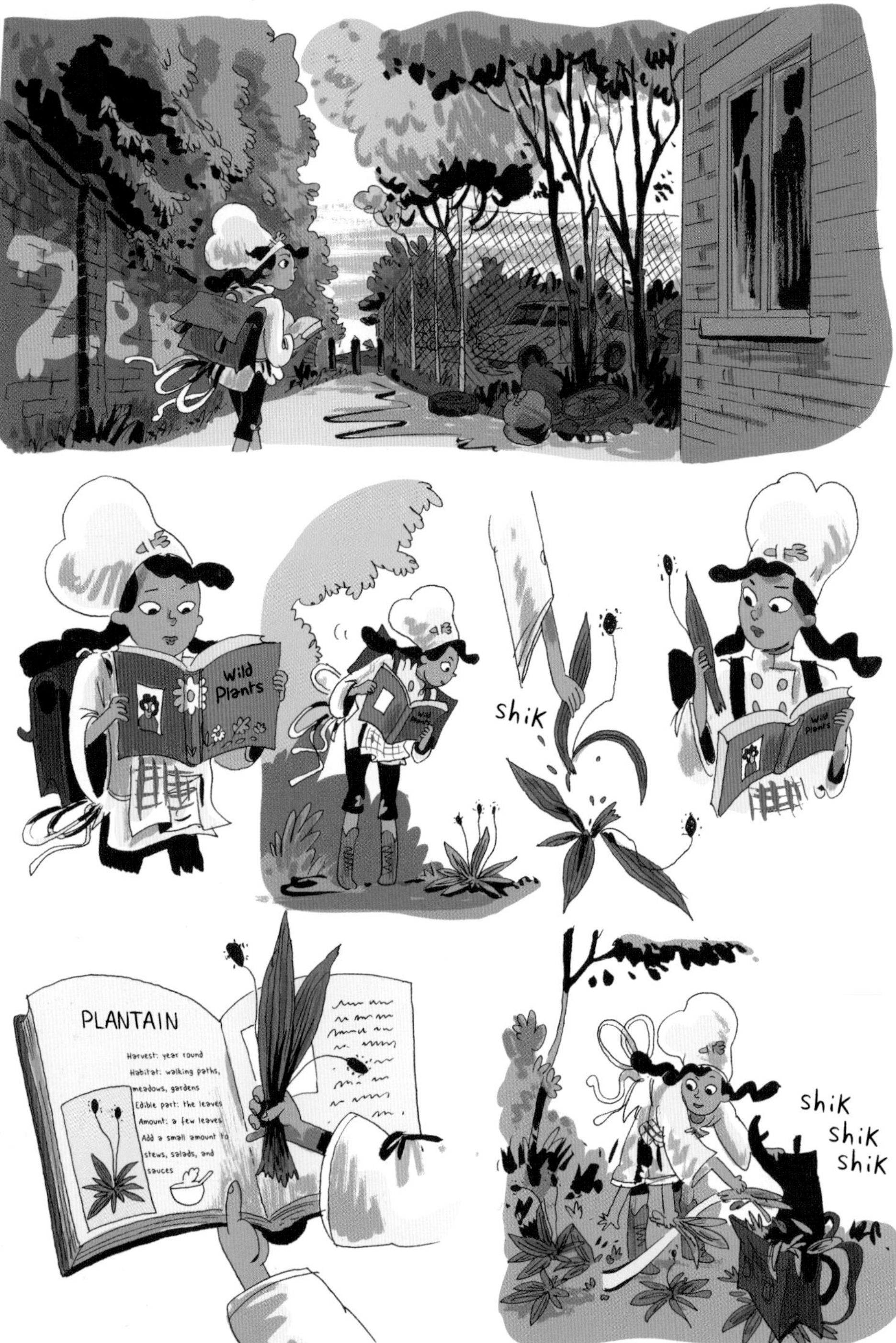
Wild Plants
shik
Wild Plants
PLANTAIN
Harvest: year round
Habitat: walking paths, meadows, gardens
Edible part: the leaves
Amount: a few leaves
Add a small amount to stews, salads, and sauces
shik
shik
shik

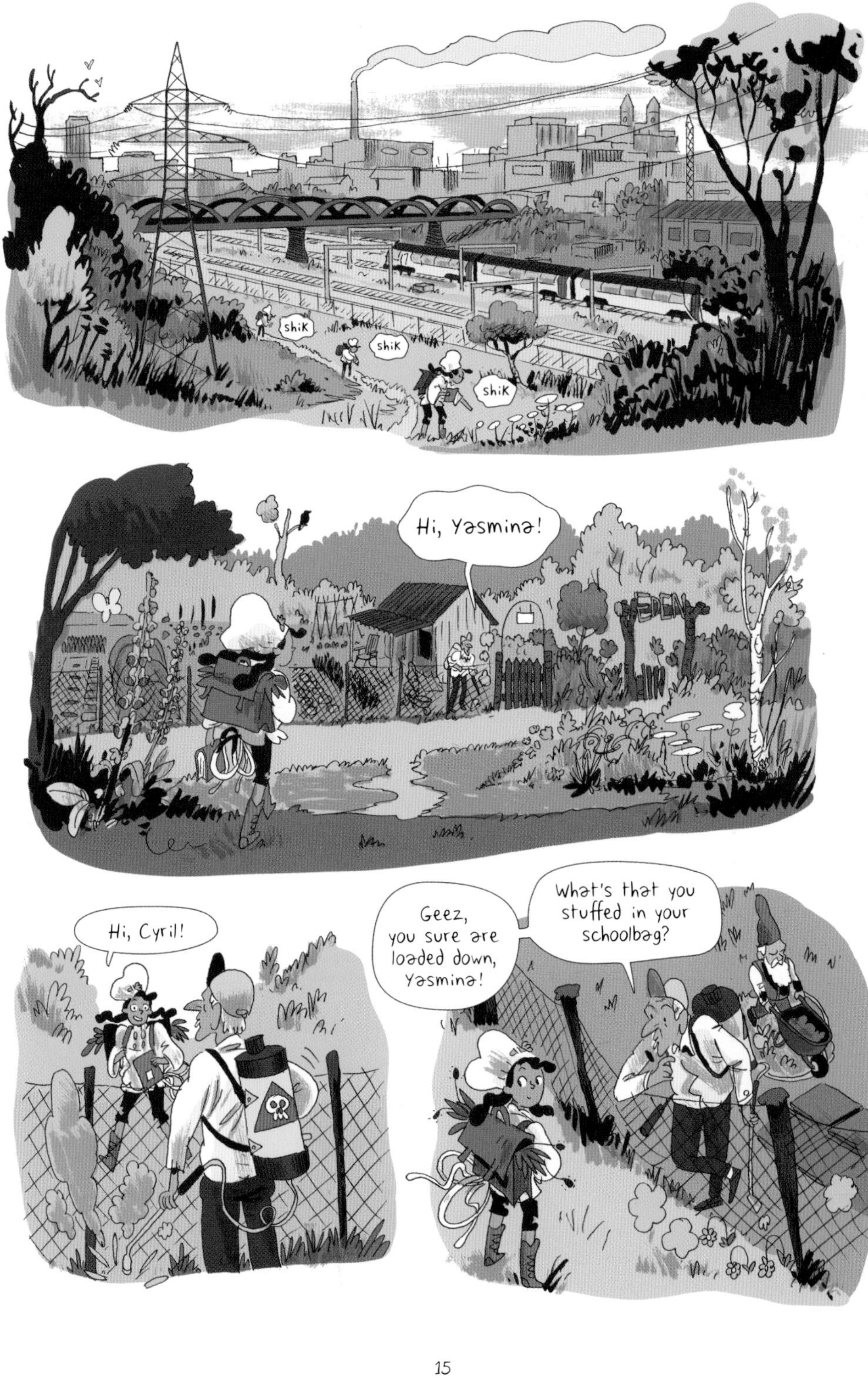
shiK
shiK
shiK
Hi, Yasmina!
EDEN
Hi, Cyril!
Geez, you sure are loaded down, Yasmina!
What's that you stuffed in your schoolbag?

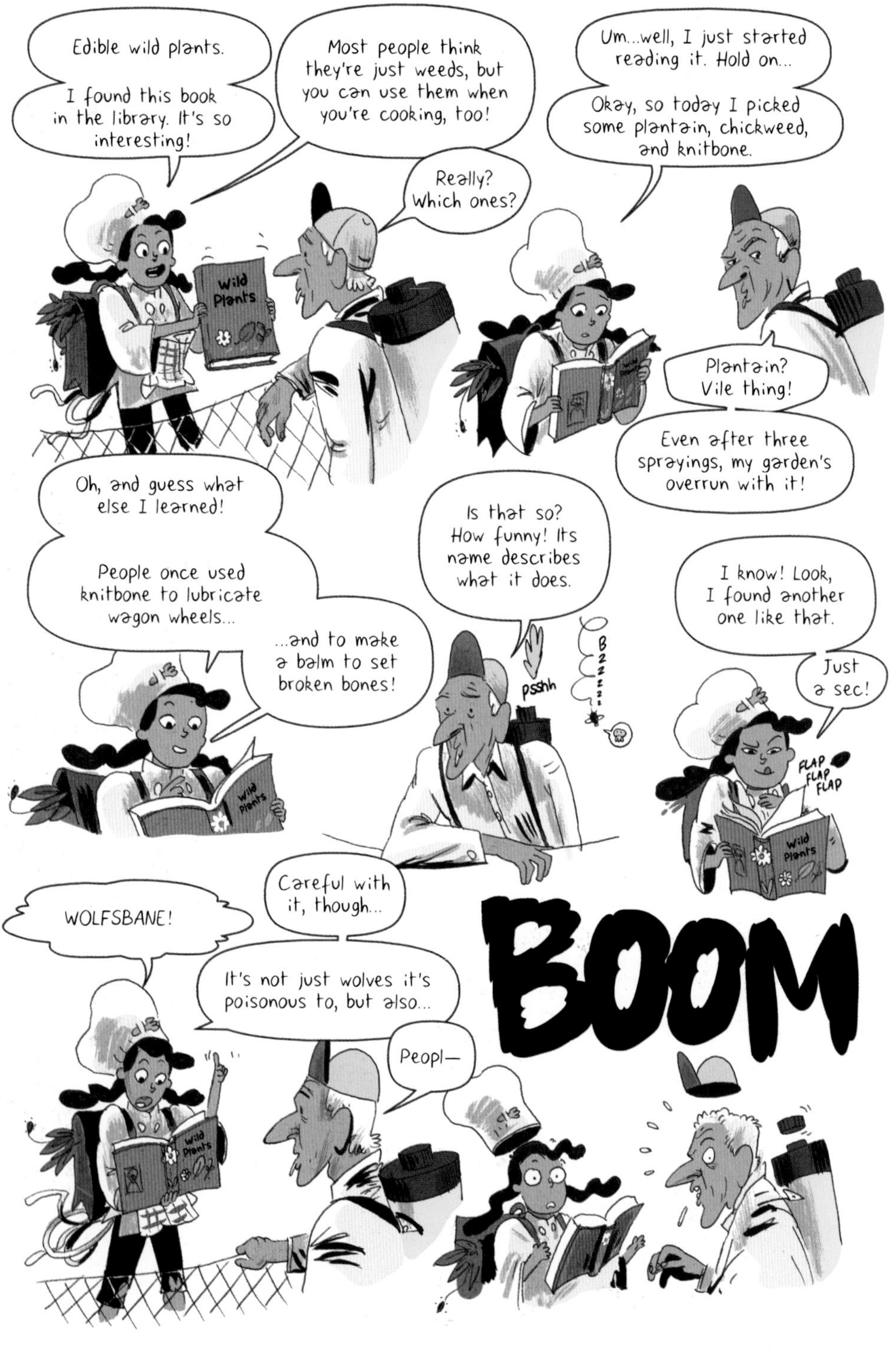
Edible wild plants.
I found this book in the library. It's so interesting!
Most people think they're just weeds, but you can use them when you're cooking, too!
Really? Which ones?
Wild Plants
Um...well, I just started reading it. Hold on...
Okay, so today I picked some plantain, chickweed, and knitbone.
Plantain? Vile thing!
Even after three sprayings, my garden's overrun with it!
Oh, and guess what else I learned!
People once used knitbone to lubricate wagon wheels...
...and to make a balm to set broken bones!
Is that so? How funny! Its name describes what it does.
psshh
BZZZZZ
I know! Look, I found another one like that.
Just a sec!
FLAP FLAP FLAP
WOLFSBANE!
Careful with it, though...
It's not just wolves it's poisonous to, but also...
Peopl—
BOOM

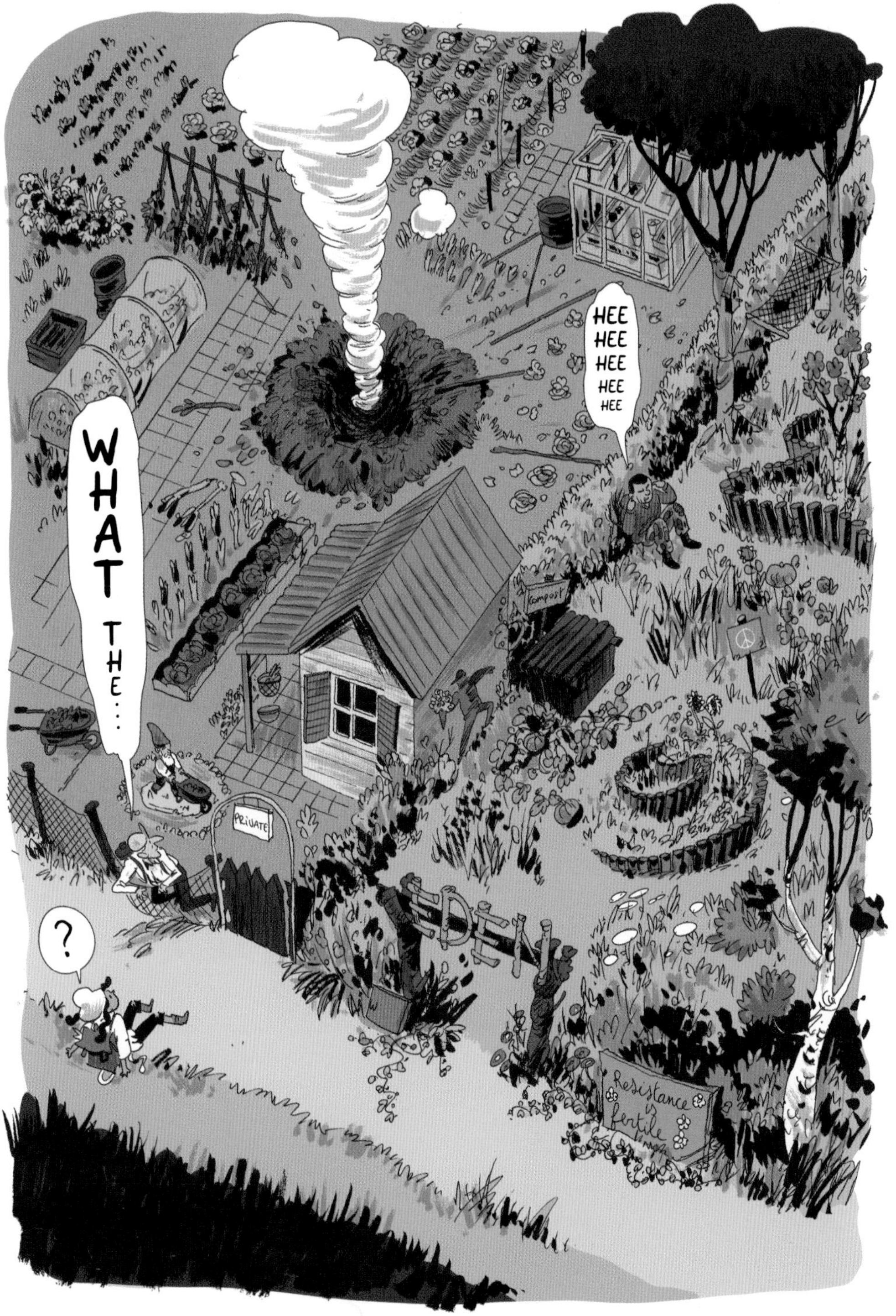
WHAT THE...
HEE HEE HEE HEE HEE
?
COMPOST
PRIVATE
EDEN
Resistance is fertile

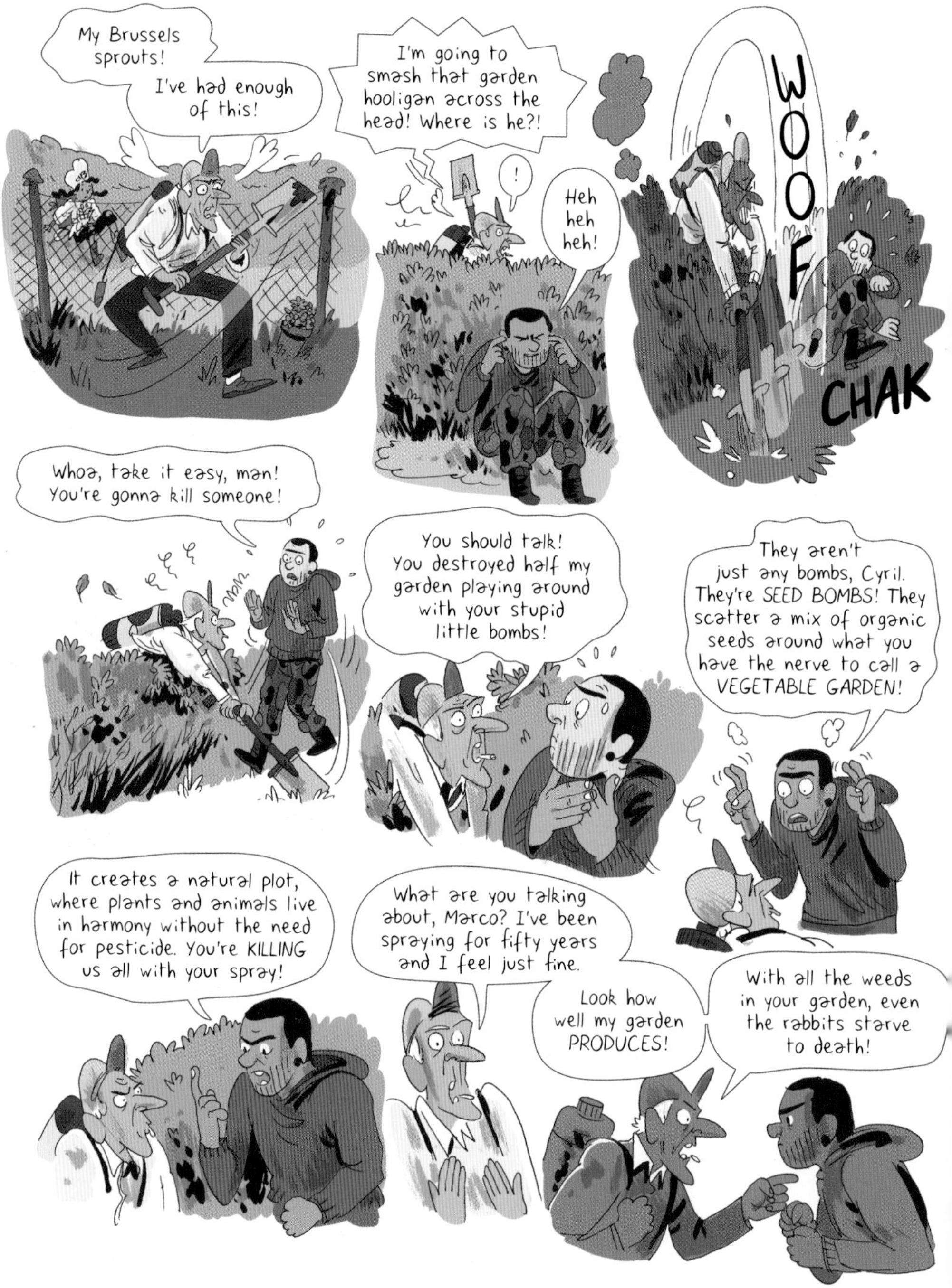

My Brussels sprouts!
I've had enough of this!
I'm going to smash that garden hooligan across the head! Where is he?!
!
Heh heh heh!
WOOF
CHAK
Whoa, take it easy, man! You're gonna kill someone!
You should talk! You destroyed half my garden playing around with your stupid little bombs!
They aren't just any bombs, Cyril. They're SEED BOMBS! They scatter a mix of organic seeds around what you have the nerve to call a VEGETABLE GARDEN!
It creates a natural plot, where plants and animals live in harmony without the need for pesticide. You're KILLING us all with your spray!
What are you talking about, Marco? I've been spraying for fifty years and I feel just fine.
Look how well my garden PRODUCES!
With all the weeds in your garden, even the rabbits starve to death!

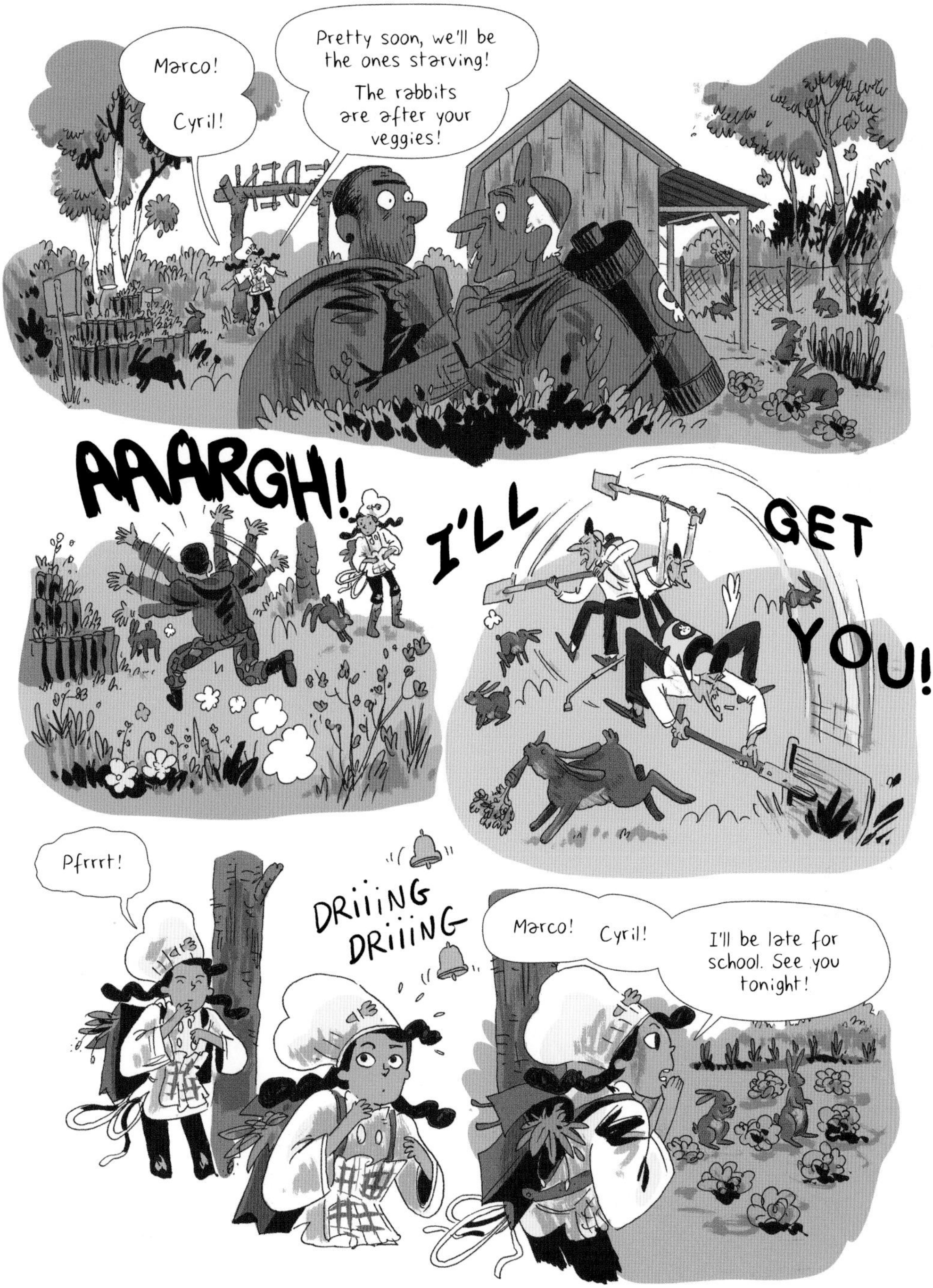
Marco!
Cyril!
Pretty soon, we'll be the ones starving!
The rabbits are after your veggies!
AAARGH!
I'LL GET YOU!
Pfrrrt!
DRiiiNG DRiiiNG
Marco! Cyril!
I'll be late for school. See you tonight!

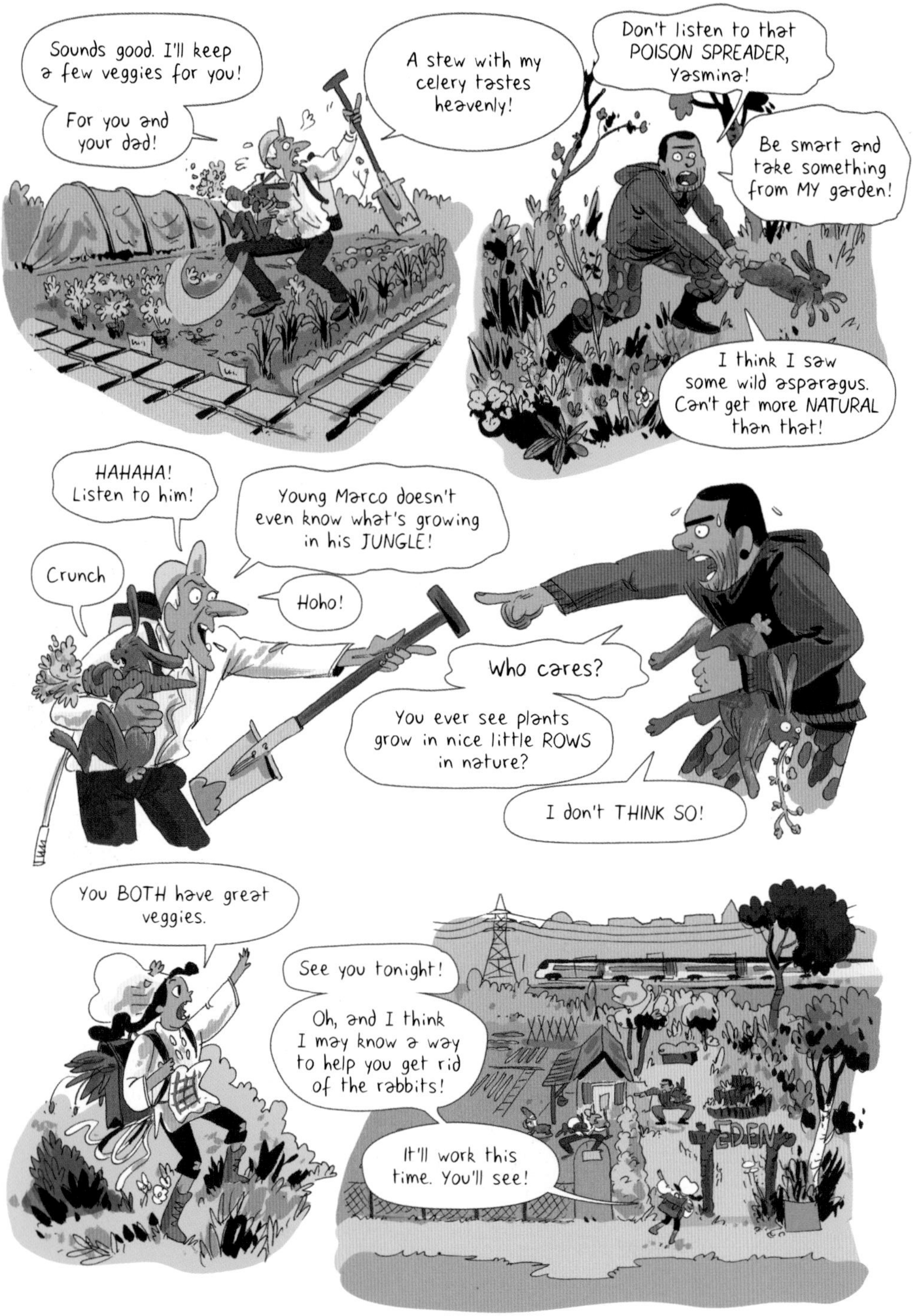
Sounds good. I'll keep a few veggies for you!
For you and your dad!
A stew with my celery tastes heavenly!
Don't listen to that POISON SPREADER, Yasmina!
Be smart and take something from MY garden!
I think I saw some wild asparagus. Can't get more NATURAL than that!
HAHAHA! Listen to him!
Young Marco doesn't even know what's growing in his JUNGLE!
Crunch
Hoho!
Who cares?
You ever see plants grow in nice little ROWS in nature?
I don't THINK SO!
You BOTH have great veggies.
See you tonight!
Oh, and I think I may know a way to help you get rid of the rabbits!
It'll work this time. You'll see!
EDEN

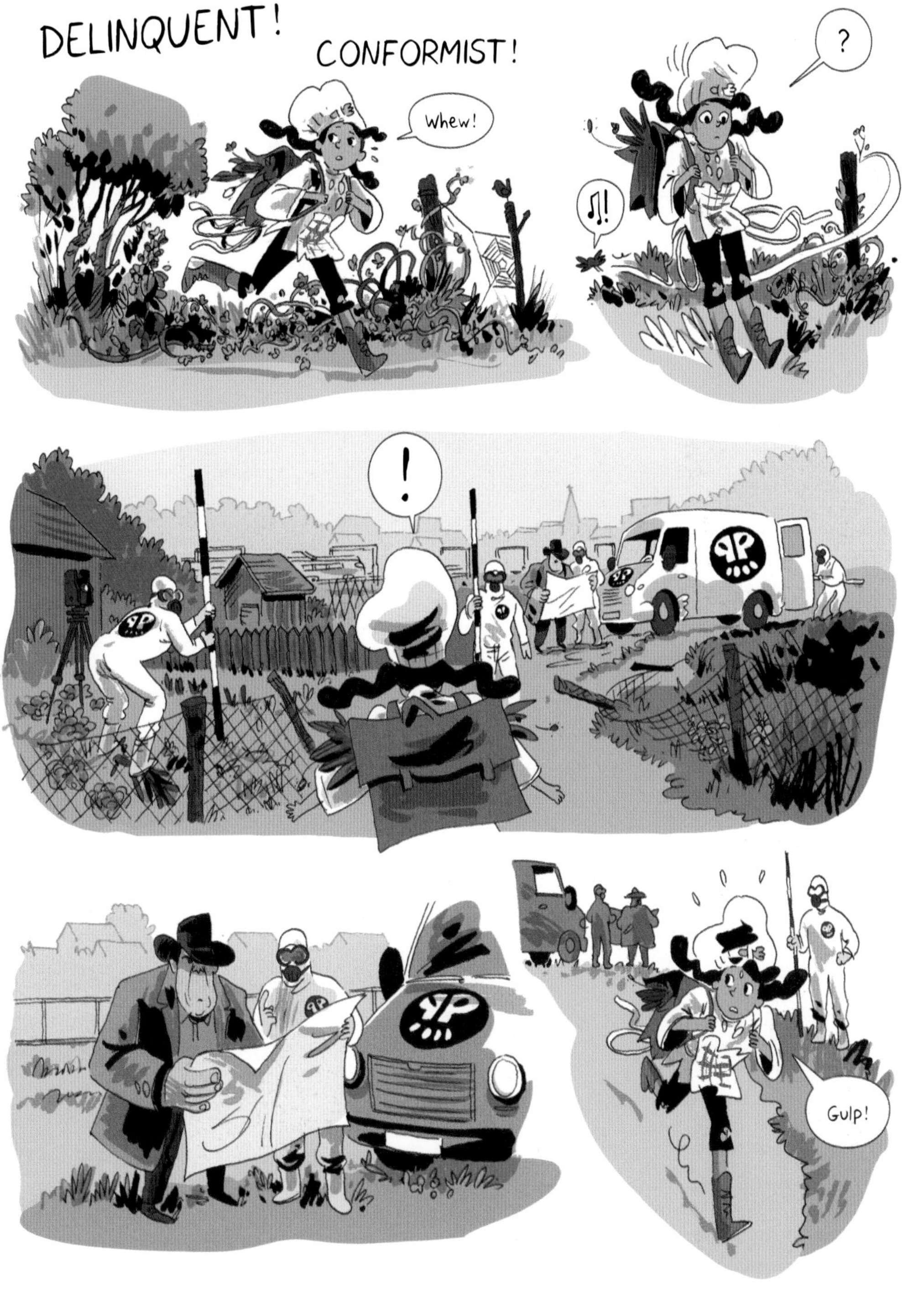
DELINQUENT!
CONFORMIST!
Whew!
?
♫!
!
Gulp!

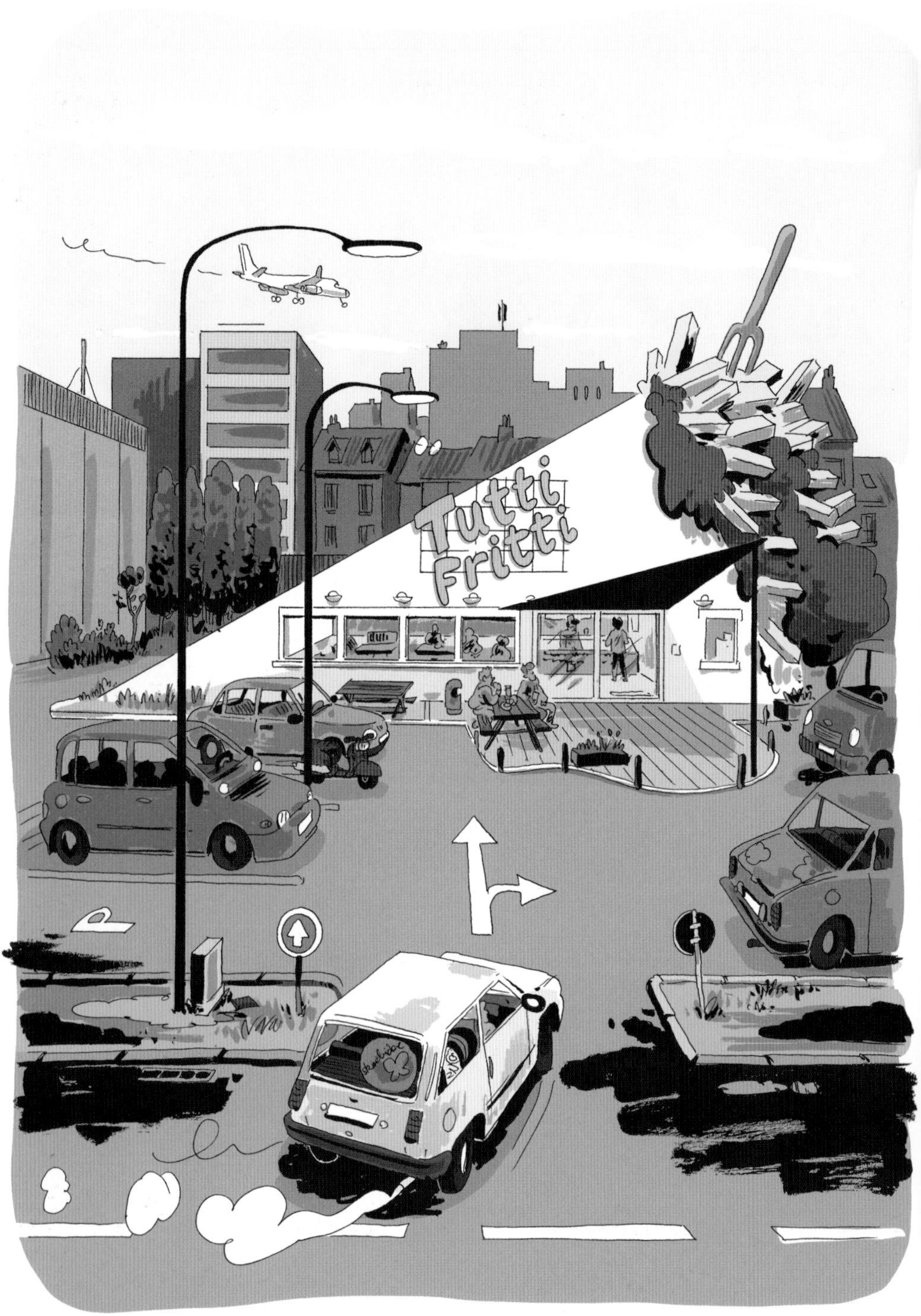
Tutti Fritti

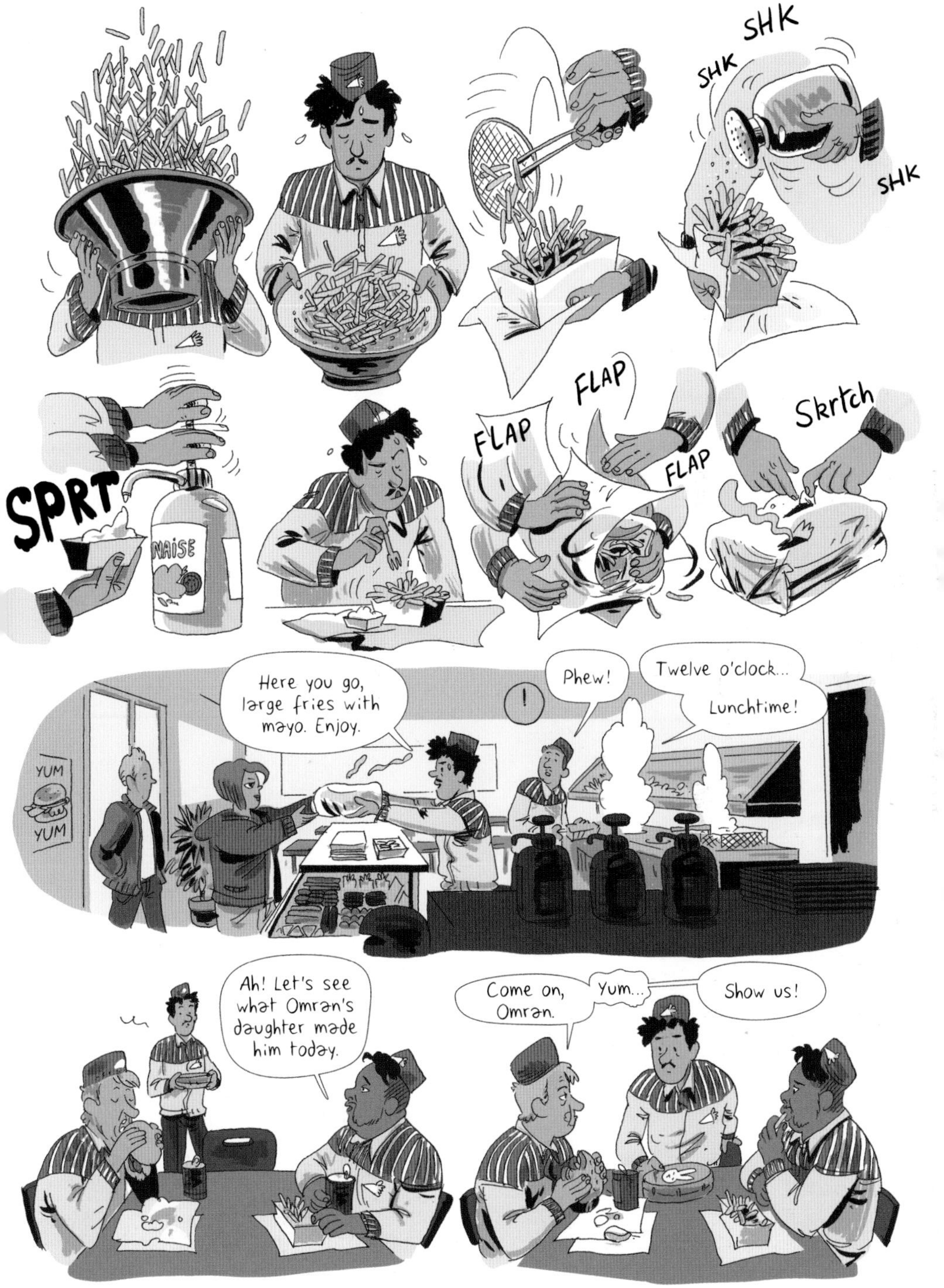
SHK
SHK
SHK
SPRT
NAISE
FLAP
FLAP
FLAP
Skrtch
Here you go, large fries with mayo. Enjoy.
YUM YUM
!
Phew!
Twelve o'clock... Lunchtime!
Ah! Let's see what Omran's daughter made him today.
Come on, Omran.
Yum...
Show us!

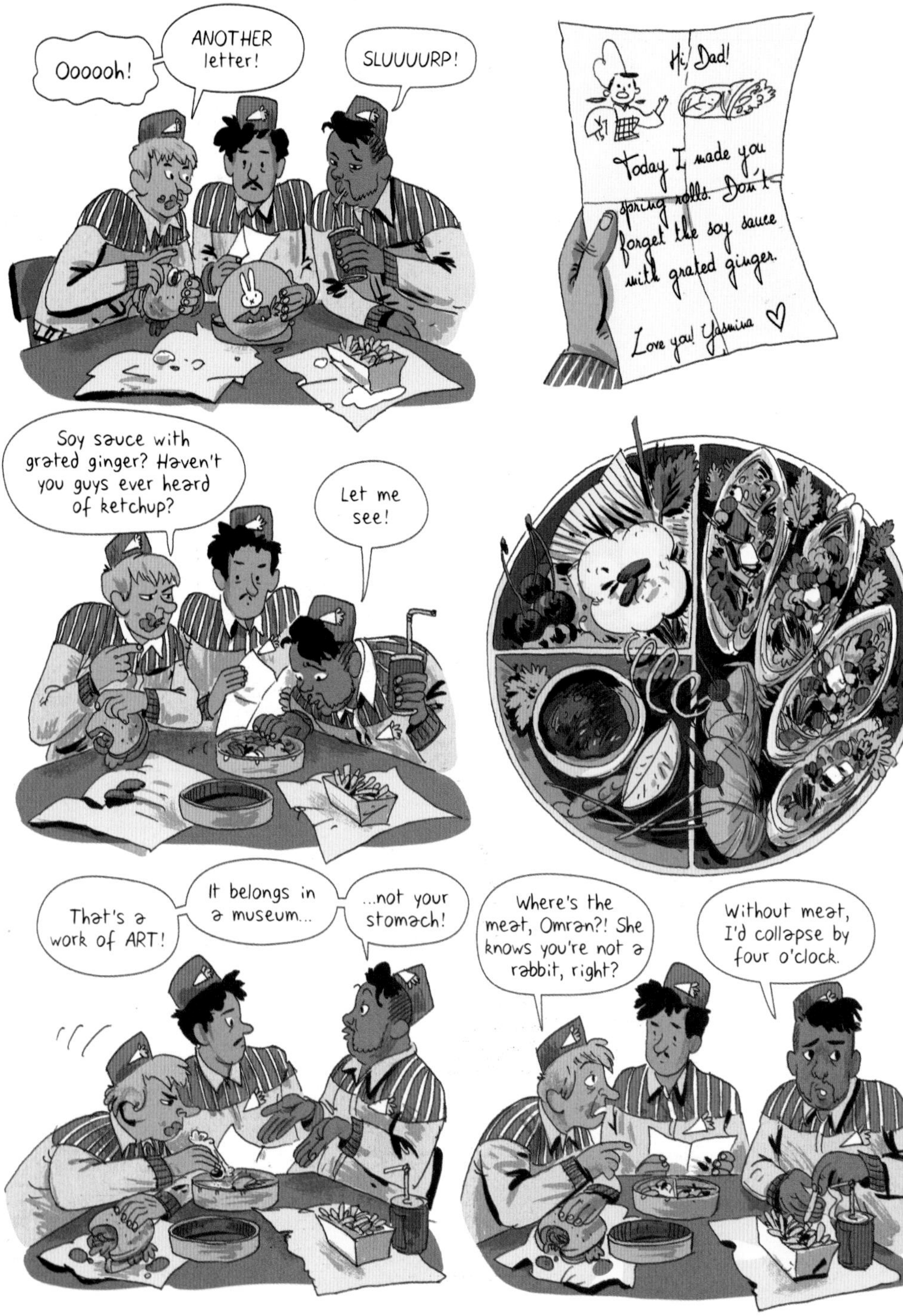

Oooooh!
ANOTHER letter!
SLUUUURP!
Hi, Dad!
Today I made you spring rolls. Don't forget the soy sauce with grated ginger.
Love you! Yasmina
Soy sauce with grated ginger? Haven't you guys ever heard of ketchup?
Let me see!
That's a work of ART!
It belongs in a museum...
...not your stomach!
Where's the meat, Omran?! She knows you're not a rabbit, right?
Without meat, I'd collapse by four o'clock.

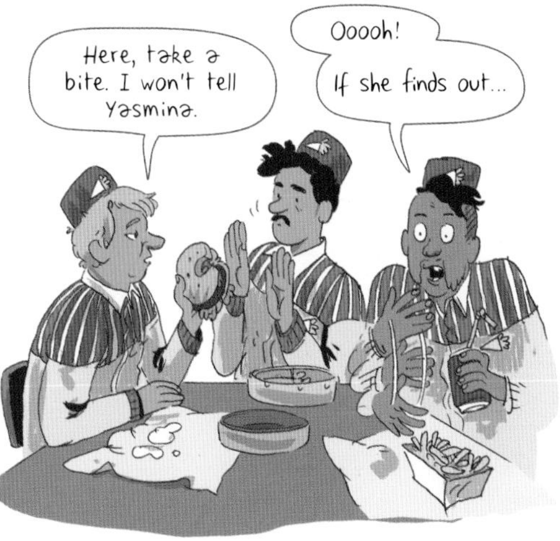
Here, take a bite. I won't tell Yasmina.
Ooooh!
If she finds out...

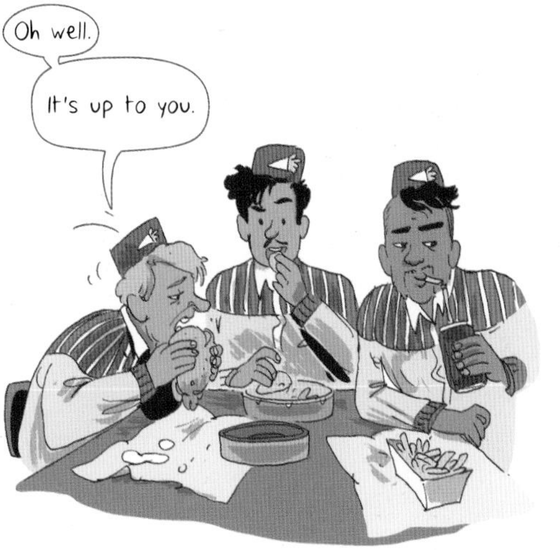
Oh well.
It's up to you.

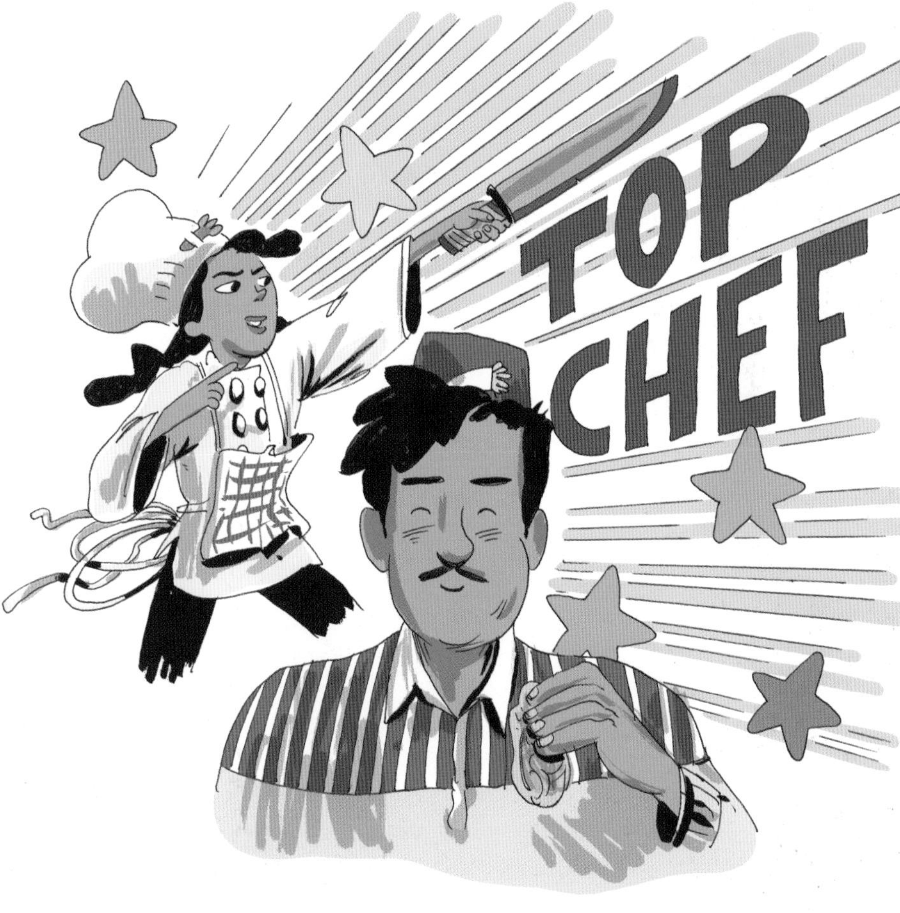
TOP CHEF

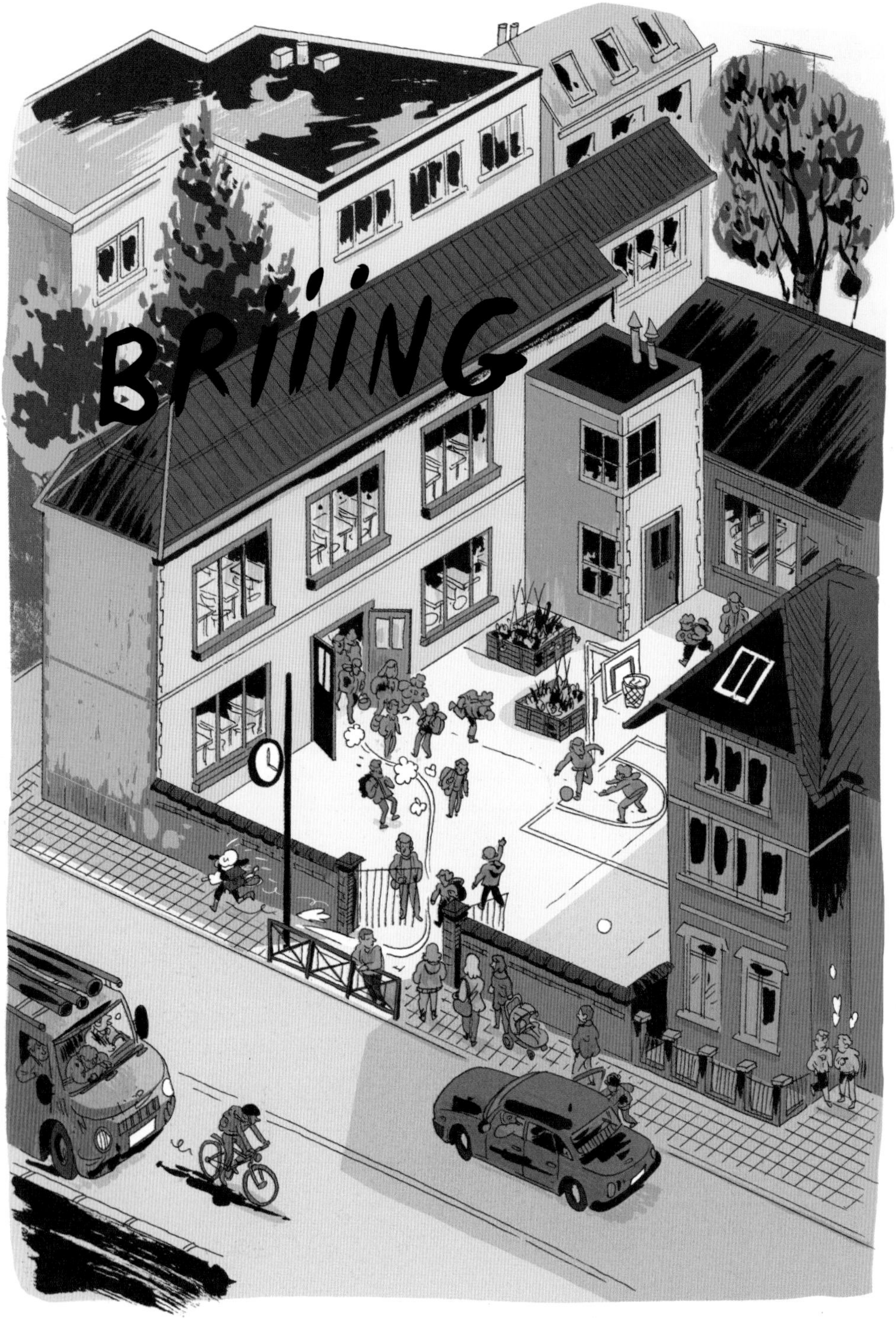
BRIiING

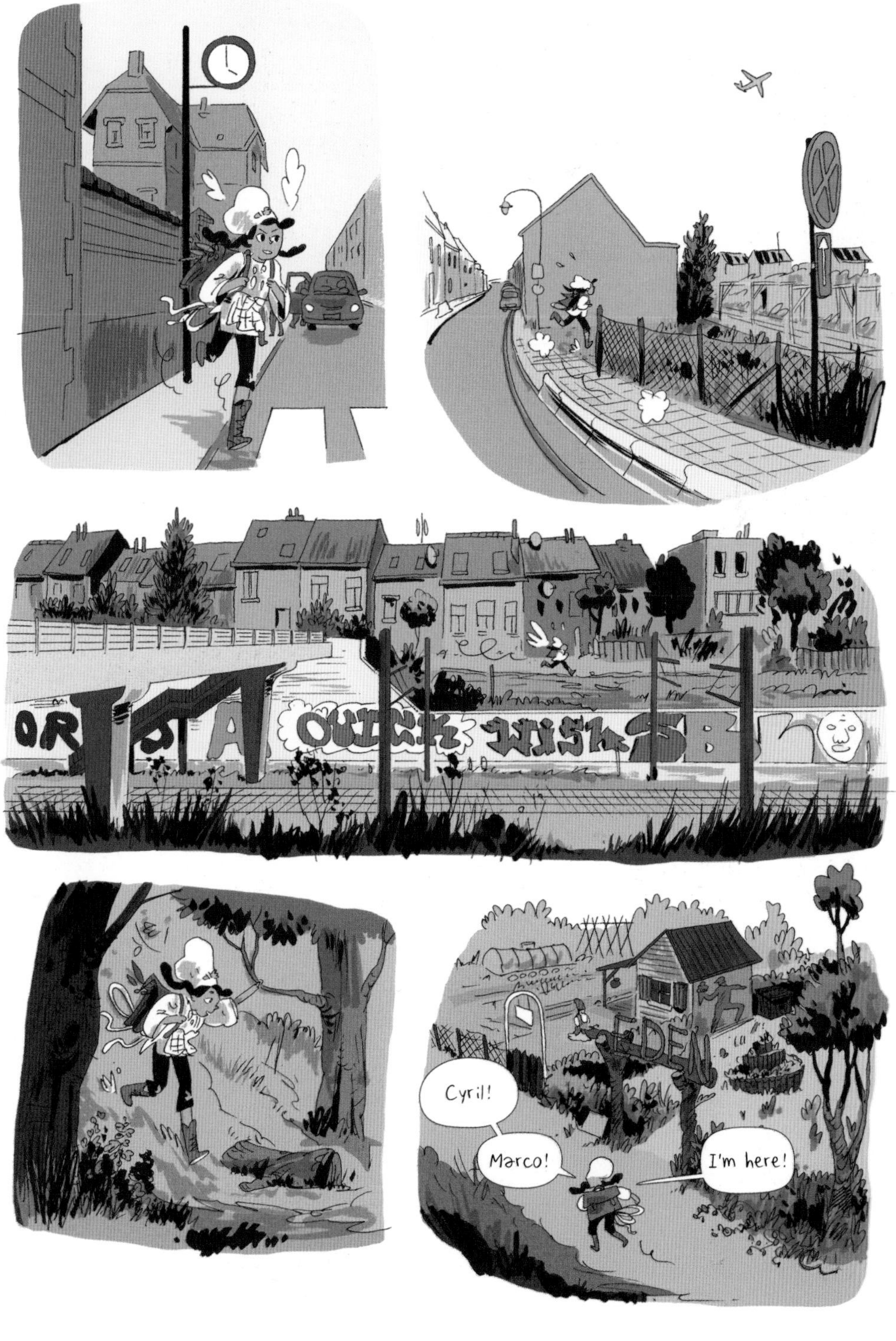
Cyril!
Marco!
I'm here!

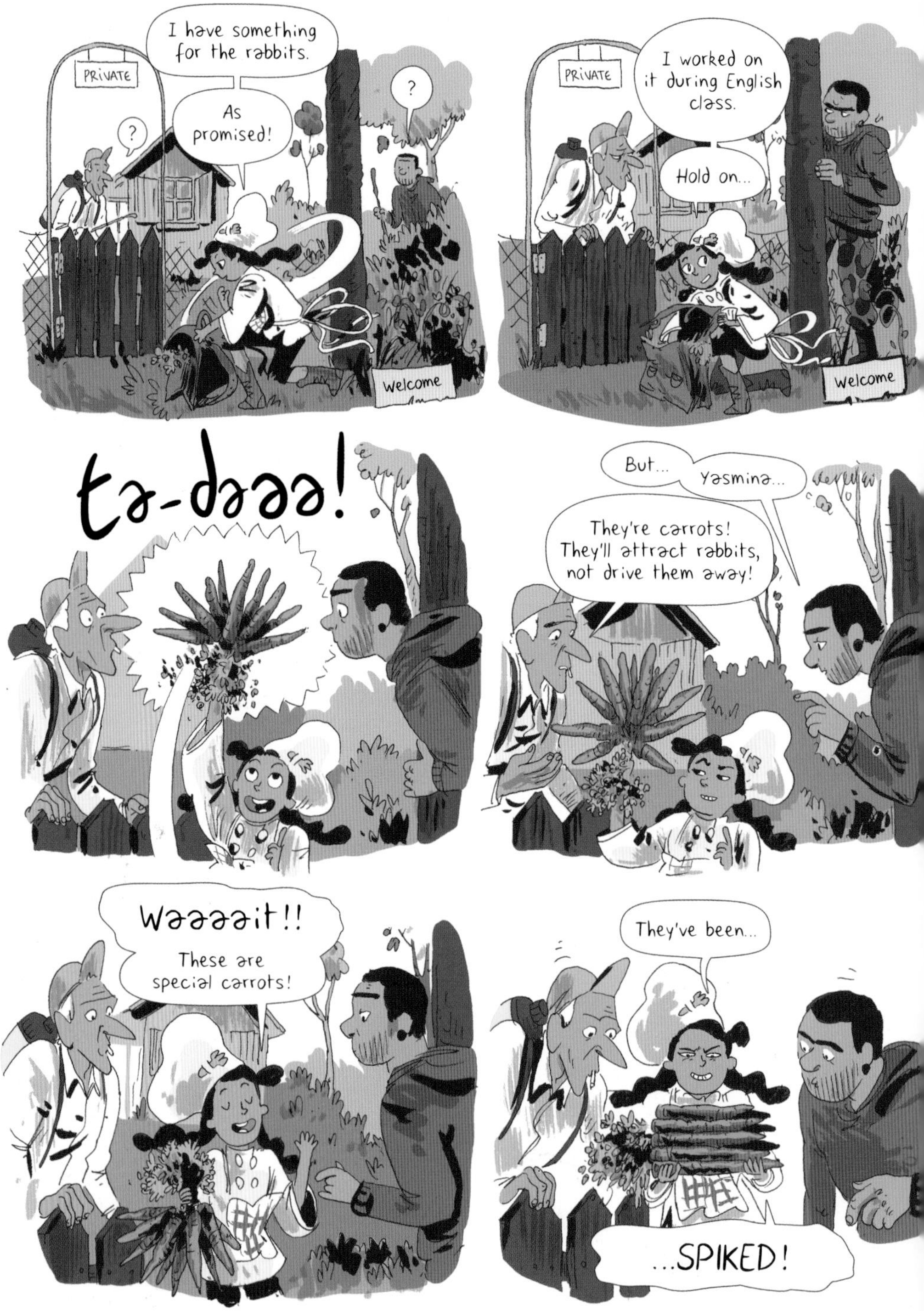
PRIVATE
I have something for the rabbits.
As promised!
?
?
Welcome
PRIVATE
I worked on it during English class.
Hold on...
Welcome
ta-daaa!
But...
Yasmina...
They're carrots! They'll attract rabbits, not drive them away!
Waaaait!!
These are special carrots!
They've been...
...SPIKED!

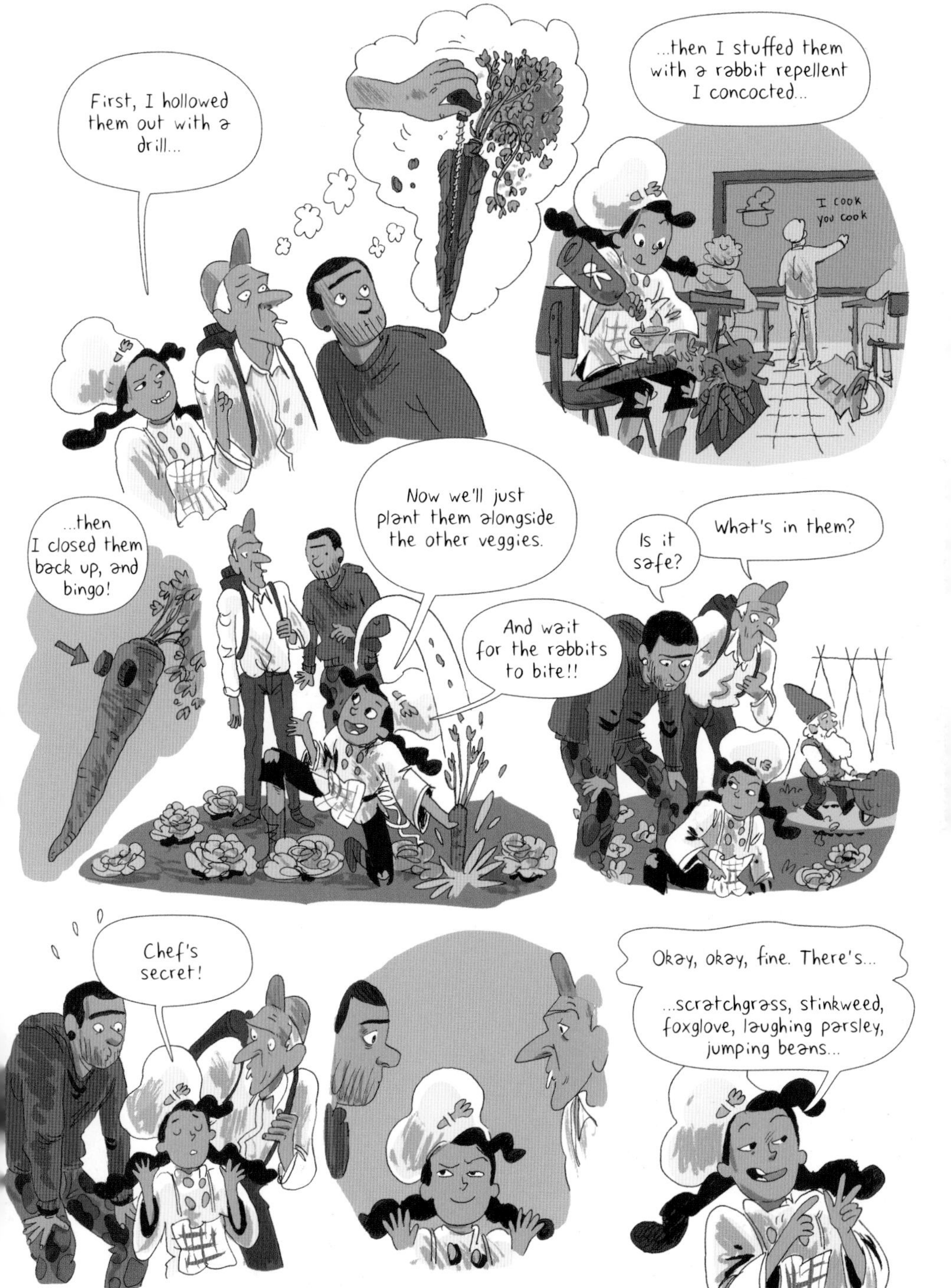
First, I hollowed them out with a drill...
...then I stuffed them with a rabbit repellent I concocted...
I COOK YOU COOK
...then I closed them back up, and bingo!
Now we'll just plant them alongside the other veggies.
And wait for the rabbits to bite!!
Is it safe?
What's in them?
Chef's secret!
Okay, okay, fine. There's...
...scratchgrass, stinkweed, foxglove, laughing parsley, jumping beans...

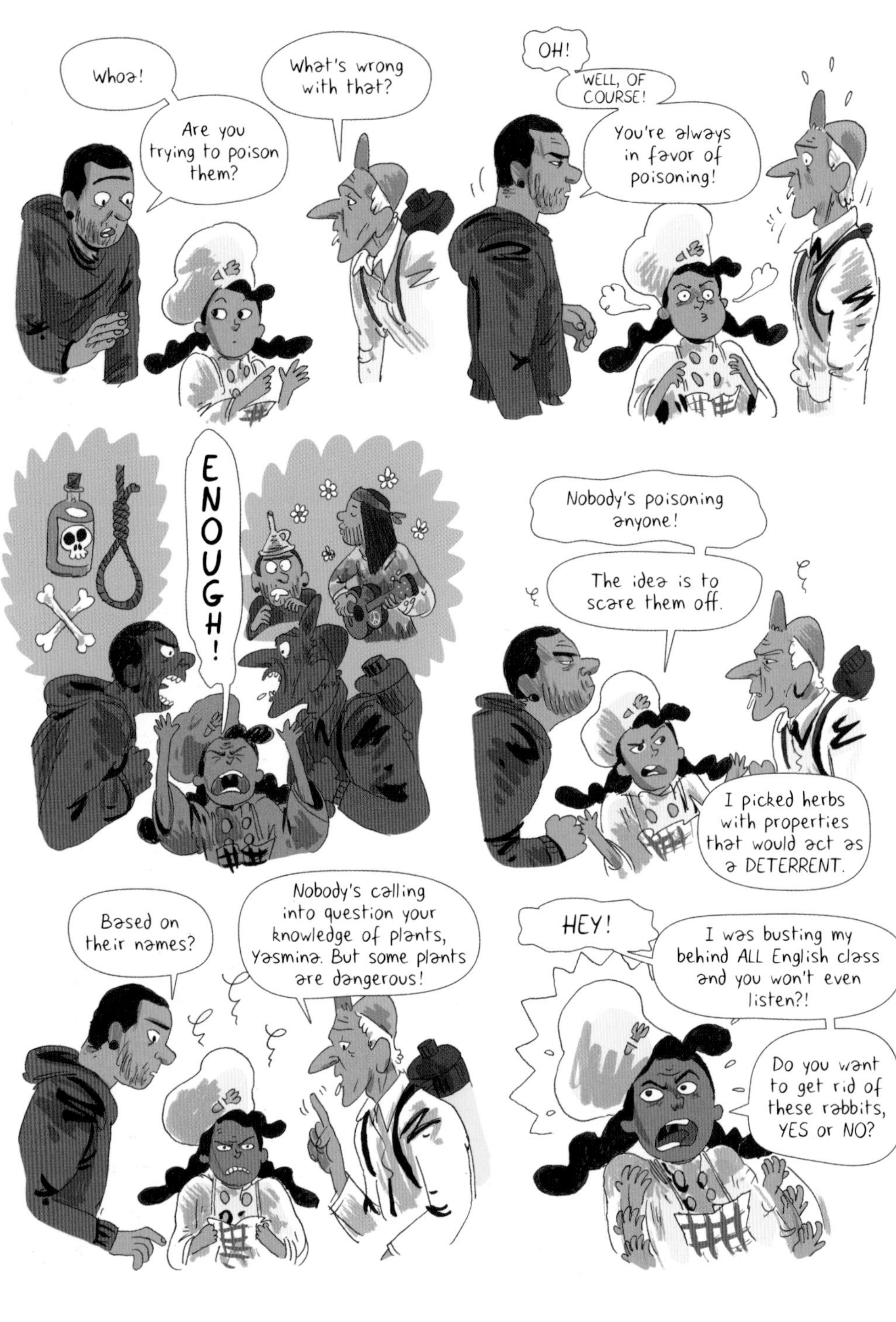
Whoa!
Are you trying to poison them?
What's wrong with that?
OH!
WELL, OF COURSE!
You're always in favor of poisoning!
ENOUGH!
Nobody's poisoning anyone!
The idea is to scare them off.
I picked herbs with properties that would act as a DETERRENT.
Based on their names?
Nobody's calling into question your knowledge of plants, Yasmina. But some plants are dangerous!
HEY!
I was busting my behind ALL English class and you won't even listen?!
Do you want to get rid of these rabbits, YES or NO?

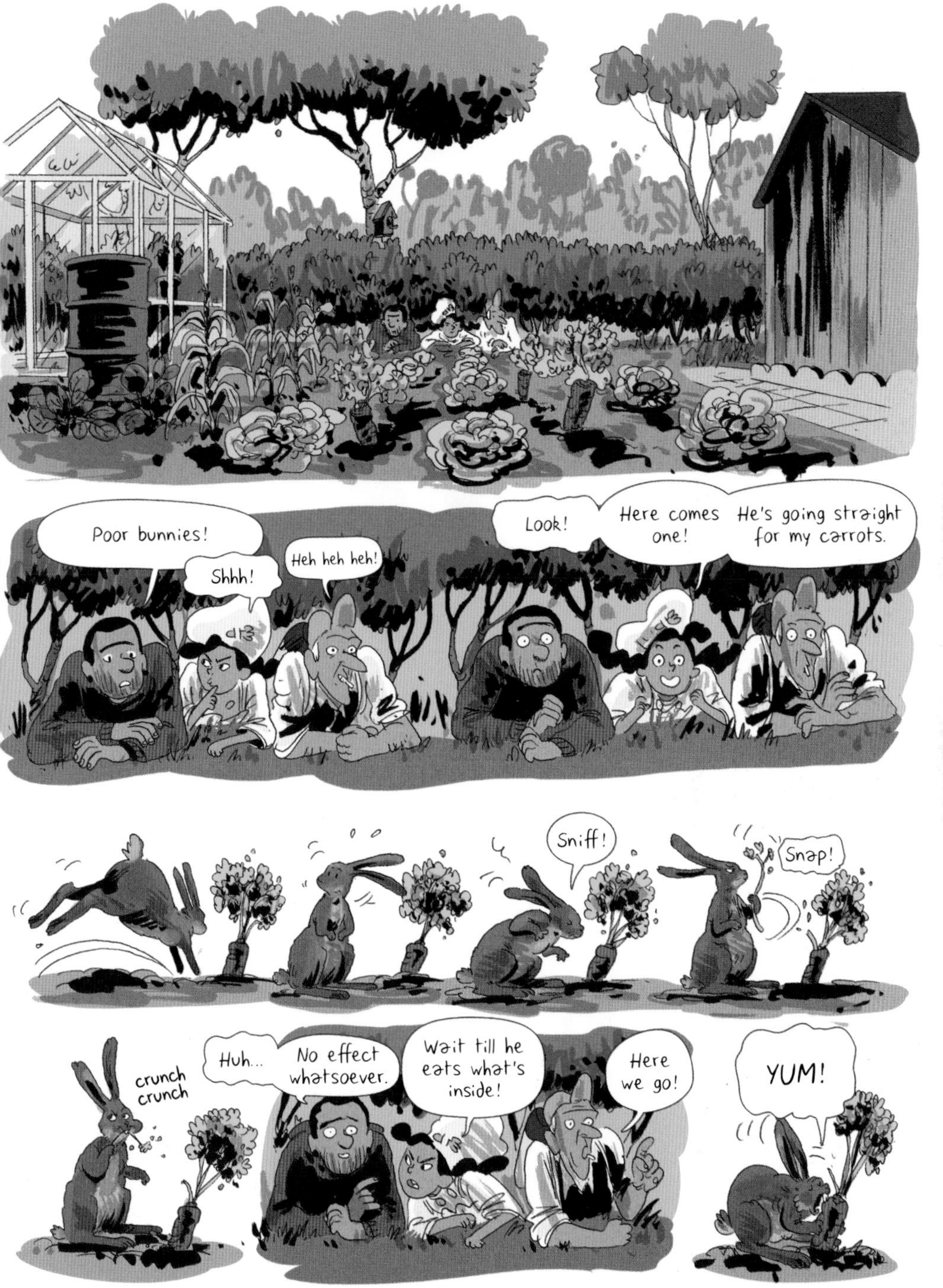
Poor bunnies!
Shhh!
Heh heh heh!
Look!
Here comes one!
He's going straight for my carrots.
Sniff!
Snap!
crunch crunch
Huh...
No effect whatsoever.
Wait till he eats what's inside!
Here we go!
YUM!

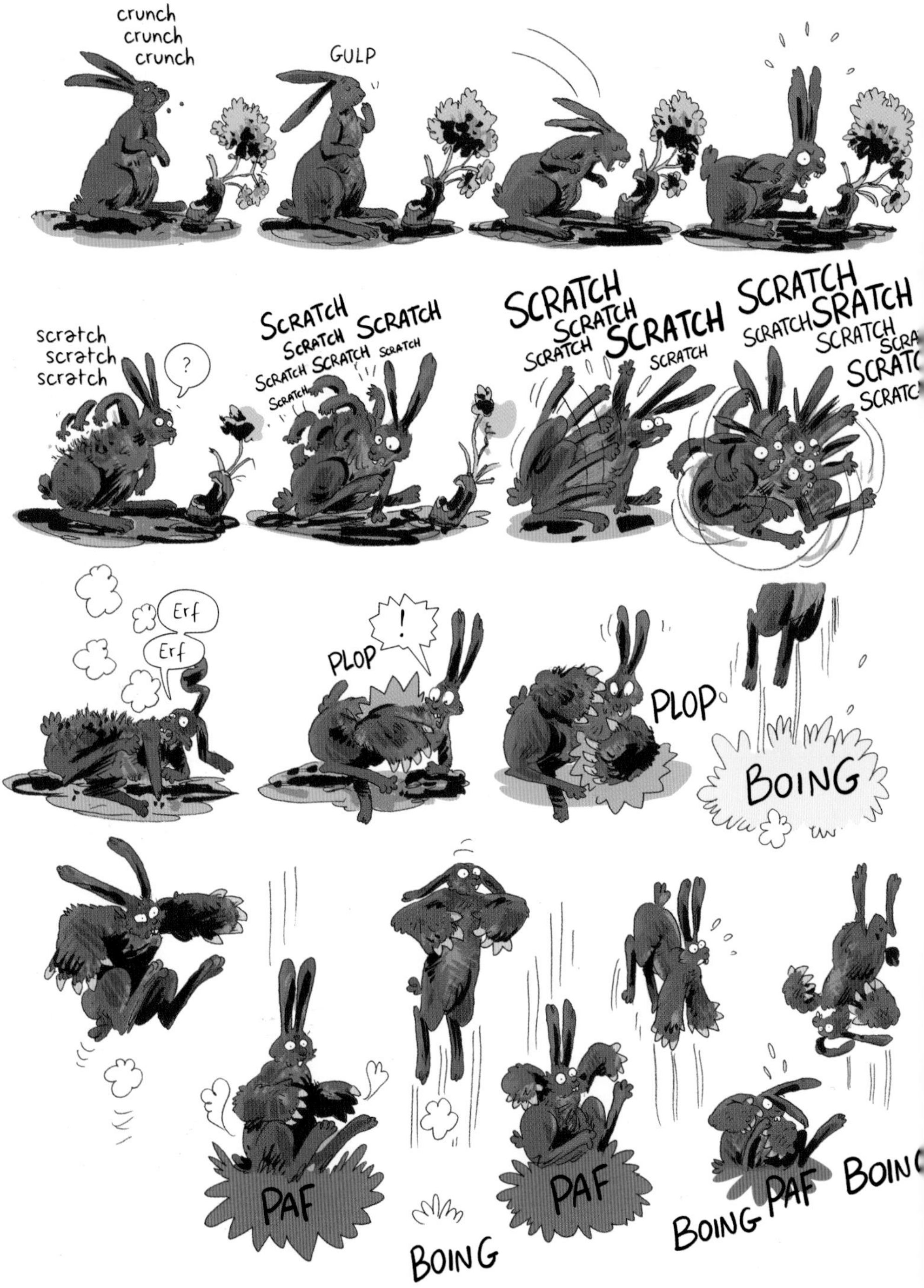

crunch
crunch
crunch
GULP
scratch
scratch
scratch
?
SCRATCH
SCRATCH SCRATCH
SCRATCH SCRATCH SCRATCH
SCRATCH
SCRATCH
SCRATCH
SCRATCH SCRATCH
SCRATCH
SCRATCH
SCRATCH SRATCH
SCRATCH
Erf
Erf
PLOP
!
PLOP
BOING
PAF
BOING
PAF
BOING PAF

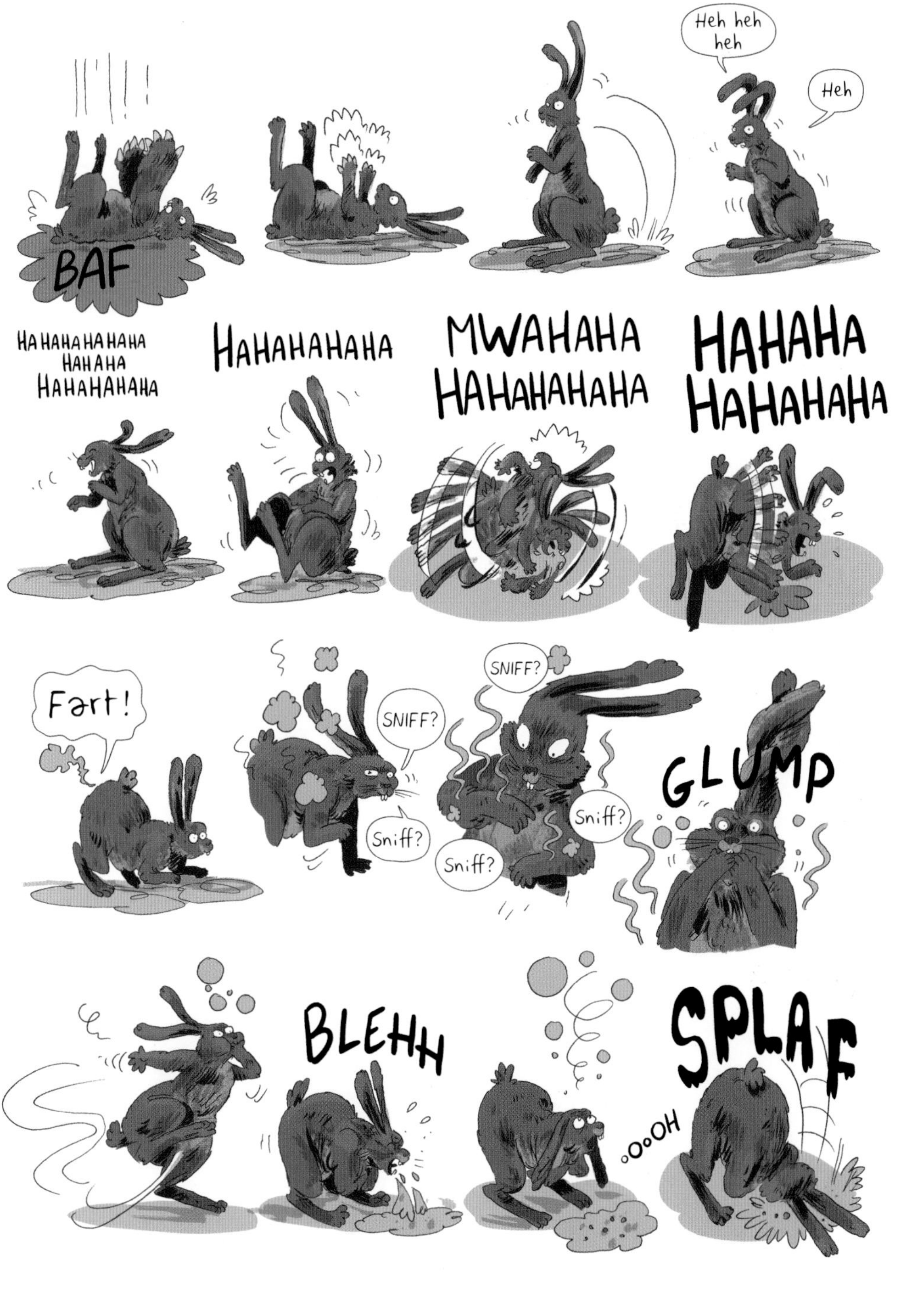
BAF
Heh heh heh
Heh
HAHAHAHAHAHA HAHAHA HAHAHAHAHA
HAHAHAHAHA
MWAHAHA HAHAHAHAHA
HAHAHA HAHAHAHA
Fart!
SNIFF?
Sniff?
SNIFF?
Sniff?
Sniff?
GLUMP
BLEHH
oOoOH
SPLAF

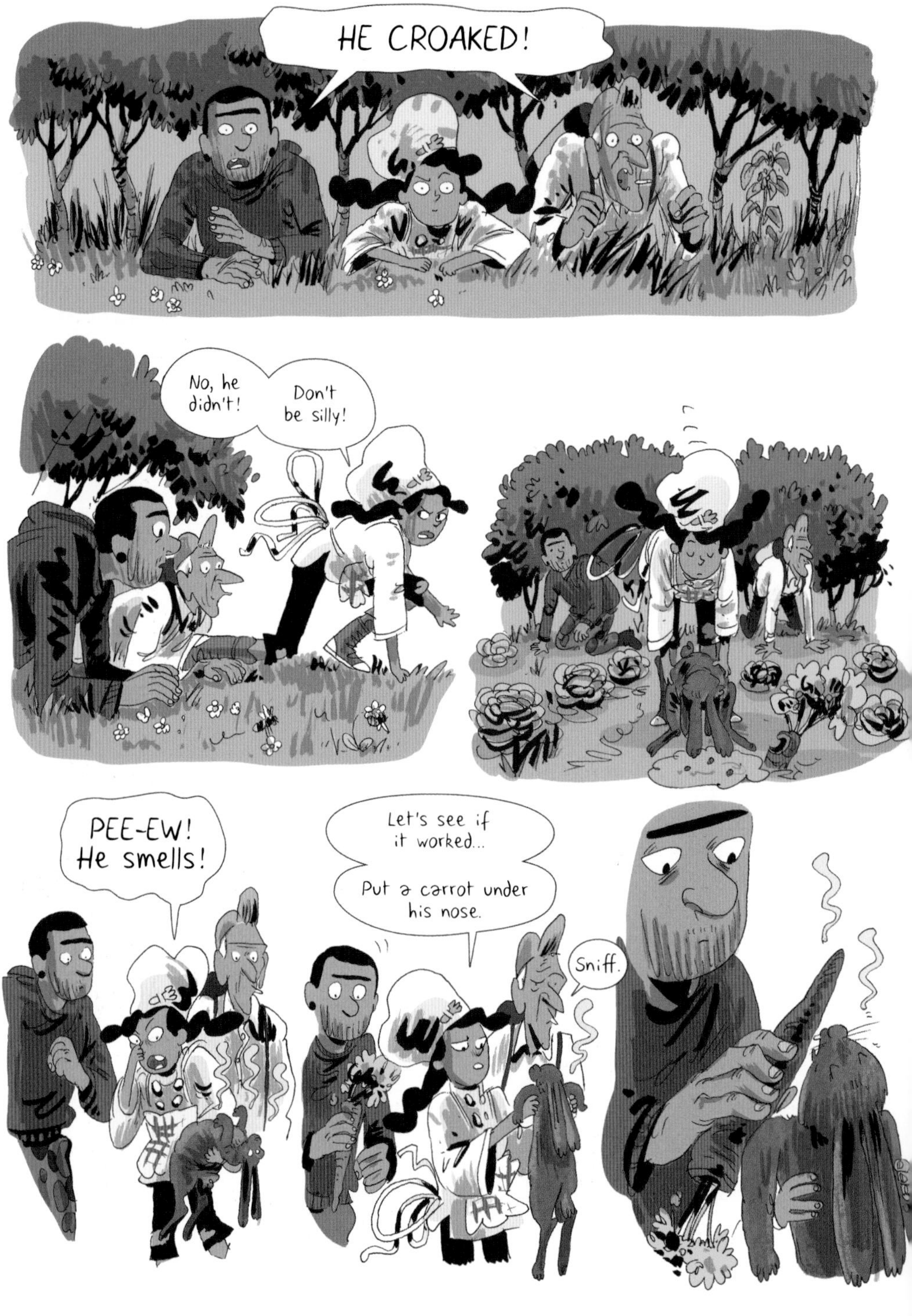
HE CROAKED!
No, he didn't!
Don't be silly!
PEE-EW! He smells!
Let's see if it worked...
Put a carrot under his nose.
Sniff.

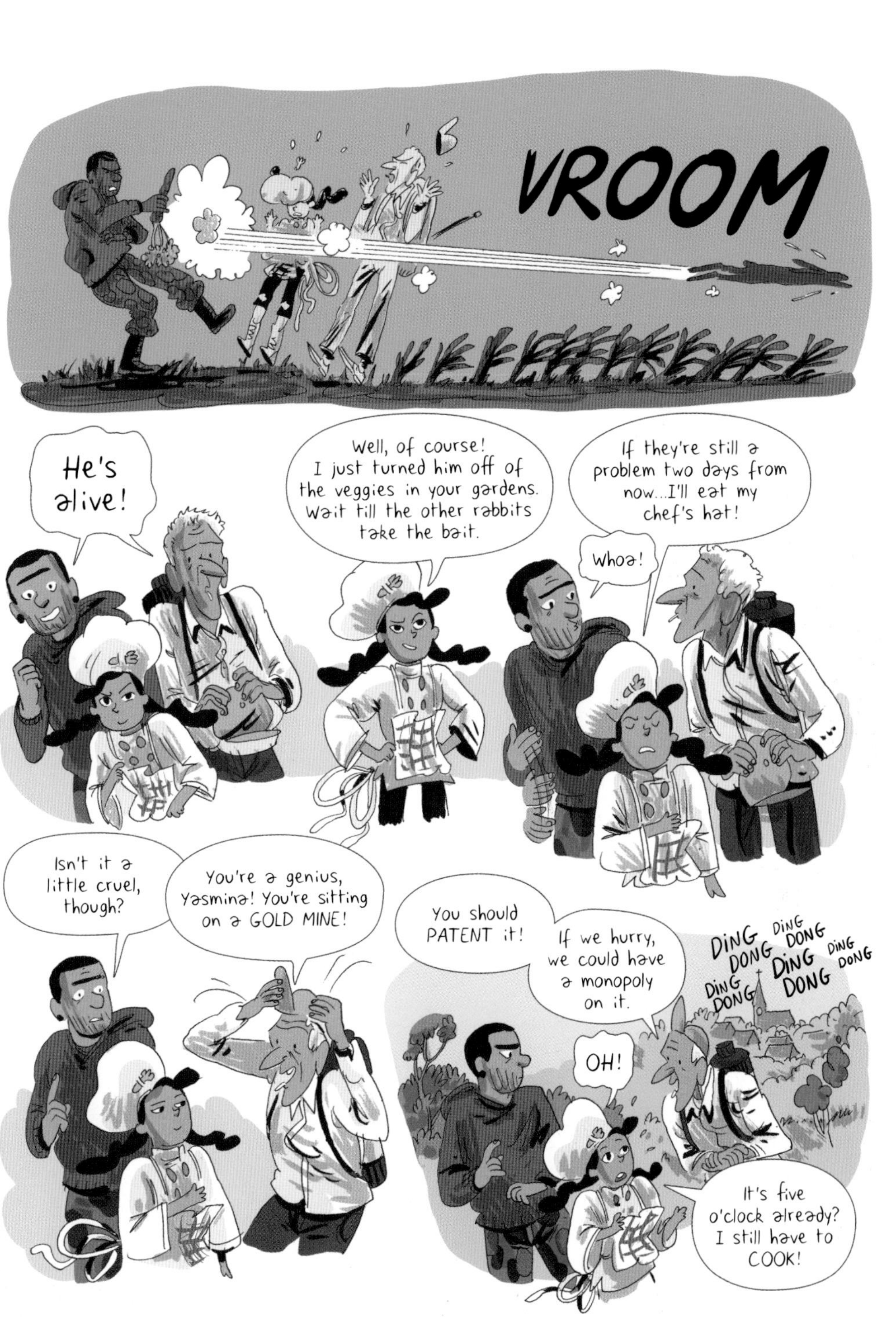
VROOM
He's alive!
Well, of course! I just turned him off of the veggies in your gardens. Wait till the other rabbits take the bait.
If they're still a problem two days from now...I'll eat my chef's hat!
Whoa!
Isn't it a little cruel, though?
You're a genius, Yasmina! You're sitting on a GOLD MINE!
You should PATENT it!
If we hurry, we could have a monopoly on it.
DING DONG DING DONG DING DONG DING DONG DING DONG
OH!
It's five o'clock already? I still have to COOK!

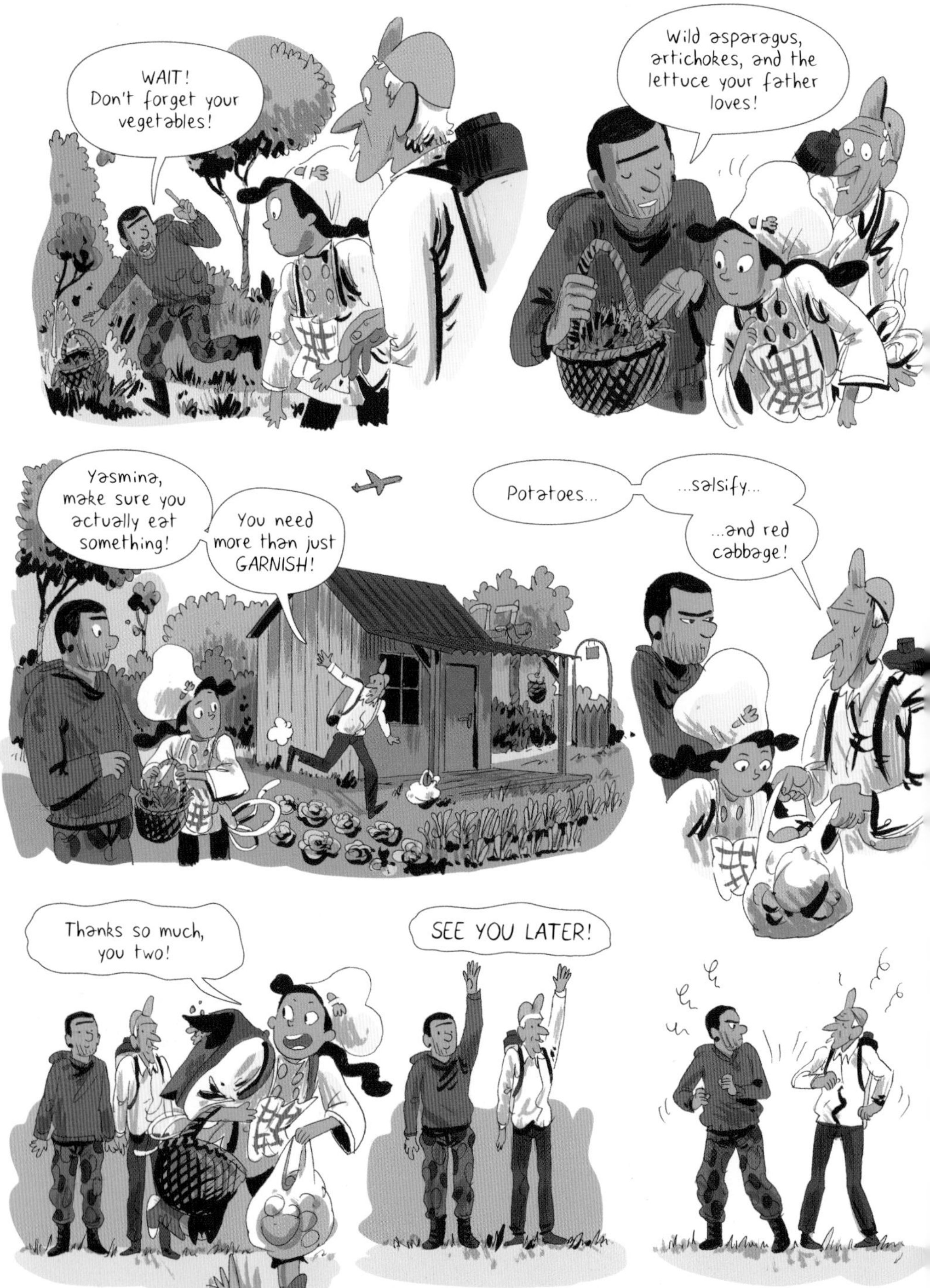
WAIT! Don't forget your vegetables!
Wild asparagus, artichokes, and the lettuce your father loves!
Yasmina, make sure you actually eat something!
You need more than just GARNISH!
Potatoes...
...salsify...
...and red cabbage!
Thanks so much, you two!
SEE YOU LATER!

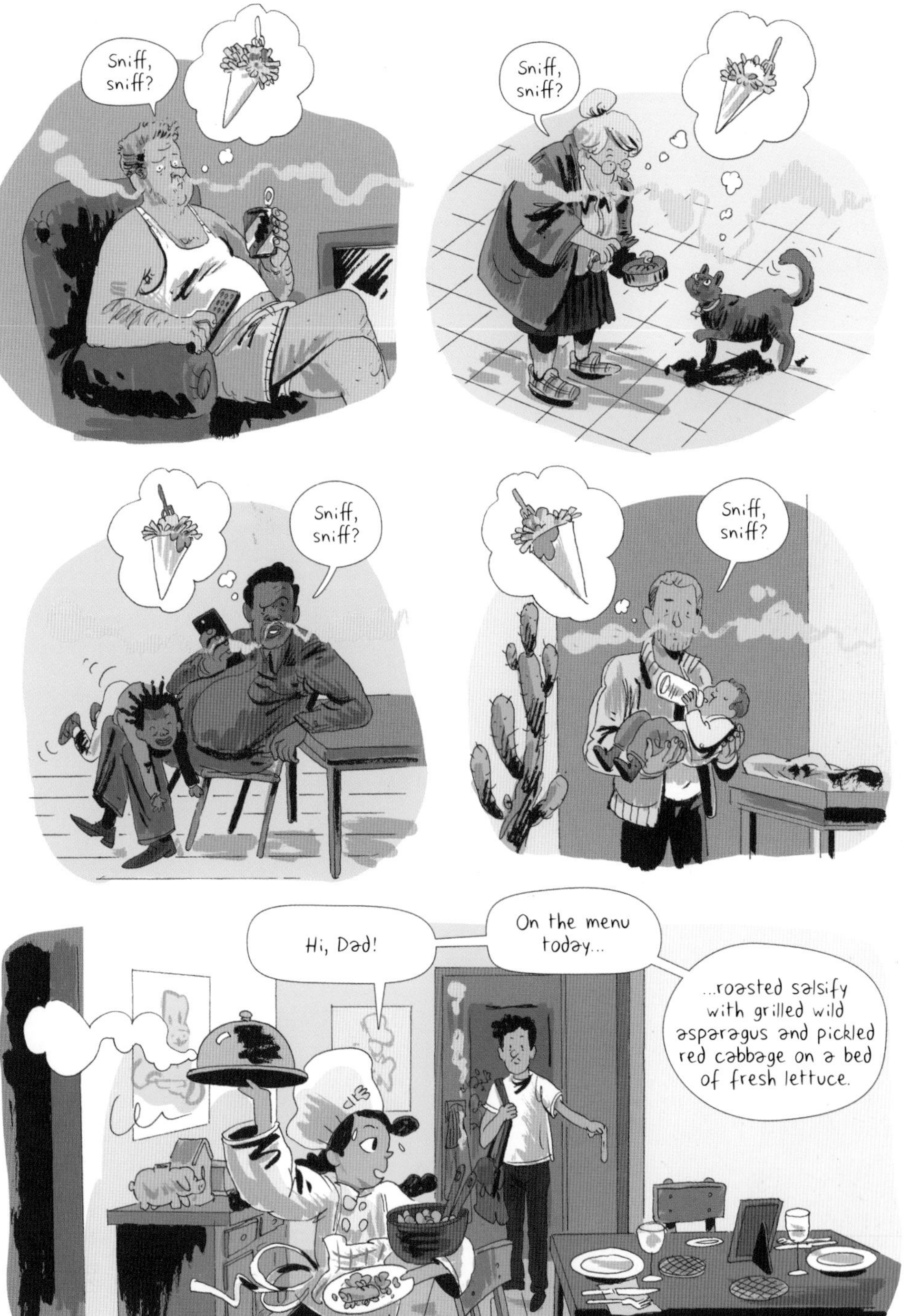
Sniff, sniff?
Sniff, sniff?
Sniff, sniff?
Sniff, sniff?
Hi, Dad!
On the menu today...
...roasted salsify with grilled wild asparagus and pickled red cabbage on a bed of fresh lettuce.

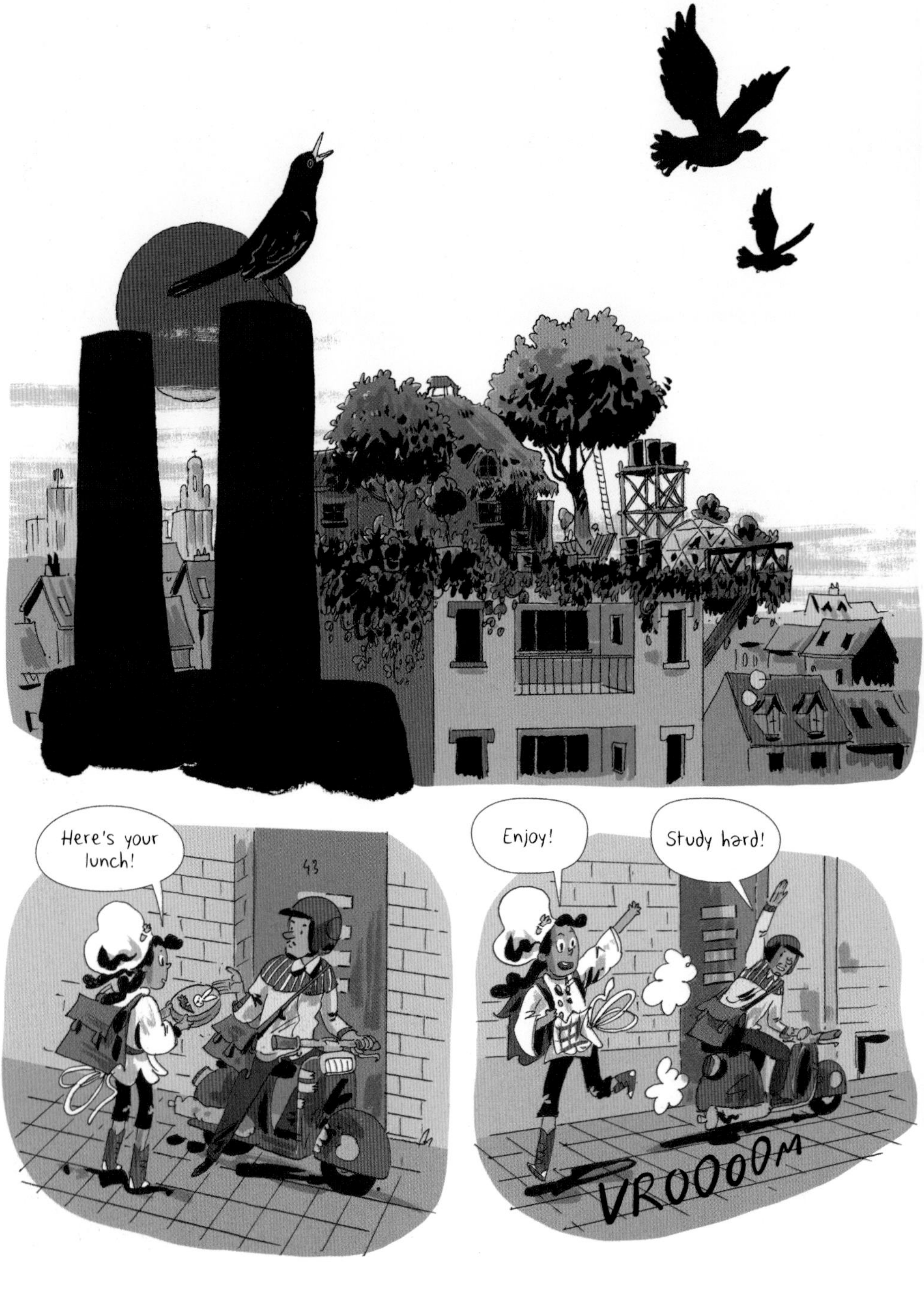
Here's your lunch!
43
Enjoy!
Study hard!
VROOOOM

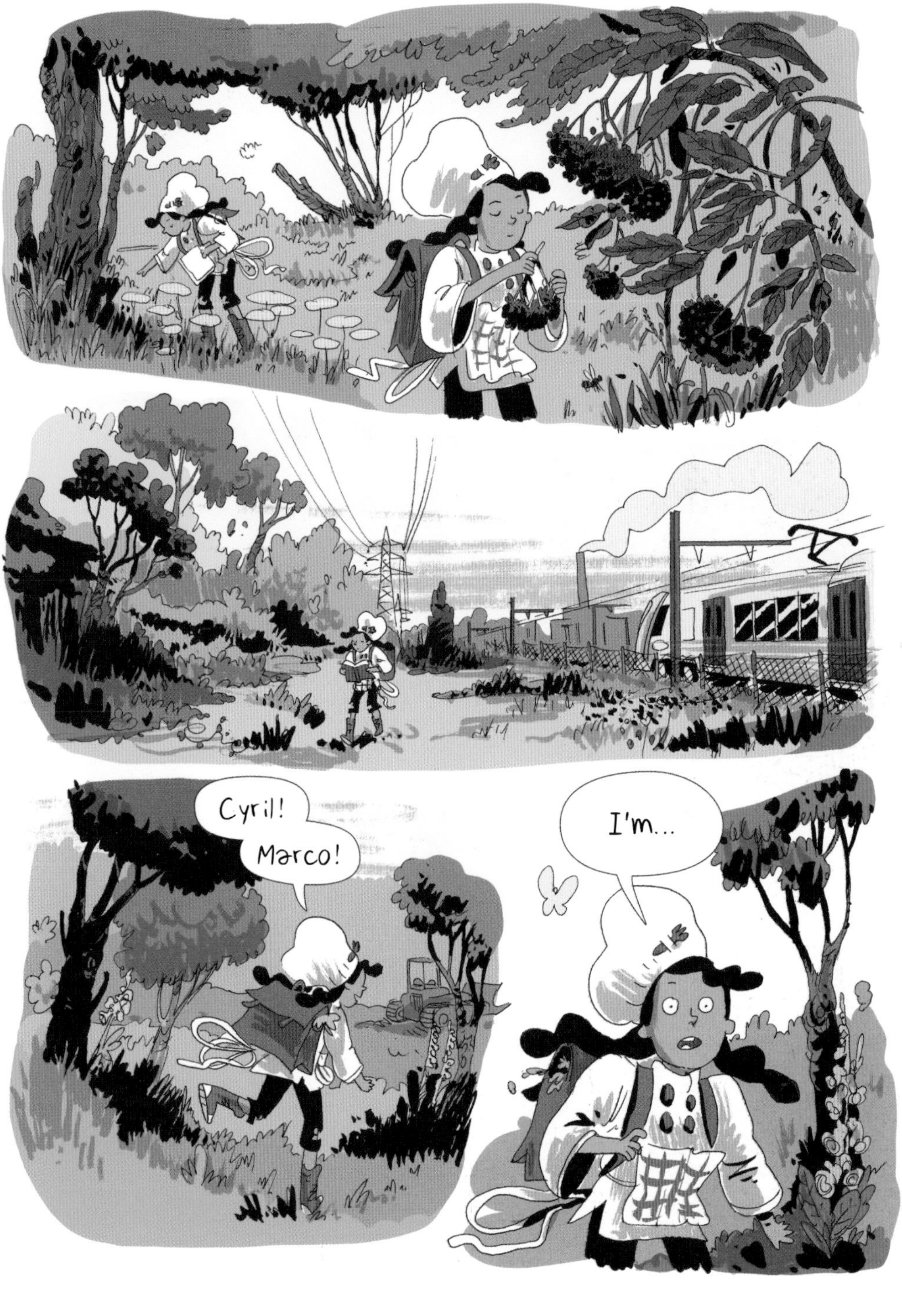
Cyril!
Marco!
I'm...

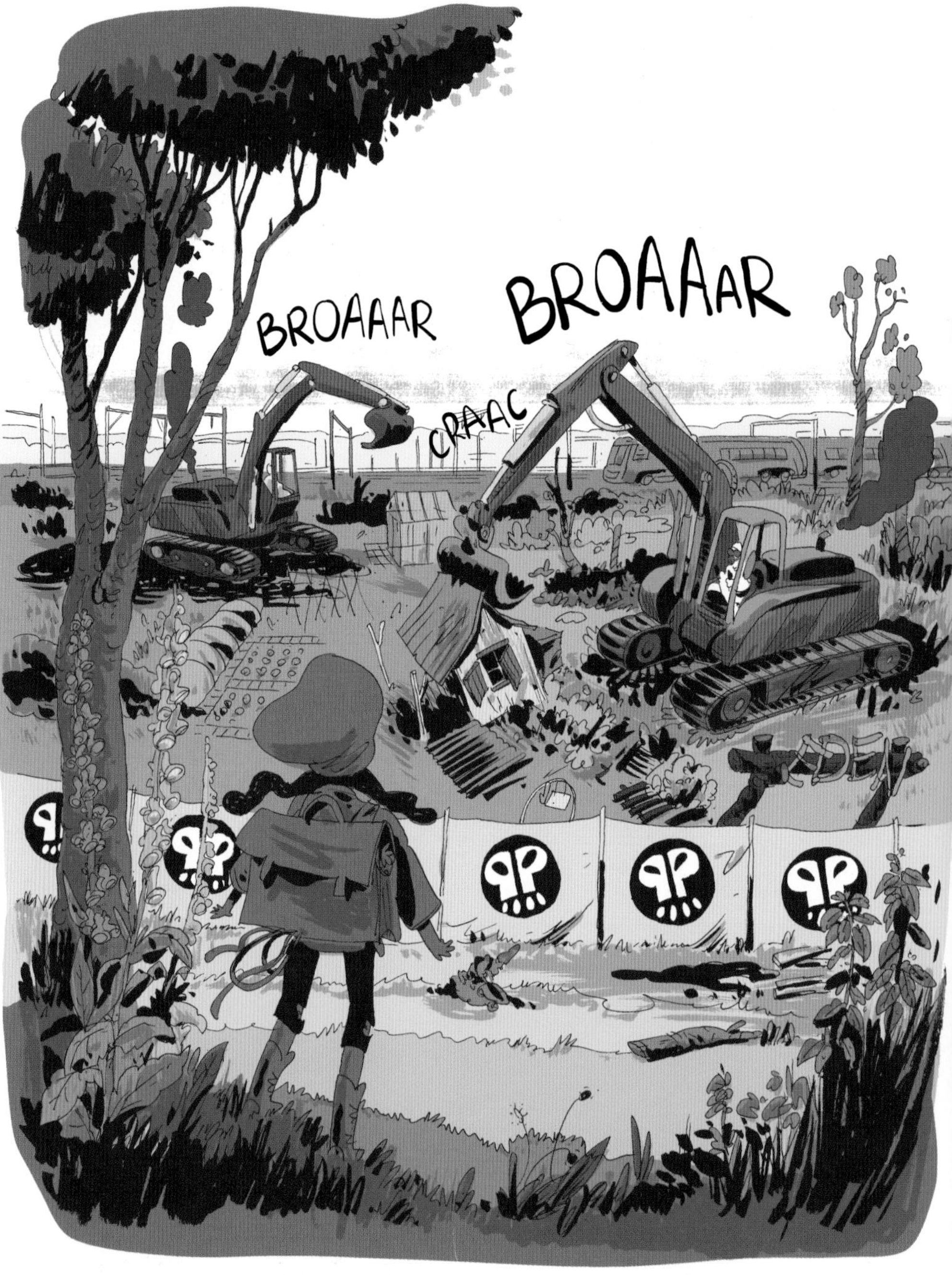
BROAAAR
BROAAAR
CRAAC

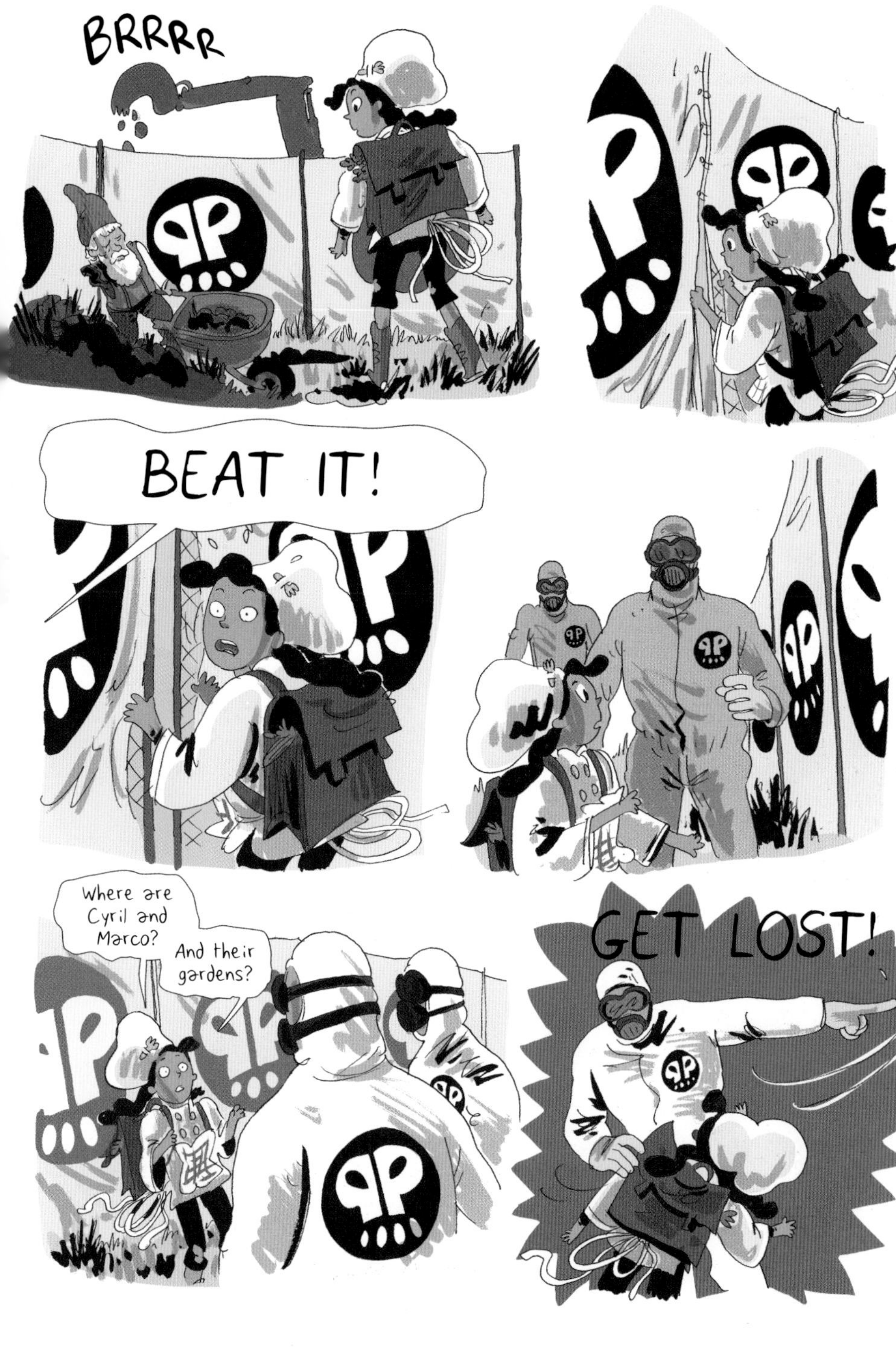
BRRRR
BEAT IT!
Where are Cyril and Marco?
And their gardens?
GET LOST!

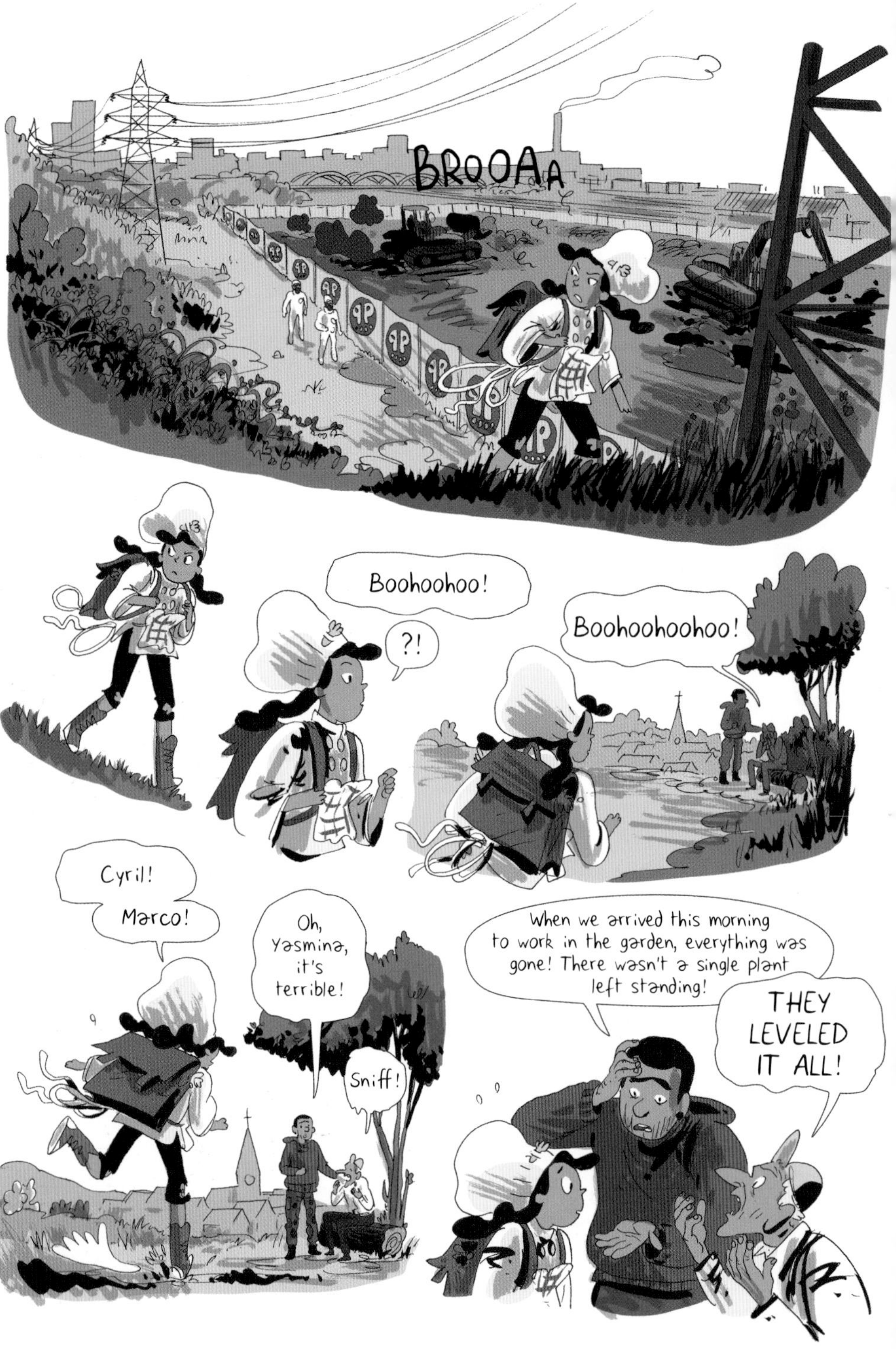
BROOAA
Boohoohoo!
?!
Boohoohoohoo!
Cyril!
Marco!
Oh, Yasmina, it's terrible!
Sniff!
When we arrived this morning to work in the garden, everything was gone! There wasn't a single plant left standing!
THEY LEVELED IT ALL!

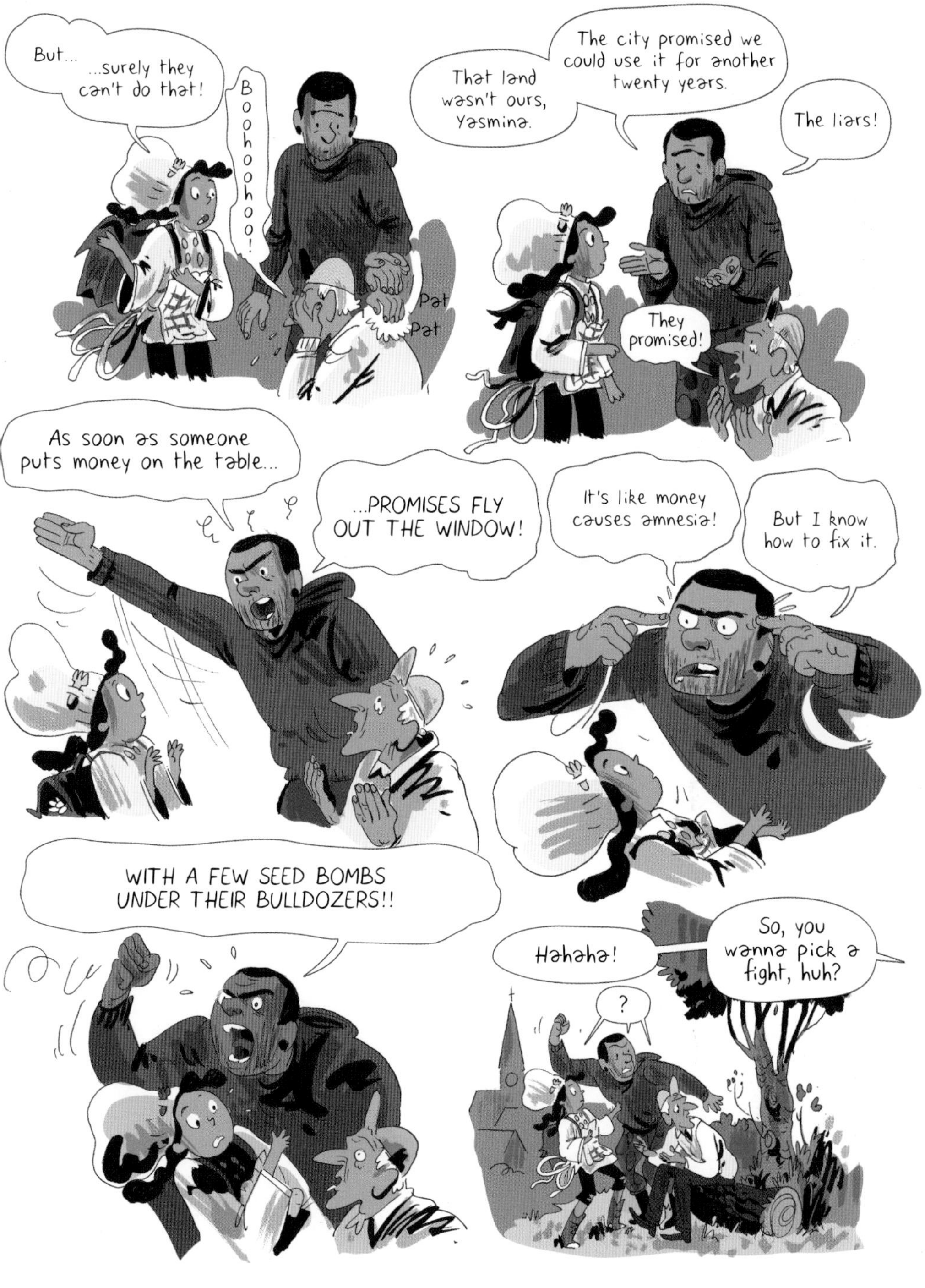
But...
...surely they can't do that!
Boohoohoo!
Pat
Pat
That land wasn't ours, Yasmina.
The city promised we could use it for another twenty years.
The liars!
They promised!
As soon as someone puts money on the table...
...PROMISES FLY OUT THE WINDOW!
It's like money causes amnesia!
But I know how to fix it.
WITH A FEW SEED BOMBS UNDER THEIR BULLDOZERS!!
Hahaha!
So, you wanna pick a fight, huh?
?

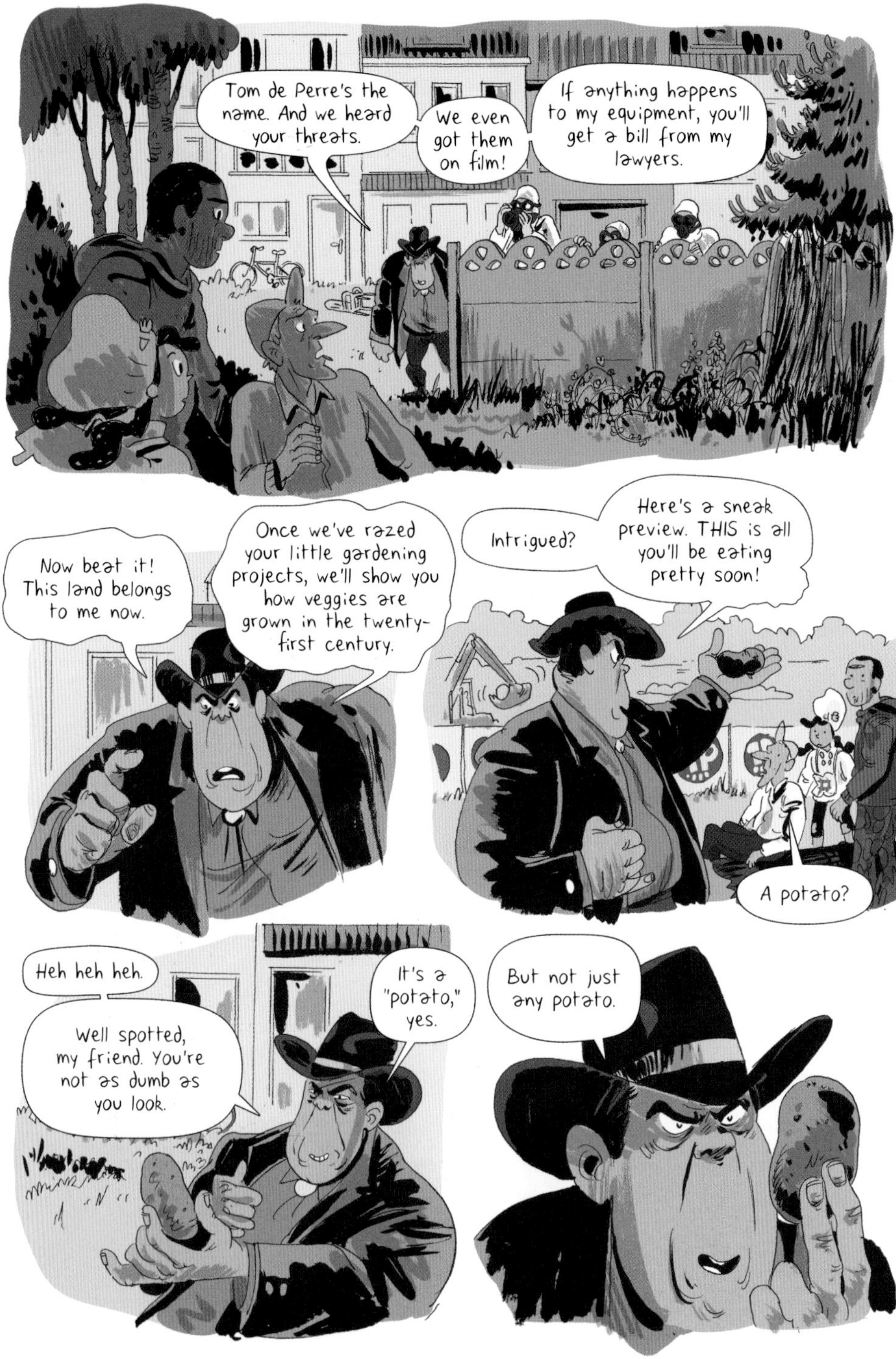
Tom de Perre's the name. And we heard your threats.
We even got them on film!
If anything happens to my equipment, you'll get a bill from my lawyers.
Now beat it! This land belongs to me now.
Once we've razed your little gardening projects, we'll show you how veggies are grown in the twenty-first century.
Intrigued?
Here's a sneak preview. THIS is all you'll be eating pretty soon!
A potato?
Heh heh heh.
Well spotted, my friend. You're not as dumb as you look.
It's a "potato," yes.
But not just any potato.

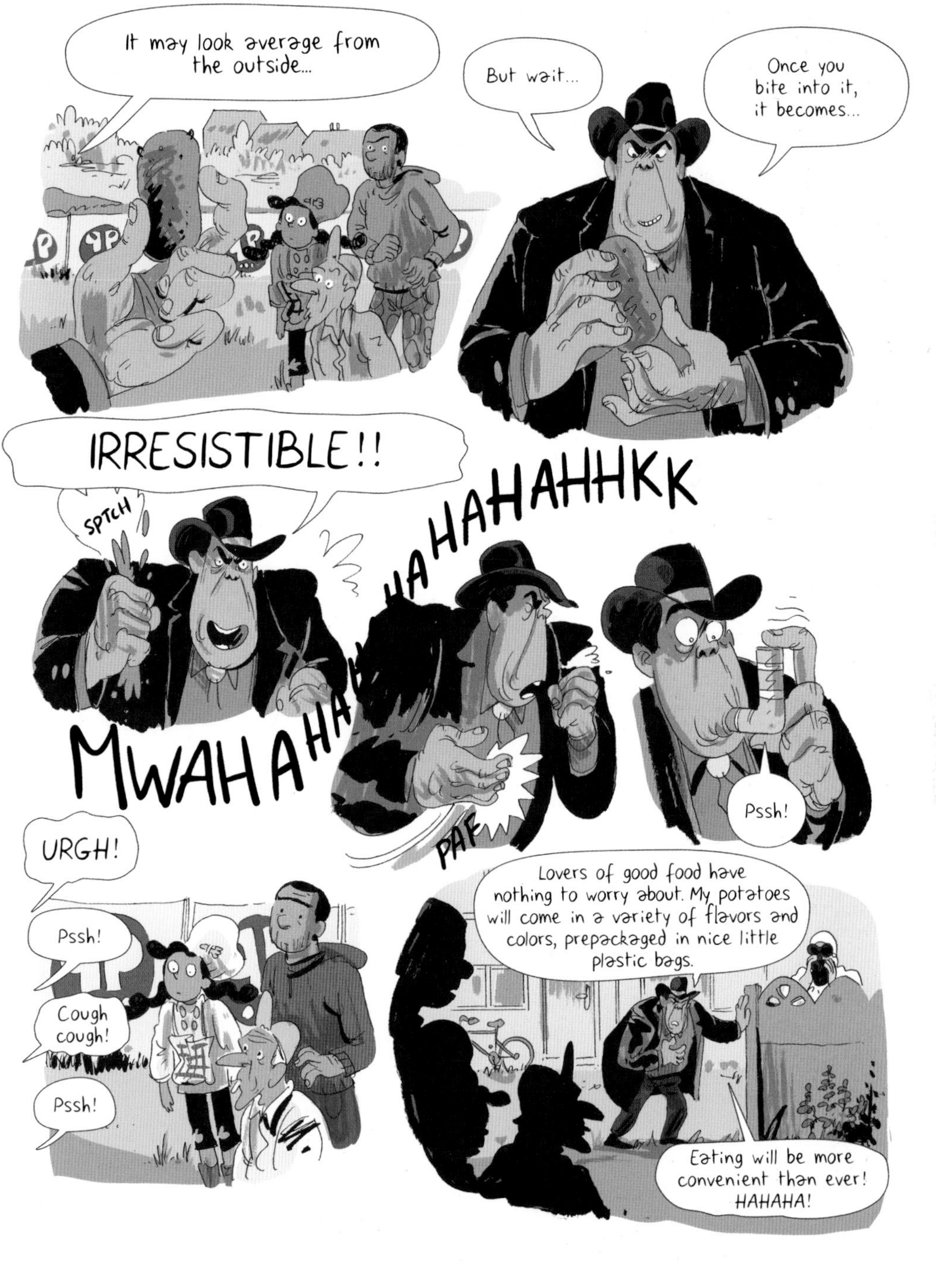
It may look average from the outside...
But wait...
Once you bite into it, it becomes...
IRRESISTIBLE!!
SPTCH
MWAHAHAHAHAHAHAHHKK
PAF
Pssh!
URGH!
Pssh!
Cough cough!
Pssh!
Lovers of good food have nothing to worry about. My potatoes will come in a variety of flavors and colors, prepackaged in nice little plastic bags.
Eating will be more convenient than ever! HAHAHA!

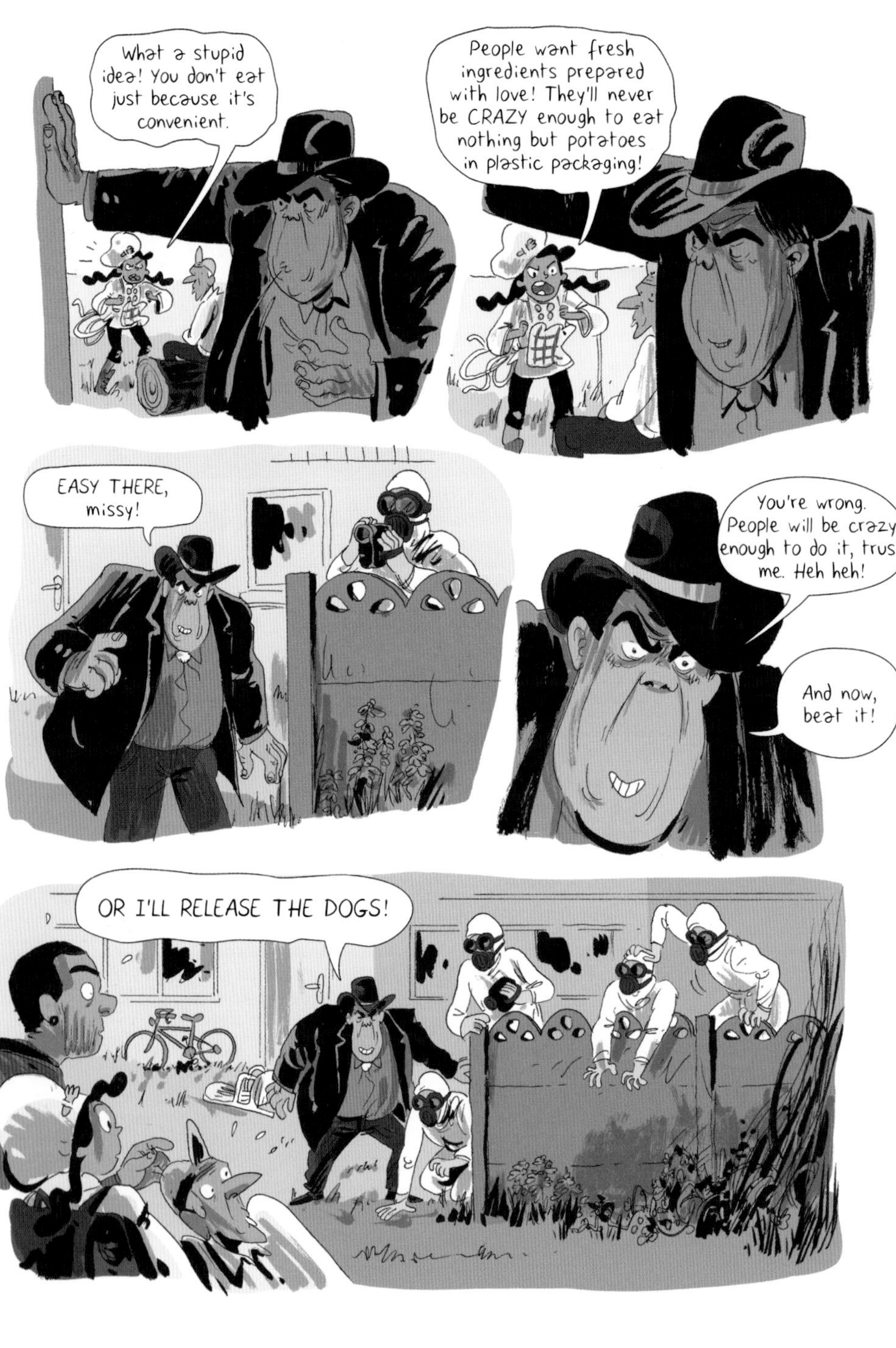
What a stupid idea! You don't eat just because it's convenient.
People want fresh ingredients prepared with love! They'll never be CRAZY enough to eat nothing but potatoes in plastic packaging!
EASY THERE, missy!
You're wrong. People will be crazy enough to do it, trust me. Heh heh!
And now, beat it!
OR I'LL RELEASE THE DOGS!

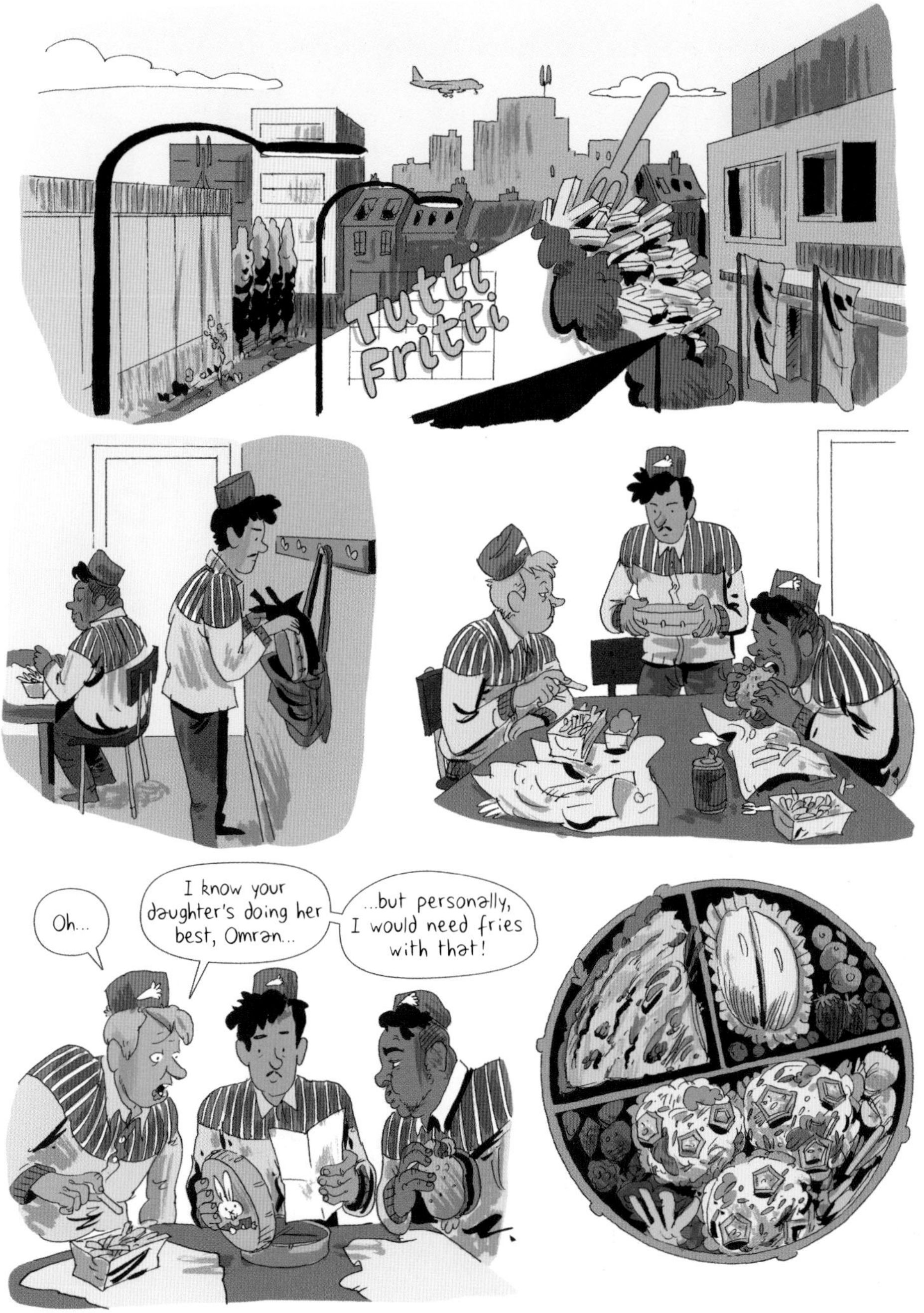
Tutti Fritti
Oh...
I know your daughter's doing her best, Omran...
...but personally, I would need fries with that!

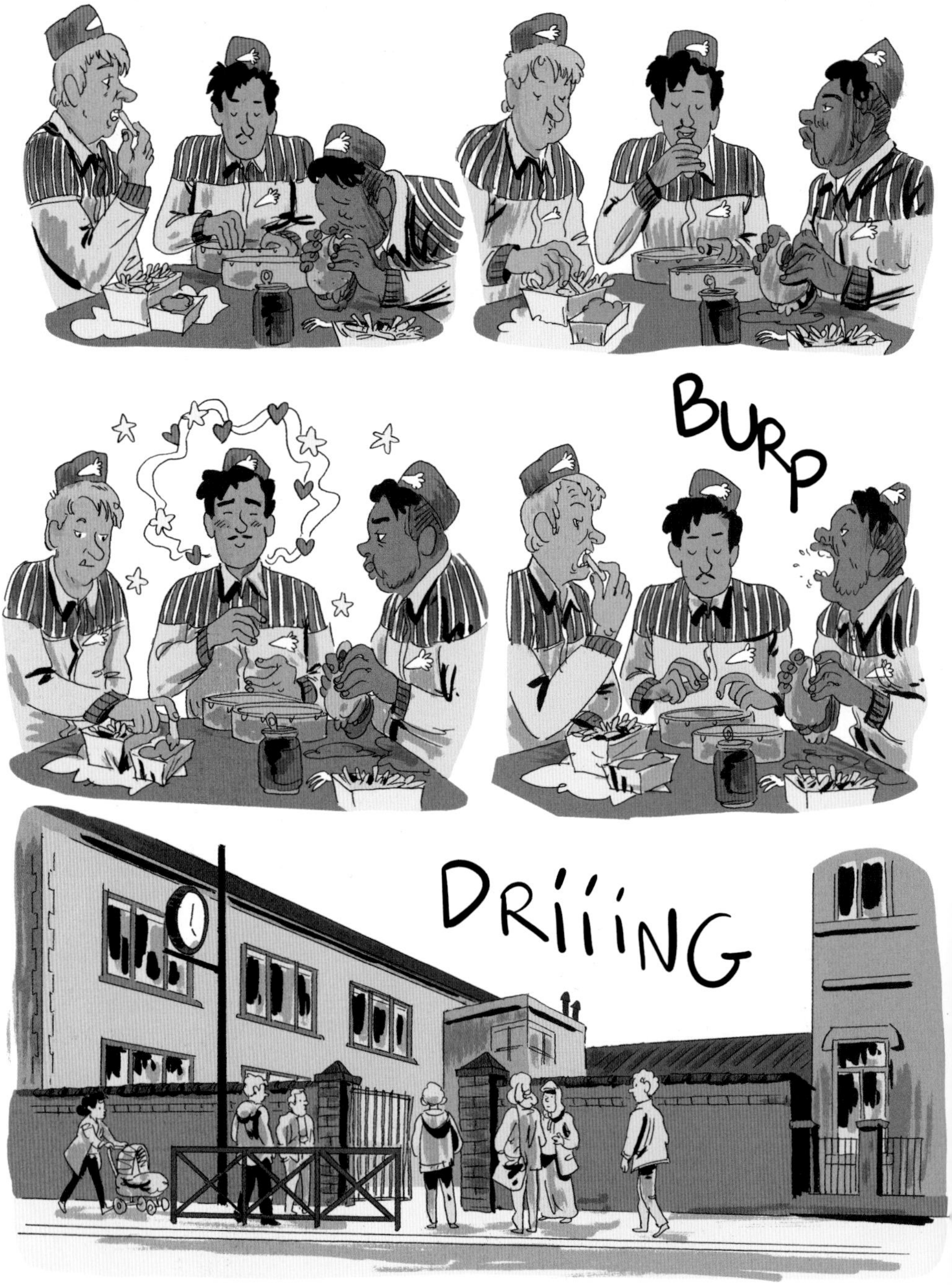
BURP
DRiiiNG

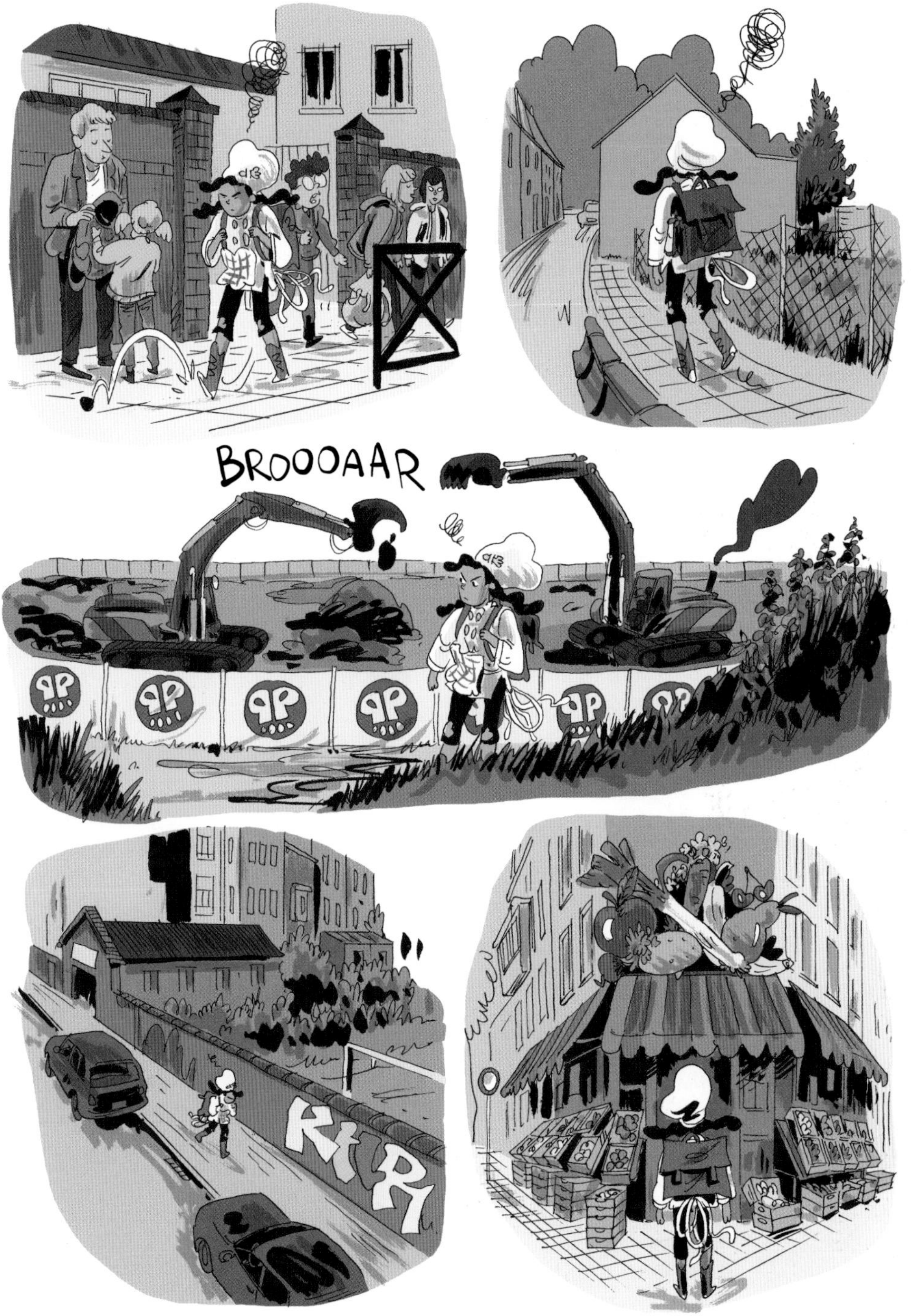
BROOOAAR

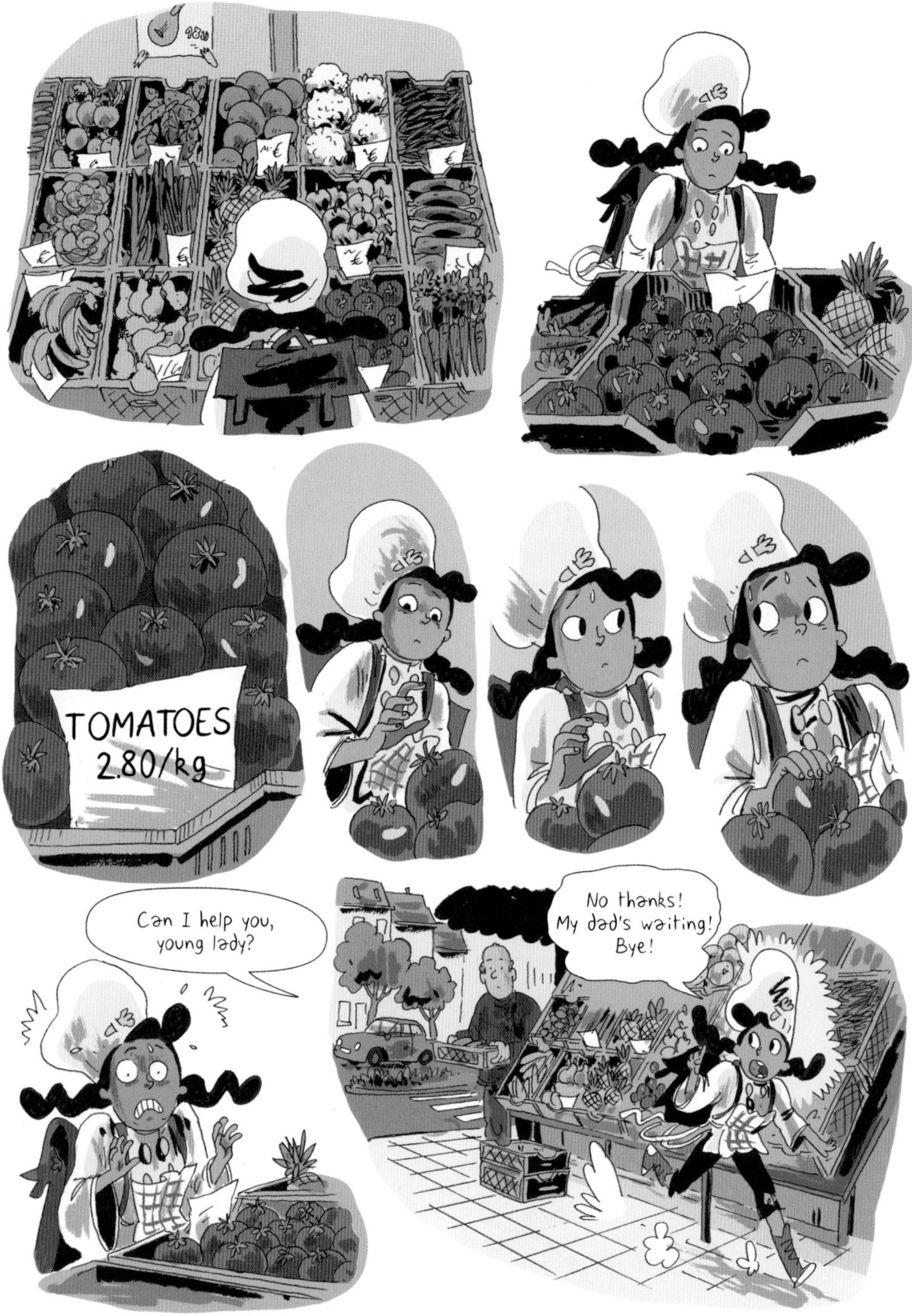
TOMATOES
2.80/kg
Can I help you, young lady?
No thanks! My dad's waiting! Bye!

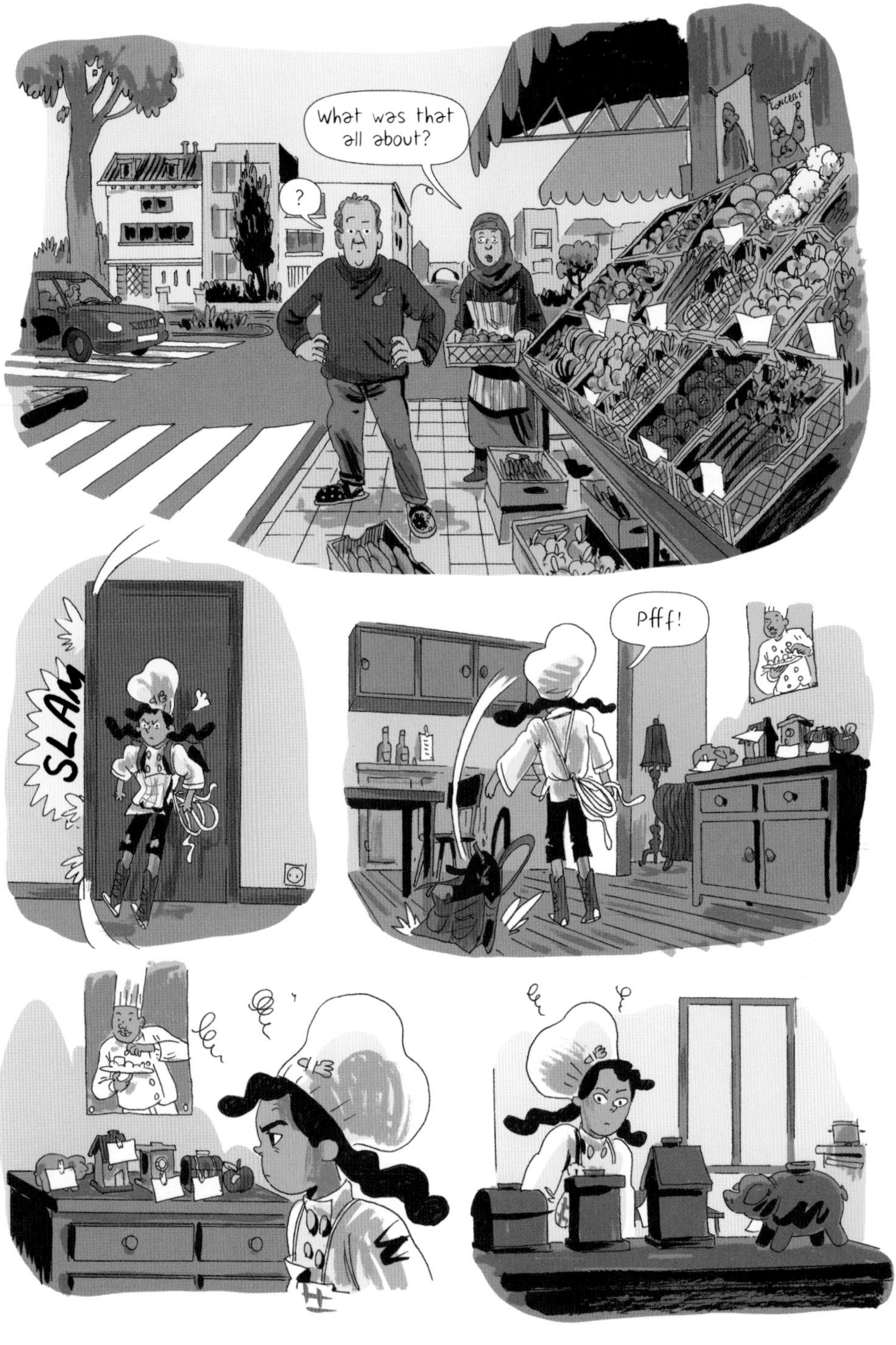
?
What was that all about?
SLAM
Pfff!

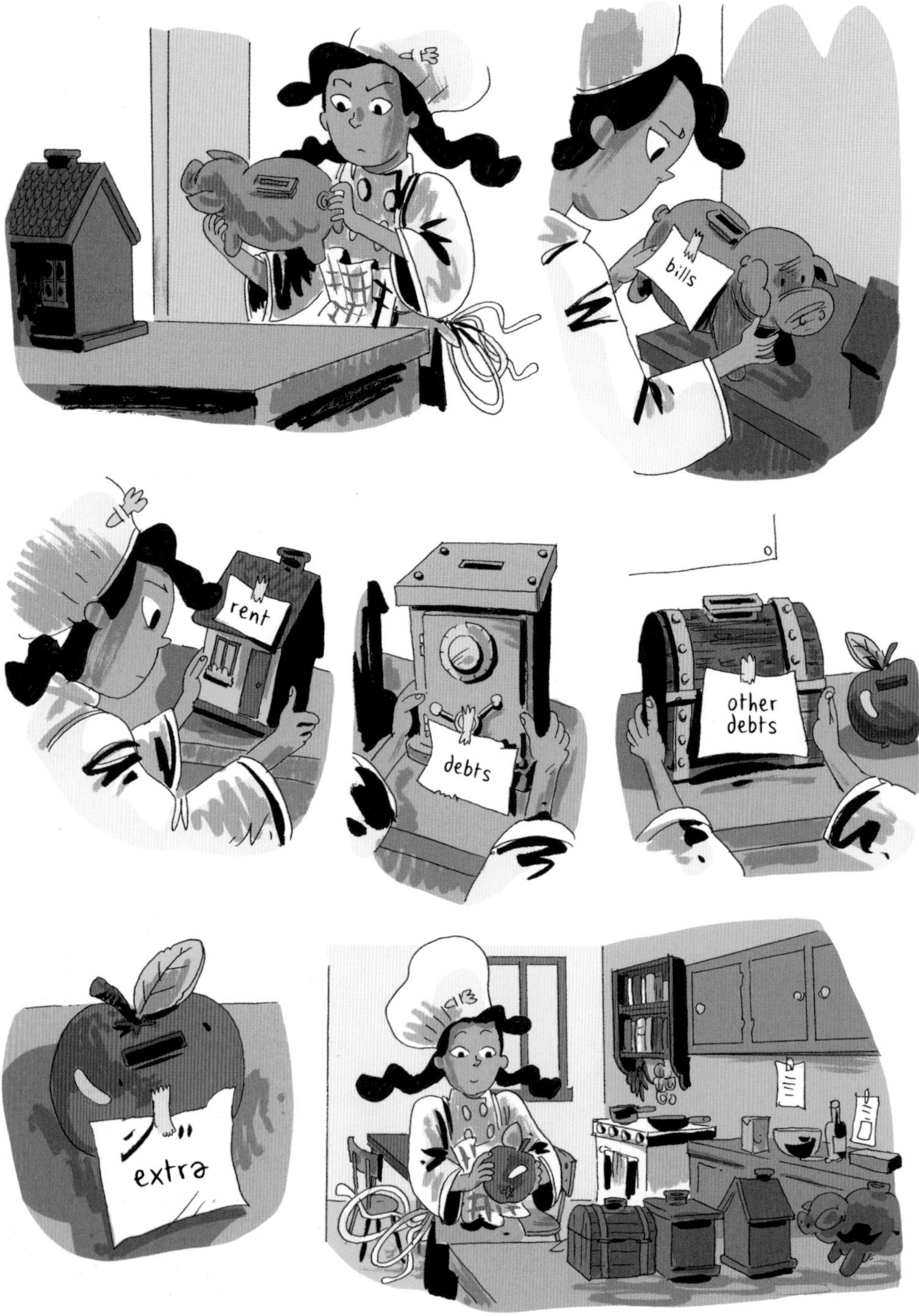
bills
rent
debts
other debts
extra

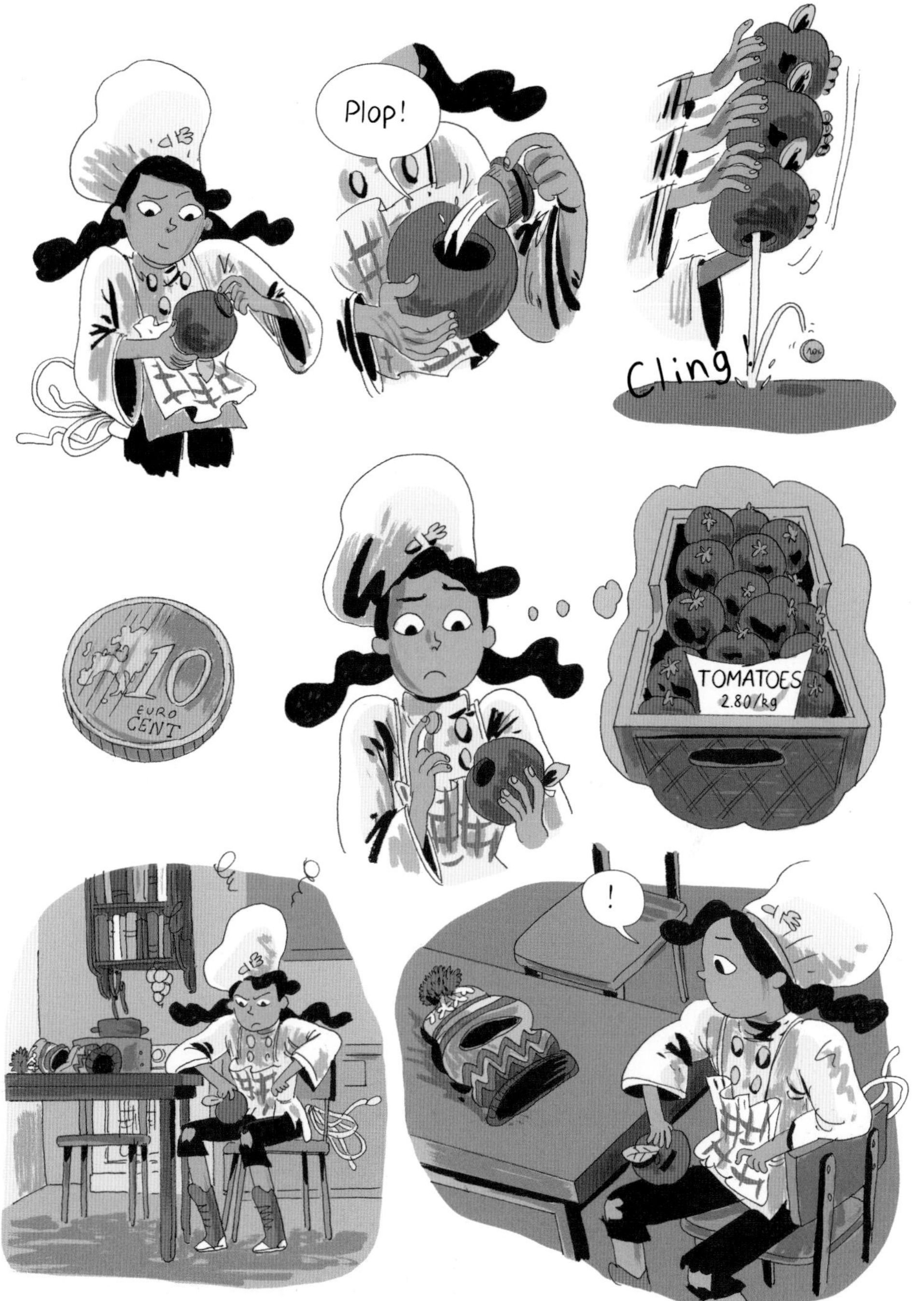
Plop!
Cling!
10
EURO CENT
TOMATOES
2.80/kg
!

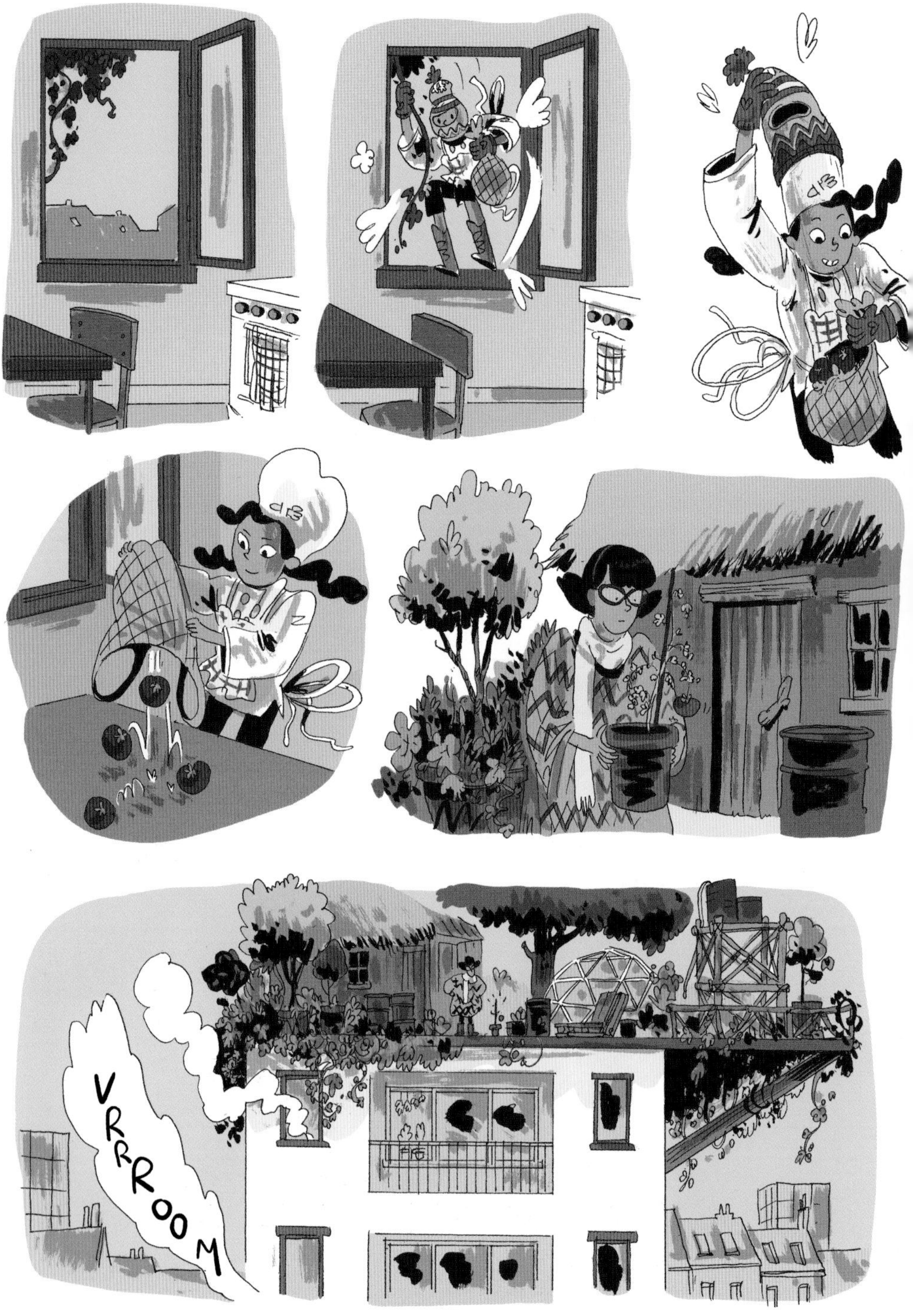
VRRROOM

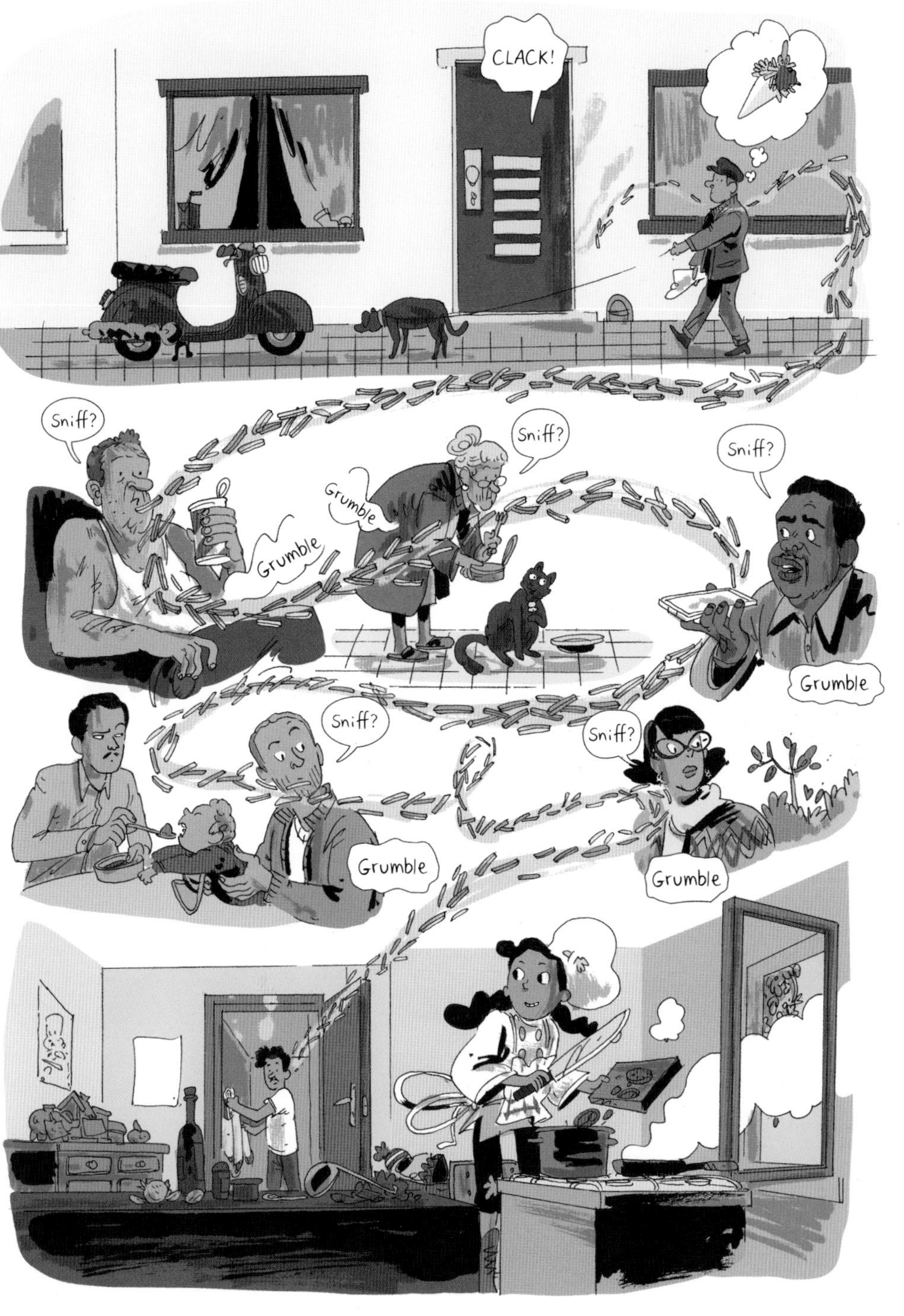
CLACK!
Sniff?
Grumble
Sniff?
Grumble
Sniff?
Grumble
Sniff?
Grumble
Sniff?
Grumble

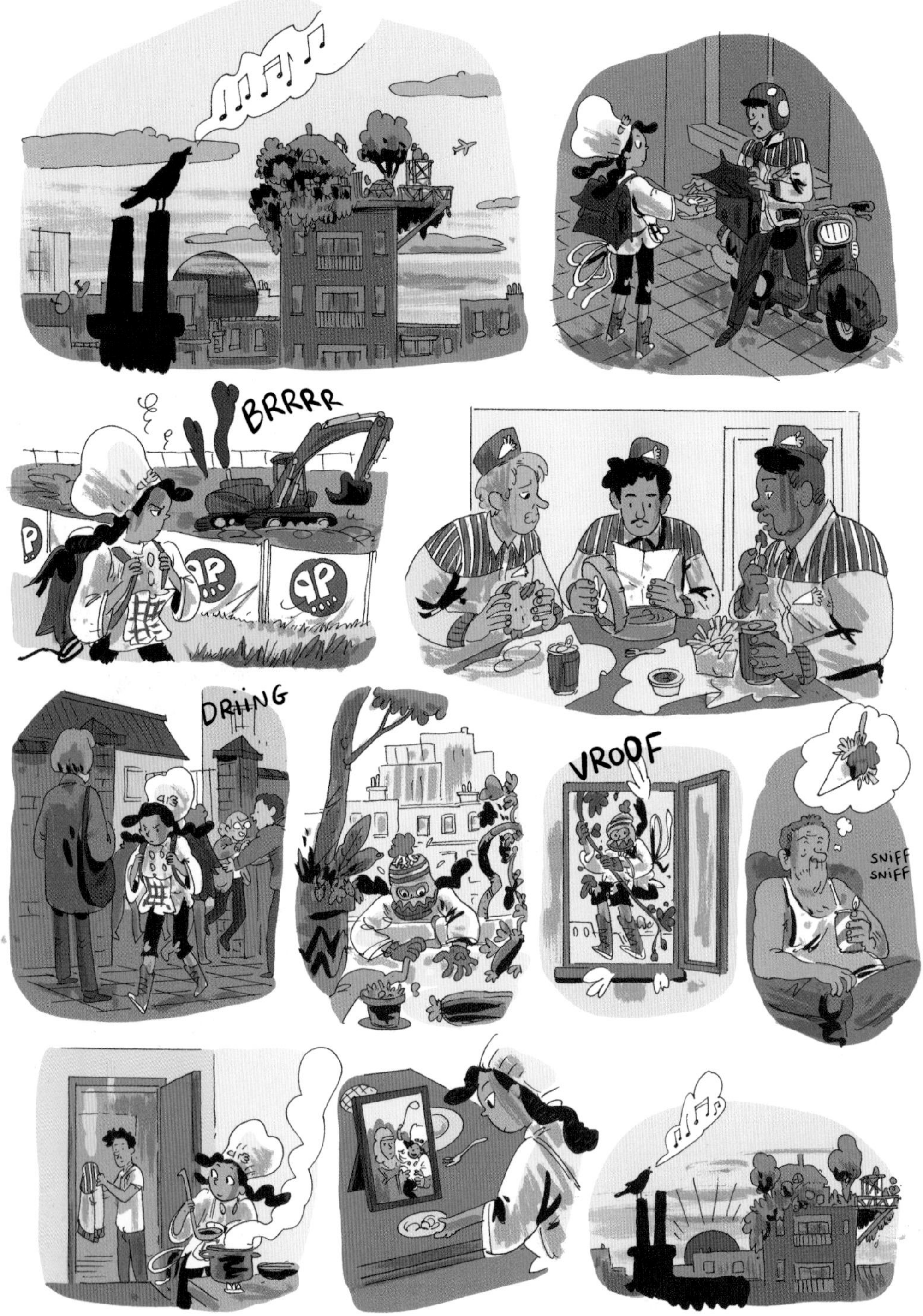
BRRRR
DRIING
VROOF
SNIFF
SNIFF

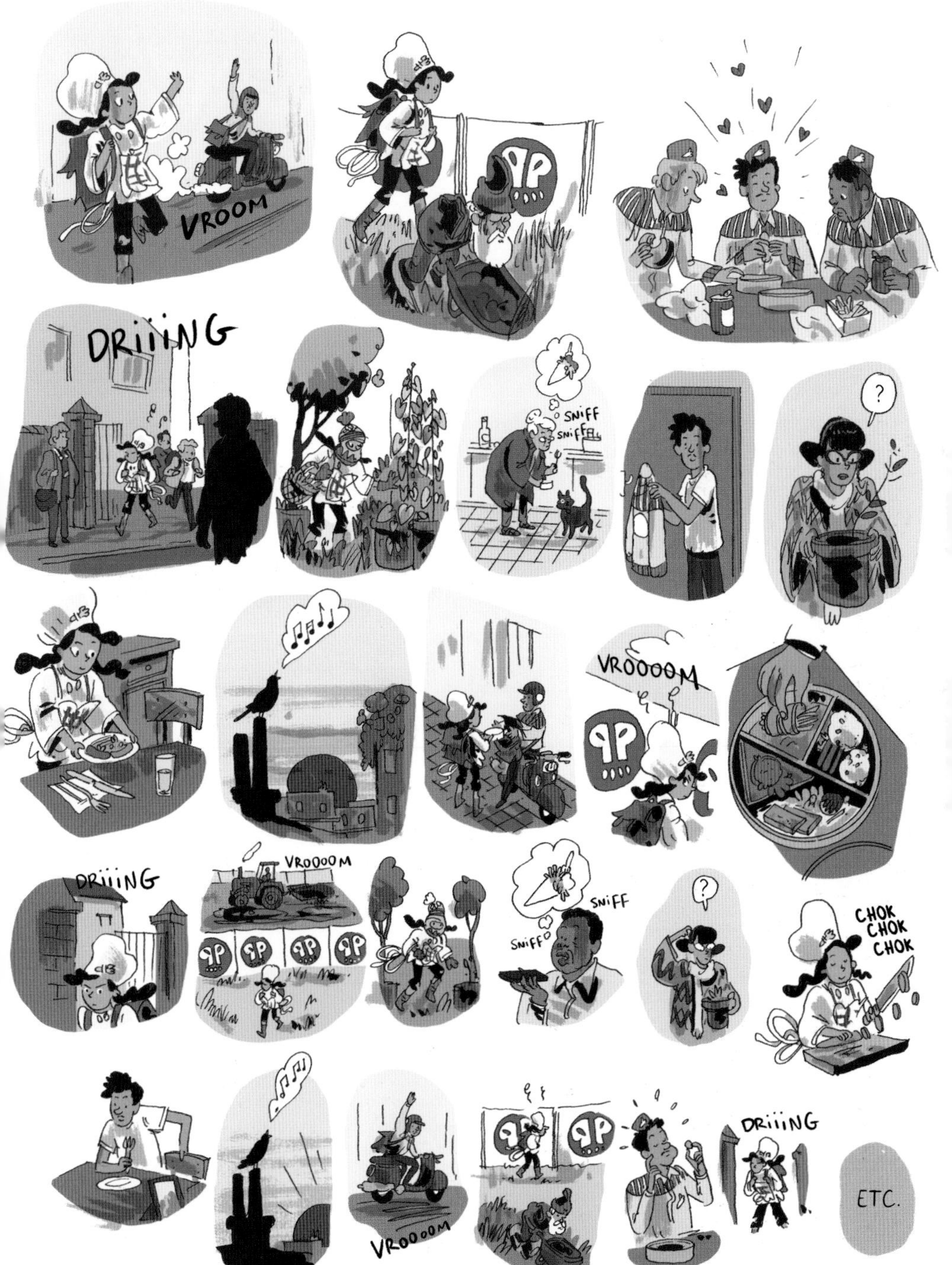
VROOM
DRiiiNG
SNiFF
SNiFF
?
VROOOOM
DRiiiNG
VROOOOM
SNiFF
SNiFF
?
CHOK
CHOK
CHOK
VROOOOM
DRiiiNG
ETC.

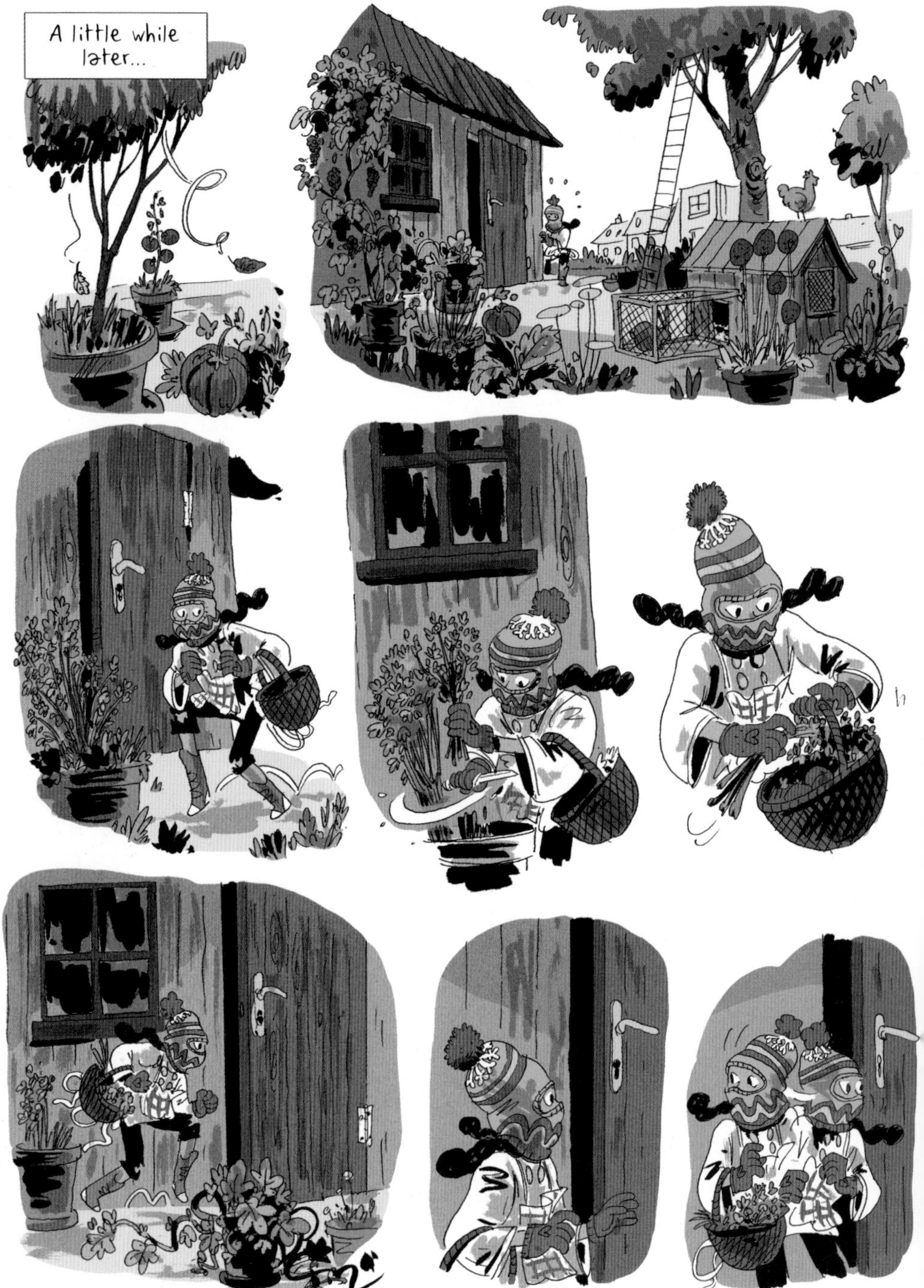
A little while later...

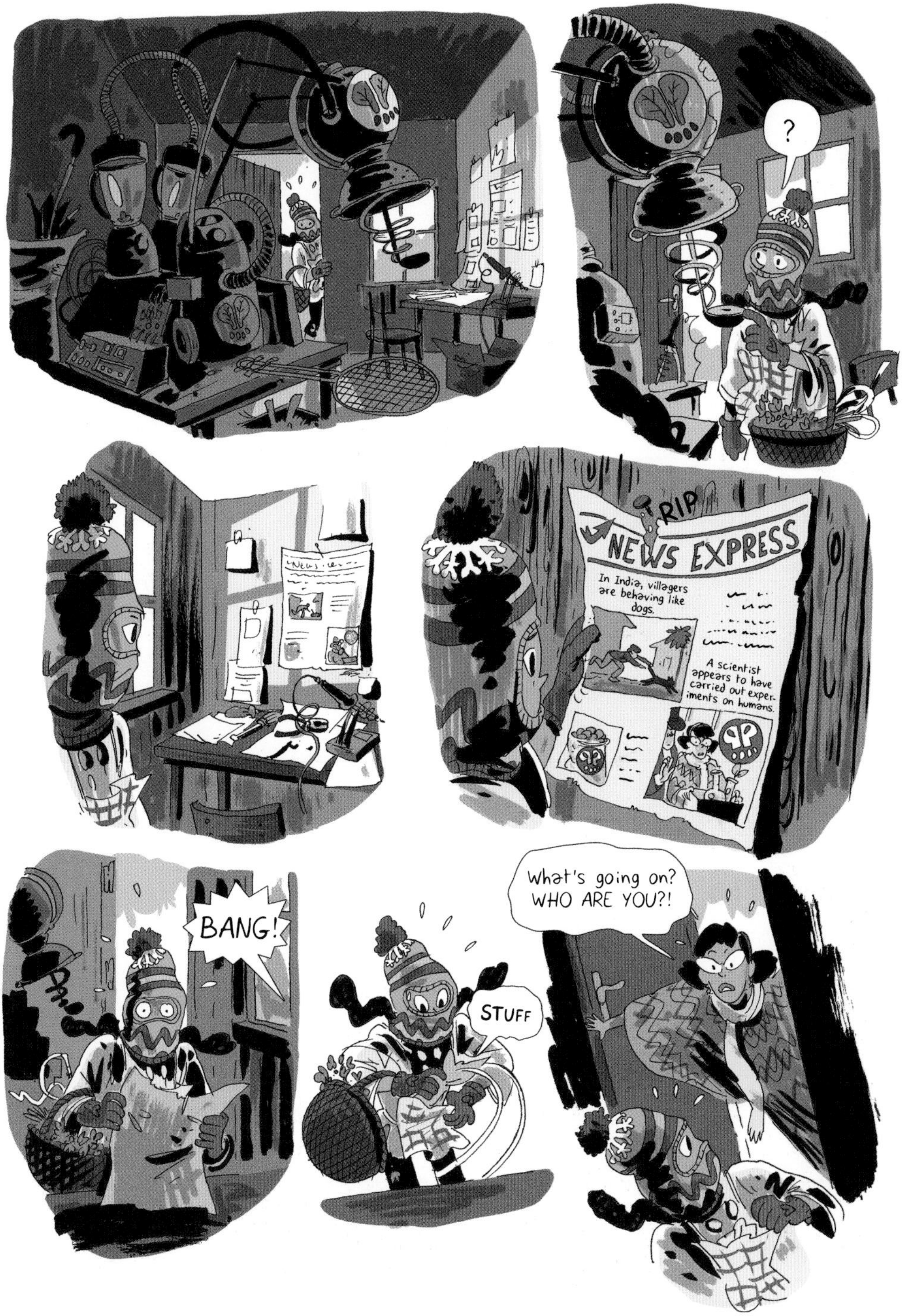
?
RIP
NEWS EXPRESS
In India, villagers are behaving like dogs.
A scientist appears to have carried out experiments on humans.
BANG!
STUFF
What's going on? WHO ARE YOU?!

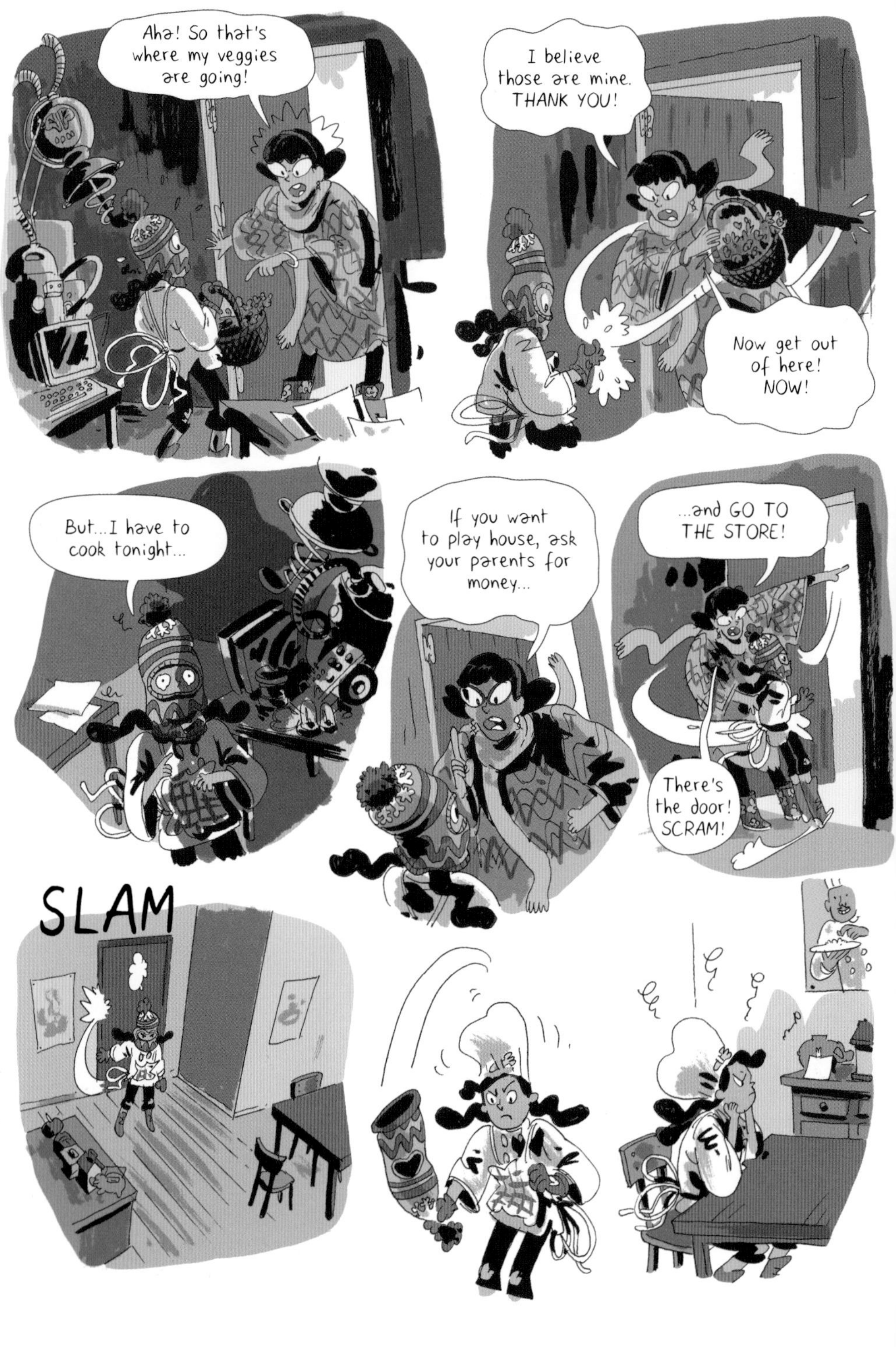
Aha! So that's where my veggies are going!
I believe those are mine. THANK YOU!
Now get out of here! NOW!
But...I have to cook tonight...
If you want to play house, ask your parents for money...
...and GO TO THE STORE!
There's the door! SCRAM!
SLAM

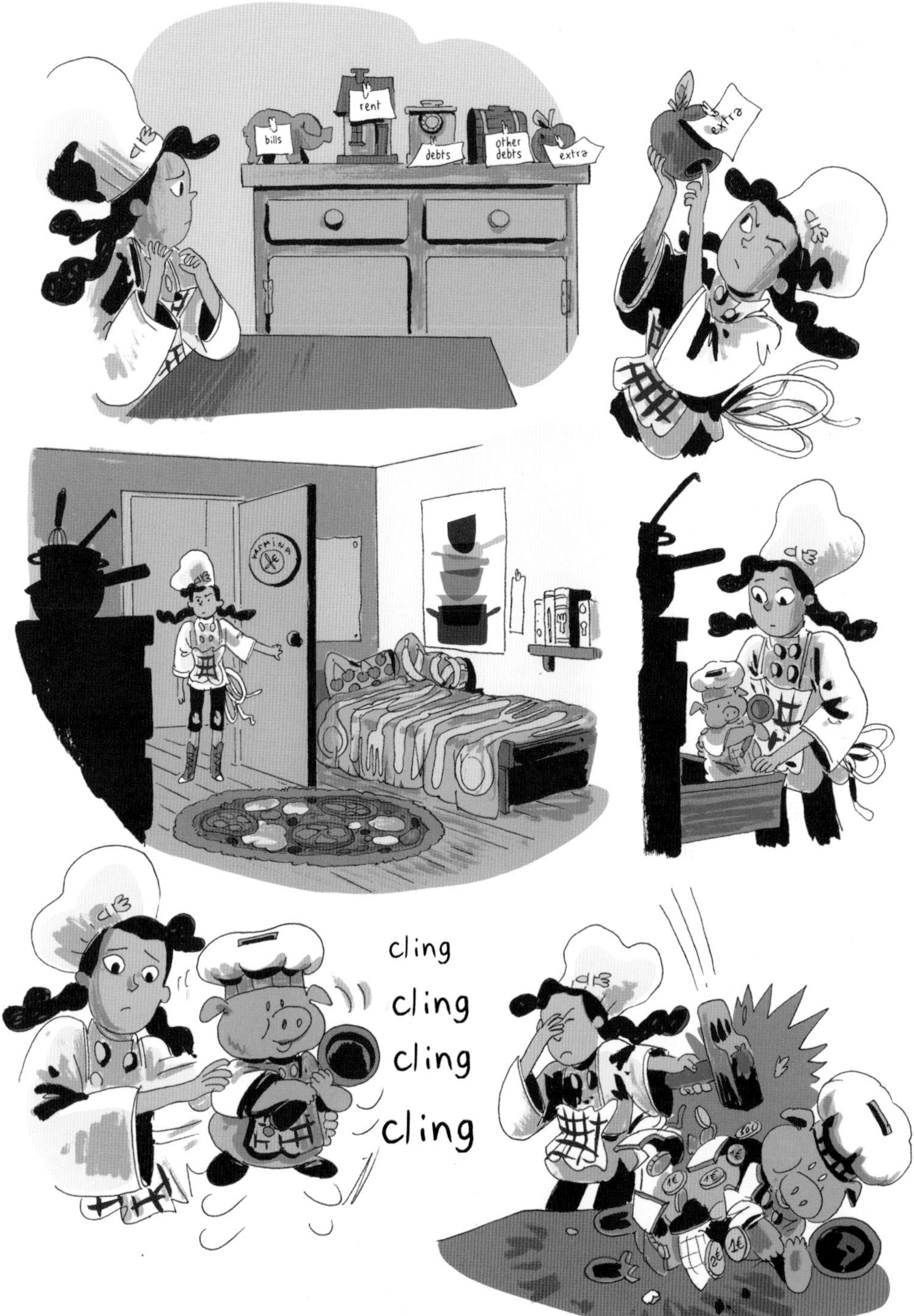
bills
rent
debts
other debts
extra
extra
cling
cling
cling
cling

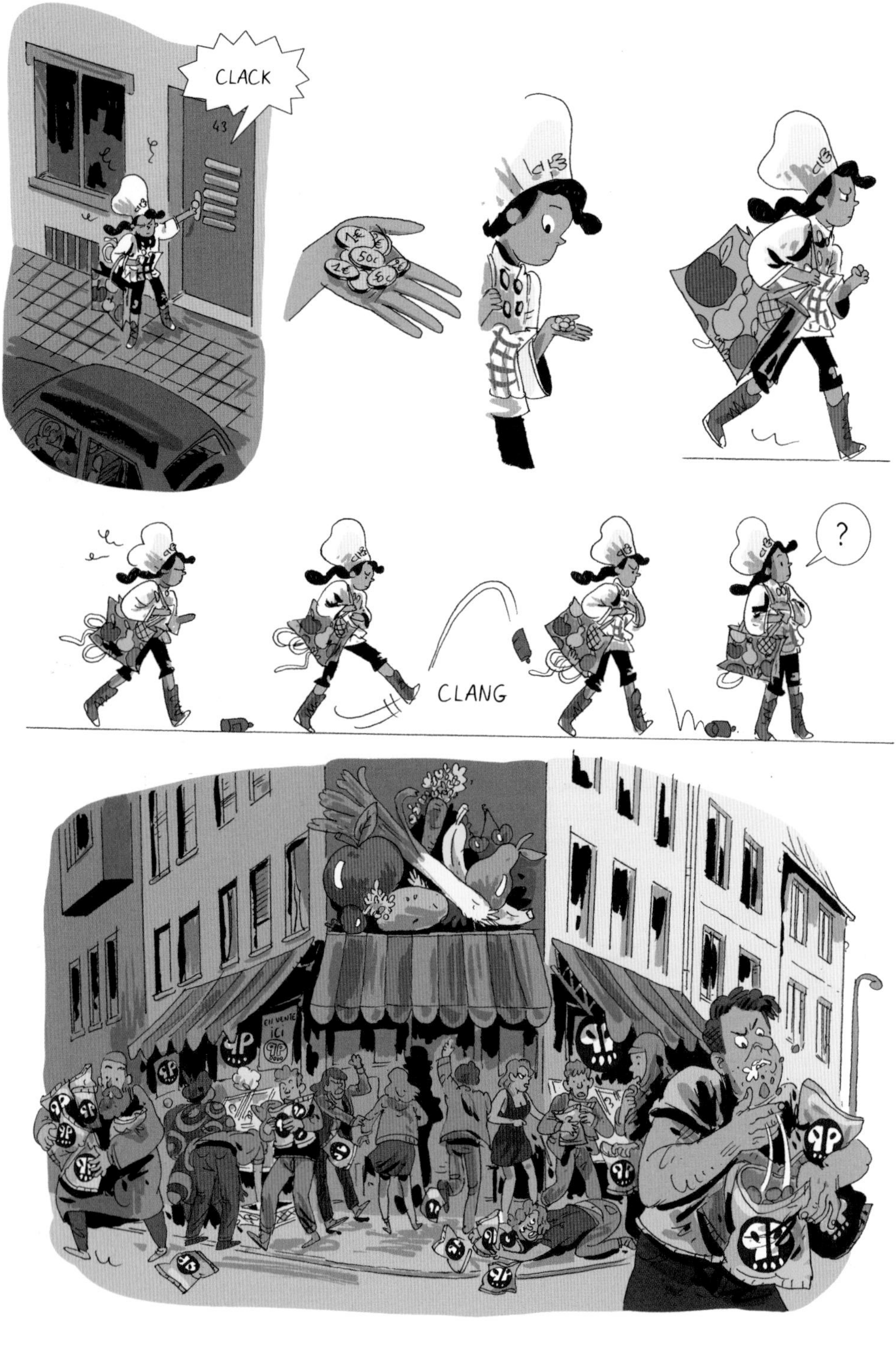
CLACK
CLANG
?

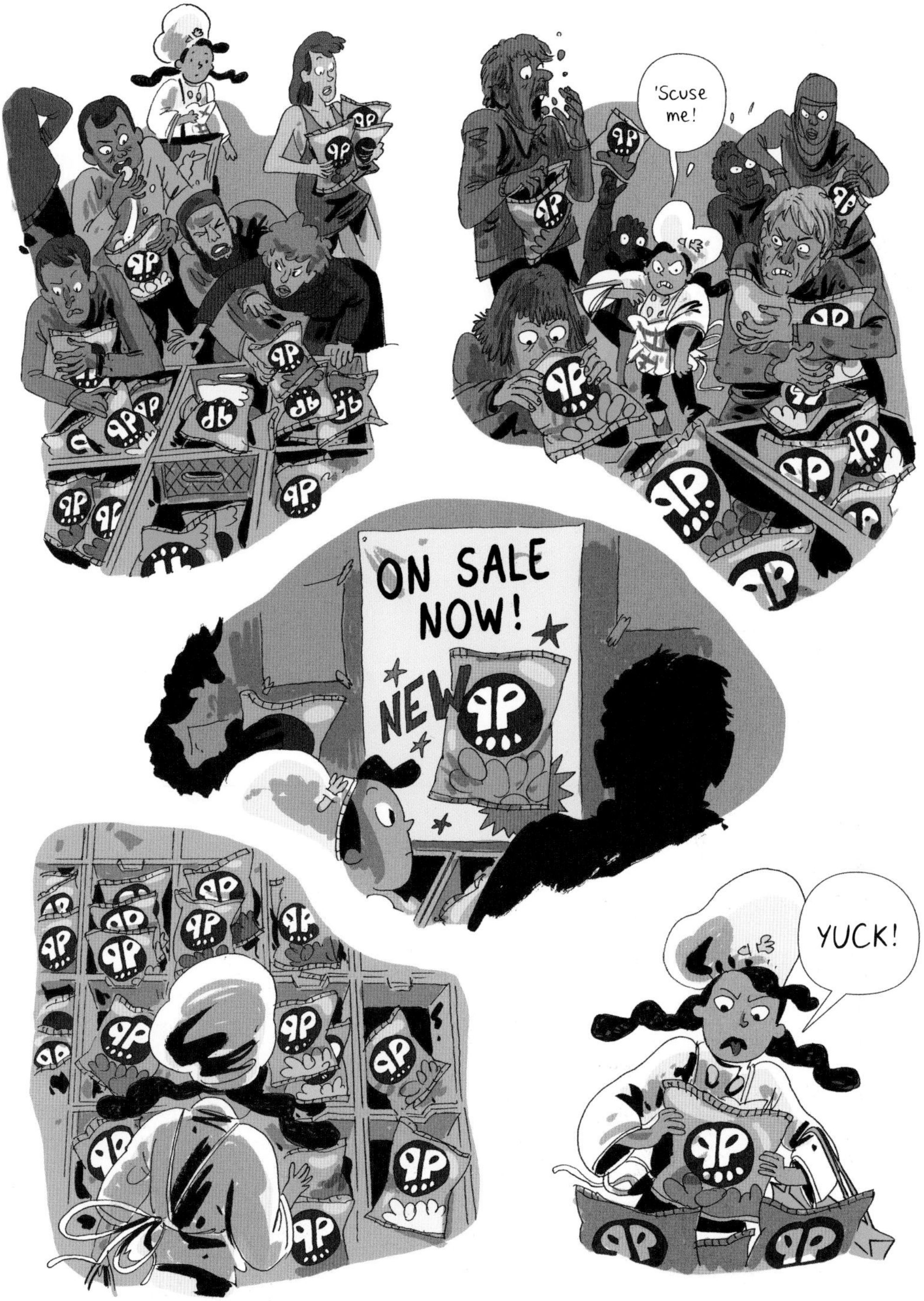
'Scuse me!
ON SALE NOW!
NEW
YUCK!

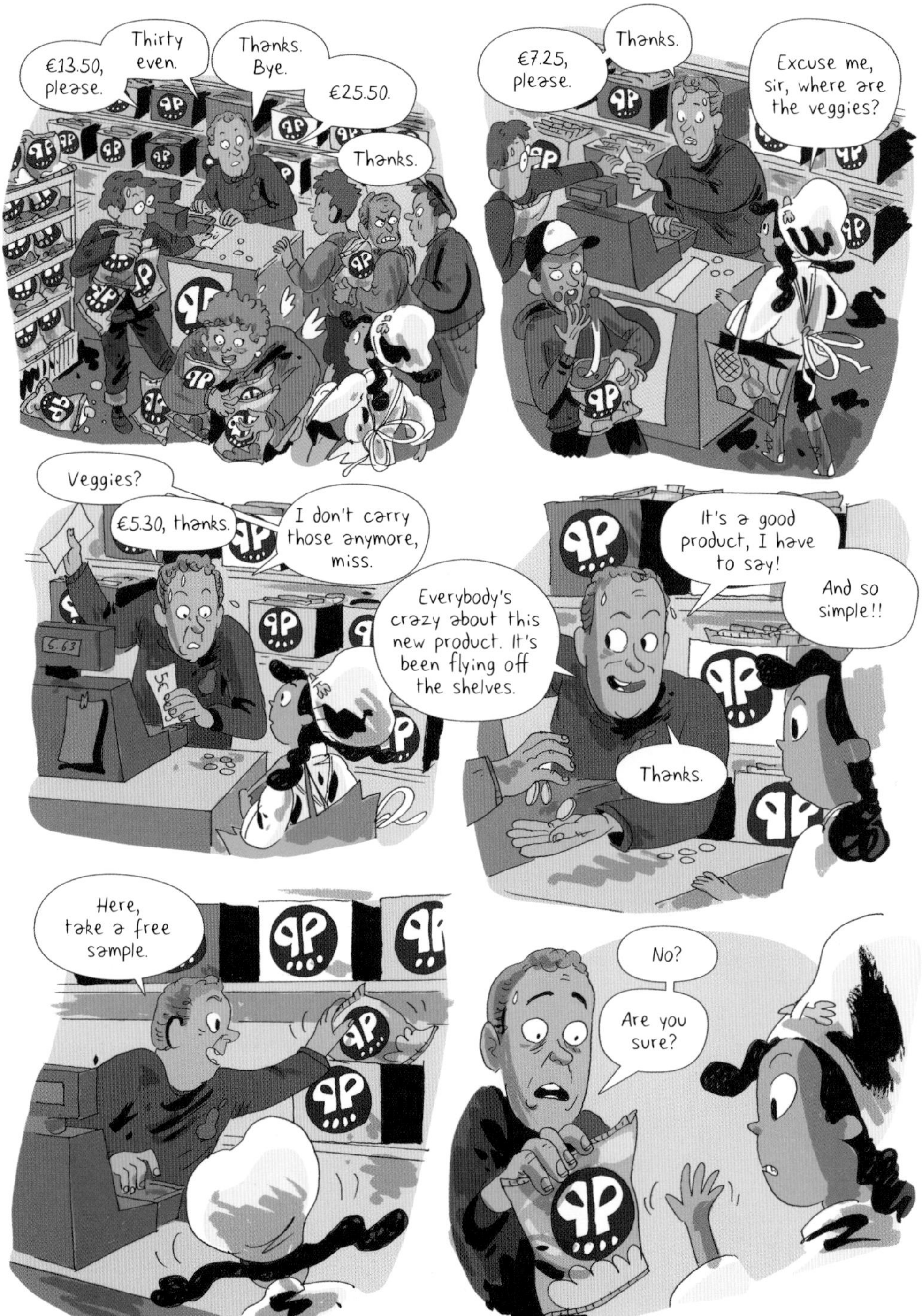
€13.50, please.
Thirty even.
Thanks. Bye.
€25.50.
Thanks.
€7.25, please.
Thanks.
Excuse me, sir, where are the veggies?
Veggies?
€5.30, thanks.
I don't carry those anymore, miss.
Everybody's crazy about this new product. It's been flying off the shelves.
It's a good product, I have to say!
And so simple!!
Thanks.
Here, take a free sample.
No?
Are you sure?

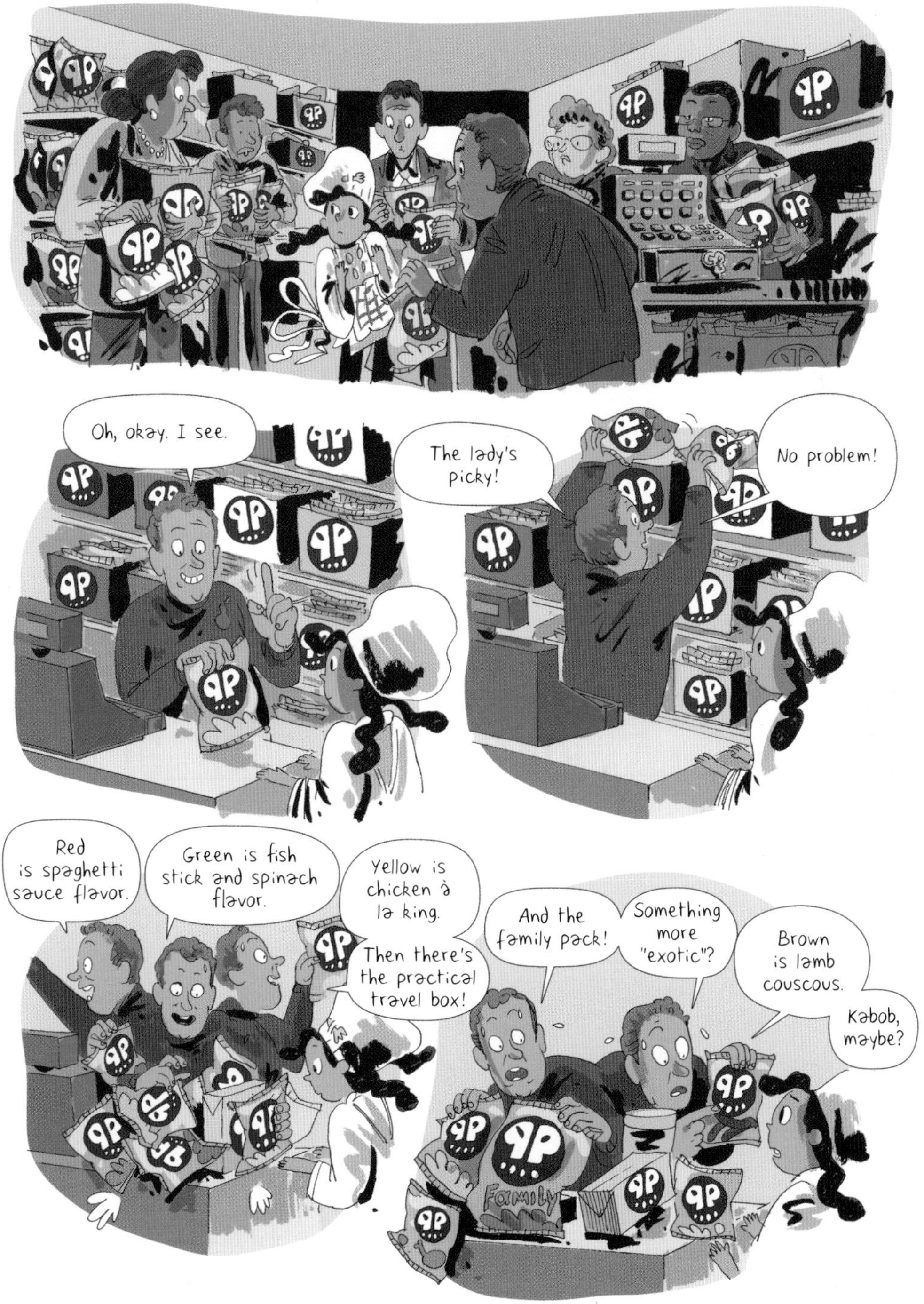

Oh, okay. I see.
The lady's picky!
No problem!
Red is spaghetti sauce flavor.
Green is fish stick and spinach flavor.
Yellow is chicken à la king.
Then there's the practical travel box!
And the family pack!
Something more "exotic"?
Brown is lamb couscous.
Kabob, maybe?

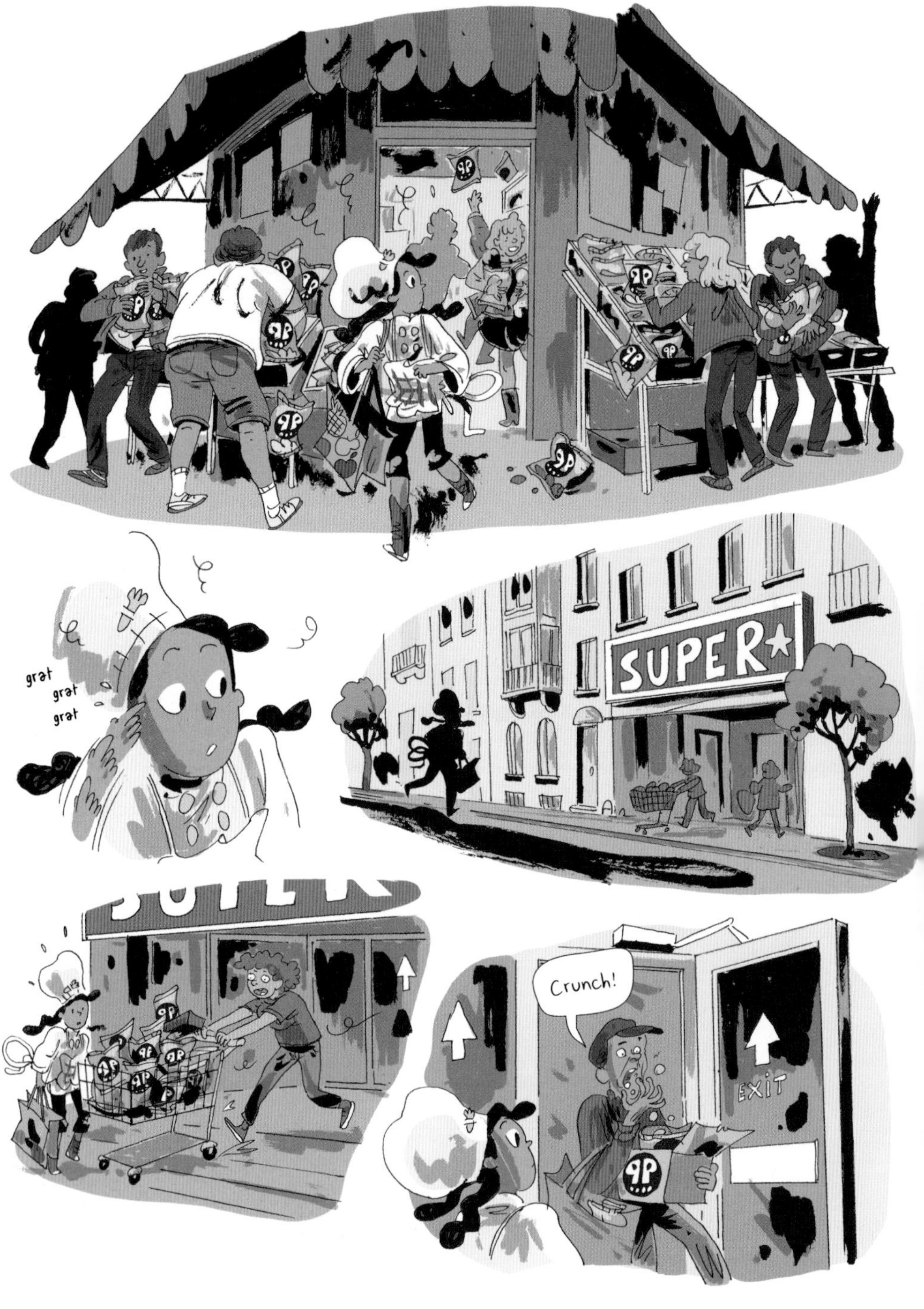
grat
grat
grat
SUPER
Crunch!
EXIT

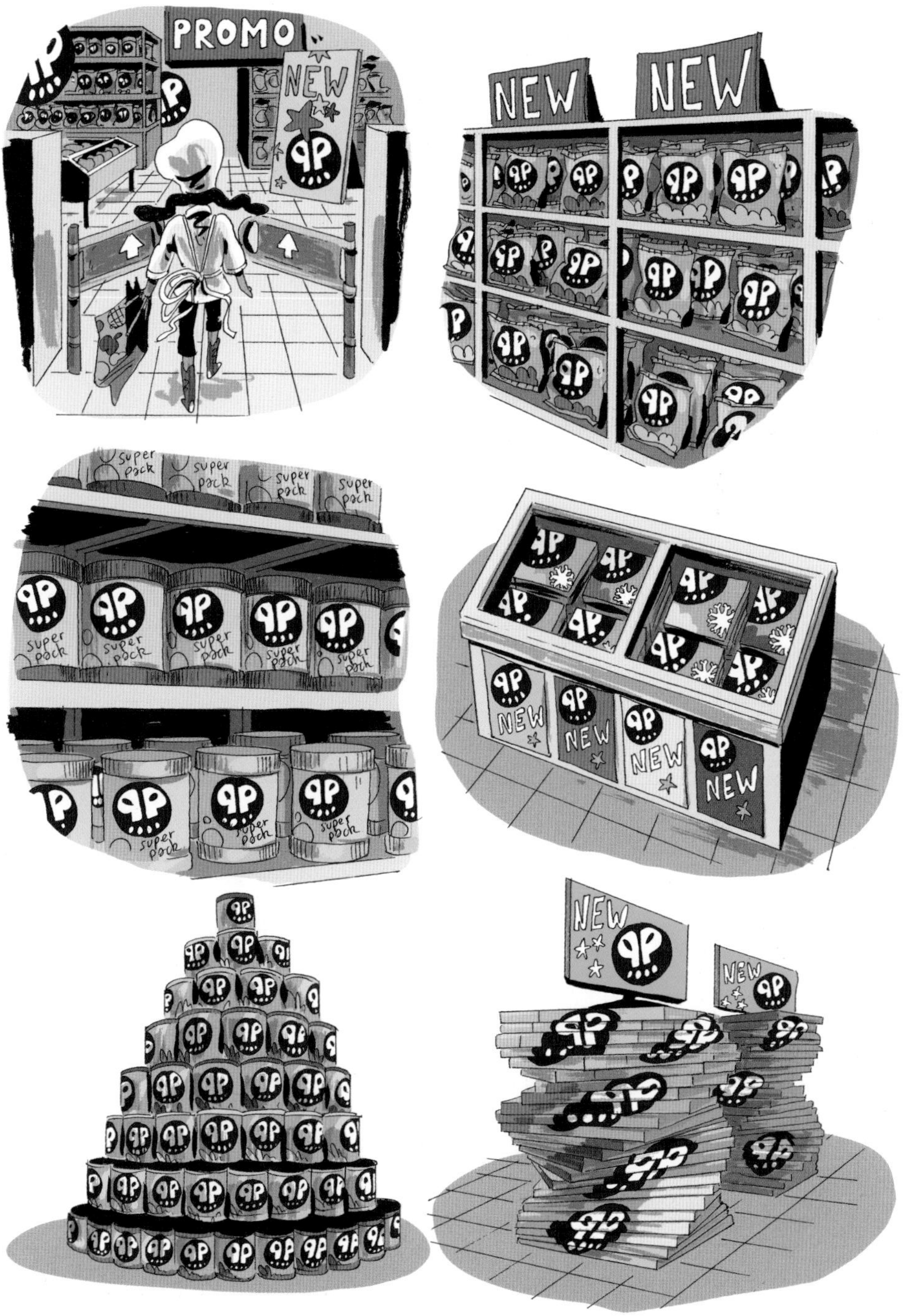
PROMO
NEW
NEW
NEW
super pack
NEW
NEW
NEW
NEW
NEW
NEW

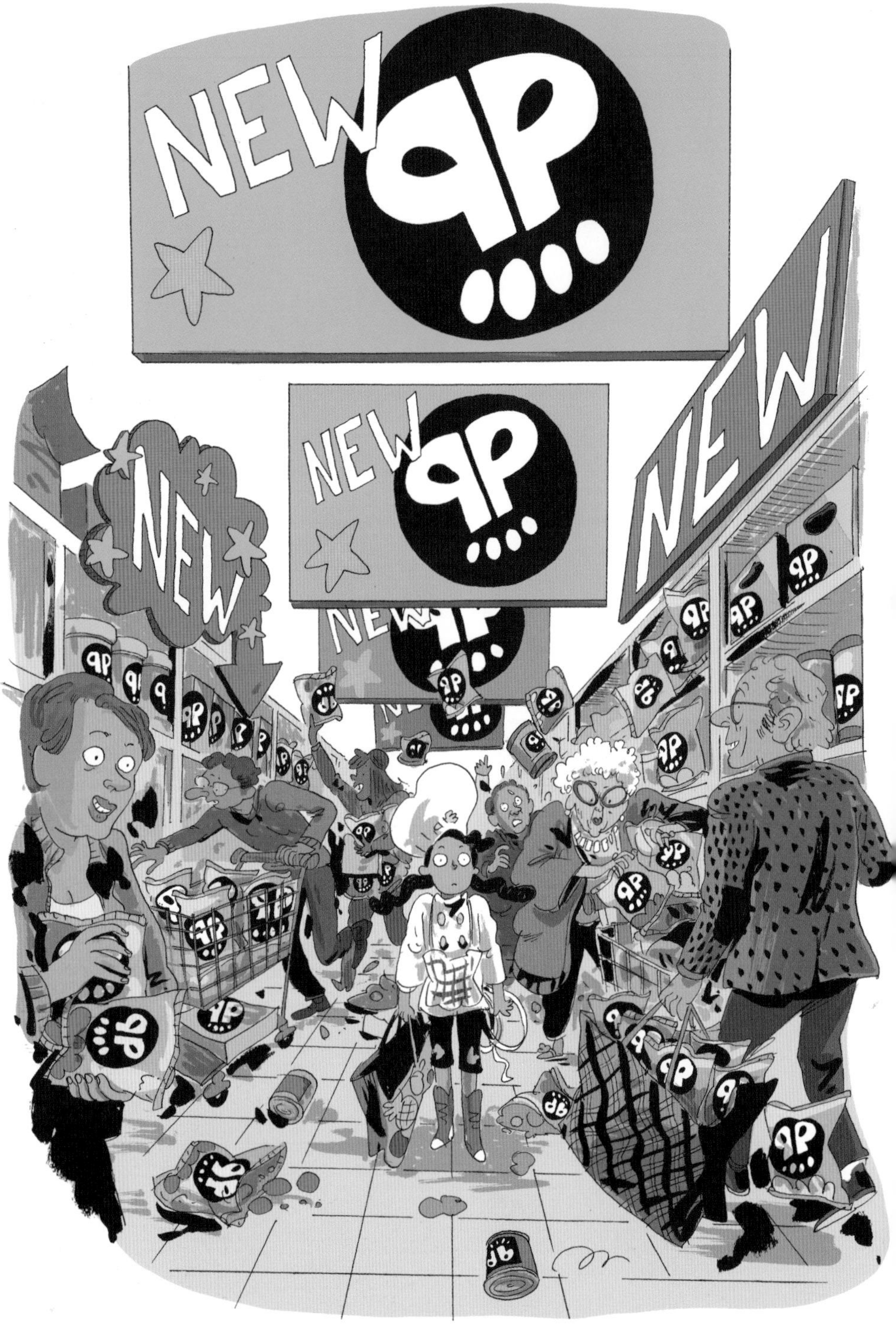
NEW
NEW
NEW
NEW

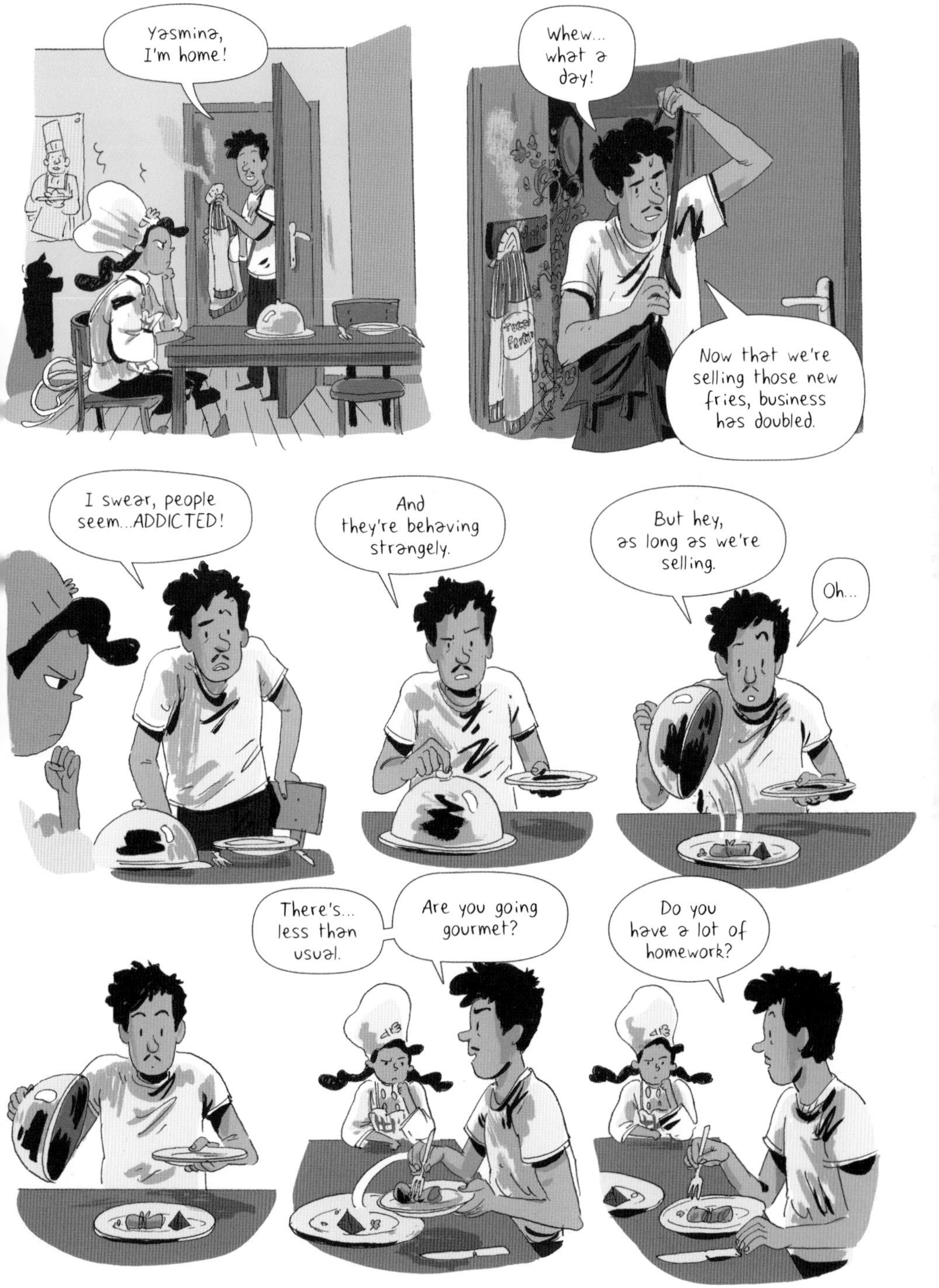
Yasmina, I'm home!
Whew... what a day!
Now that we're selling those new fries, business has doubled.
I swear, people seem...ADDICTED!
And they're behaving strangely.
But hey, as long as we're selling.
Oh...
There's... less than usual.
Are you going gourmet?
Do you have a lot of homework?

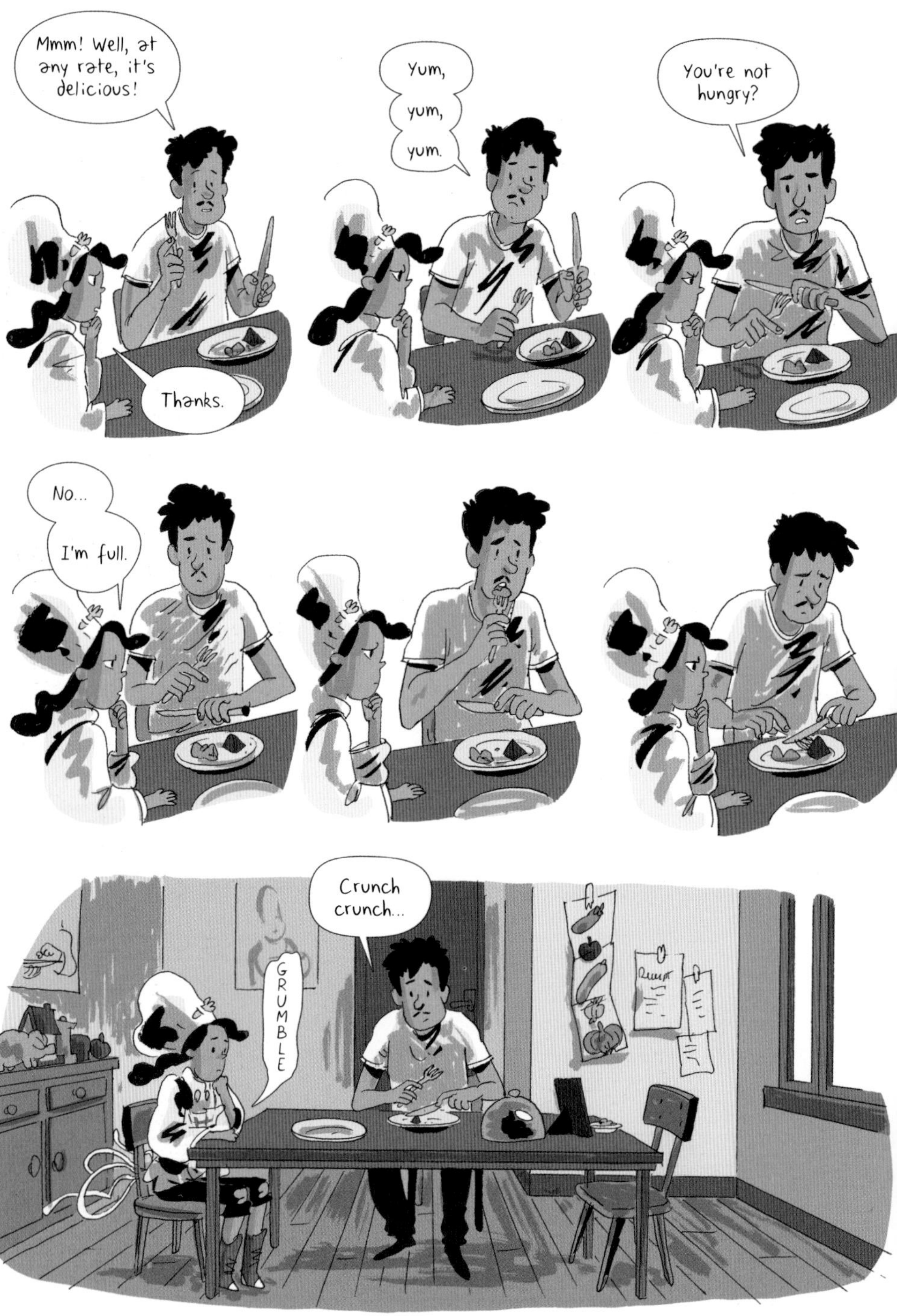

Mmm! Well, at any rate, it's delicious!
Thanks.
Yum,
yum,
yum.
You're not hungry?
No...
I'm full.
Crunch crunch...
GRUMBLE

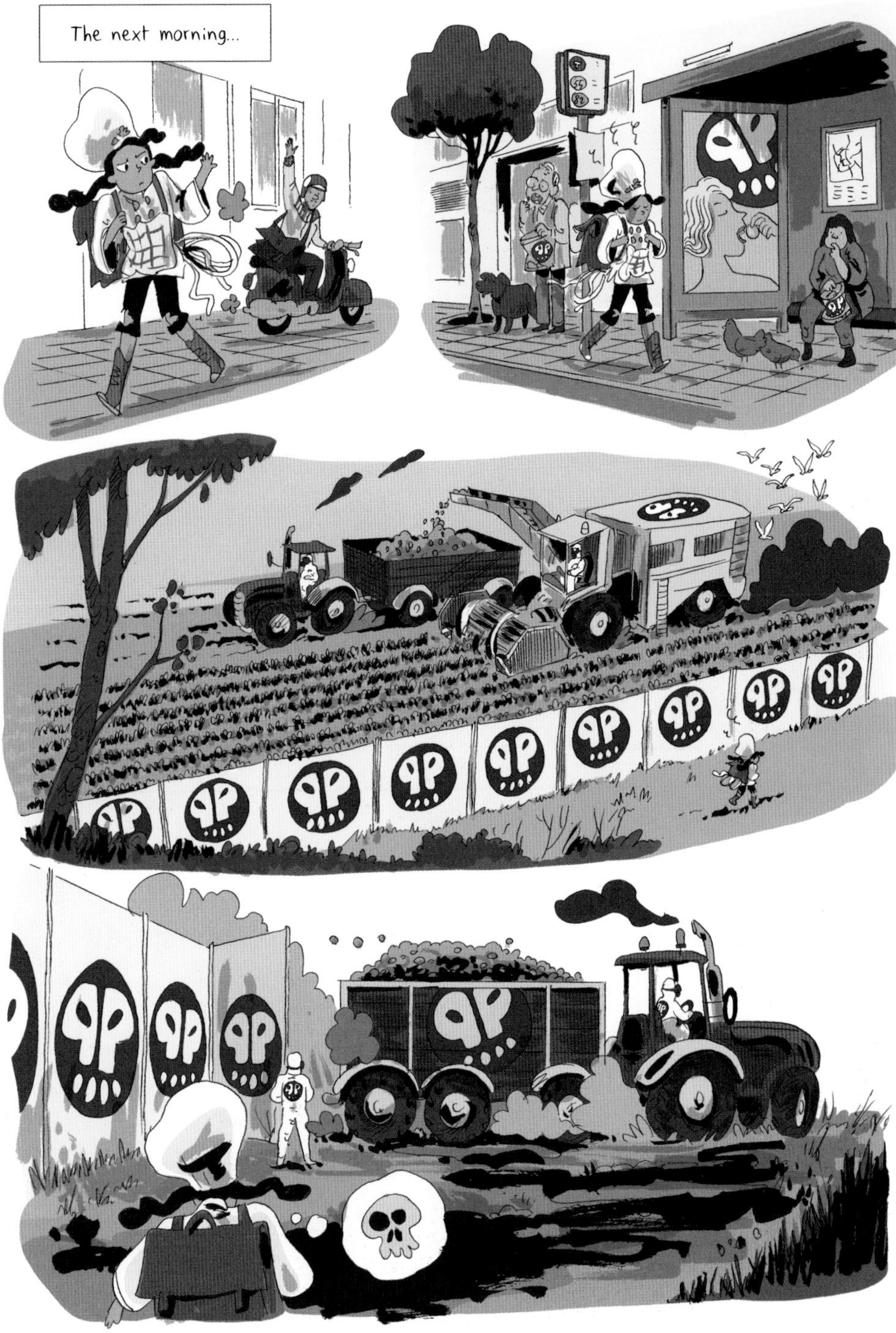
The next morning...

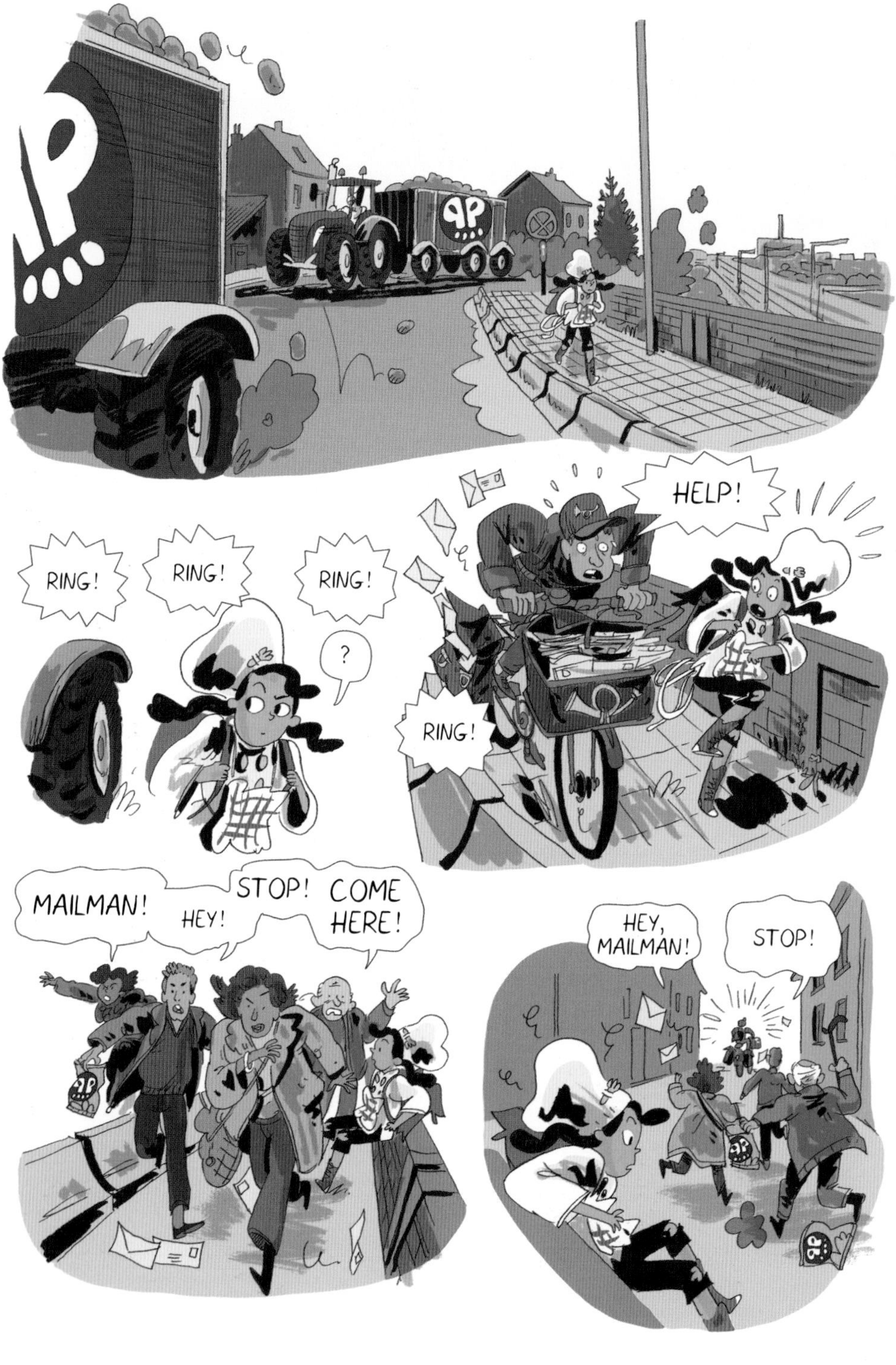
RING!
RING!
RING!
?
HELP!
RING!
MAILMAN!
HEY!
STOP!
COME HERE!
HEY, MAILMAN!
STOP!

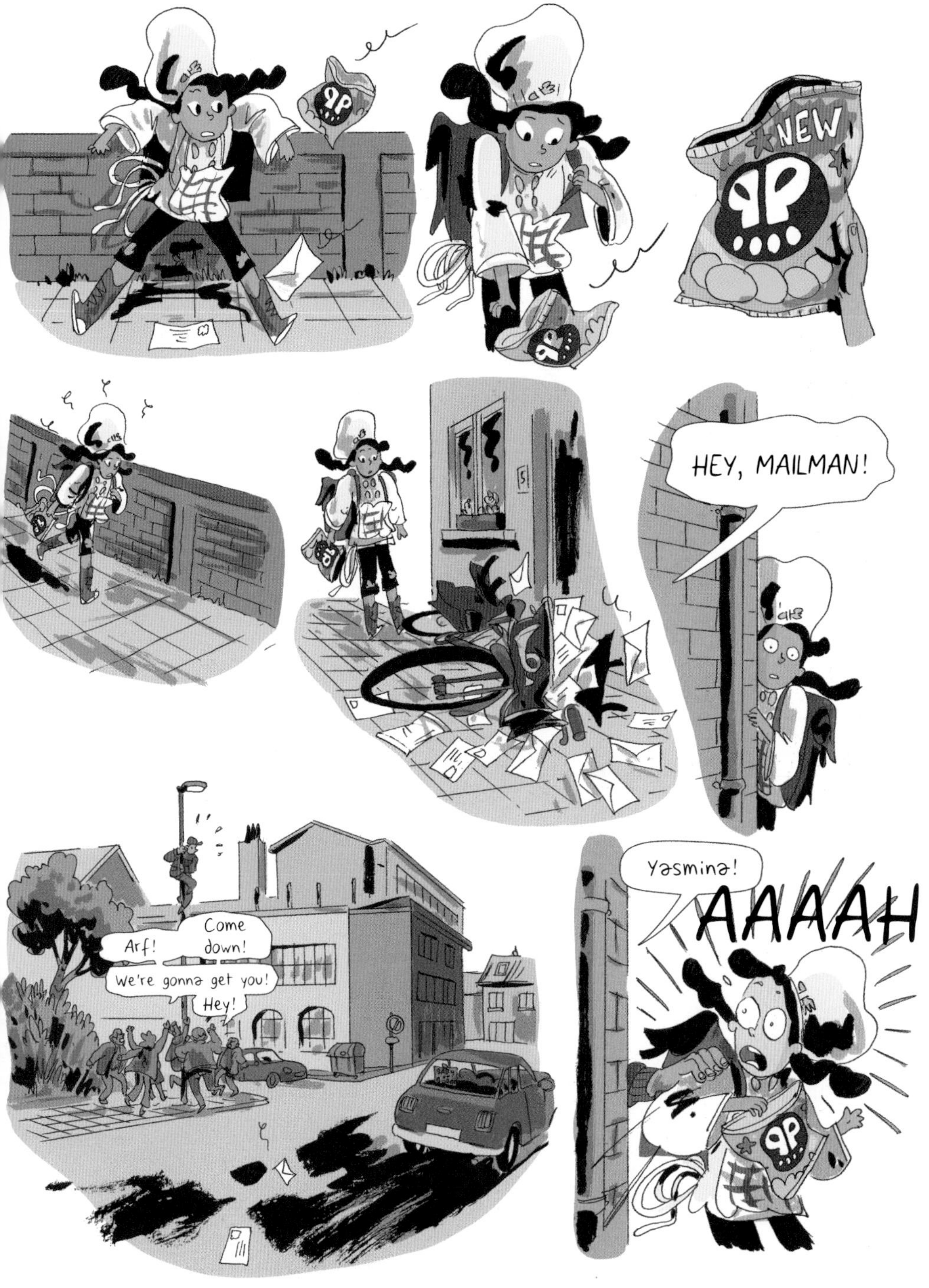
NEW
HEY, MAILMAN!
Arf!
Come down!
We're gonna get you!
Hey!
Yasmina!
AAAAH

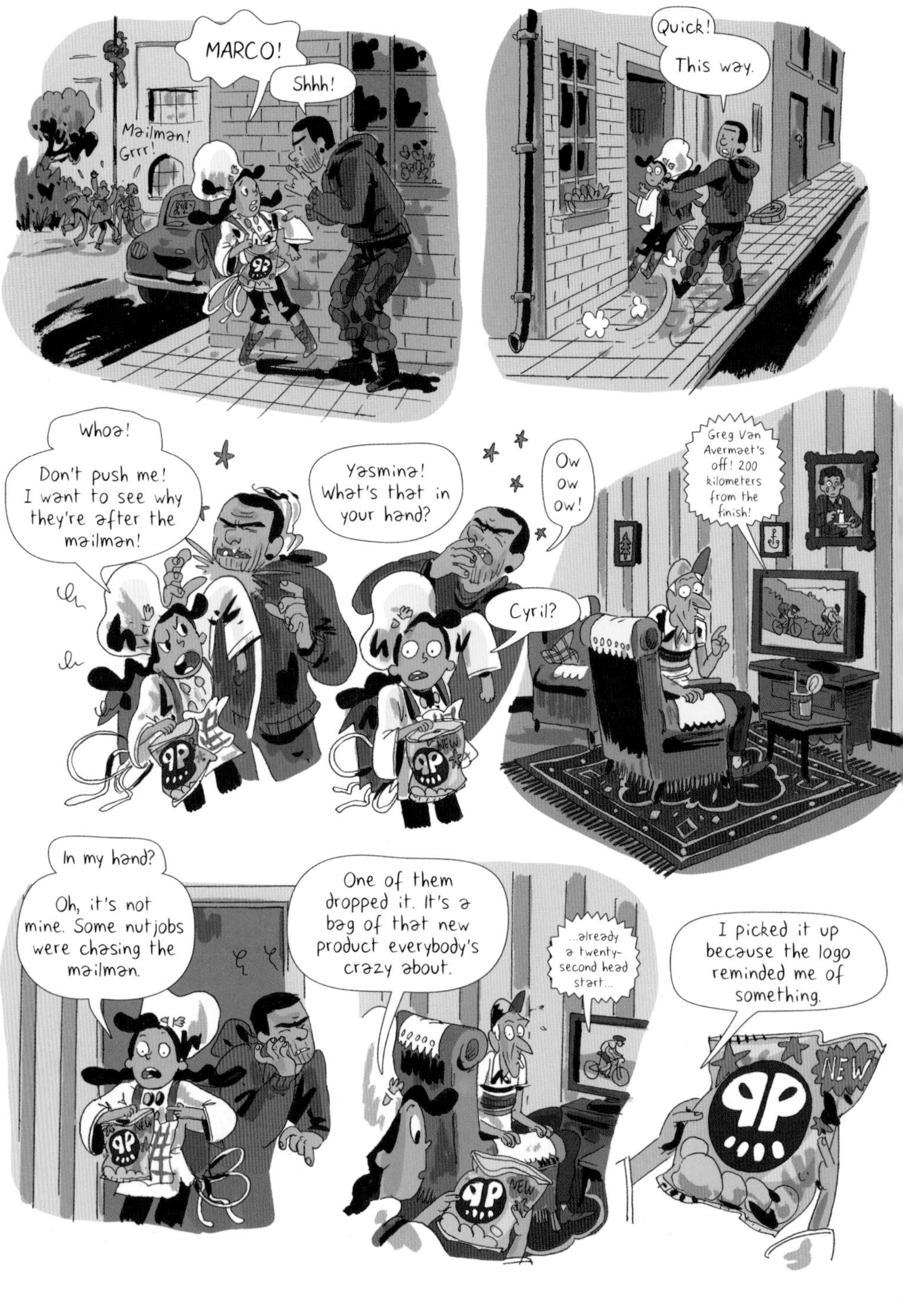

MARCO!
Shhh!
Mailman! Grrr!
Quick!
This way.
Whoa!
Don't push me! I want to see why they're after the mailman!
Yasmina! What's that in your hand?
Ow ow ow!
Cyril?
Greg Van Avermaet's off! 200 kilometers from the finish!
In my hand?
Oh, it's not mine. Some nutjobs were chasing the mailman.
One of them dropped it. It's a bag of that new product everybody's crazy about.
...already a twenty-second head start...
I picked it up because the logo reminded me of something.
NEW

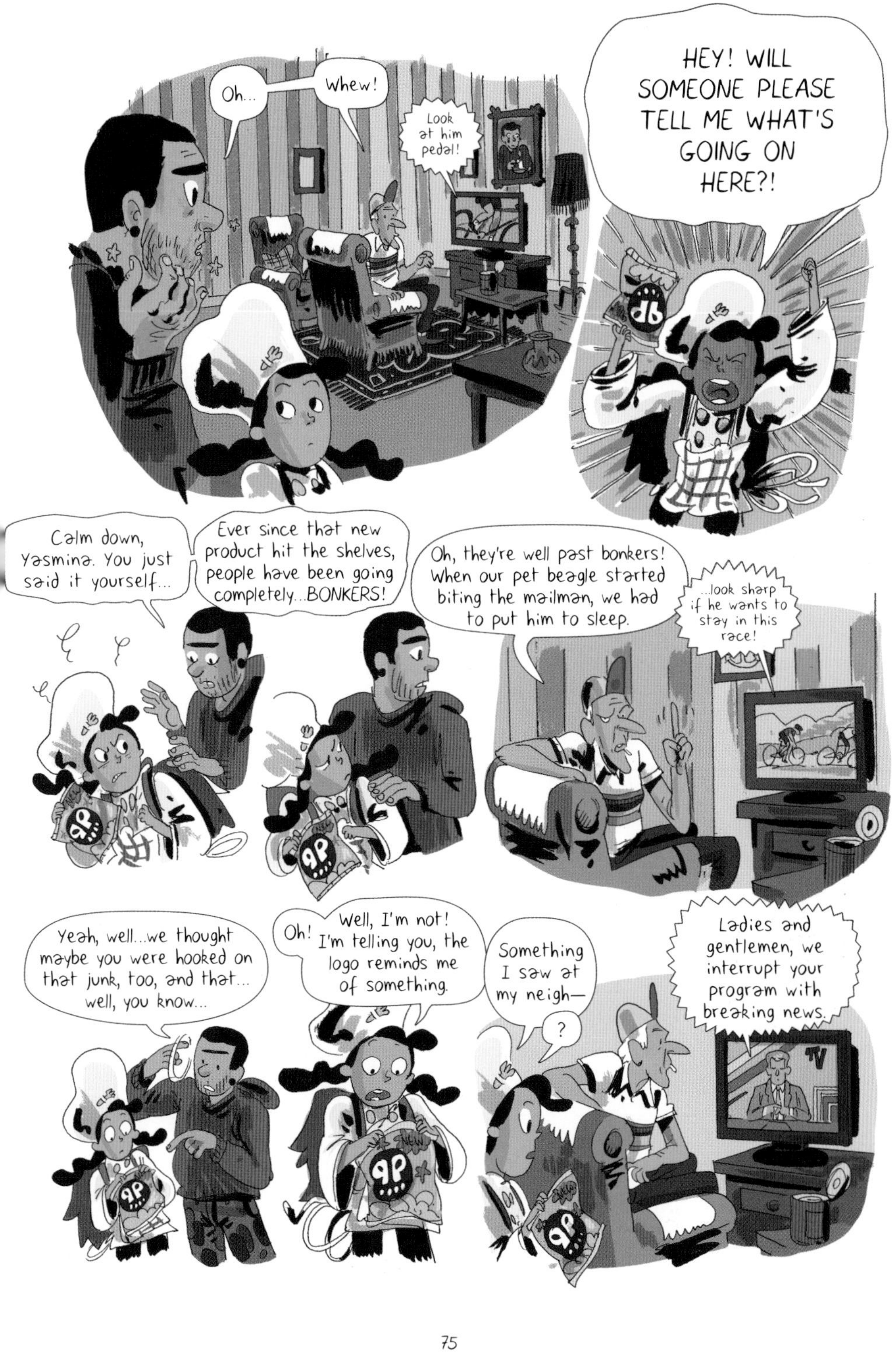
Oh...
Whew!
Look at him pedal!
HEY! WILL SOMEONE PLEASE TELL ME WHAT'S GOING ON HERE?!
Calm down, Yasmina. You just said it yourself...
Ever since that new product hit the shelves, people have been going completely...BONKERS!
Oh, they're well past bonkers! When our pet beagle started biting the mailman, we had to put him to sleep.
...look sharp if he wants to stay in this race!
Yeah, well...we thought maybe you were hooked on that junk, too, and that... well, you know...
Oh!
Well, I'm not! I'm telling you, the logo reminds me of something.
Something I saw at my neigh—
?
Ladies and gentlemen, we interrupt your program with breaking news.

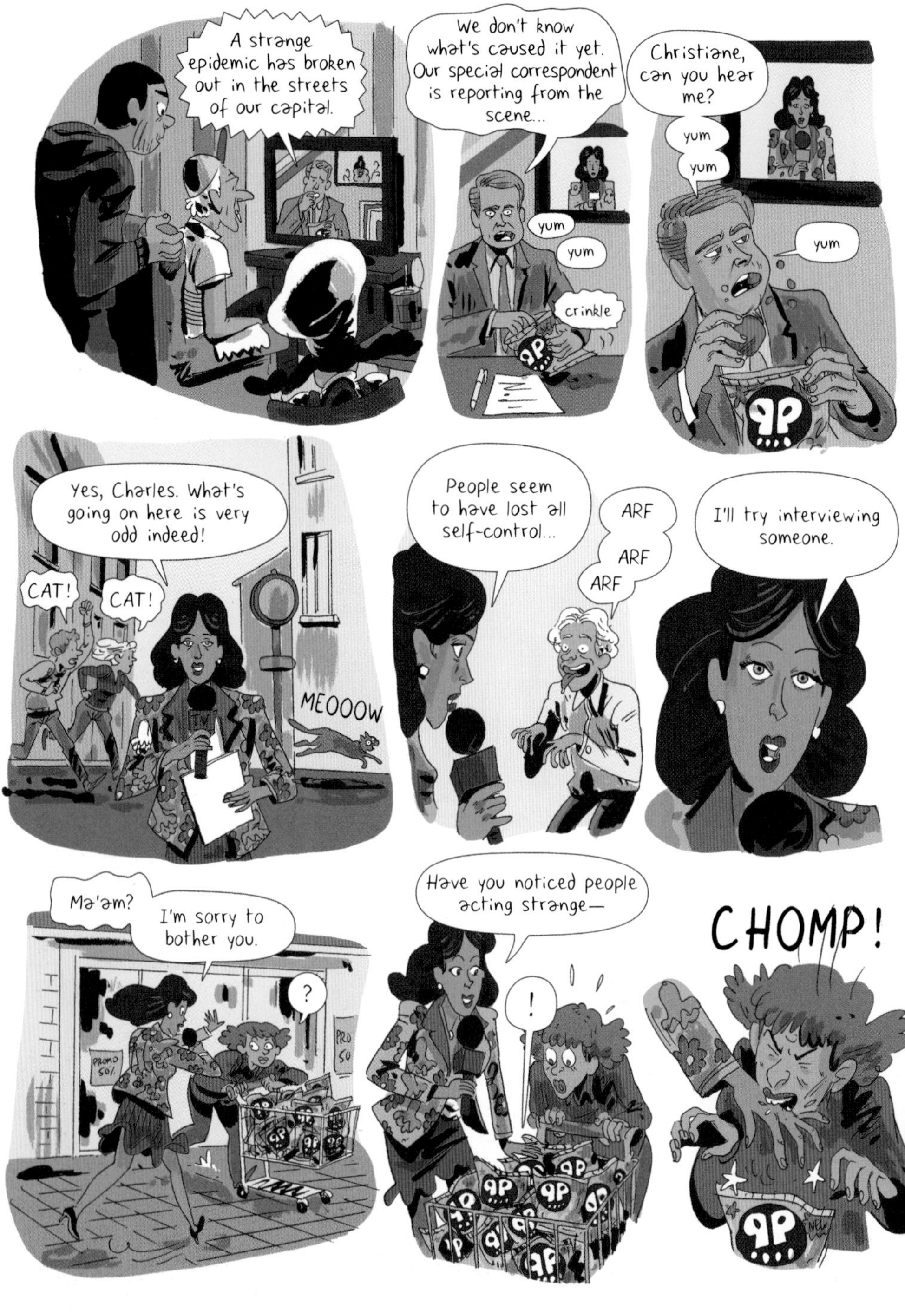
A strange epidemic has broken out in the streets of our capital.
We don't know what's caused it yet. Our special correspondent is reporting from the scene...
yum
yum
crinkle
Christiane, can you hear me?
yum
yum
yum
Yes, Charles. What's going on here is very odd indeed!
CAT!
CAT!
MEOOOW
People seem to have lost all self-control...
ARF
ARF
ARF
I'll try interviewing someone.
Ma'am?
I'm sorry to bother you.
?
Have you noticed people acting strange—
!
CHOMP!

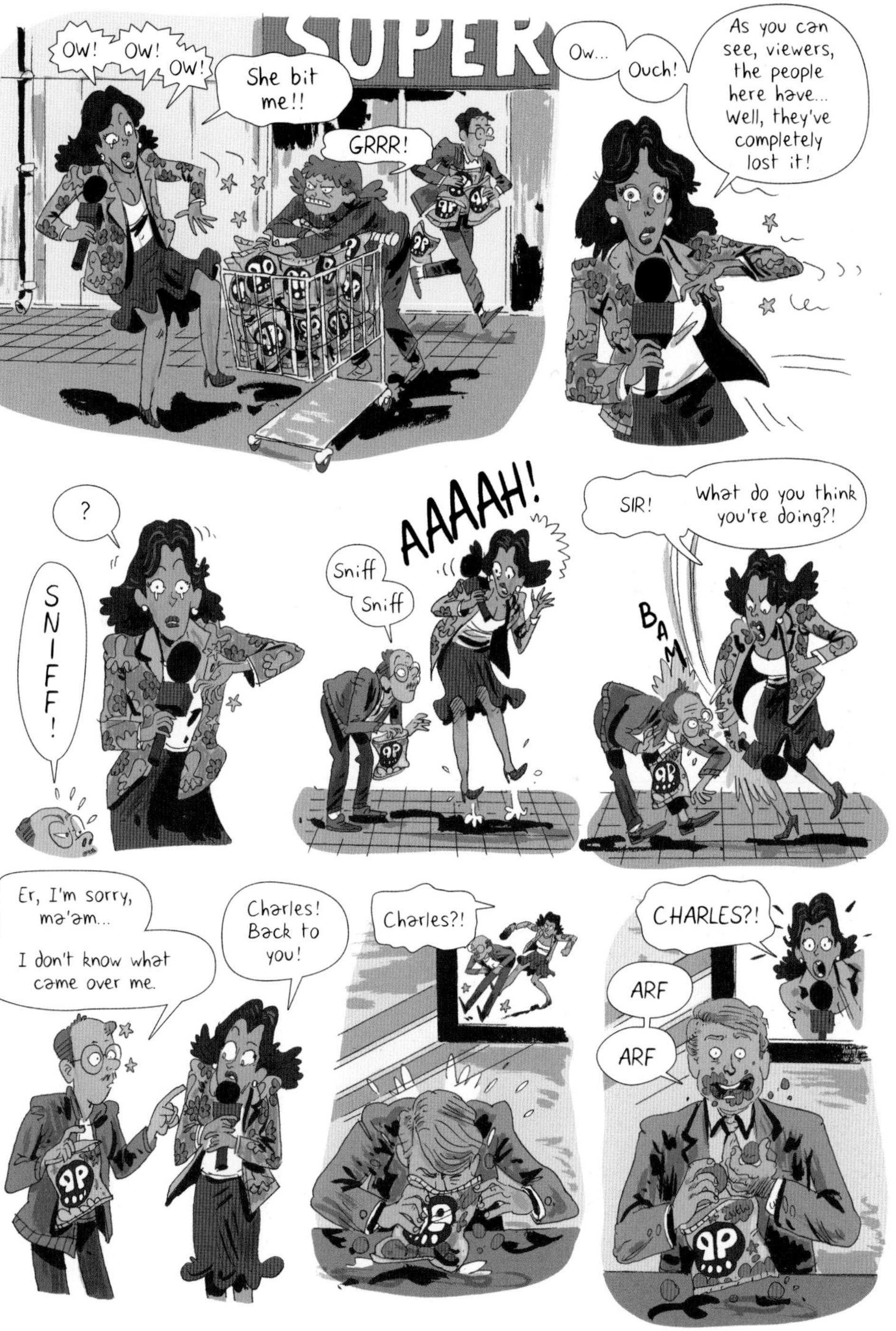
SUPER
OW! OW! OW!
She bit me!!
GRRR!
Ow...
Ouch!
As you can see, viewers, the people here have... Well, they've completely lost it!
?
SNIFF!
Sniff
Sniff
AAAAH!
SIR!
What do you think you're doing?!
BAM
Er, I'm sorry, ma'am...
I don't know what came over me.
Charles! Back to you!
Charles?!
CHARLES?!
ARF
ARF

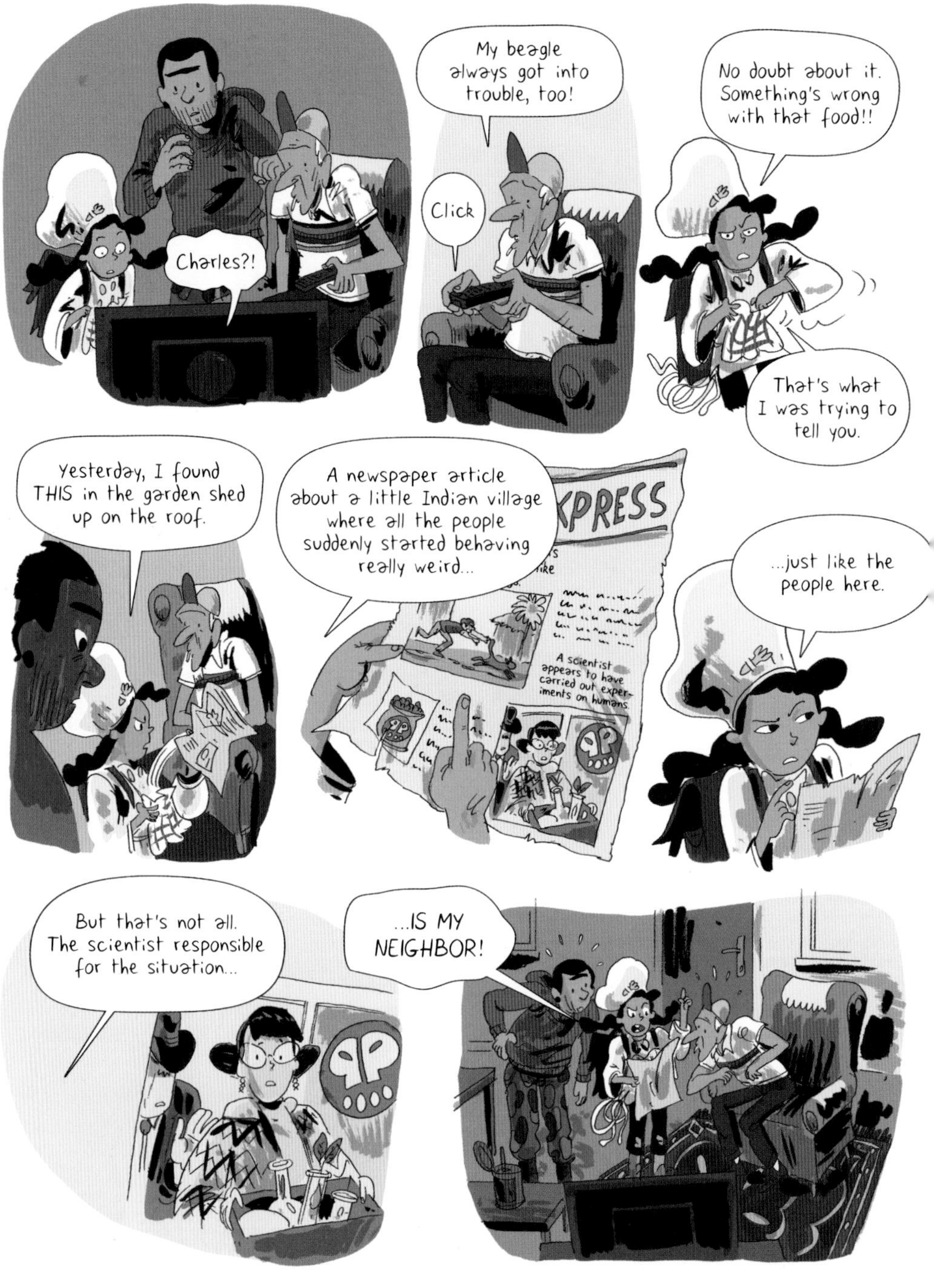
Charles?!
My beagle always got into trouble, too!
Click
No doubt about it. Something's wrong with that food!!
That's what I was trying to tell you.
Yesterday, I found THIS in the garden shed up on the roof.
A newspaper article about a little Indian village where all the people suddenly started behaving really weird...
XPRESS
A scientist appears to have carried out experiments on humans.
...just like the people here.
But that's not all. The scientist responsible for the situation...
...IS MY NEIGHBOR!

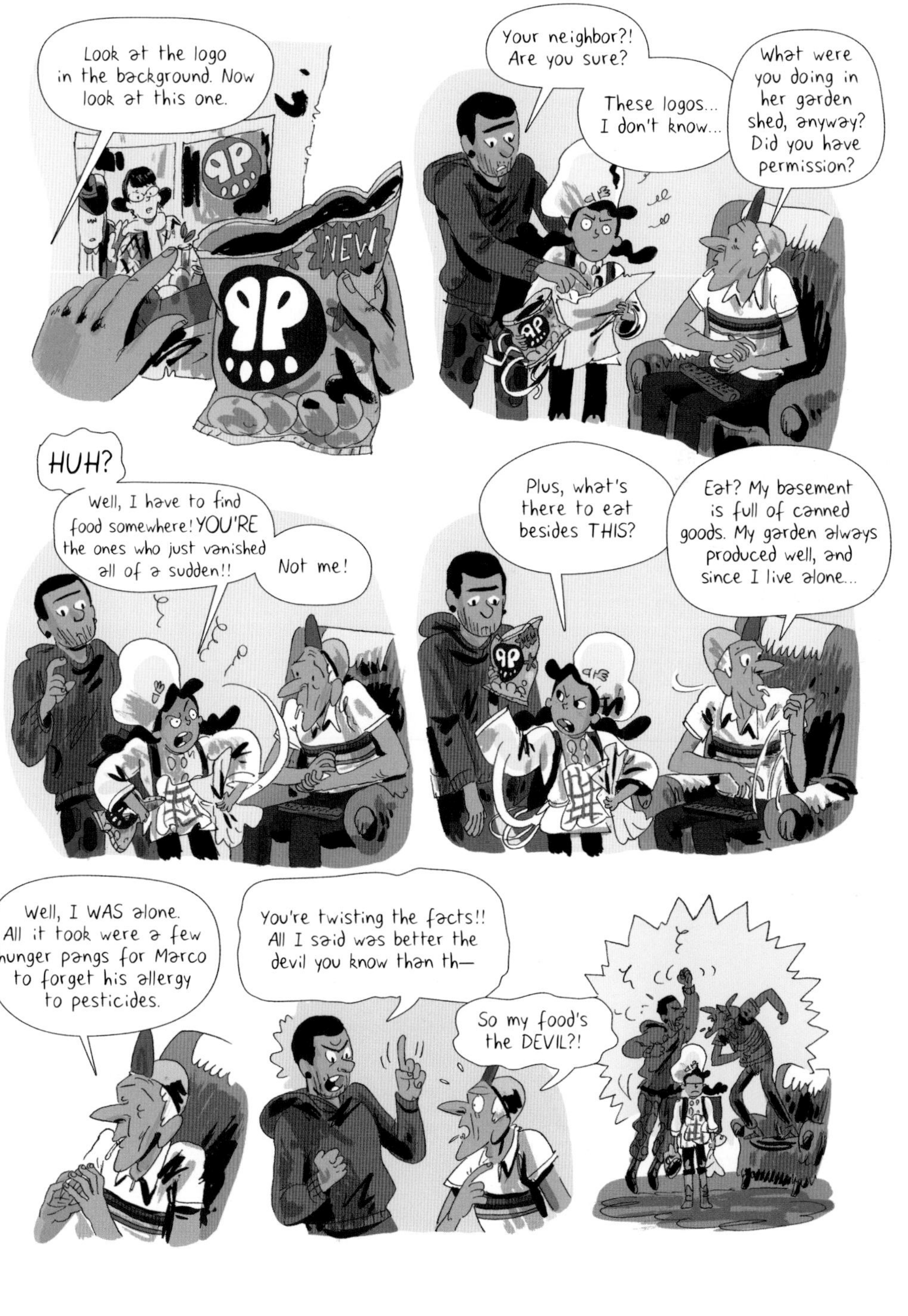
Look at the logo in the background. Now look at this one.
NEW
Your neighbor?! Are you sure?
These logos... I don't know...
What were you doing in her garden shed, anyway? Did you have permission?
HUH?
Well, I have to find food somewhere! YOU'RE the ones who just vanished all of a sudden!!
Not me!
Plus, what's there to eat besides THIS?
Eat? My basement is full of canned goods. My garden always produced well, and since I live alone...
Well, I WAS alone. All it took were a few hunger pangs for Marco to forget his allergy to pesticides.
You're twisting the facts!! All I said was better the devil you know than th—
So my food's the DEVIL?!

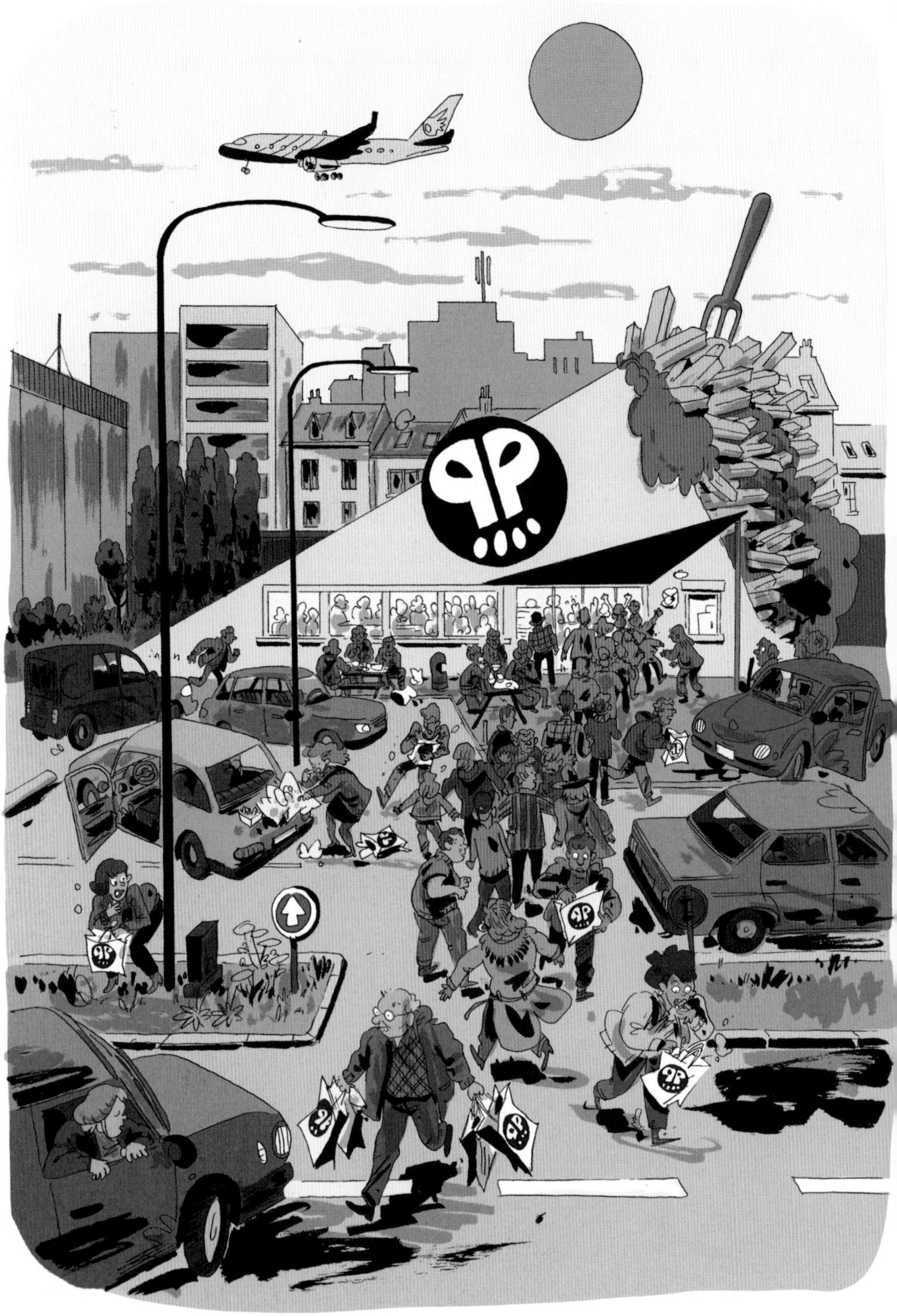

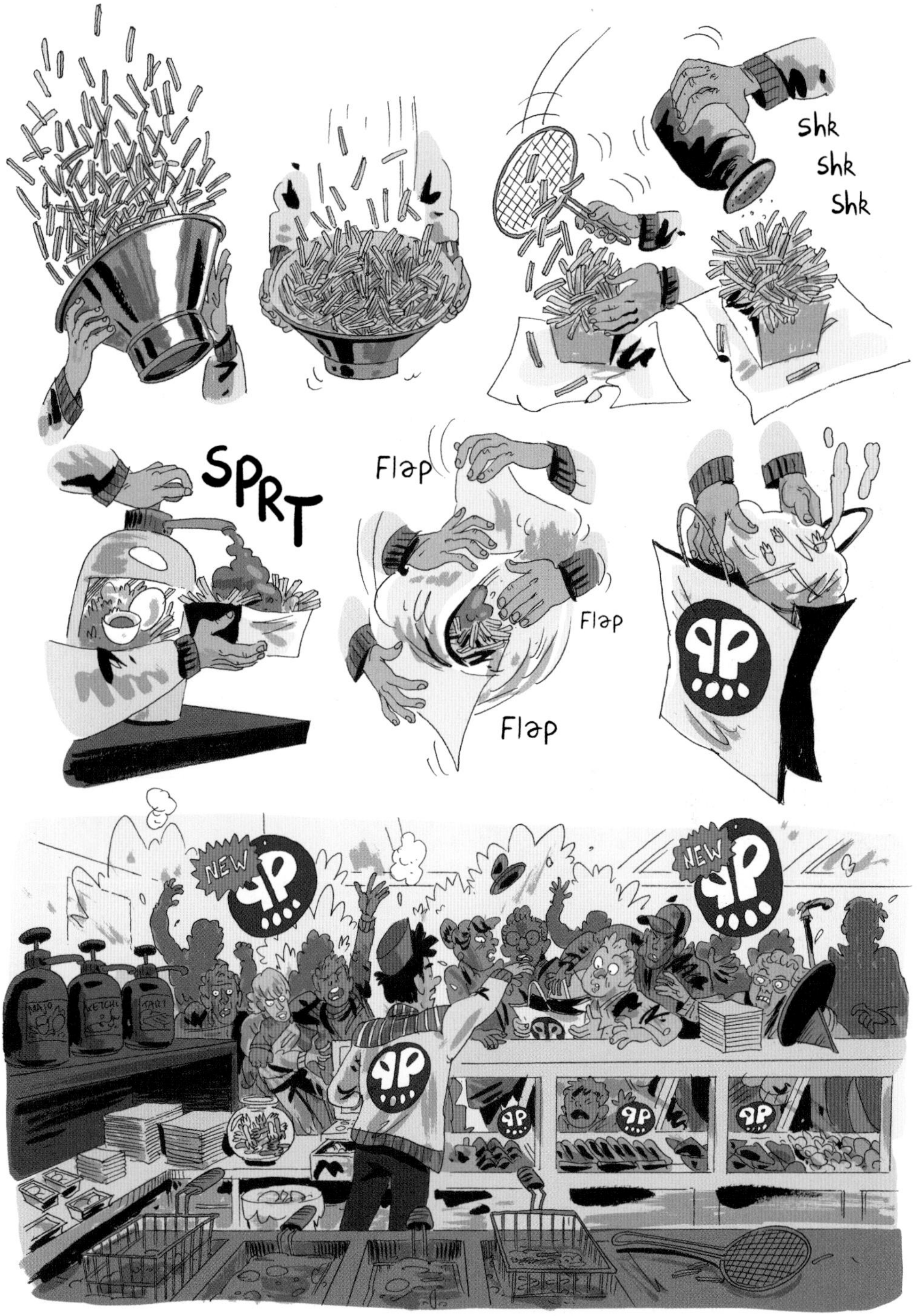
Shk
Shk
Shk
SPRT
Flap
Flap
Flap
NEW
NEW

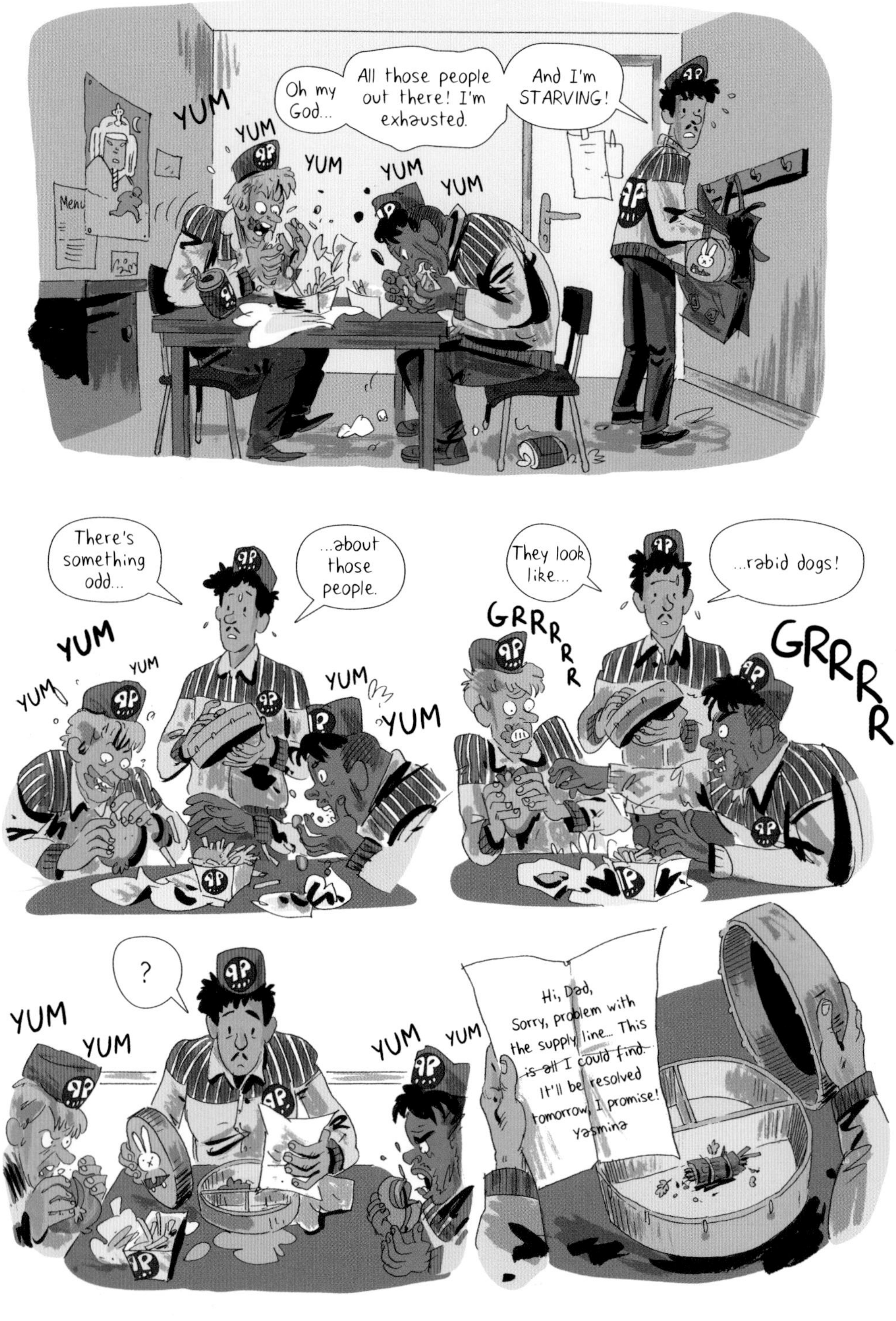
YUM
YUM
YUM
YUM
YUM
Oh my God...
All those people out there! I'm exhausted.
And I'm STARVING!
Menu
There's something odd...
...about those people.
YUM
YUM
YUM
YUM
YUM
They look like...
...rabid dogs!
GRRRRR
GRRRRR
?
YUM
YUM
YUM
YUM
Hi, Dad,
Sorry, problem with the supply line... This is all I could find. It'll be resolved tomorrow, I promise!
Yasmina

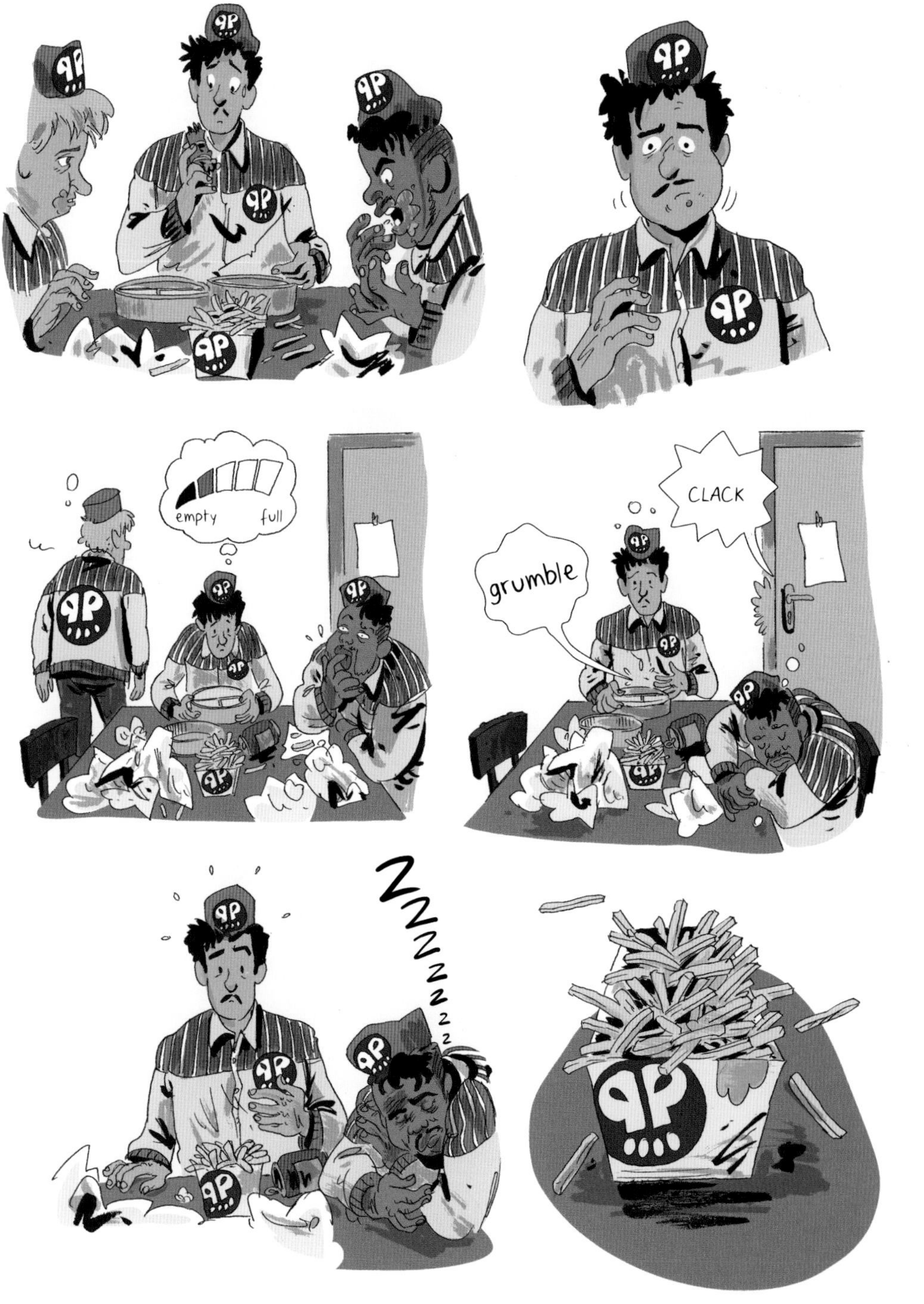
empty
full
grumble
CLACK
ZZZZZZZ

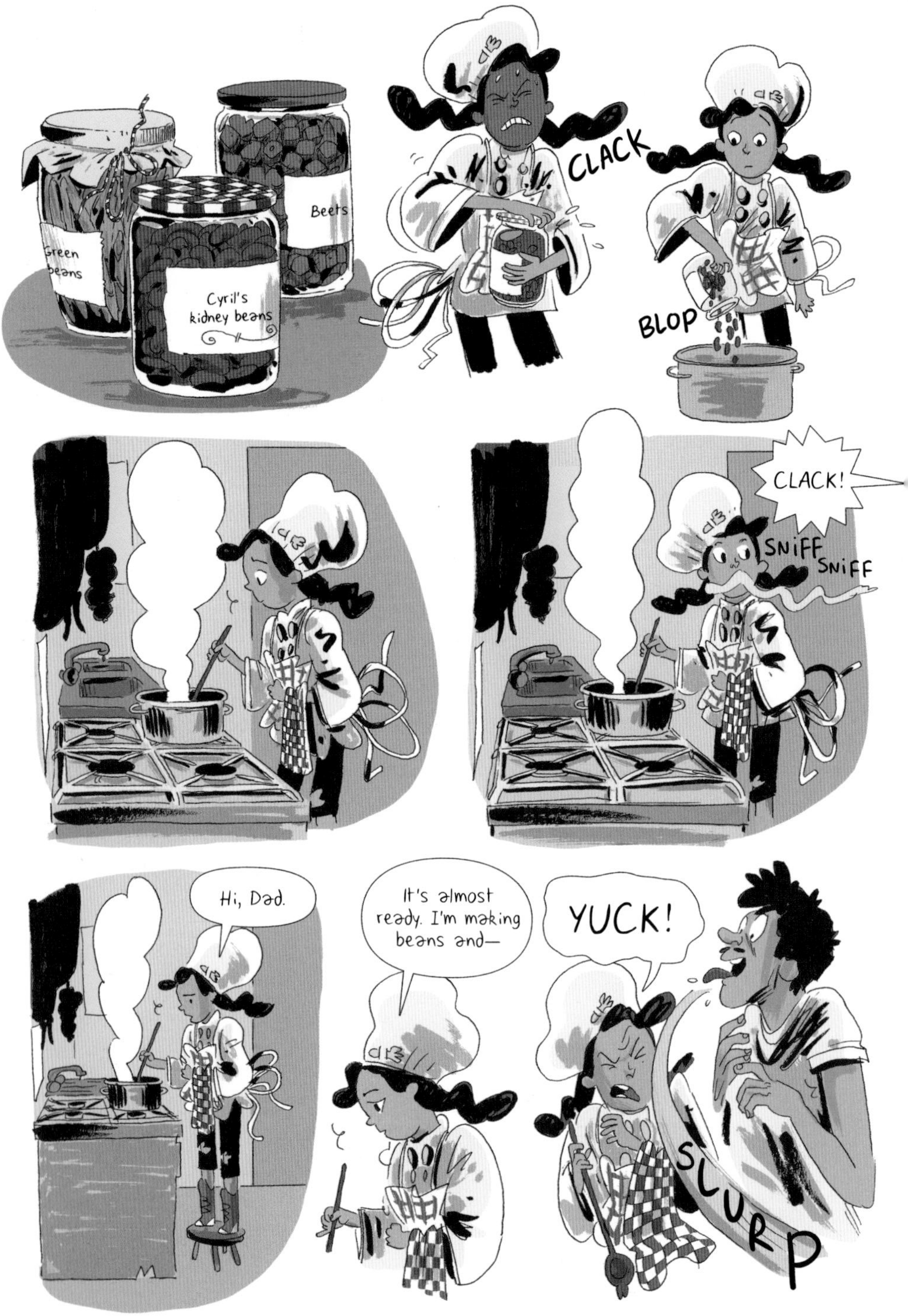
Green beans
Beets
Cyril's kidney beans
CLACK
BLOP
CLACK!
SNIFF SNIFF
Hi, Dad.
It's almost ready. I'm making beans and—
YUCK!
SLURP

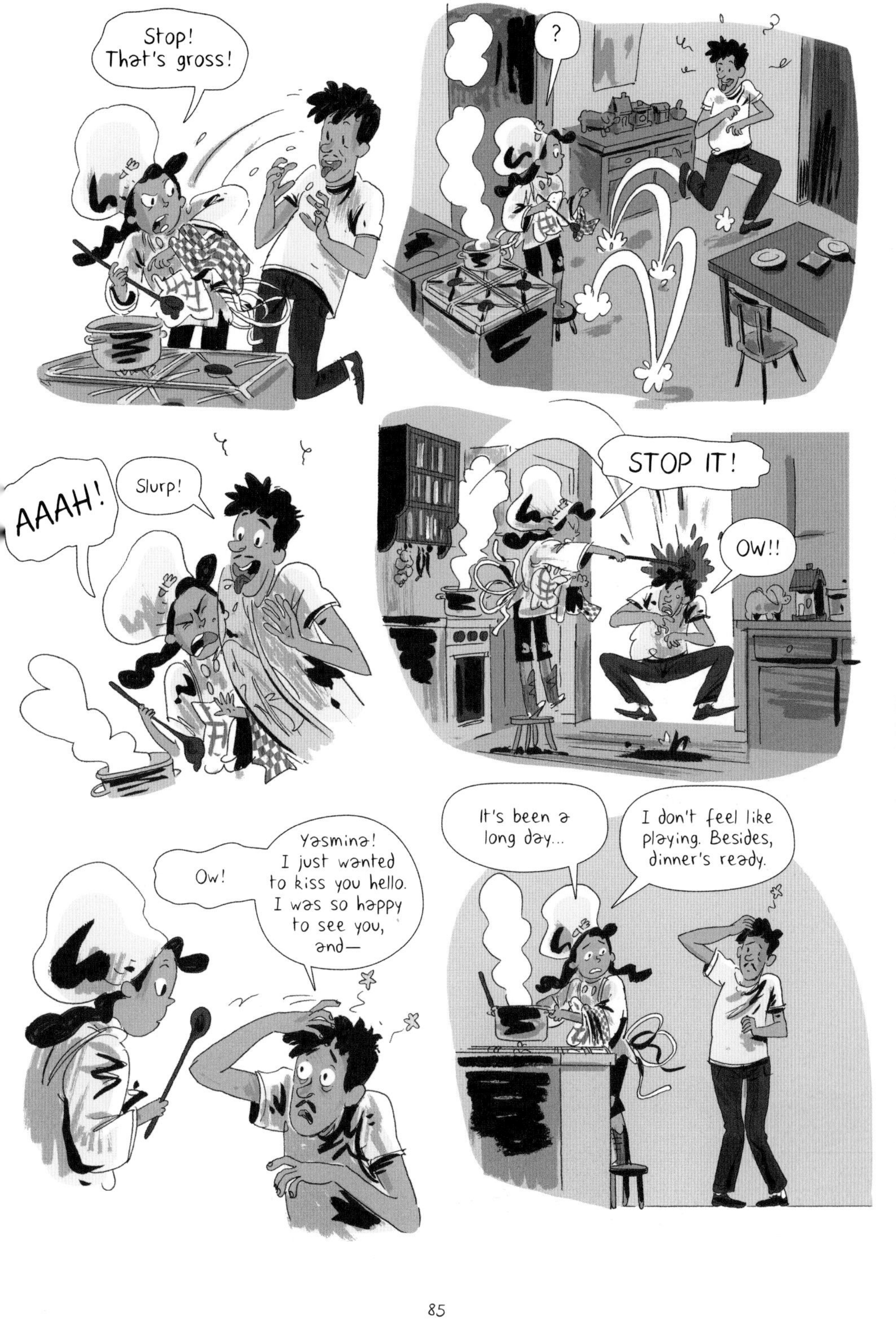
Stop!
That's gross!
?
AAAH!
Slurp!
STOP IT!
OW!!
Ow!
Yasmina!
I just wanted
to kiss you hello.
I was so happy
to see you,
and—
It's been a
long day...
I don't feel like
playing. Besides,
dinner's ready.

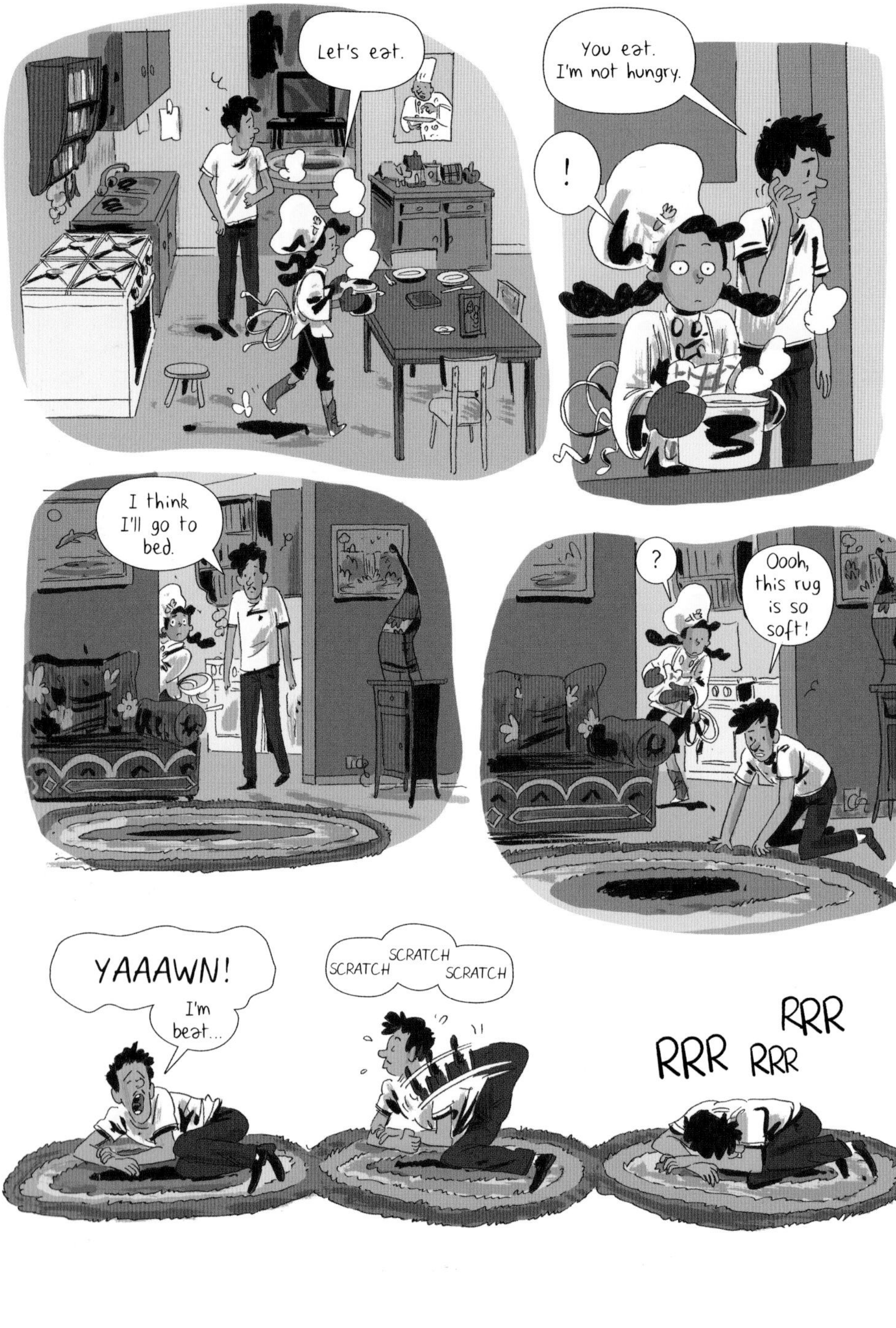
Let's eat.
You eat. I'm not hungry.
!
I think I'll go to bed.
?
Oooh, this rug is so soft!
YAAAWN! I'm beat...
SCRATCH SCRATCH SCRATCH
RRR RRR RRR

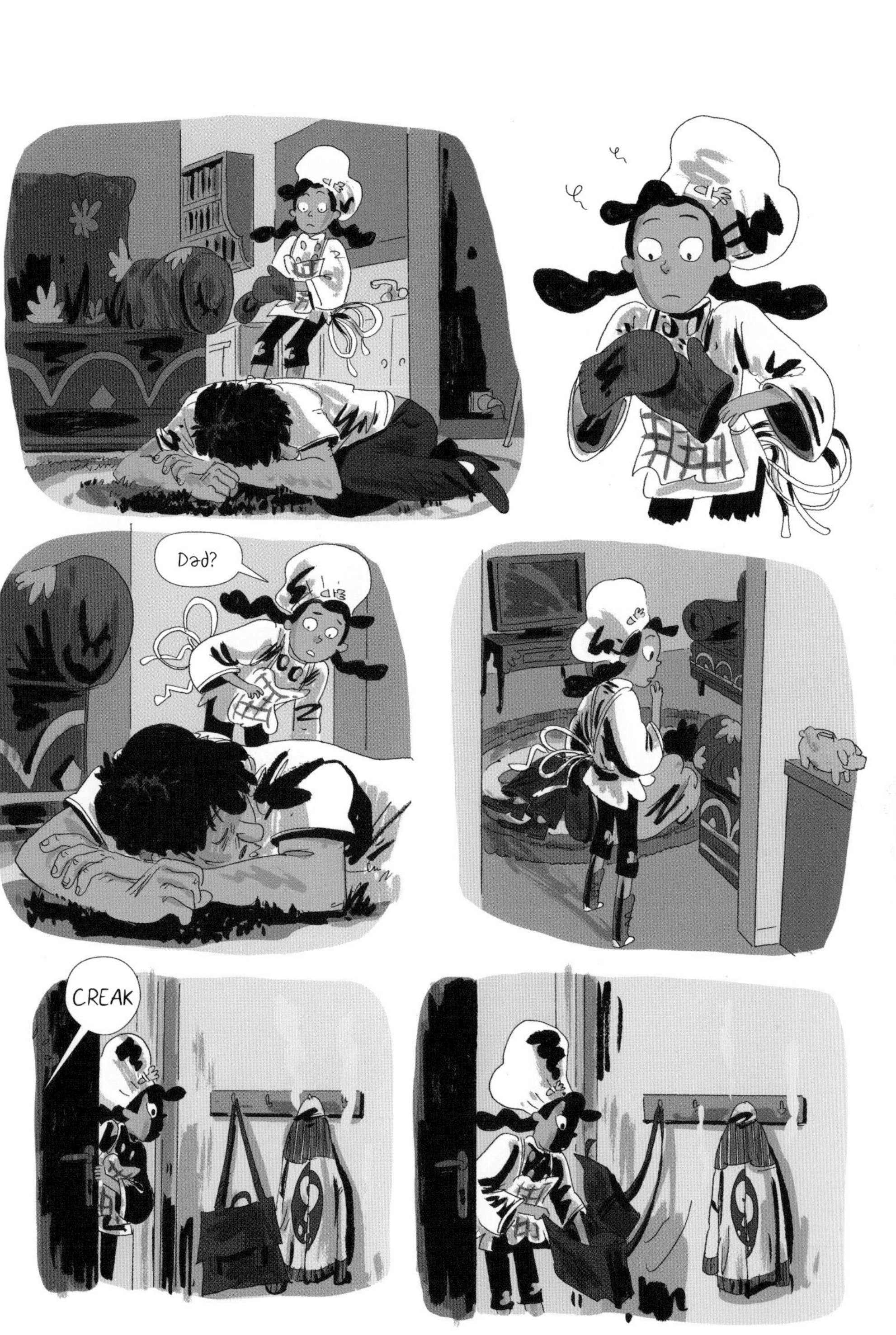
Dad?
CREAK

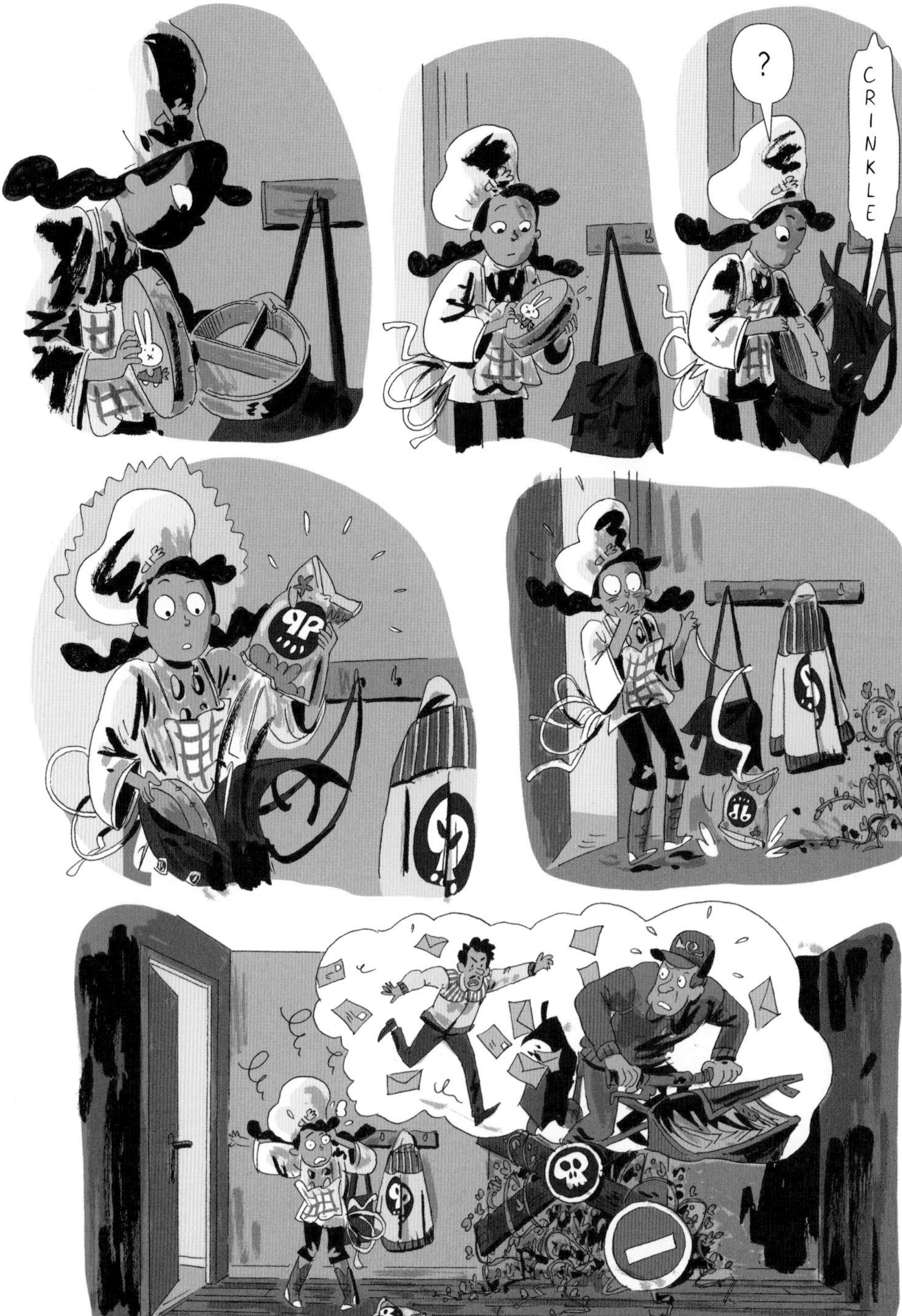
?
CRINKLE

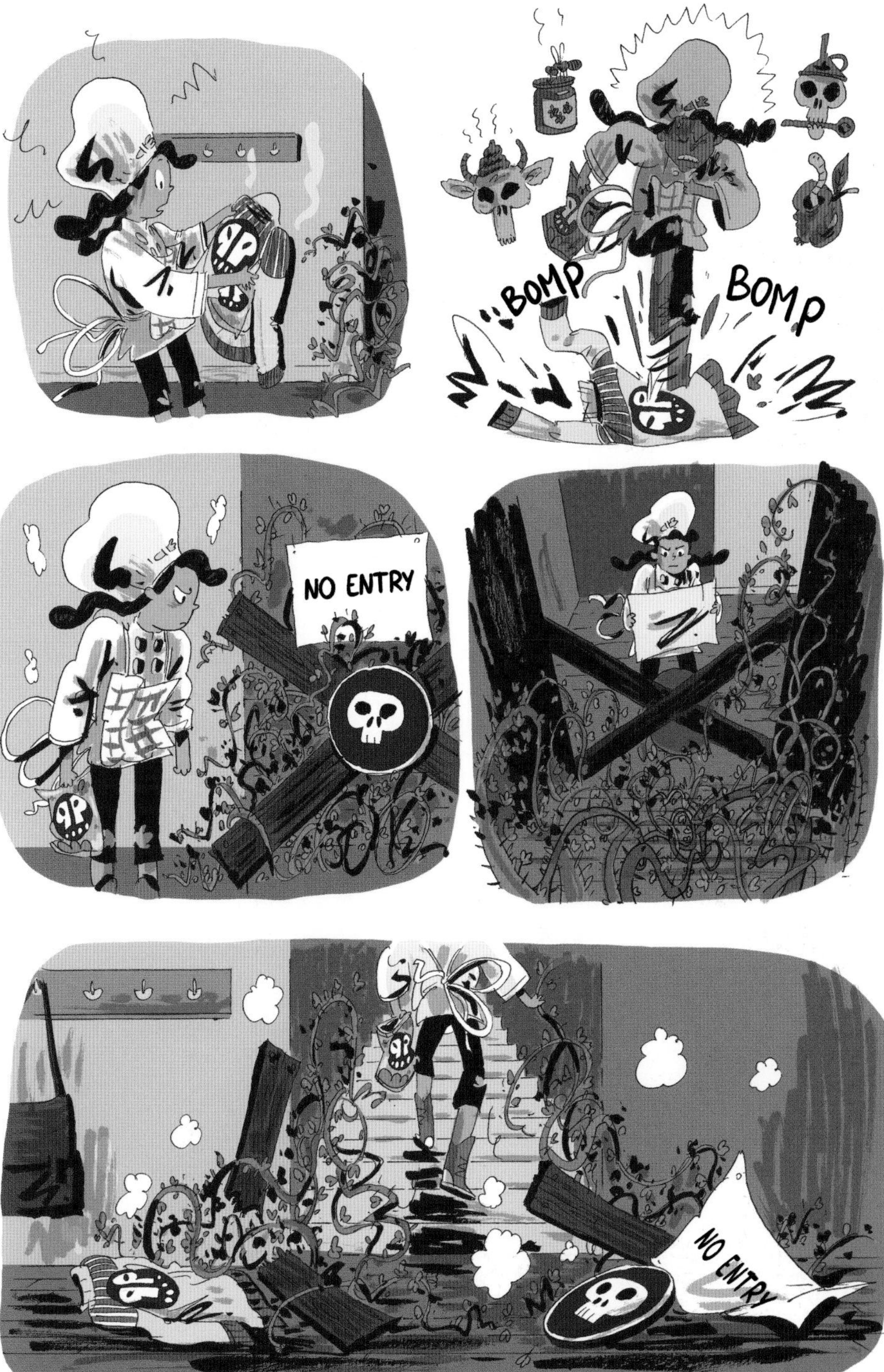
BOMP
BOMP
NO ENTRY
NO ENTRY

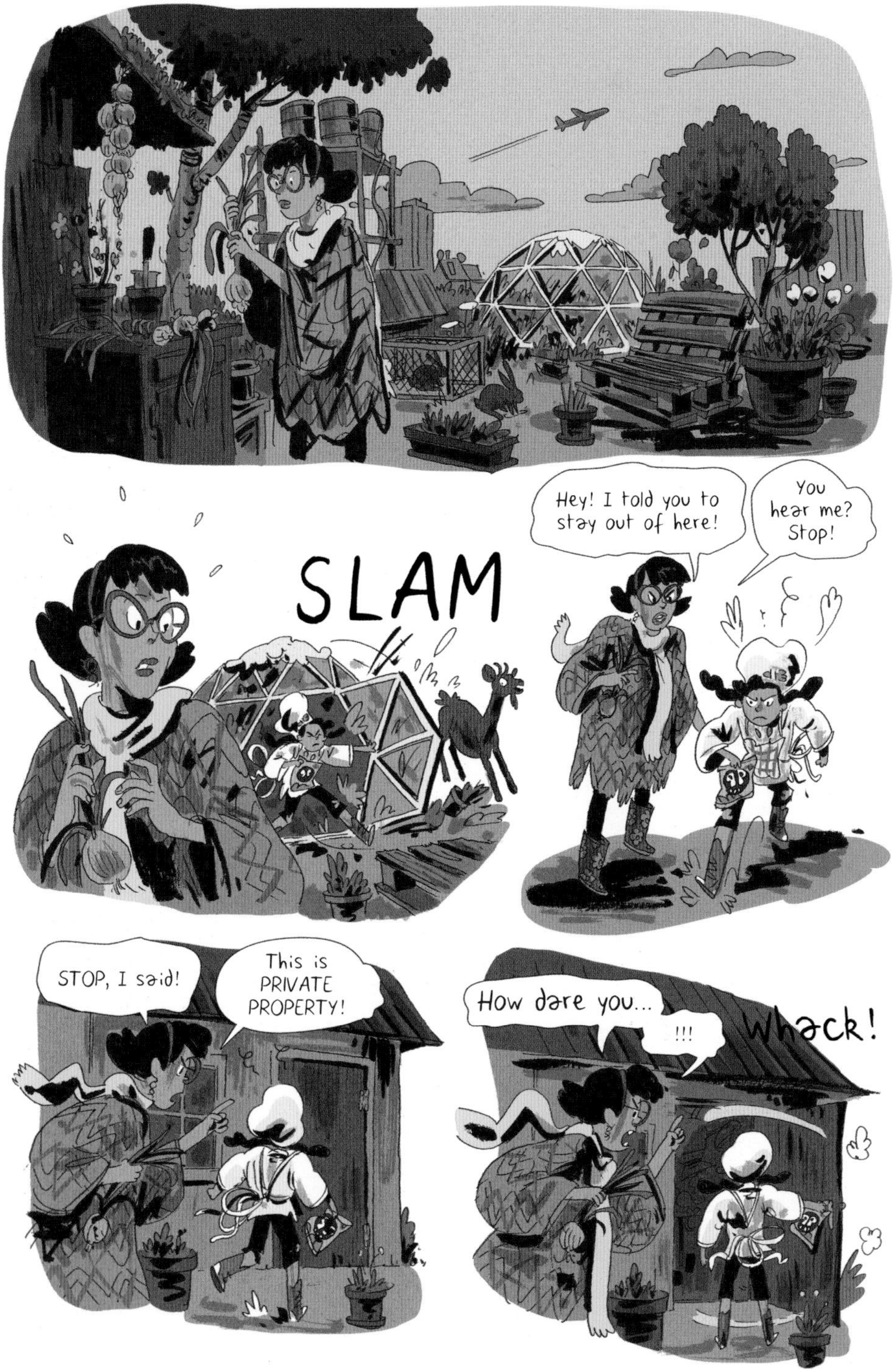
SLAM
Hey! I told you to stay out of here!
You hear me? Stop!
STOP, I said!
This is PRIVATE PROPERTY!
How dare you...
!!!
whack!

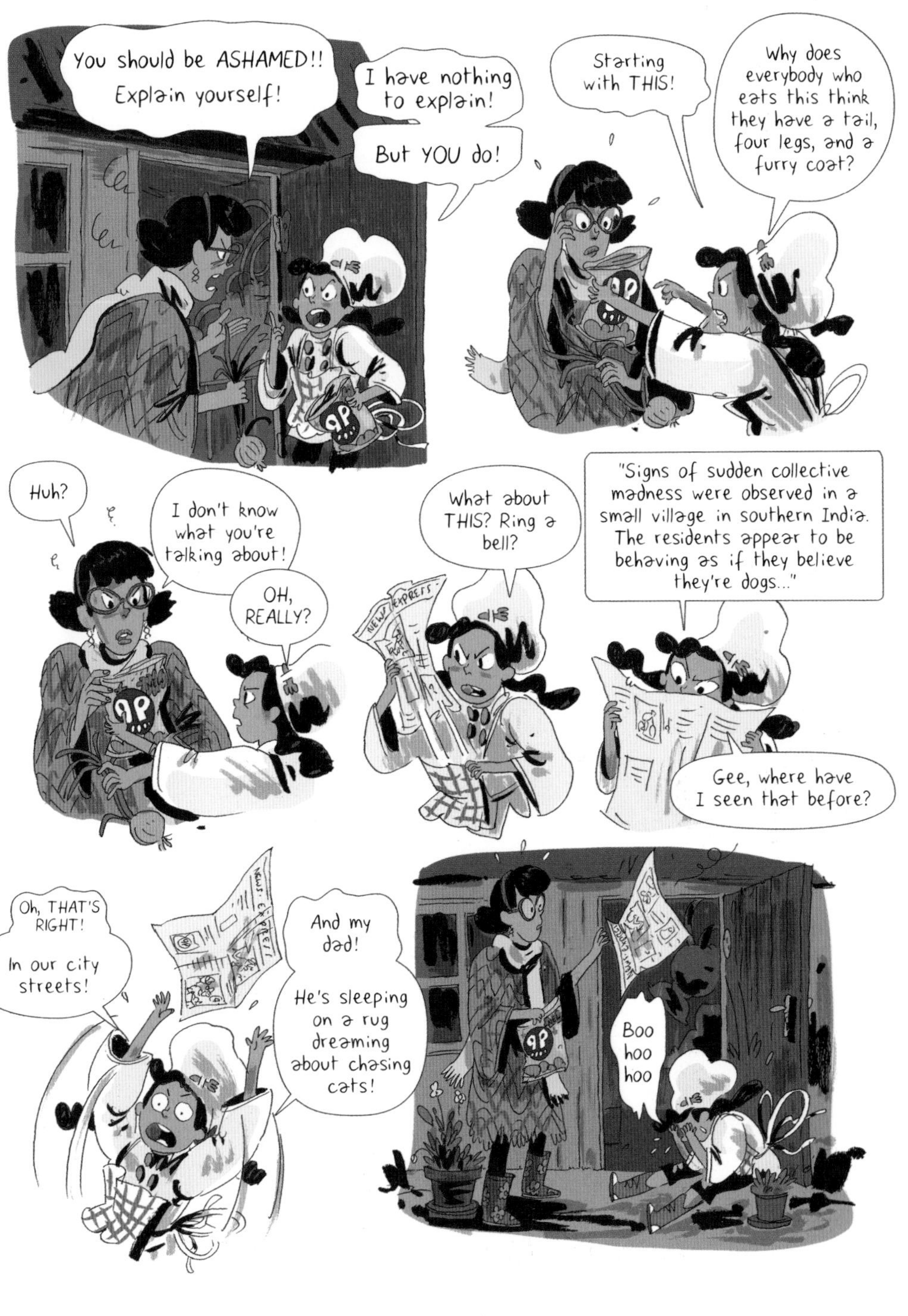
You should be ASHAMED!! Explain yourself!
I have nothing to explain!
But YOU do!
Starting with THIS!
Why does everybody who eats this think they have a tail, four legs, and a furry coat?
Huh?
I don't know what you're talking about!
OH, REALLY?
What about THIS? Ring a bell?
"Signs of sudden collective madness were observed in a small village in southern India. The residents appear to be behaving as if they believe they're dogs..."
Gee, where have I seen that before?
Oh, THAT'S RIGHT!
In our city streets!
And my dad!
He's sleeping on a rug dreaming about chasing cats!
Boo hoo hoo

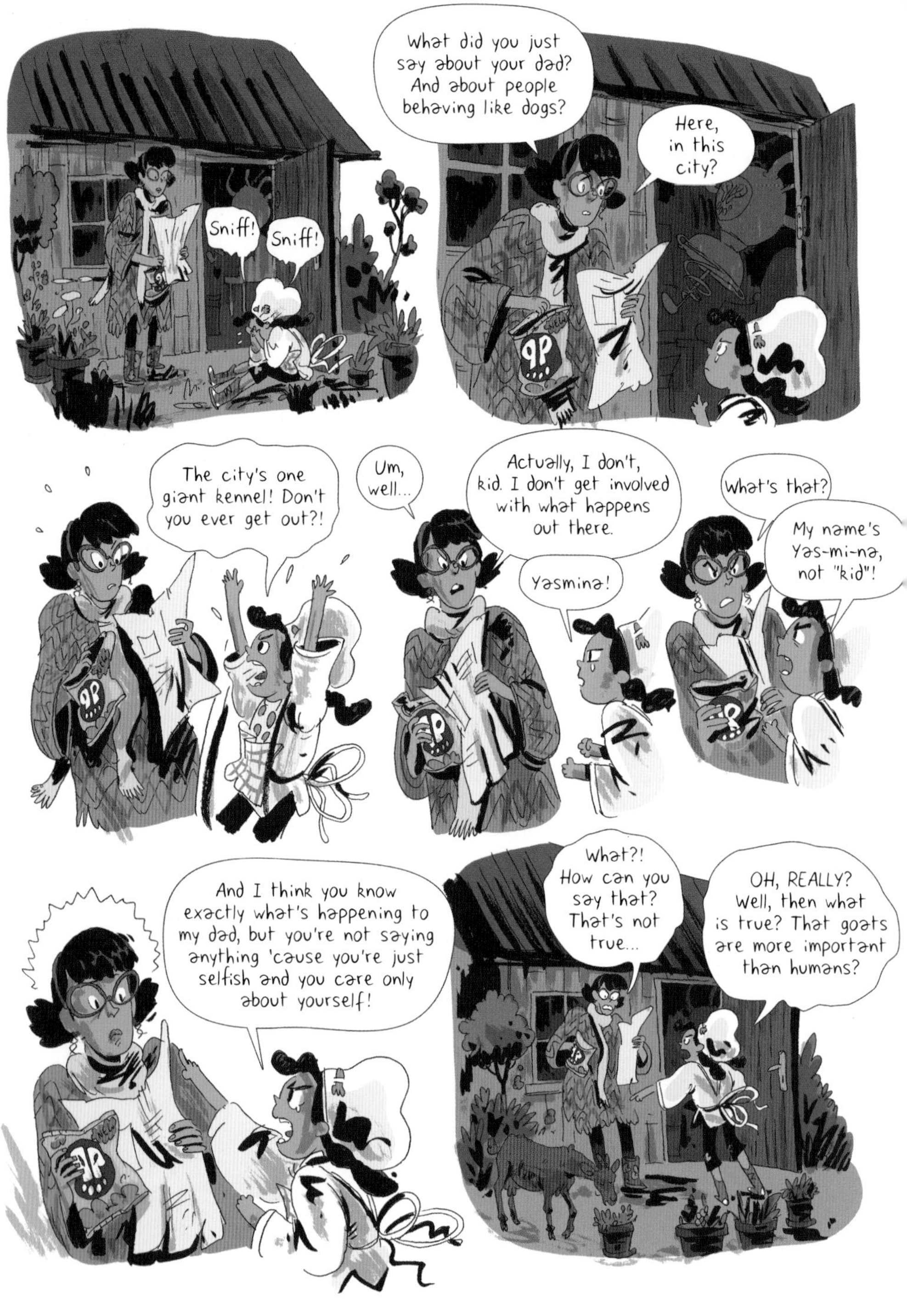
Sniff!
Sniff!
What did you just say about your dad? And about people behaving like dogs?
Here, in this city?
The city's one giant kennel! Don't you ever get out?!
Um, well...
Actually, I don't, kid. I don't get involved with what happens out there.
Yasmina!
What's that?
My name's Yas-mi-na, not "kid"!
And I think you know exactly what's happening to my dad, but you're not saying anything 'cause you're just selfish and you care only about yourself!
What?! How can you say that? That's not true...
OH, REALLY? Well, then what is true? That goats are more important than humans?

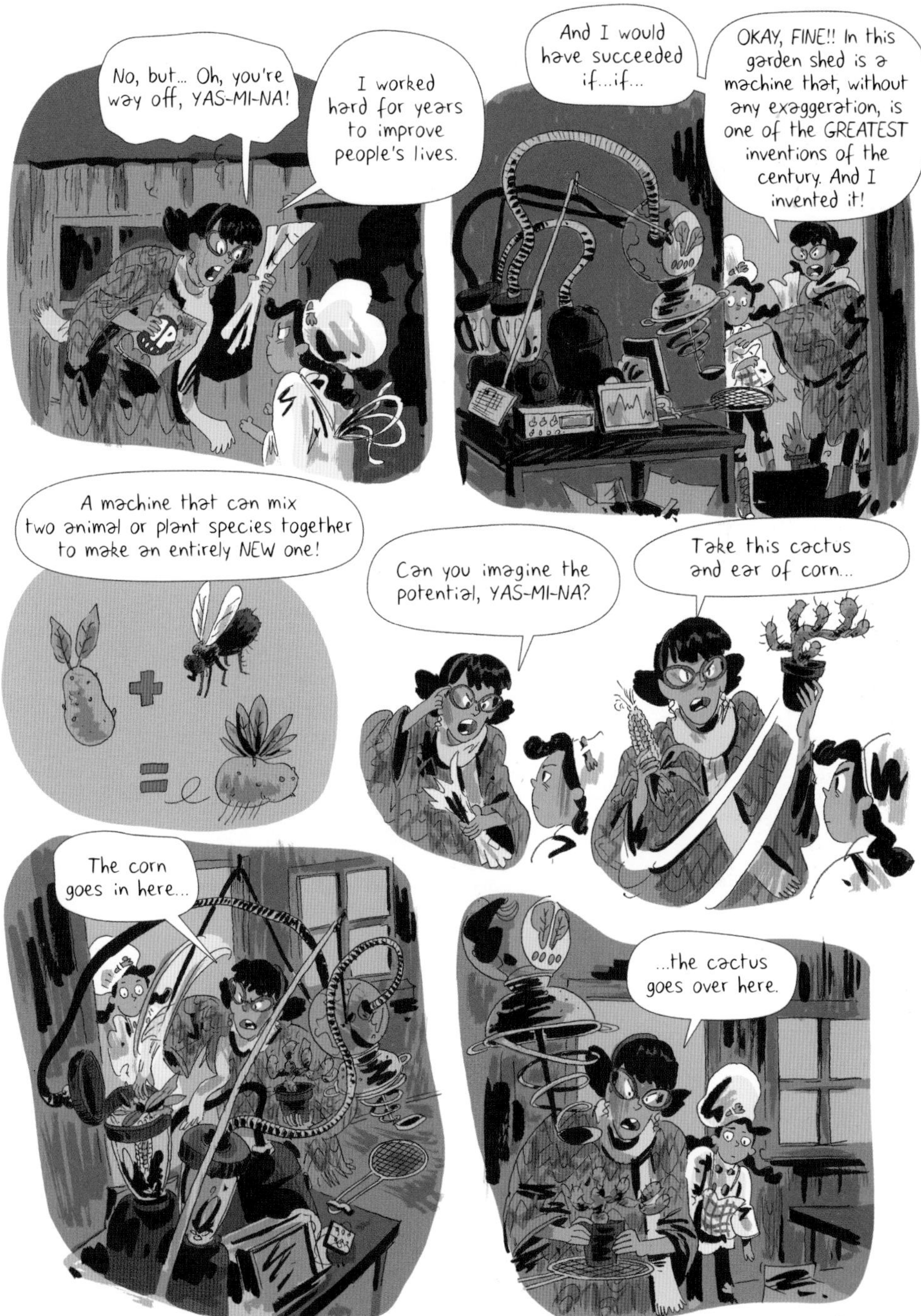
No, but... Oh, you're way off, YAS-MI-NA!
I worked hard for years to improve people's lives.
And I would have succeeded if...if...
OKAY, FINE!! In this garden shed is a machine that, without any exaggeration, is one of the GREATEST inventions of the century. And I invented it!
A machine that can mix two animal or plant species together to make an entirely NEW one!
Can you imagine the potential, YAS-MI-NA?
Take this cactus and ear of corn...
The corn goes in here...
...the cactus goes over here.

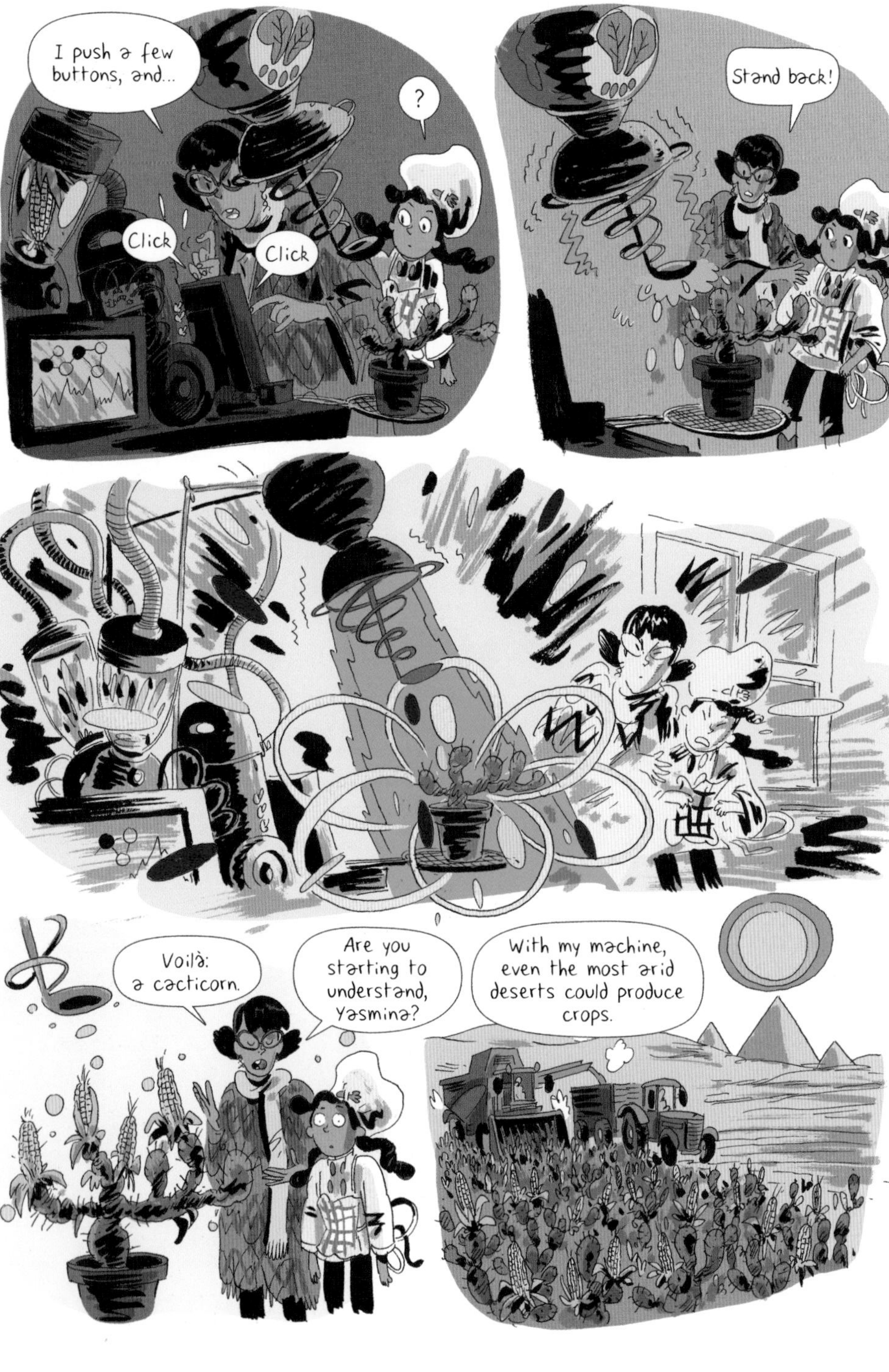
I push a few buttons, and...
?
Click
Click
Stand back!
Voilà: a cacticorn.
Are you starting to understand, Yasmina?
With my machine, even the most arid deserts could produce crops.

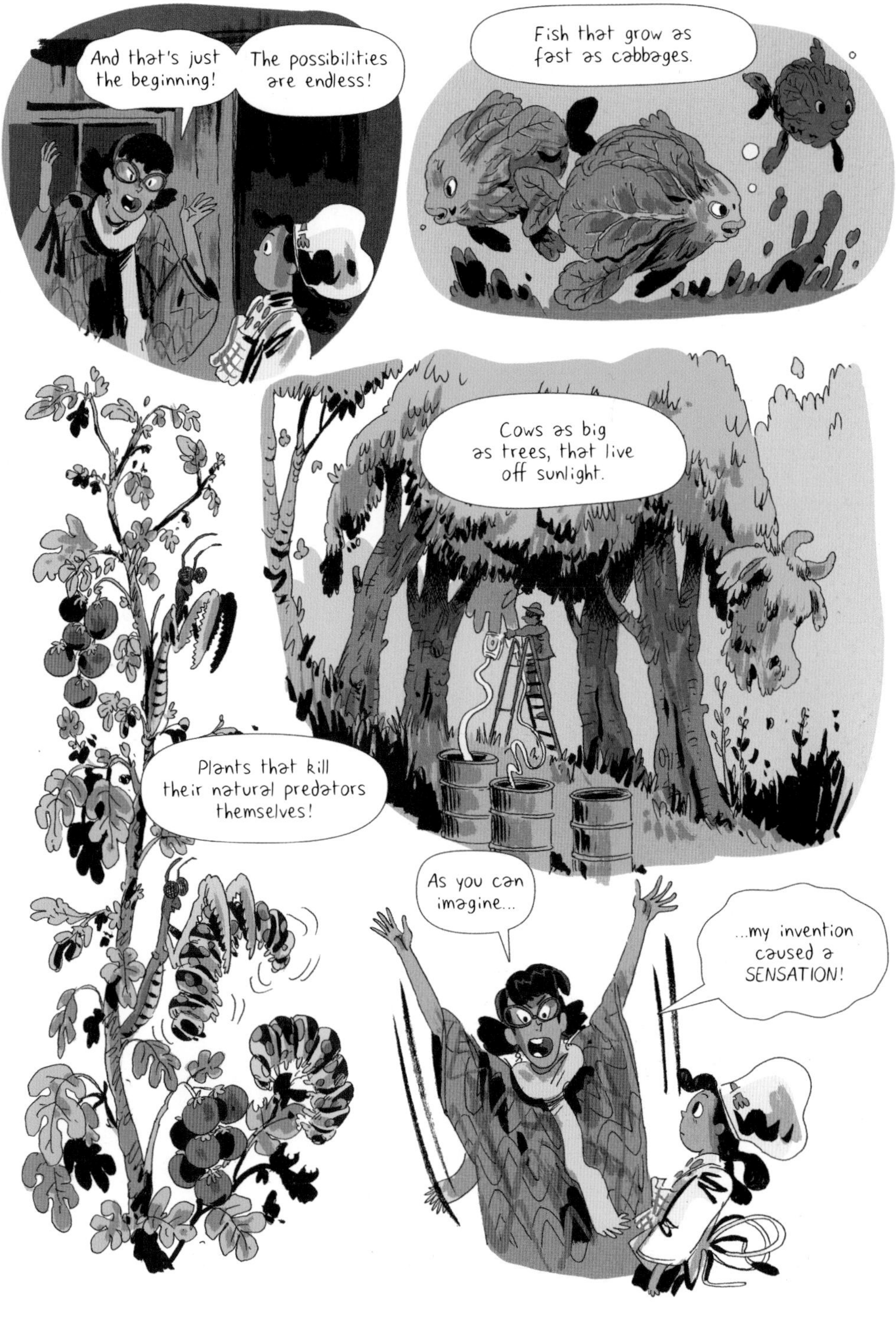
And that's just the beginning!
The possibilities are endless!
Fish that grow as fast as cabbages.
Cows as big as trees, that live off sunlight.
Plants that kill their natural predators themselves!
As you can imagine...
...my invention caused a SENSATION!

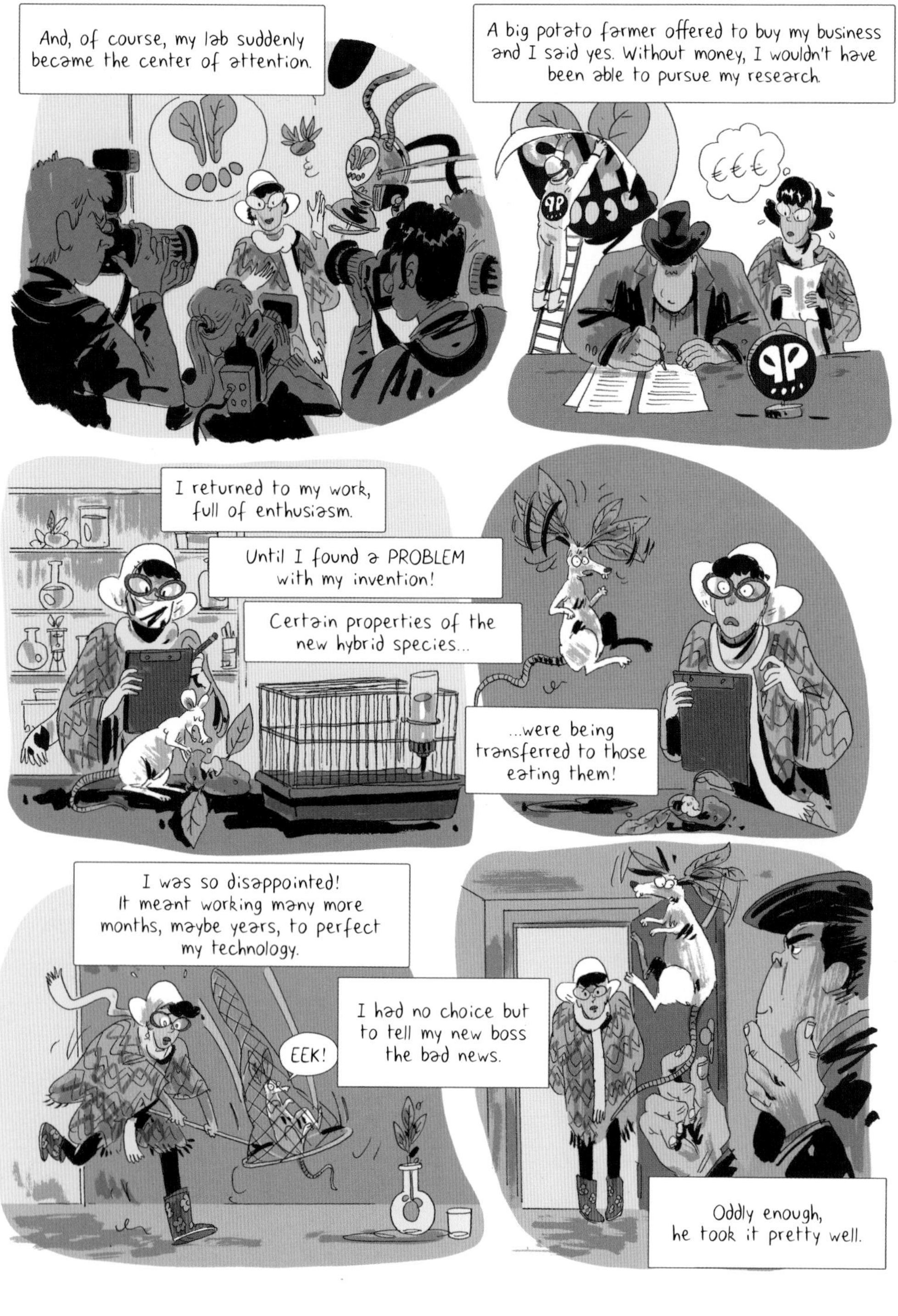
And, of course, my lab suddenly became the center of attention.
A big potato farmer offered to buy my business and I said yes. Without money, I wouldn't have been able to pursue my research.
€€€
I returned to my work, full of enthusiasm.
Until I found a PROBLEM with my invention!
Certain properties of the new hybrid species...
...were being transferred to those eating them!
I was so disappointed! It meant working many more months, maybe years, to perfect my technology.
EEK!
I had no choice but to tell my new boss the bad news.
Oddly enough, he took it pretty well.

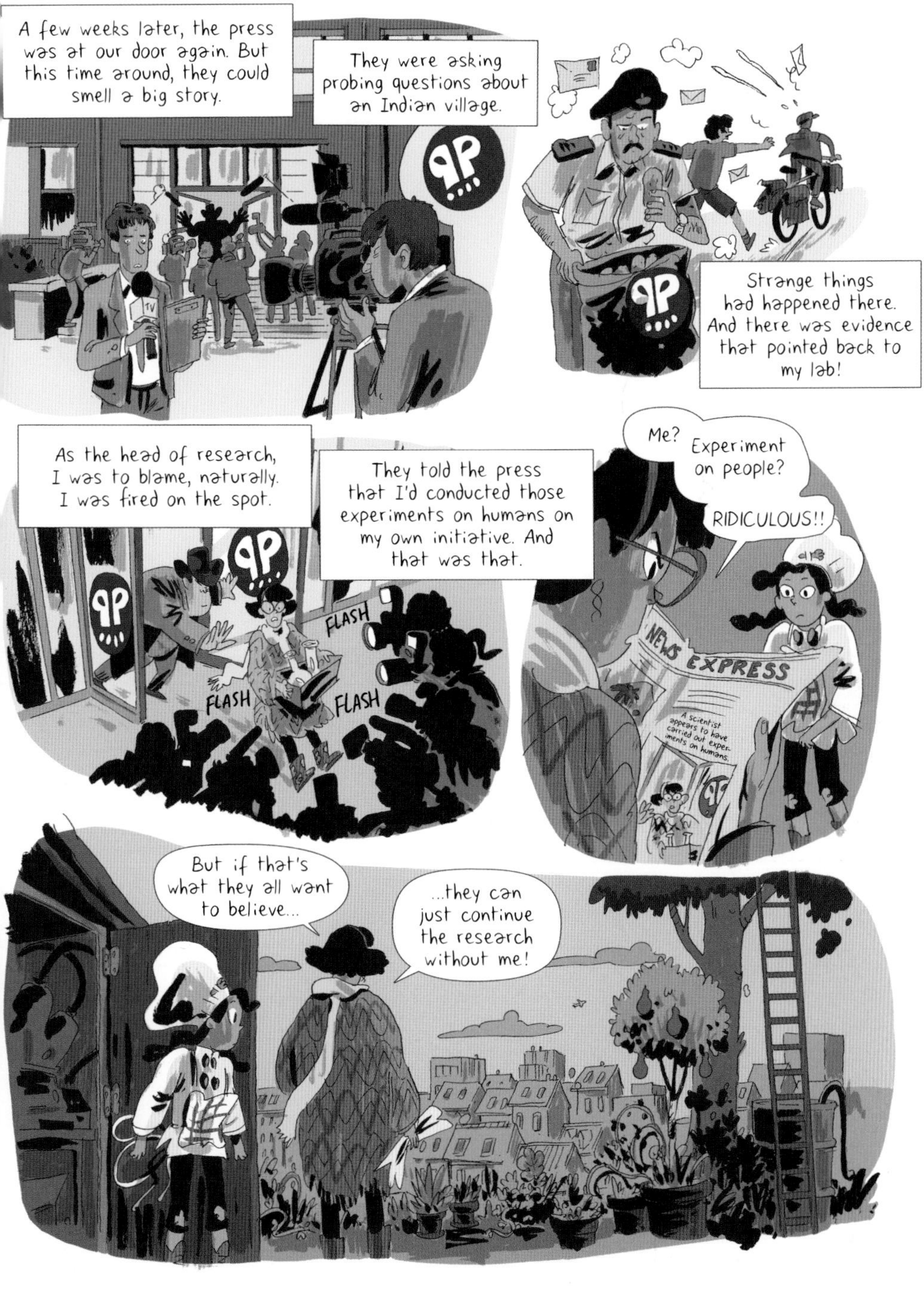
A few weeks later, the press was at our door again. But this time around, they could smell a big story.
They were asking probing questions about an Indian village.
Strange things had happened there. And there was evidence that pointed back to my lab!
As the head of research, I was to blame, naturally. I was fired on the spot.
They told the press that I'd conducted those experiments on humans on my own initiative. And that was that.
FLASH
FLASH
FLASH
Me?
Experiment on people?
RIDICULOUS!!
NEWS EXPRESS
A scientist appears to have carried out experiments on humans.
But if that's what they all want to believe...
...they can just continue the research without me!

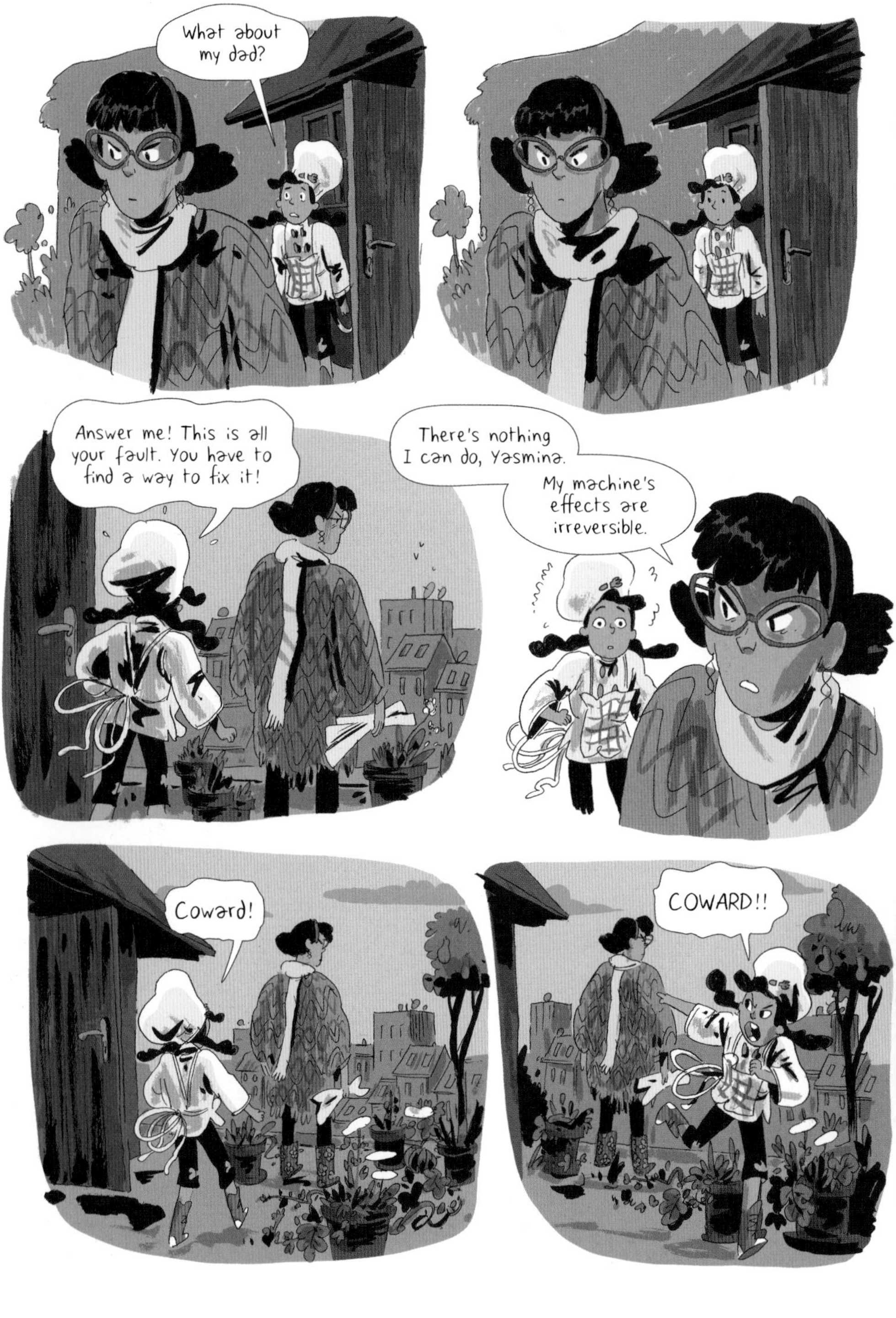
What about my dad?
Answer me! This is all your fault. You have to find a way to fix it!
There's nothing I can do, Yasmina.
My machine's effects are irreversible.
Coward!
COWARD!!

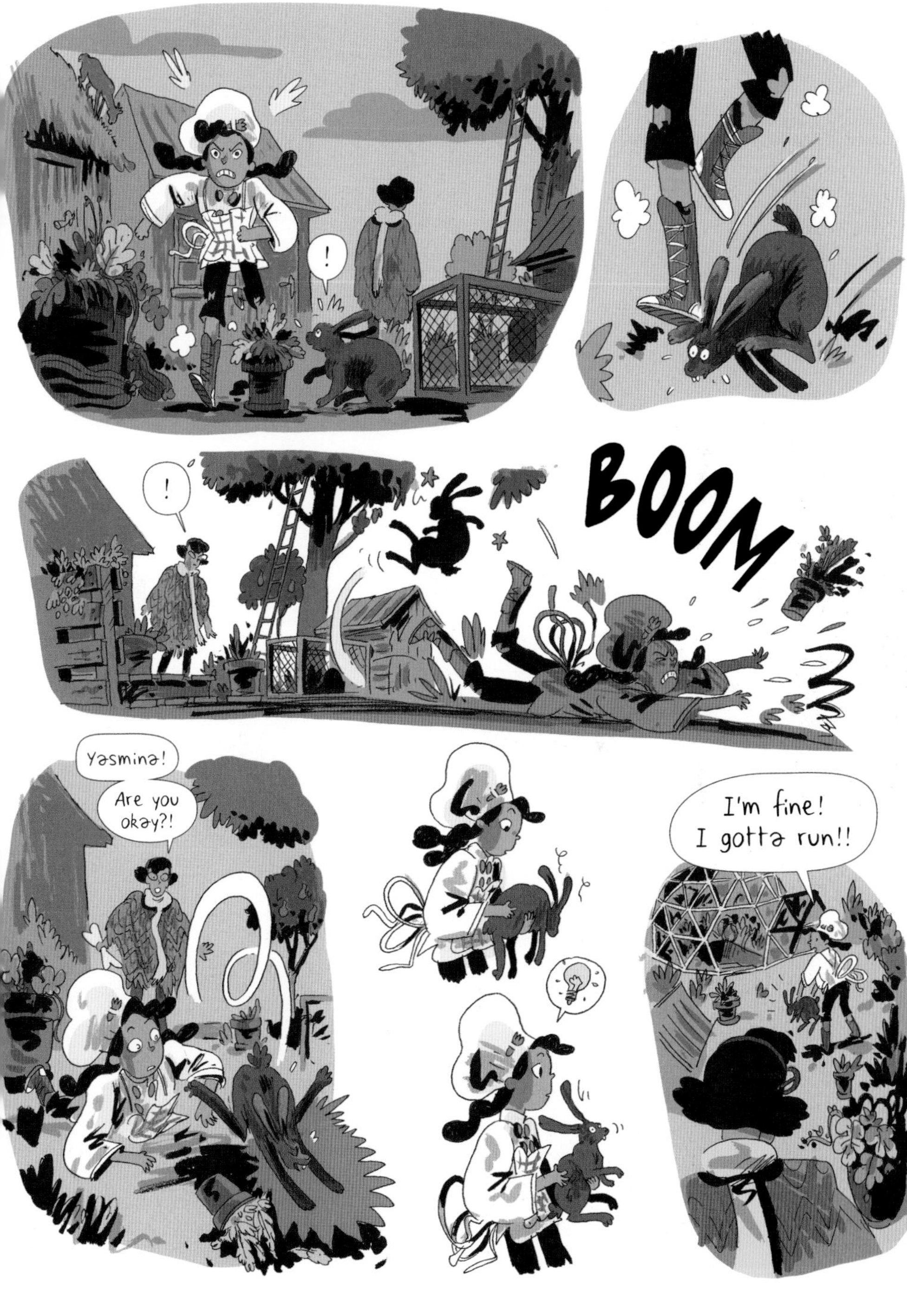
!
!
BOOM
Yasmina!
Are you okay?!
I'm fine!
I gotta run!!

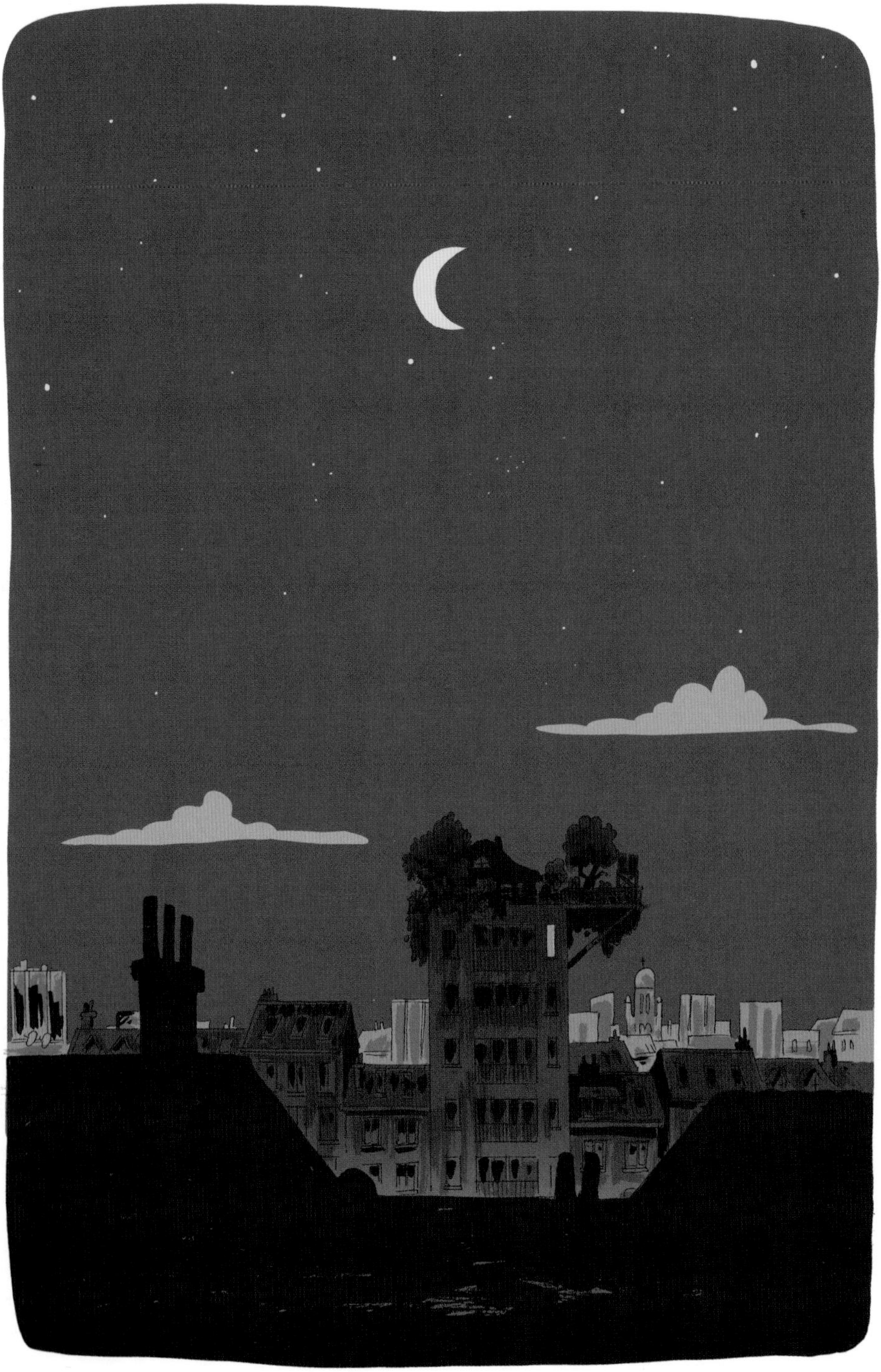

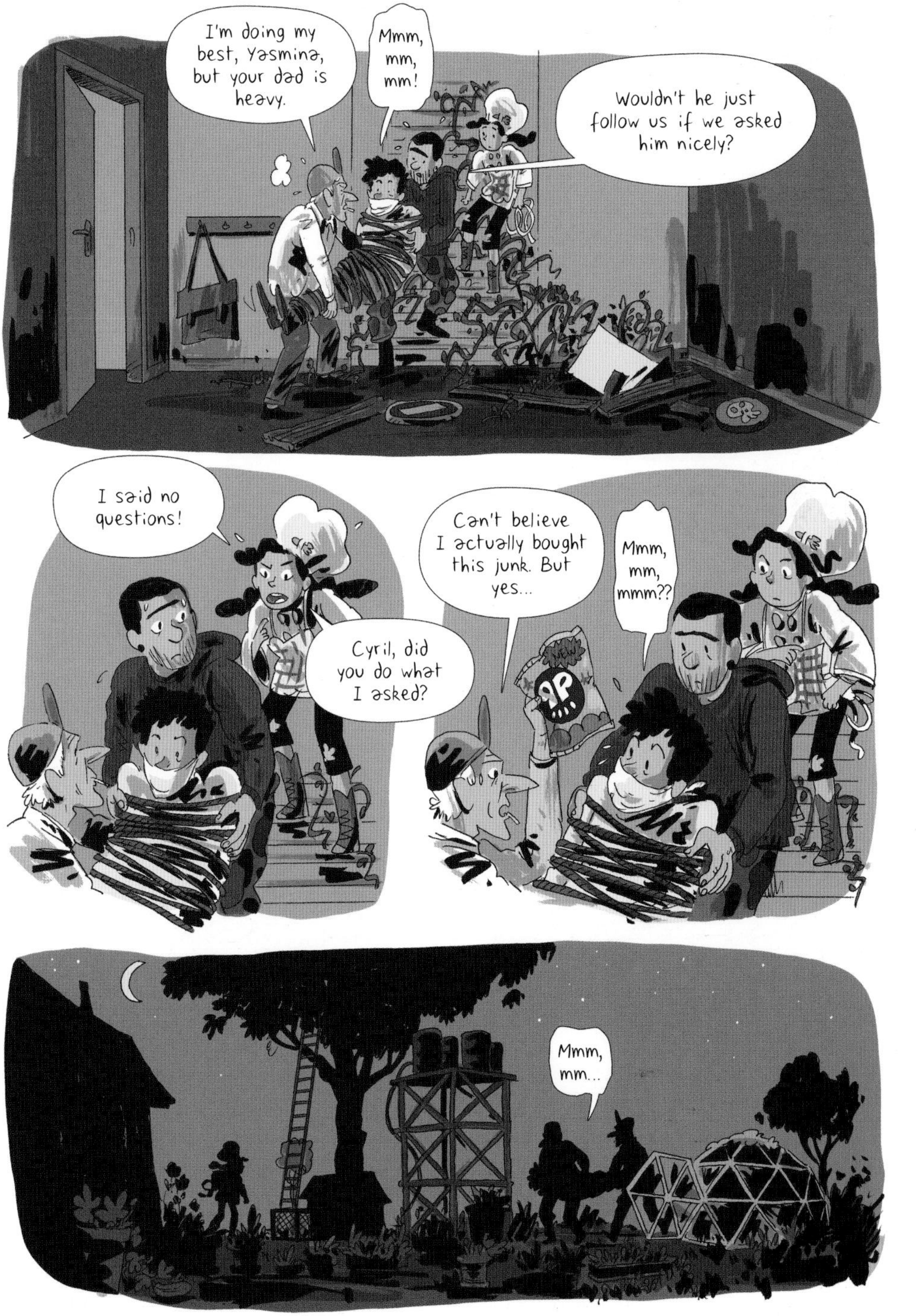
I'm doing my best, Yasmina, but your dad is heavy.
Mmm, mm, mm!
Wouldn't he just follow us if we asked him nicely?
I said no questions!
Cyril, did you do what I asked?
Can't believe I actually bought this junk. But yes...
Mmm, mm, mmm??
Mmm, mm...

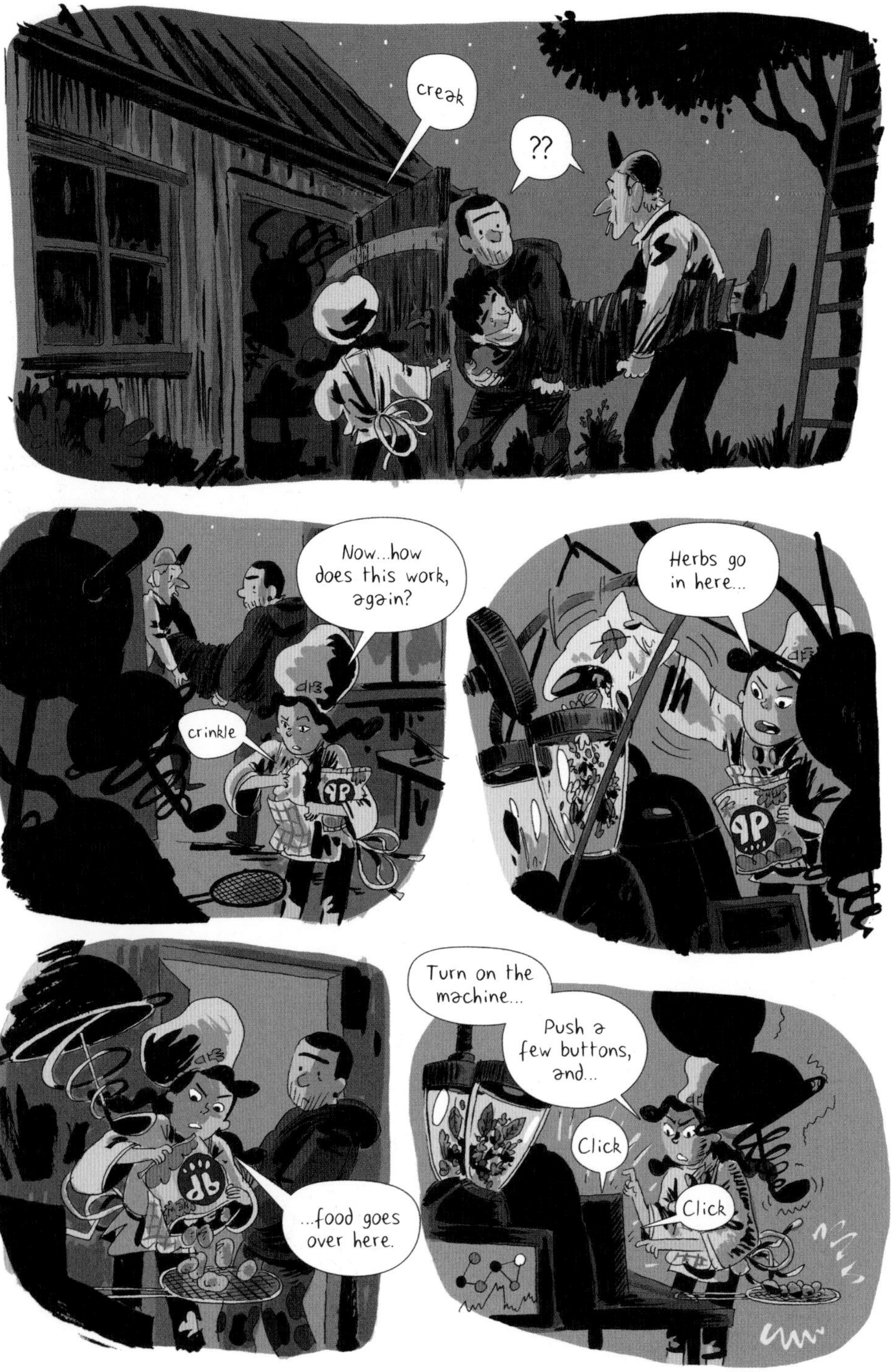
creak
??
Now...how does this work, again?
crinkle
Herbs go in here...
...food goes over here.
Turn on the machine...
Push a few buttons, and...
Click
Click

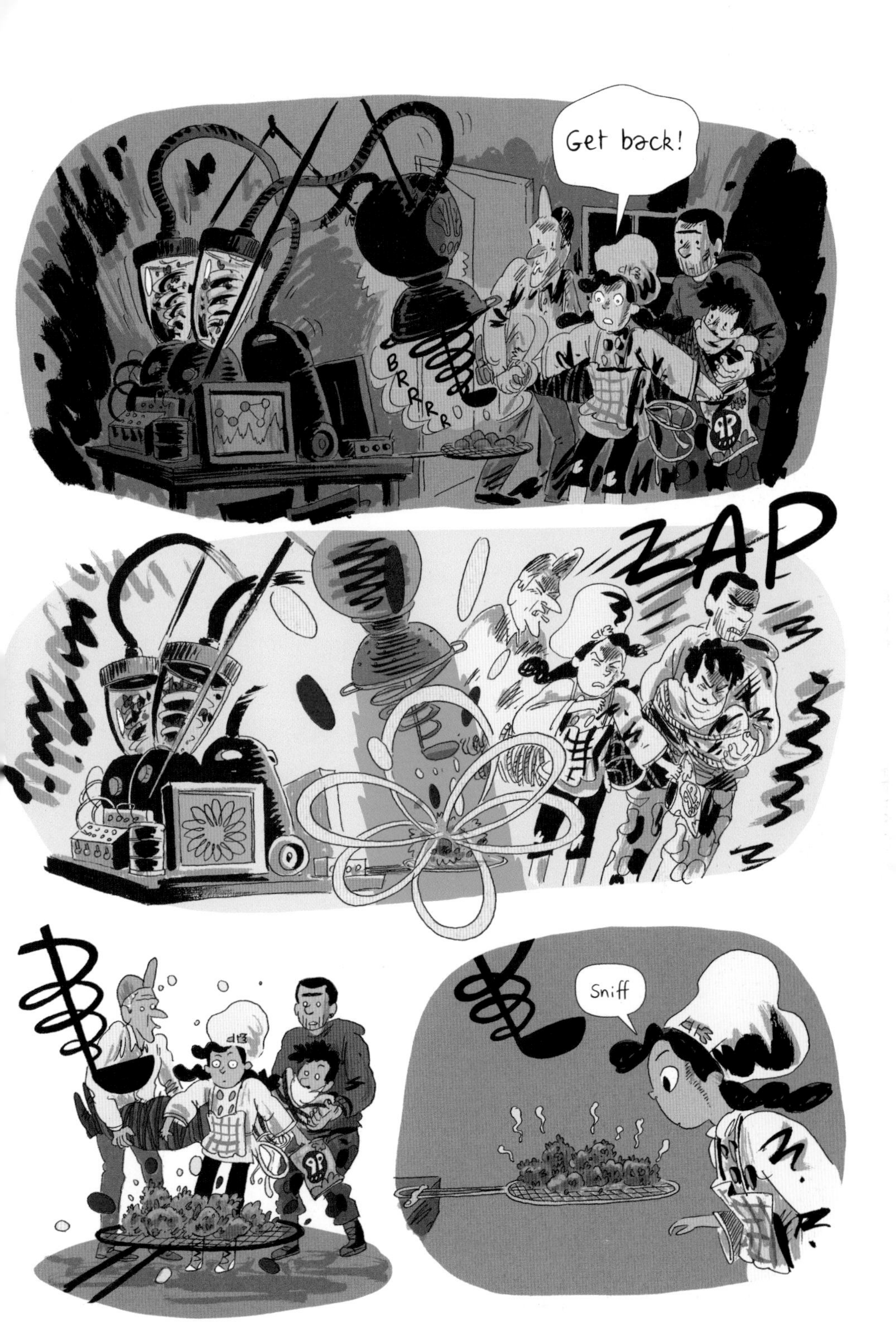
Get back!
BRRRRR
ZAP
Sniff

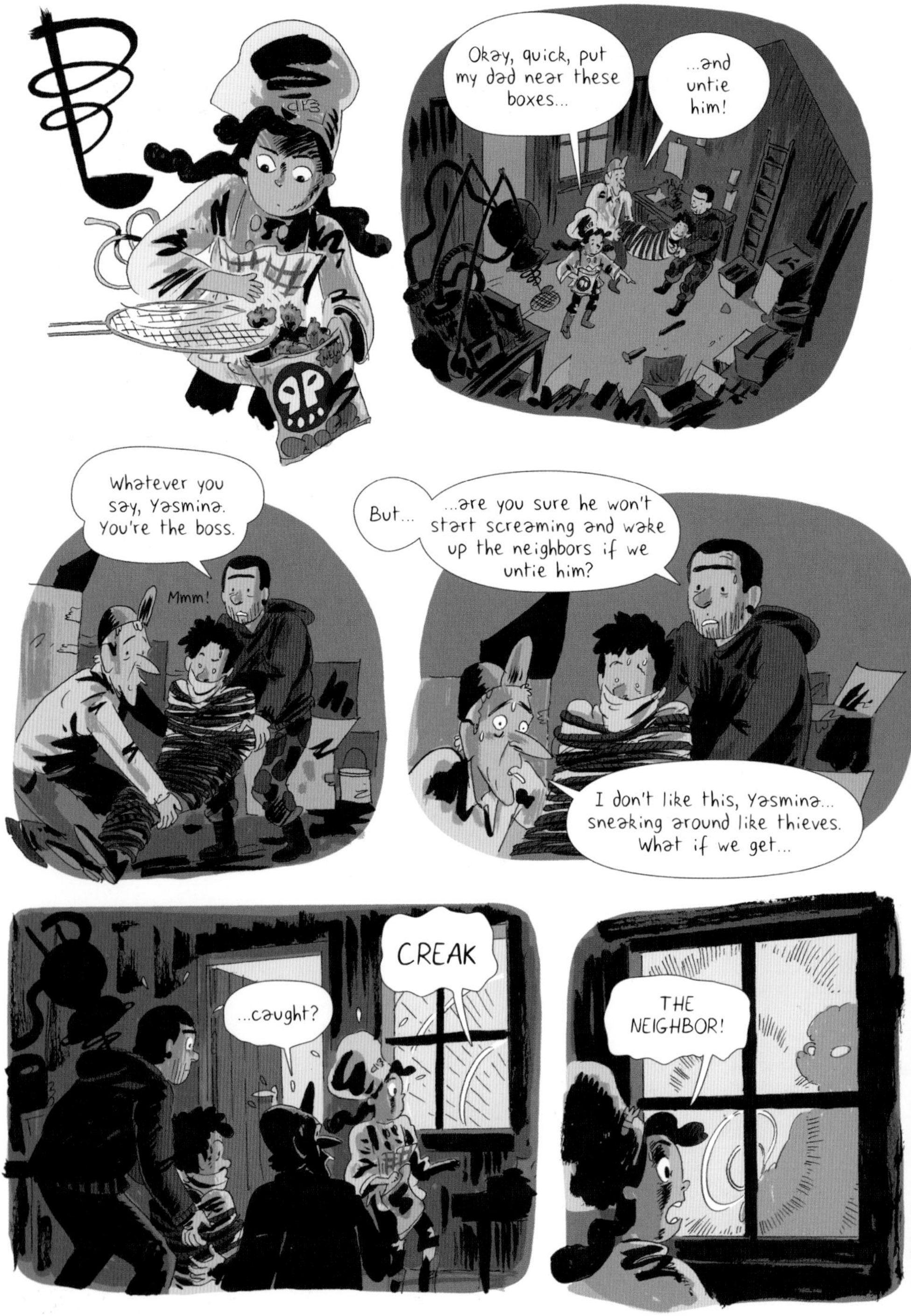
Okay, quick, put my dad near these boxes...
...and untie him!
Whatever you say, Yasmina. You're the boss.
Mmm!
But...
...are you sure he won't start screaming and wake up the neighbors if we untie him?
I don't like this, Yasmina... sneaking around like thieves. What if we get...
...caught?
CREAK
THE NEIGHBOR!

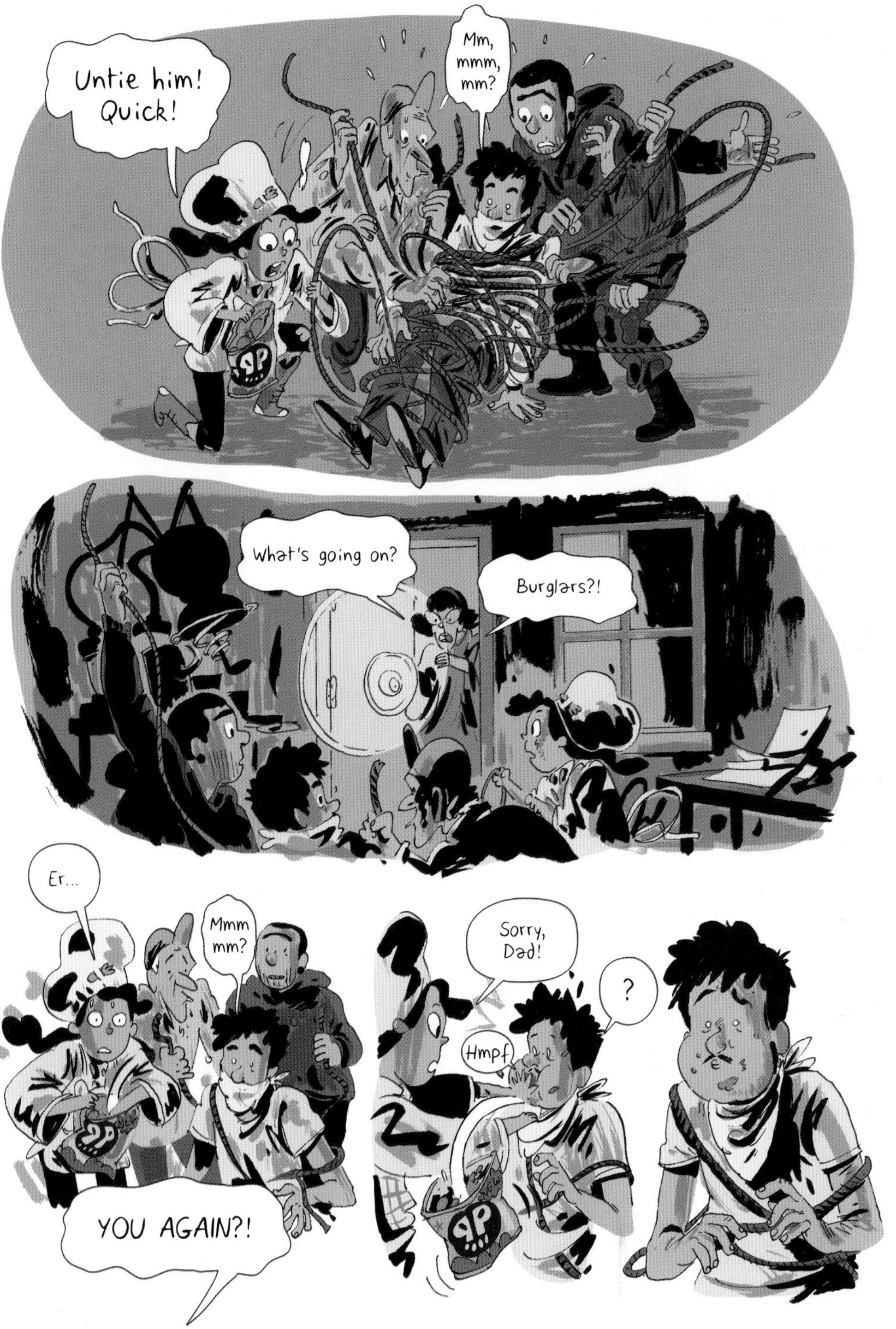

Untie him! Quick!
Mm, mmm, mm?
What's going on?
Burglars?!
Er...
Mmm mm?
YOU AGAIN?!
Sorry, Dad!
?
Hmpf

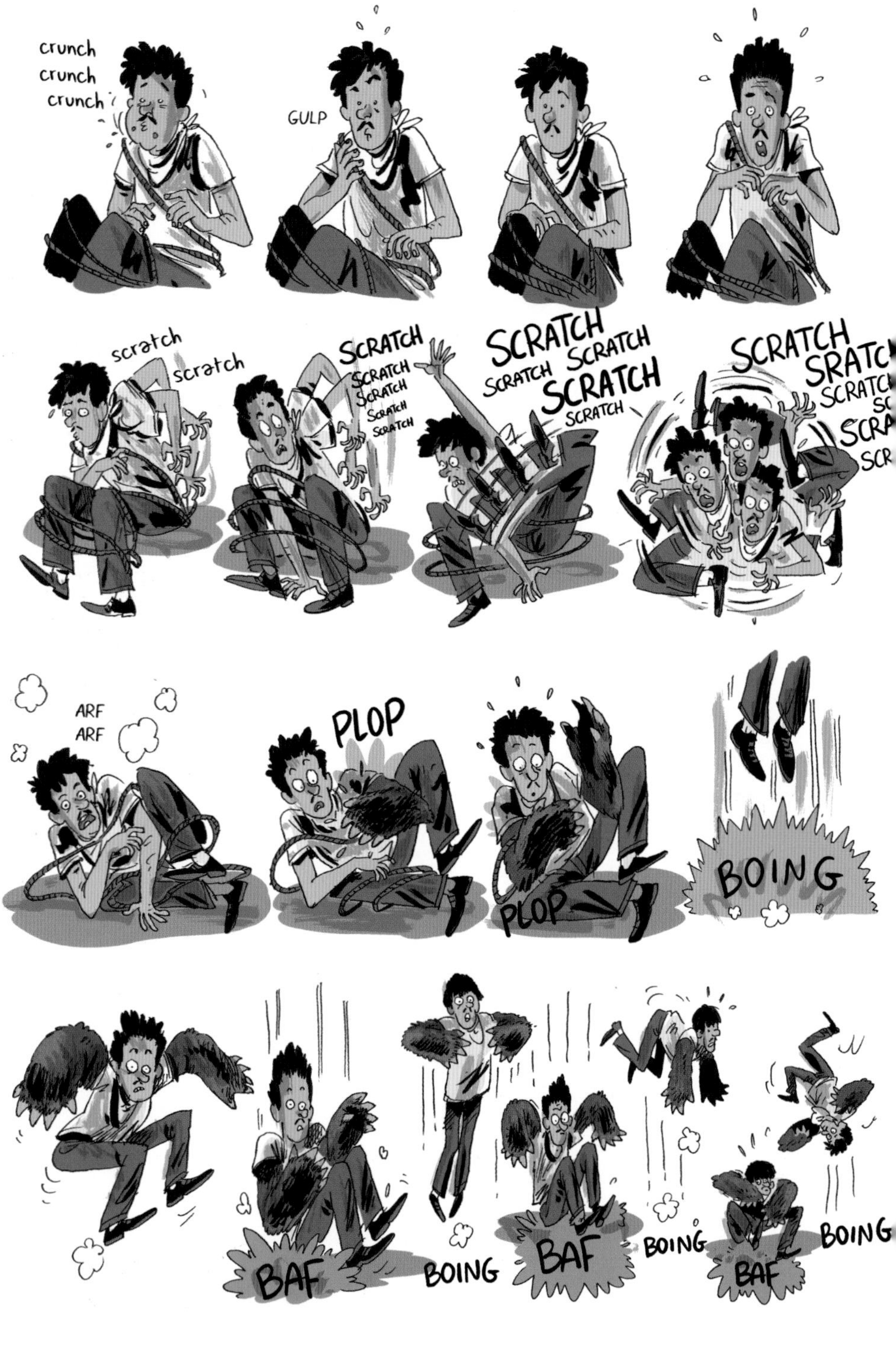
crunch
crunch
crunch
GULP
scratch
scratch
SCRATCH
SCRATCH
SCRATCH
SCRATCH
SCRATCH
SCRATCH
SCRATCH SCRATCH
SCRATCH
SCRATCH
SCRATCH
SRATC
ARF
ARF
PLOP
PLOP
BOING
BAF
BOING
BAF
BOING
BAF
BOING

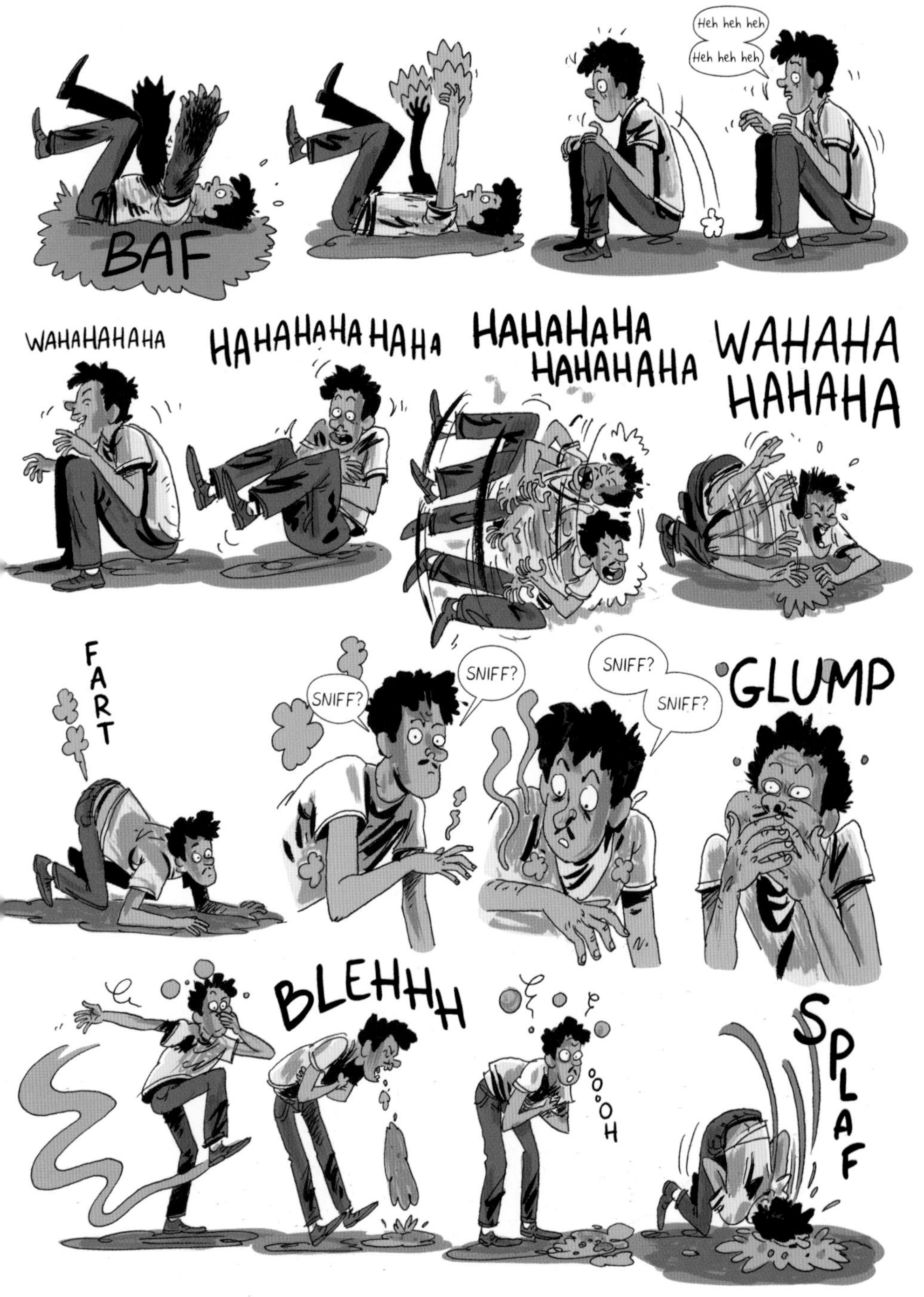
BAF
Heh heh heh
Heh heh heh
WAHAHAHAHA
HAHAHAHAHAHA
HAHAHAHA
HAHAHAHA
WAHAHA
HAHAHA
FART
SNIFF?
SNIFF?
SNIFF?
SNIFF?
GLUMP
BLEHHH
OOOOH
SPLAF

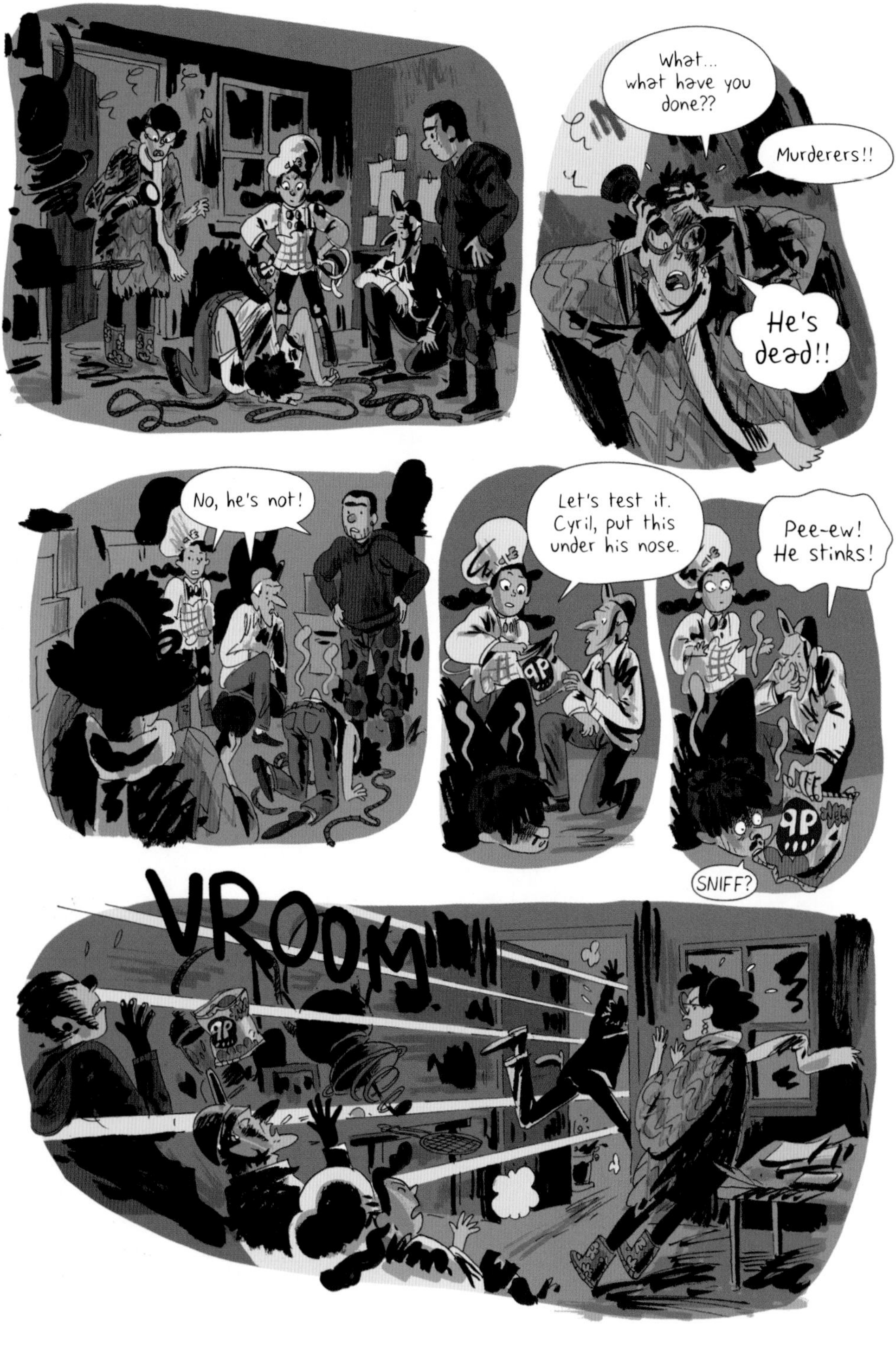
What... what have you done??
Murderers!!
He's dead!!
No, he's not!
Let's test it. Cyril, put this under his nose.
Pee-ew! He stinks!
SNIFF?
VROOM

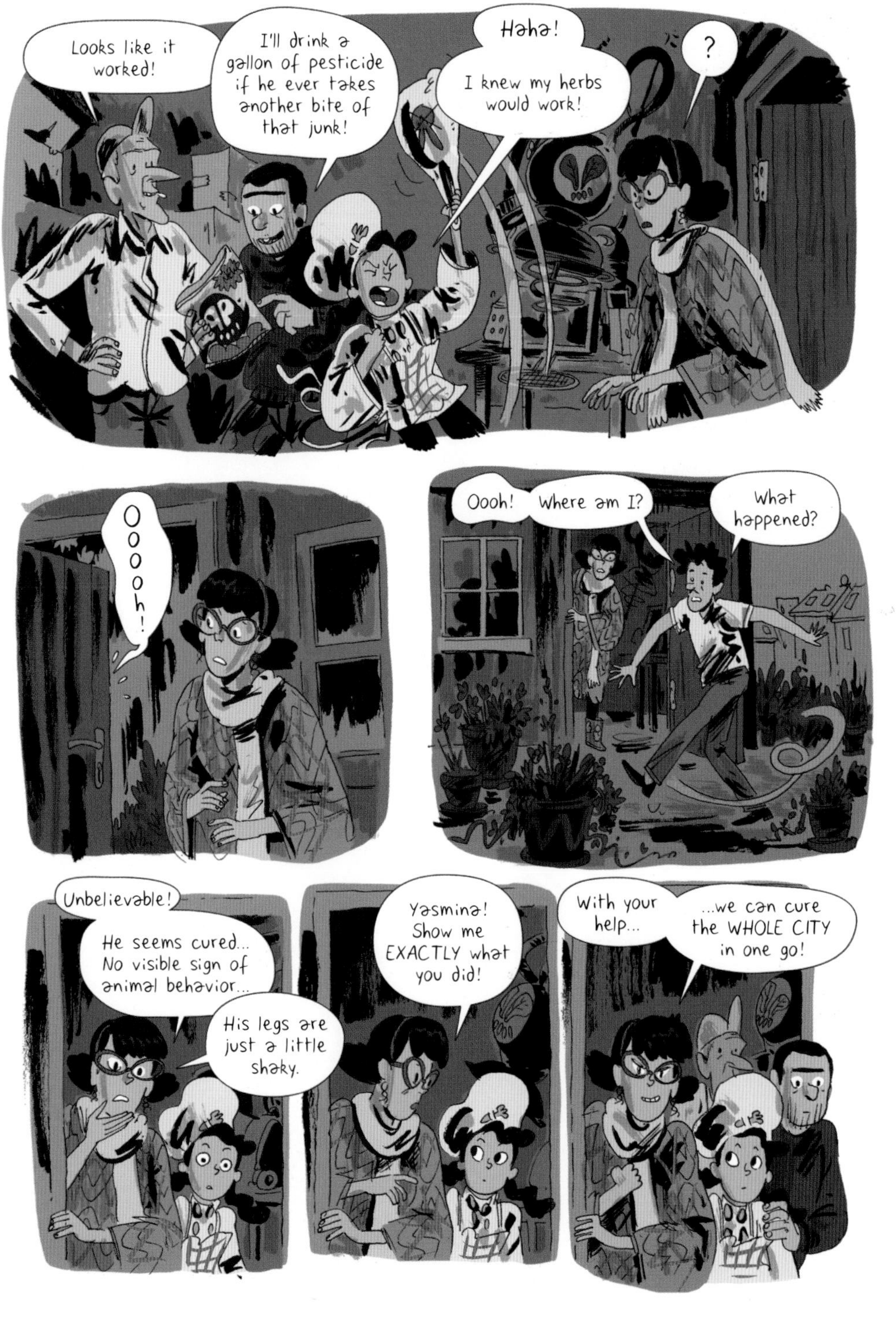
Looks like it worked!
I'll drink a gallon of pesticide if he ever takes another bite of that junk!
Haha!
I knew my herbs would work!
?
Ooooh!
Oooh!
Where am I?
What happened?
Unbelievable!
He seems cured... No visible sign of animal behavior...
His legs are just a little shaky.
Yasmina! Show me EXACTLY what you did!
With your help...
...we can cure the WHOLE CITY in one go!

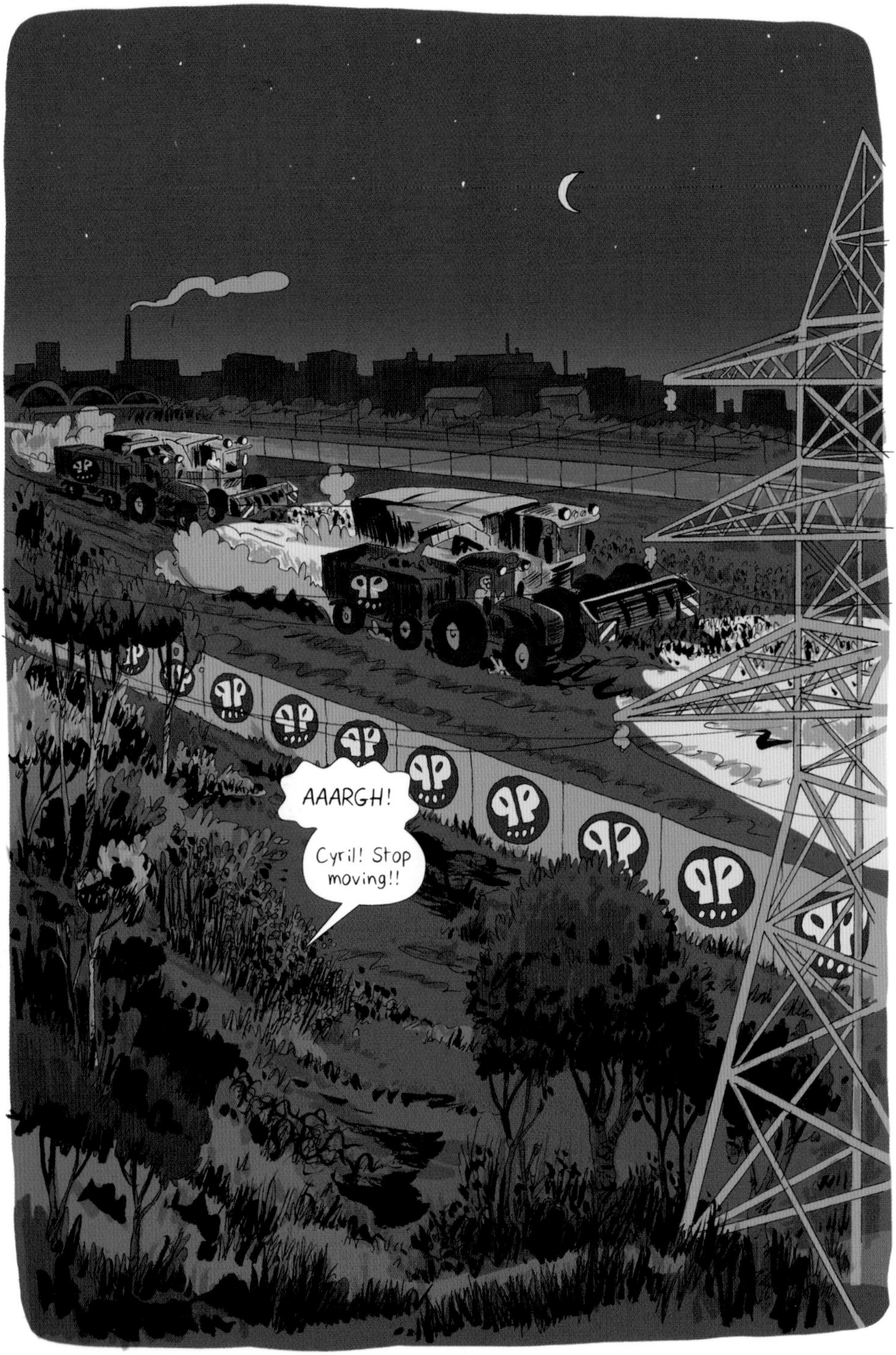
AAARGH!
Cyril! Stop moving!!

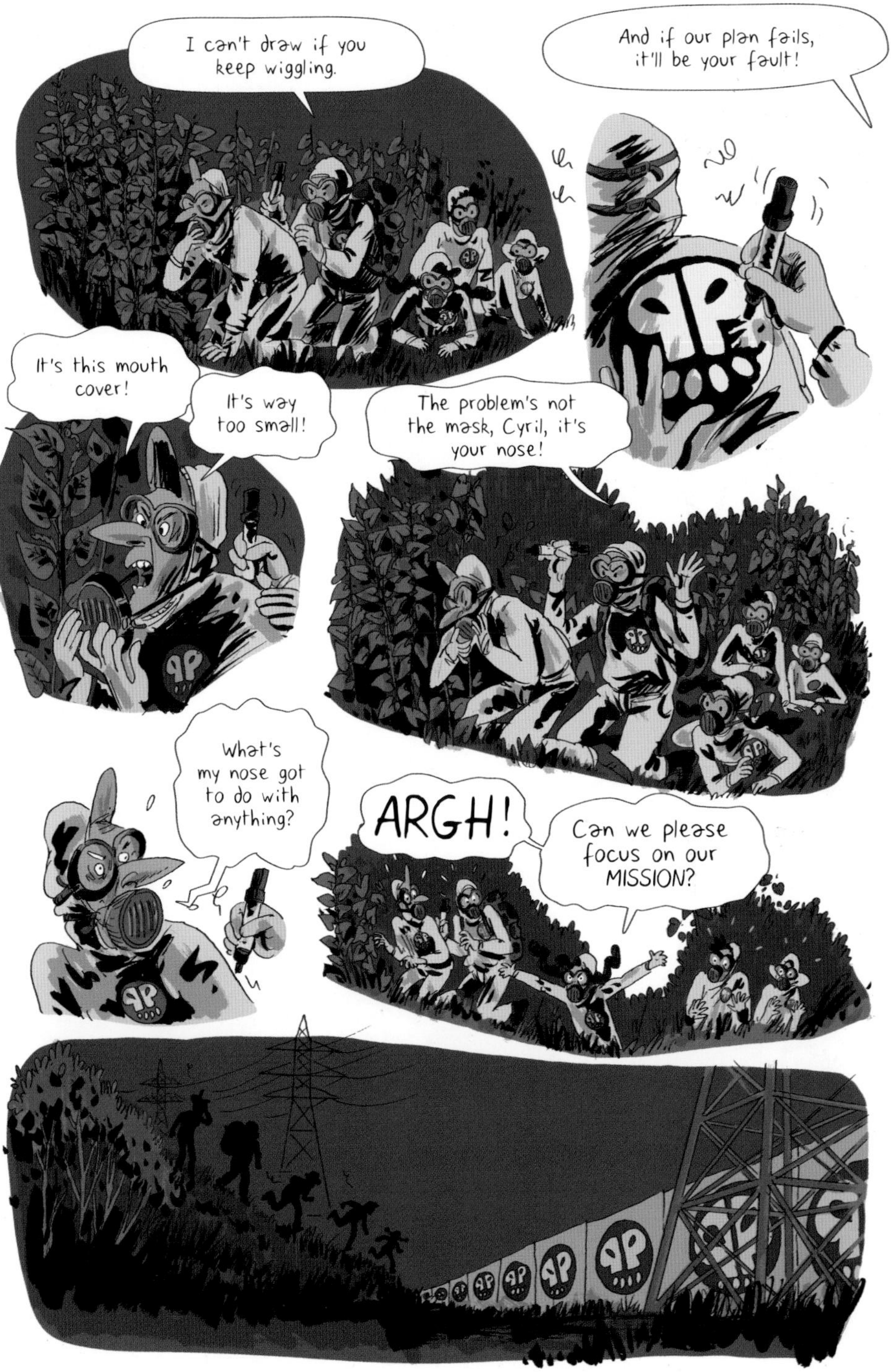

I can't draw if you keep wiggling.
And if our plan fails, it'll be your fault!
It's this mouth cover!
It's way too small!
The problem's not the mask, Cyril, it's your nose!
What's my nose got to do with anything?
ARGH!
Can we please focus on our MISSION?

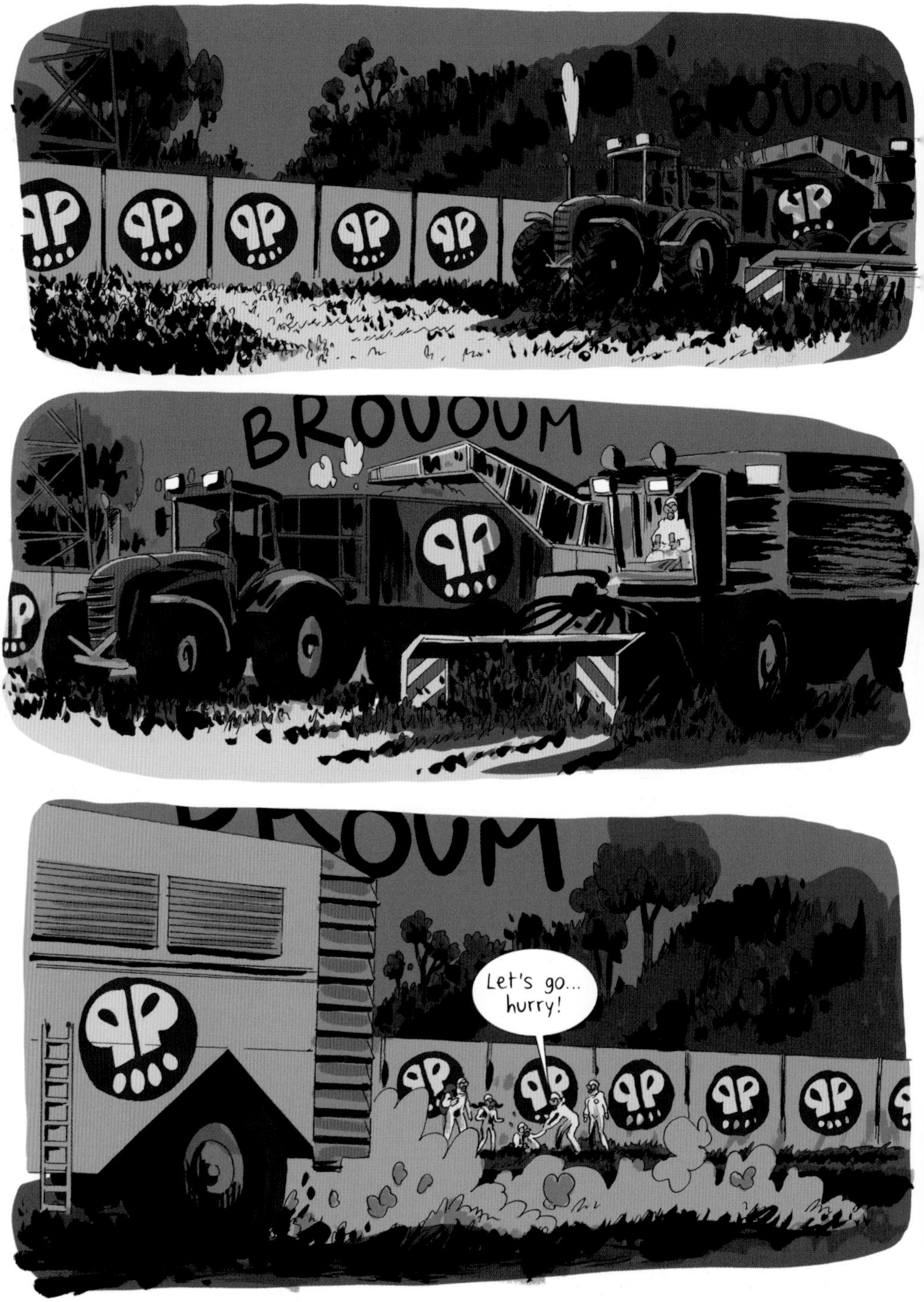
BROUOUM
BROUOUM
ROUM
Let's go... hurry!

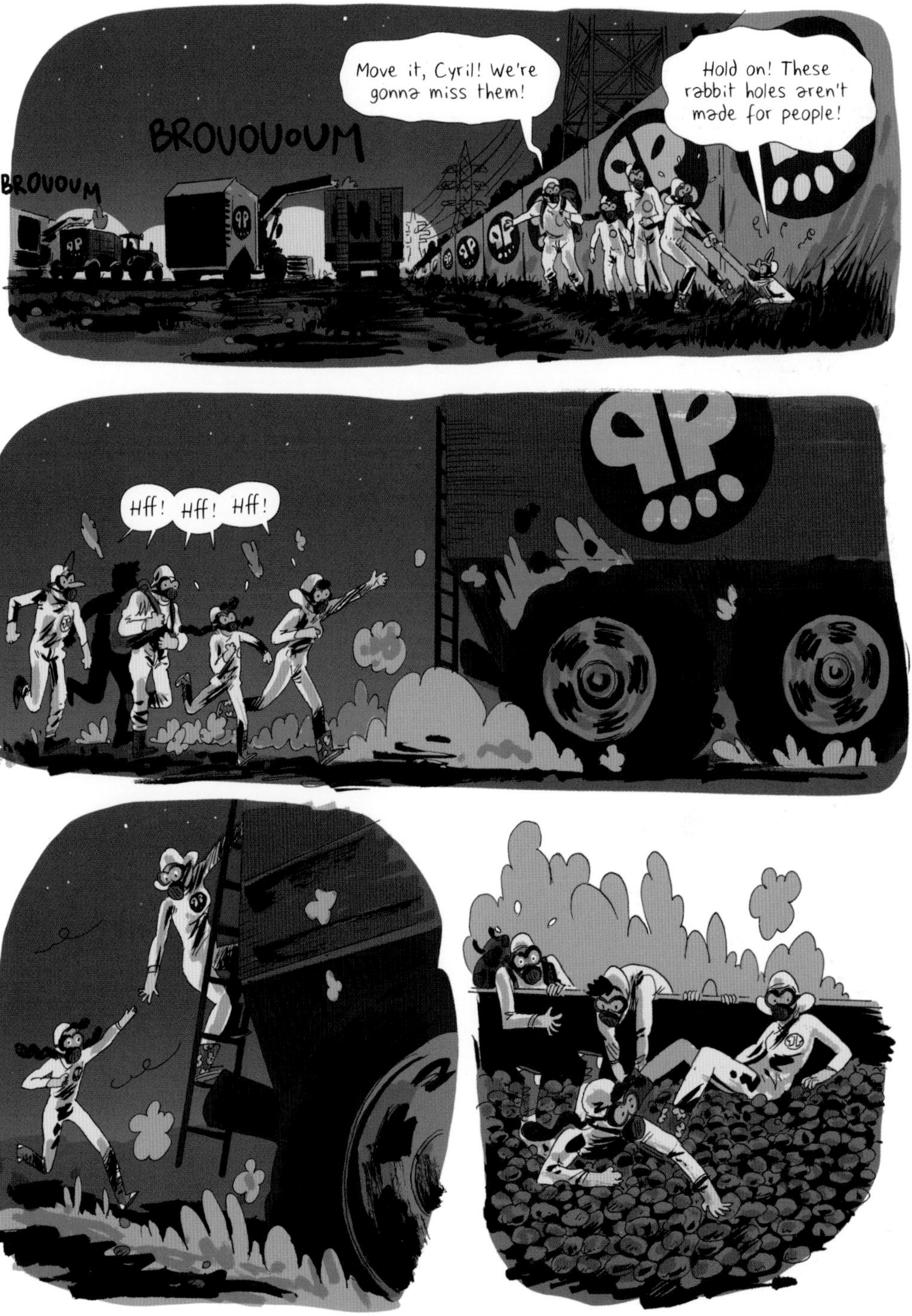
BROUOUM
BROUOUOUM
Move it, Cyril! We're gonna miss them!
Hold on! These rabbit holes aren't made for people!
Hff!
Hff!
Hff!

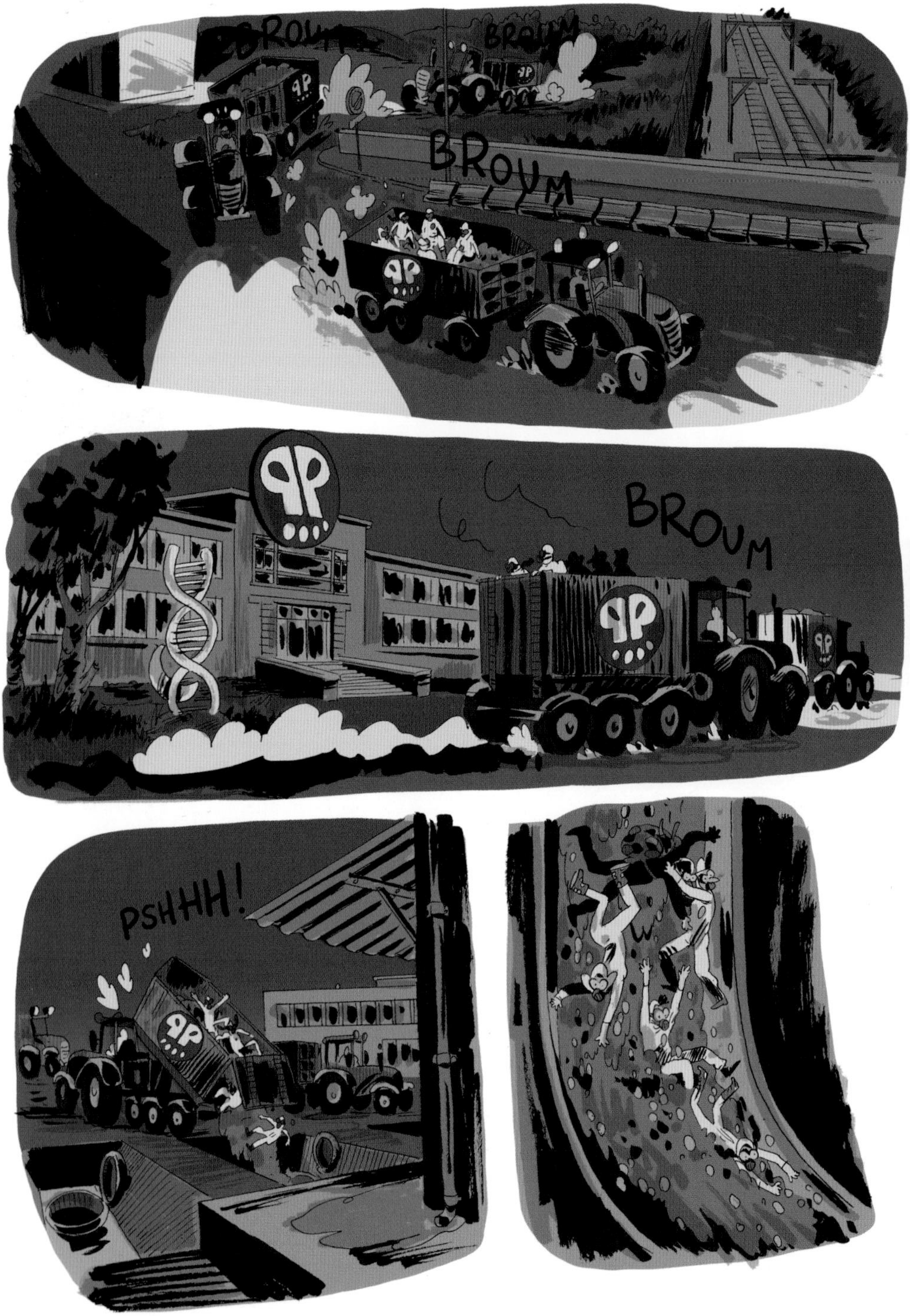
BROUM
BROUM
BROUM
PSHHH!

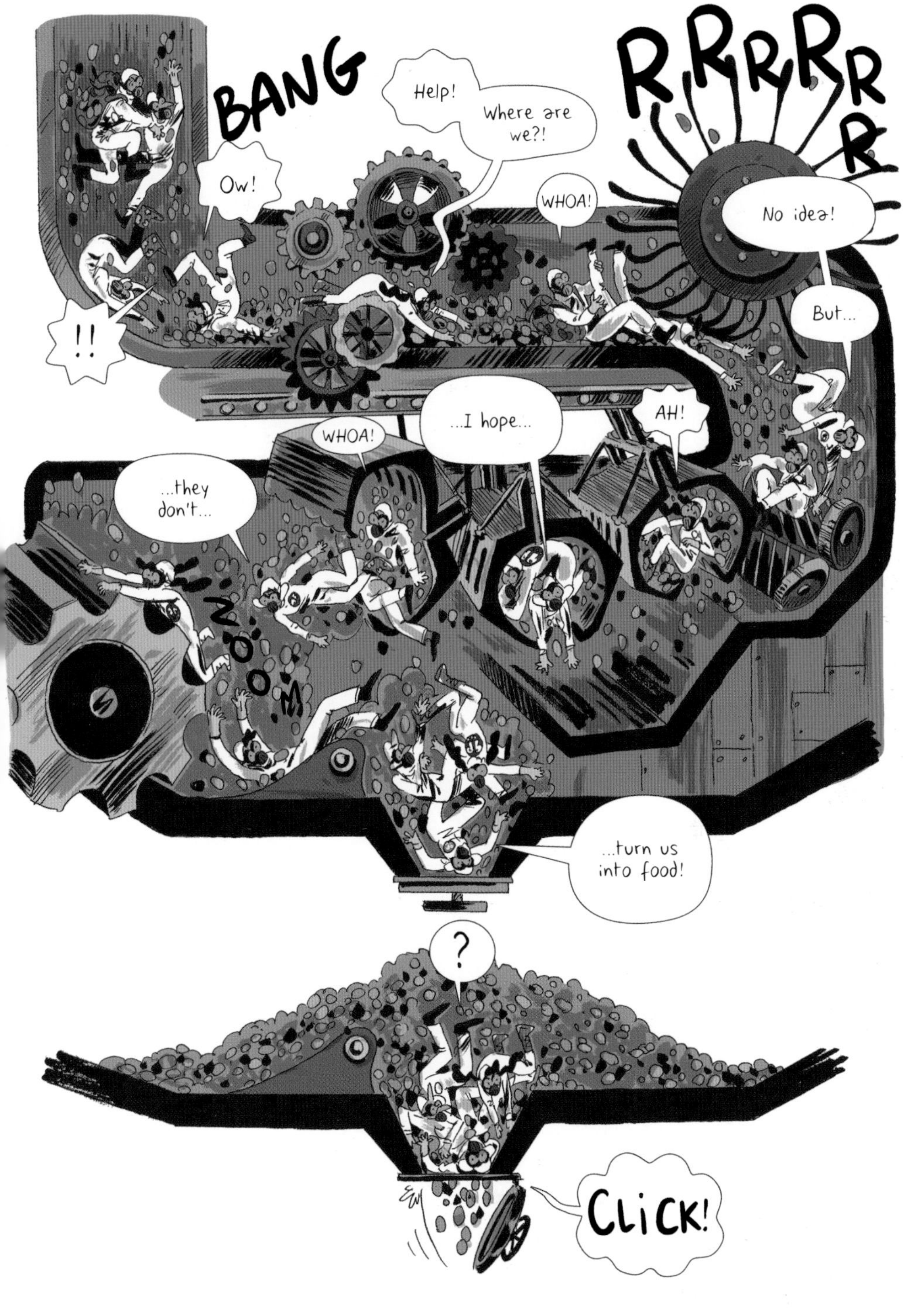

BANG
Help!
Where are we?!
RRRRRRR
Ow!
WHOA!
No idea!
!!
But...
...I hope...
WHOA!
AH!
...they don't...
ZOOOM
...turn us into food!
?
CLICK!

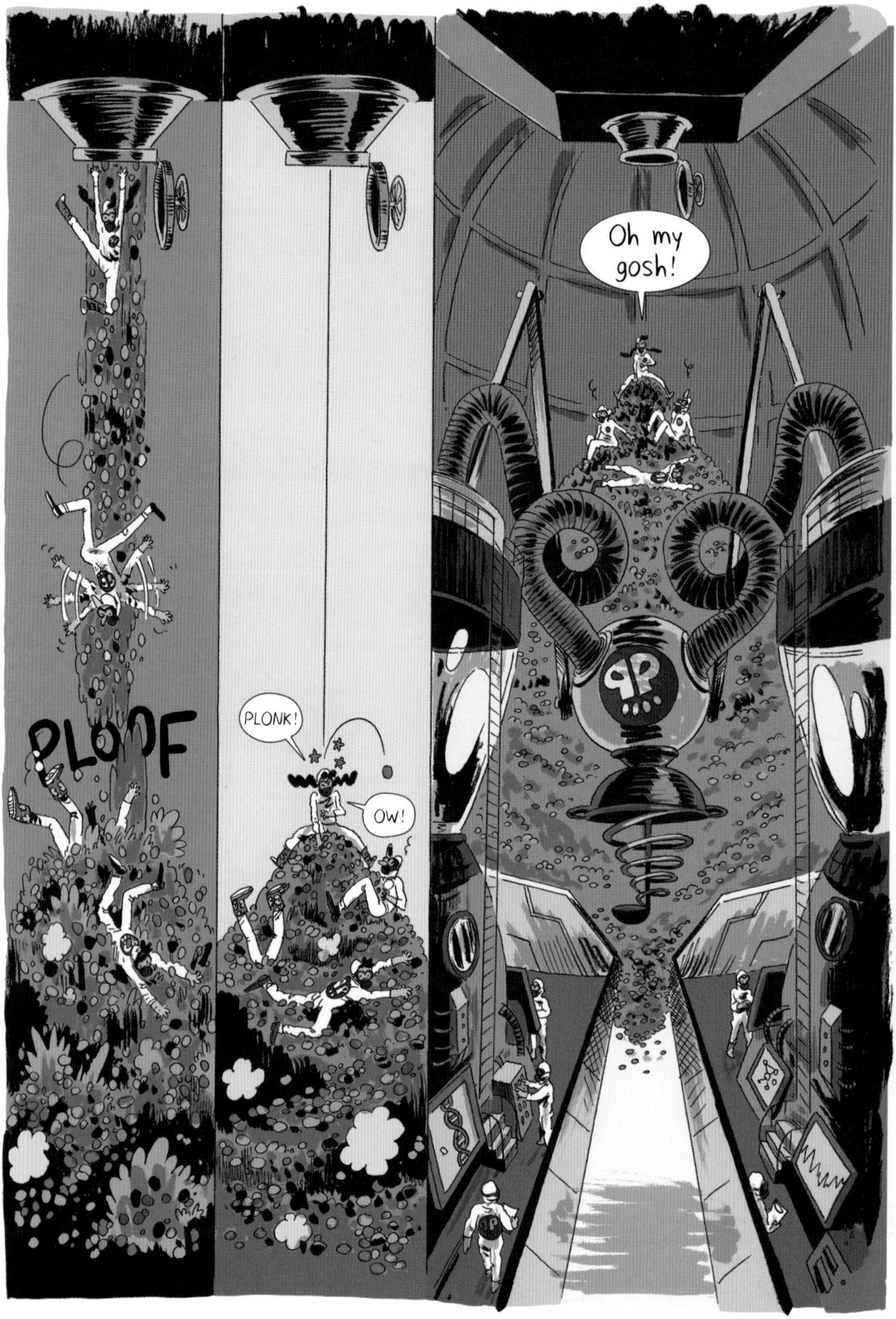
PLOOF
PLONK!
OW!
Oh my gosh!

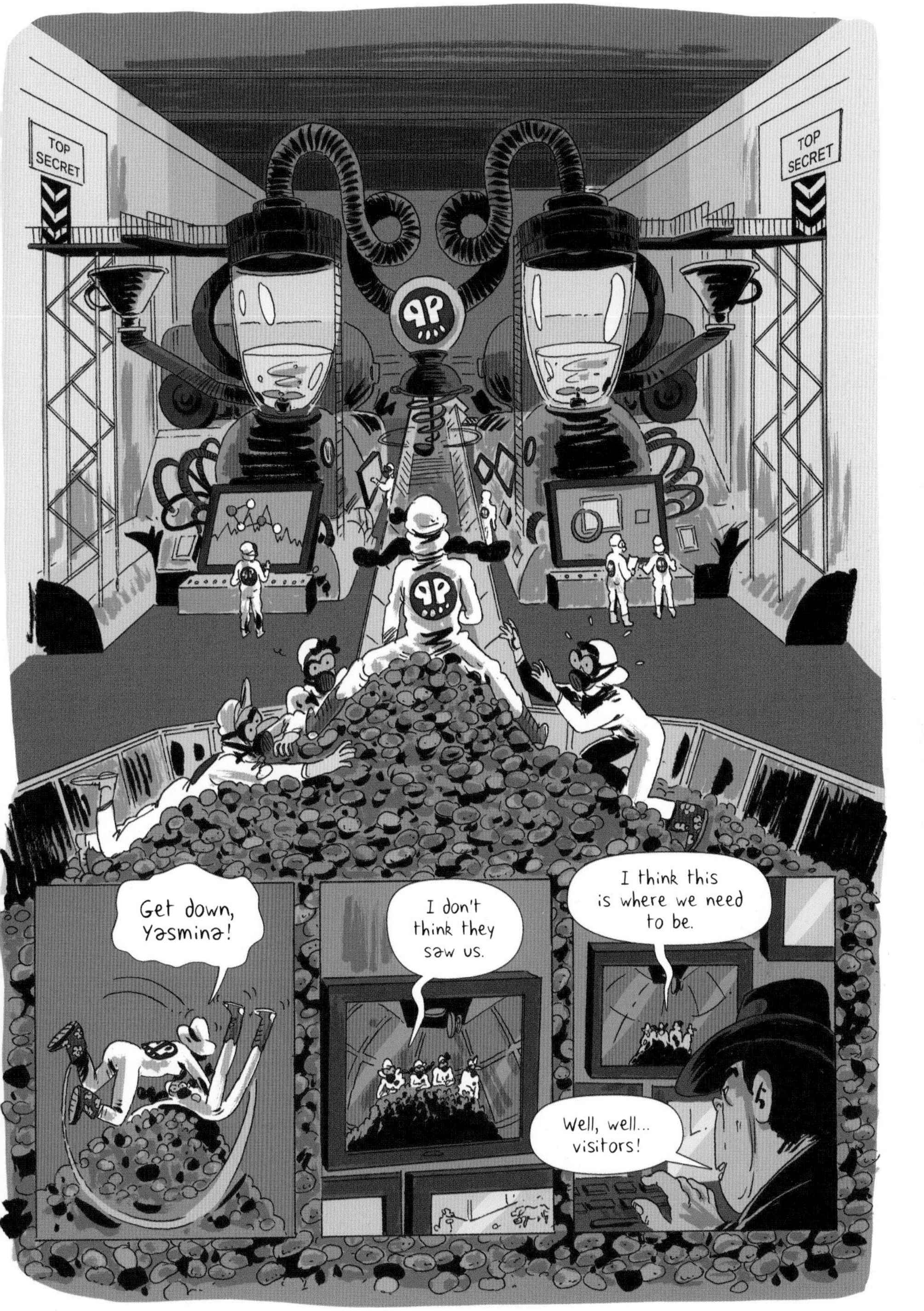
TOP SECRET
TOP SECRET
Get down, Yasmina!
I don't think they saw us.
I think this is where we need to be.
Well, well... visitors!

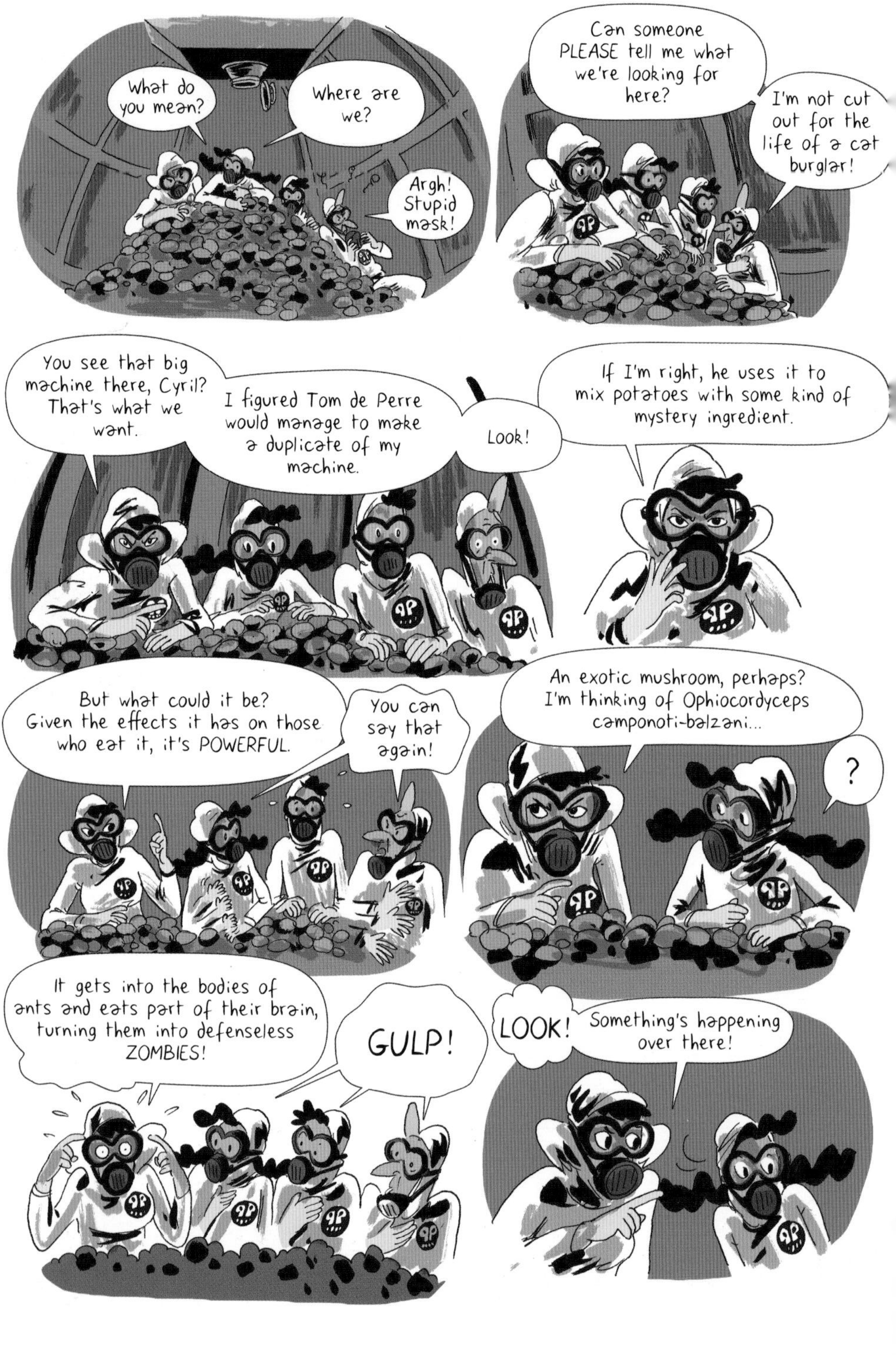
What do you mean?
Where are we?
Argh! Stupid mask!
Can someone PLEASE tell me what we're looking for here?
I'm not cut out for the life of a cat burglar!
You see that big machine there, Cyril? That's what we want.
I figured Tom de Perre would manage to make a duplicate of my machine.
Look!
If I'm right, he uses it to mix potatoes with some kind of mystery ingredient.
But what could it be? Given the effects it has on those who eat it, it's POWERFUL.
You can say that again!
An exotic mushroom, perhaps? I'm thinking of Ophiocordyceps camponoti-balzani...
?
It gets into the bodies of ants and eats part of their brain, turning them into defenseless ZOMBIES!
GULP!
LOOK!
Something's happening over there!

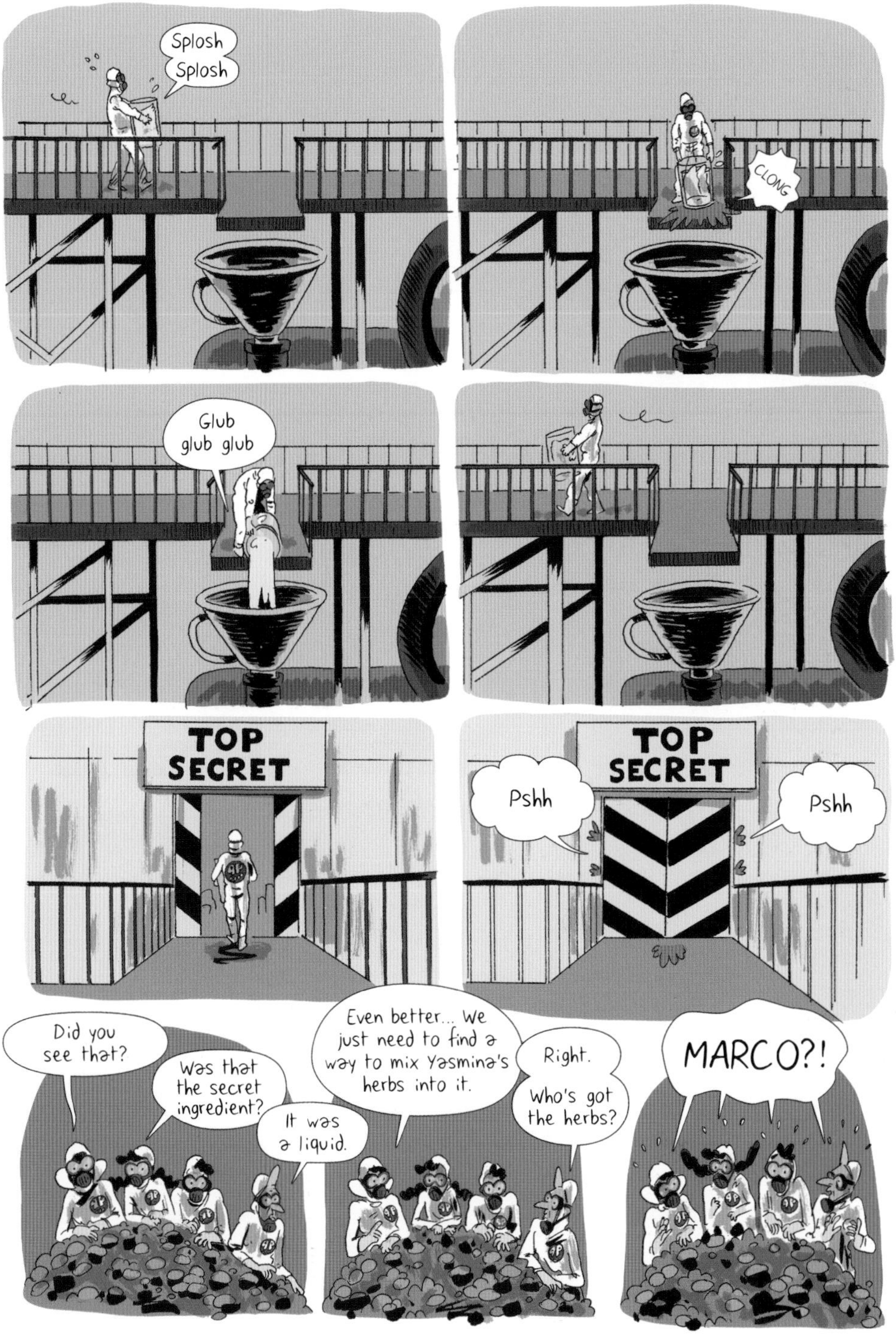
Splosh
Splosh
CLONG
Glub
glub glub
TOP SECRET
TOP SECRET
Pshh
Pshh
Did you see that?
Was that the secret ingredient?
It was a liquid.
Even better... We just need to find a way to mix Yasmina's herbs into it.
Right.
Who's got the herbs?
MARCO?!

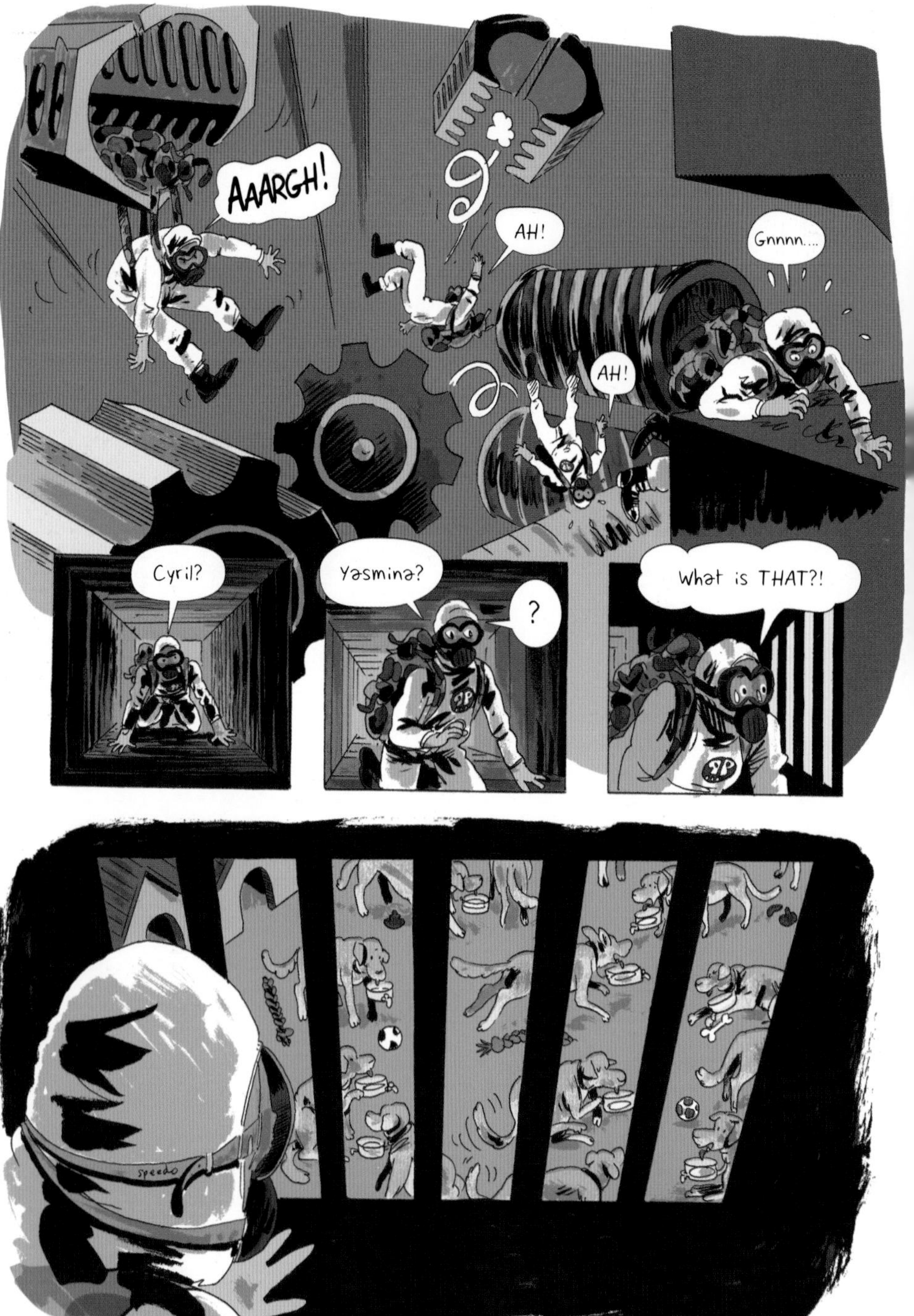
AAARGH!
AH!
Gnnnn....
AH!
Cyril?
Yasmina?
?
What is THAT?!
speedo

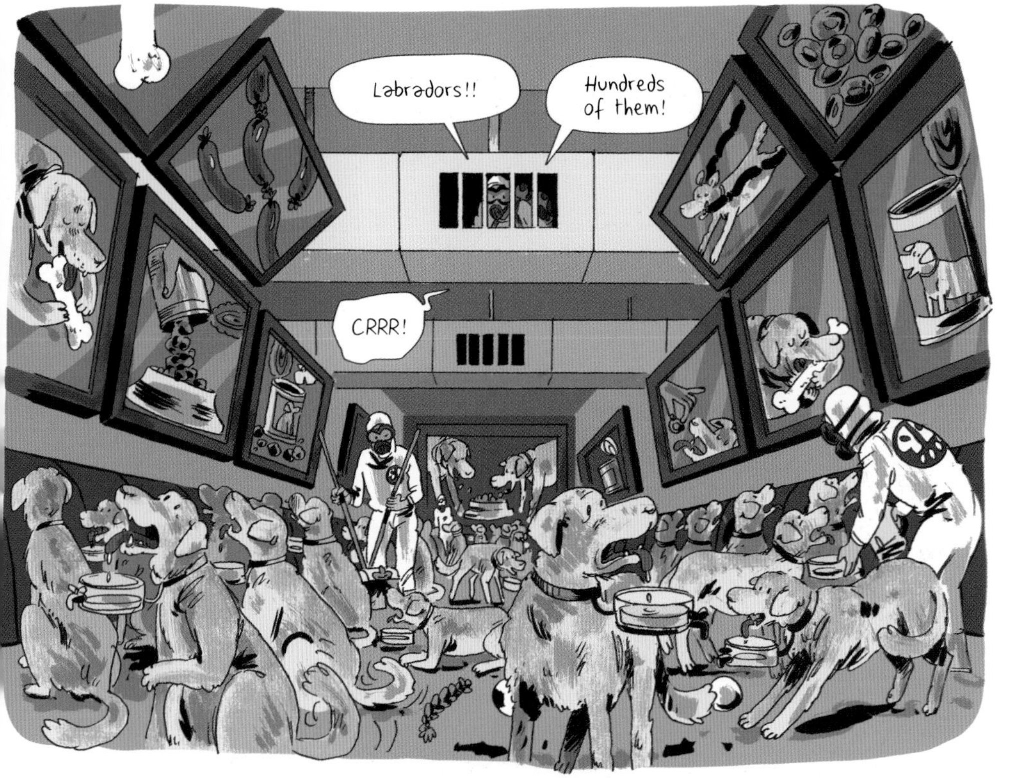
Labradors!!
Hundreds of them!
CRRR!

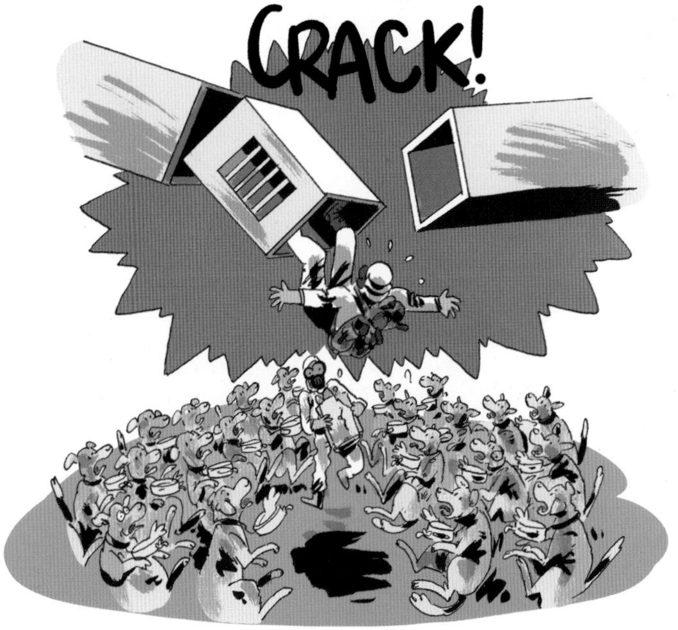
CRACK!

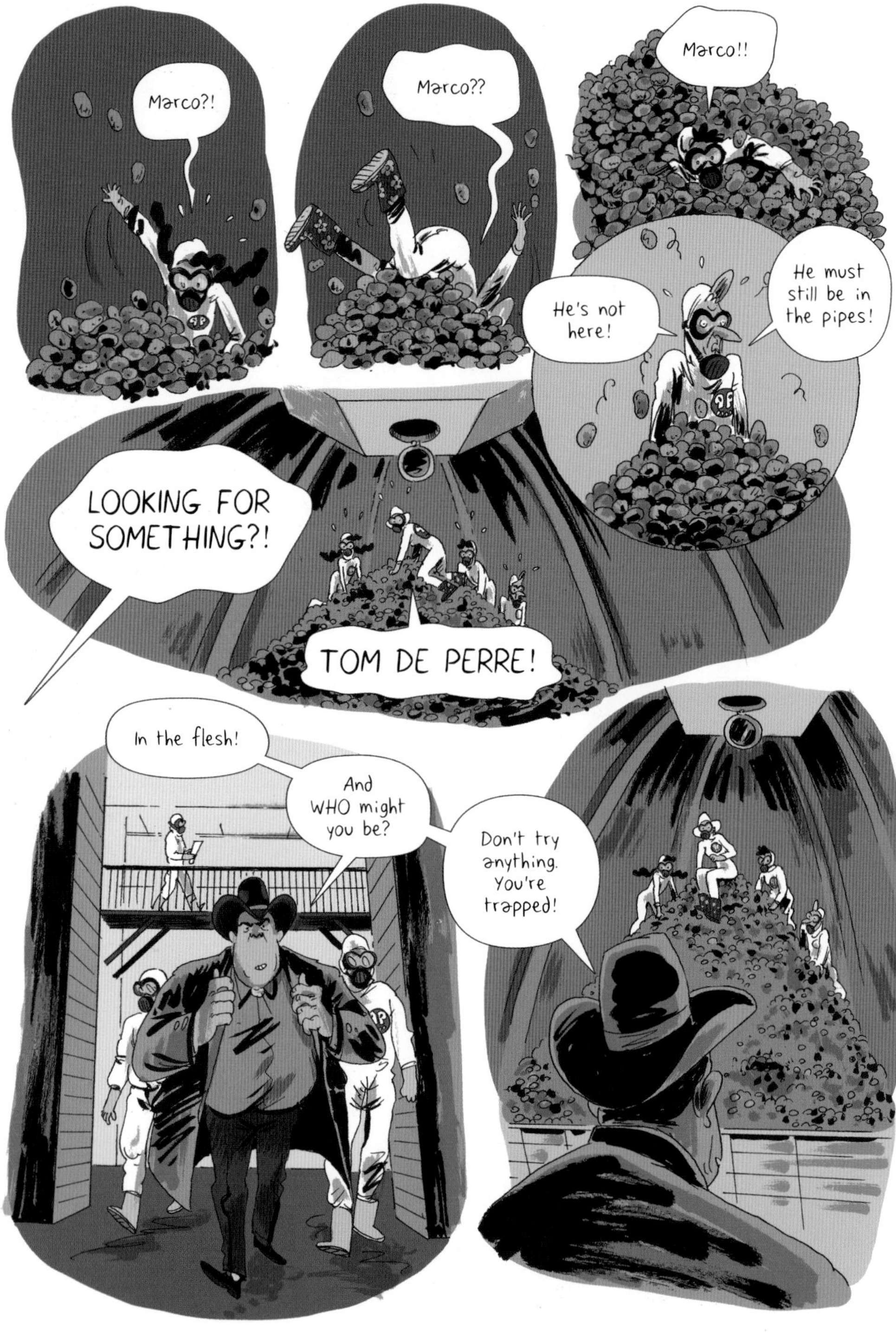
Marco?!
Marco??
Marco!!
He's not here!
He must still be in the pipes!
LOOKING FOR SOMETHING?!
TOM DE PERRE!
In the flesh!
And WHO might you be?
Don't try anything. You're trapped!

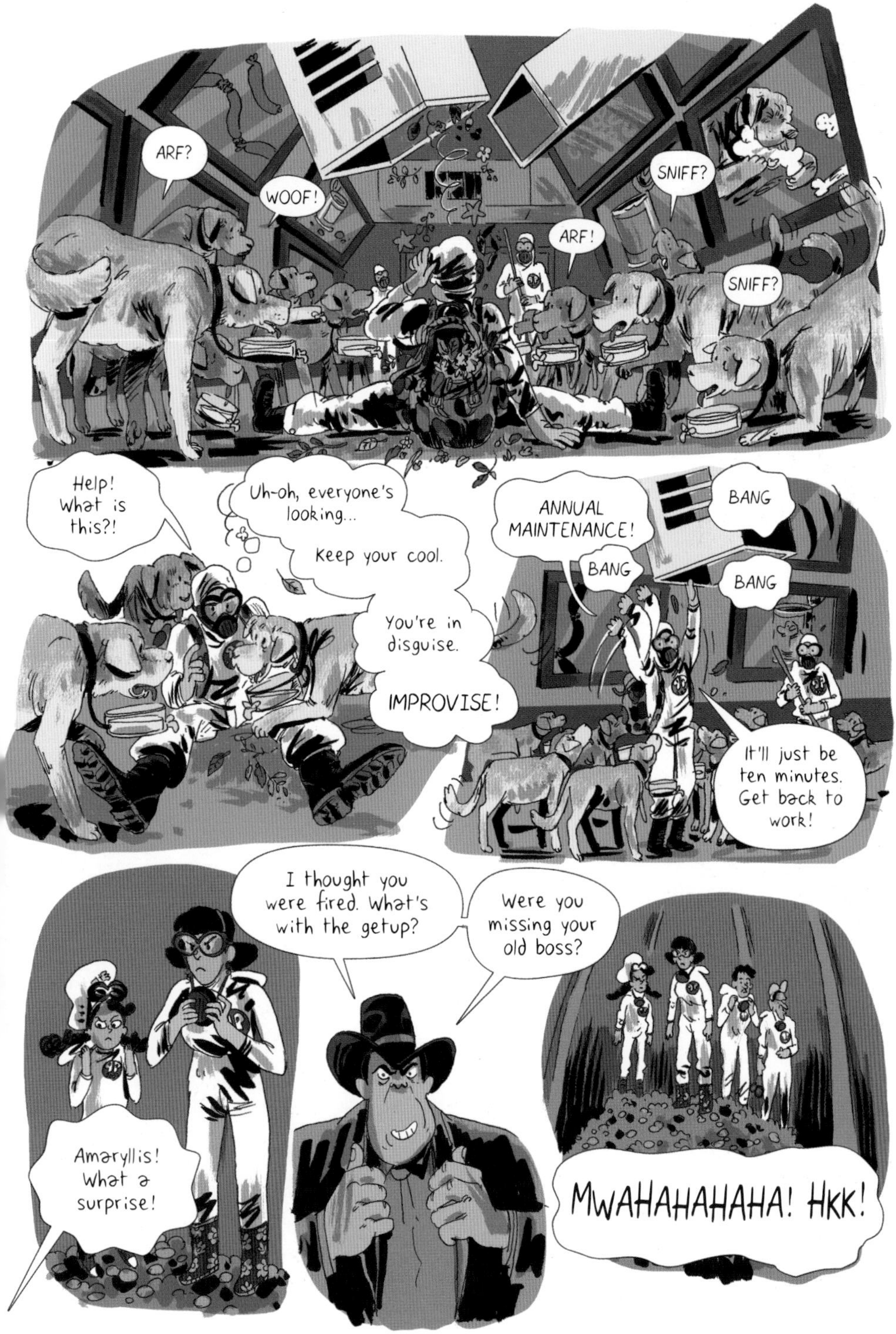
ARF?
WOOF!
ARF!
SNIFF?
SNIFF?
Help! What is this?!
Uh-oh, everyone's looking...
Keep your cool.
You're in disguise.
IMPROVISE!
ANNUAL MAINTENANCE!
BANG
BANG
BANG
It'll just be ten minutes. Get back to work!
Amaryllis! What a surprise!
I thought you were fired. What's with the getup?
Were you missing your old boss?
MWAHAHAHAHA! HKK!

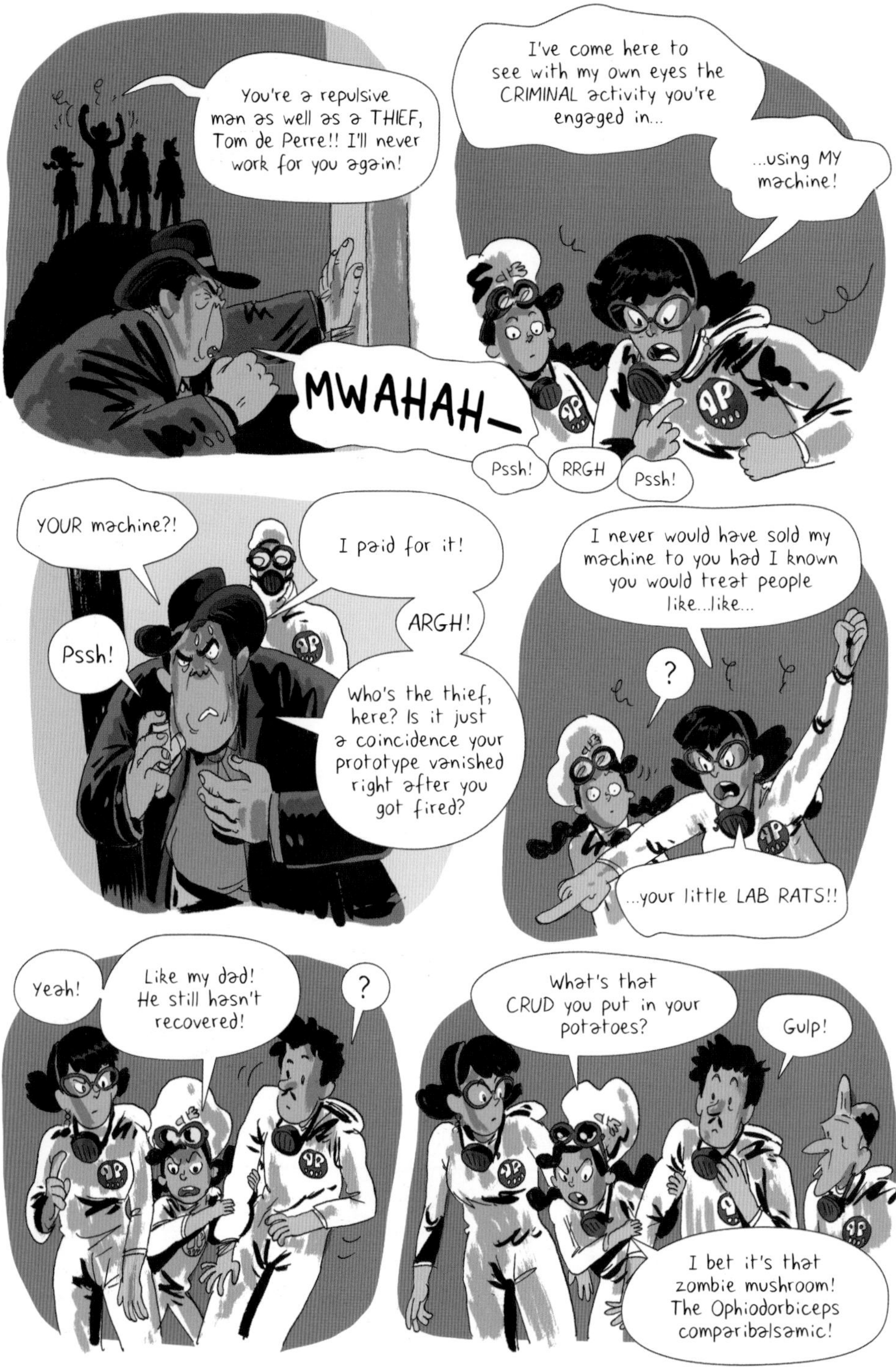
You're a repulsive man as well as a THIEF, Tom de Perre!! I'll never work for you again!
MWAHAH—
I've come here to see with my own eyes the CRIMINAL activity you're engaged in...
...using MY machine!
Pssh!
RRGH
Pssh!
YOUR machine?!
I paid for it!
ARGH!
Pssh!
Who's the thief, here? Is it just a coincidence your prototype vanished right after you got fired?
I never would have sold my machine to you had I known you would treat people like...like...
?
...your little LAB RATS!!
Yeah!
Like my dad! He still hasn't recovered!
?
What's that CRUD you put in your potatoes?
Gulp!
I bet it's that zombie mushroom! The Ophiodorbiceps comparibalsamic!

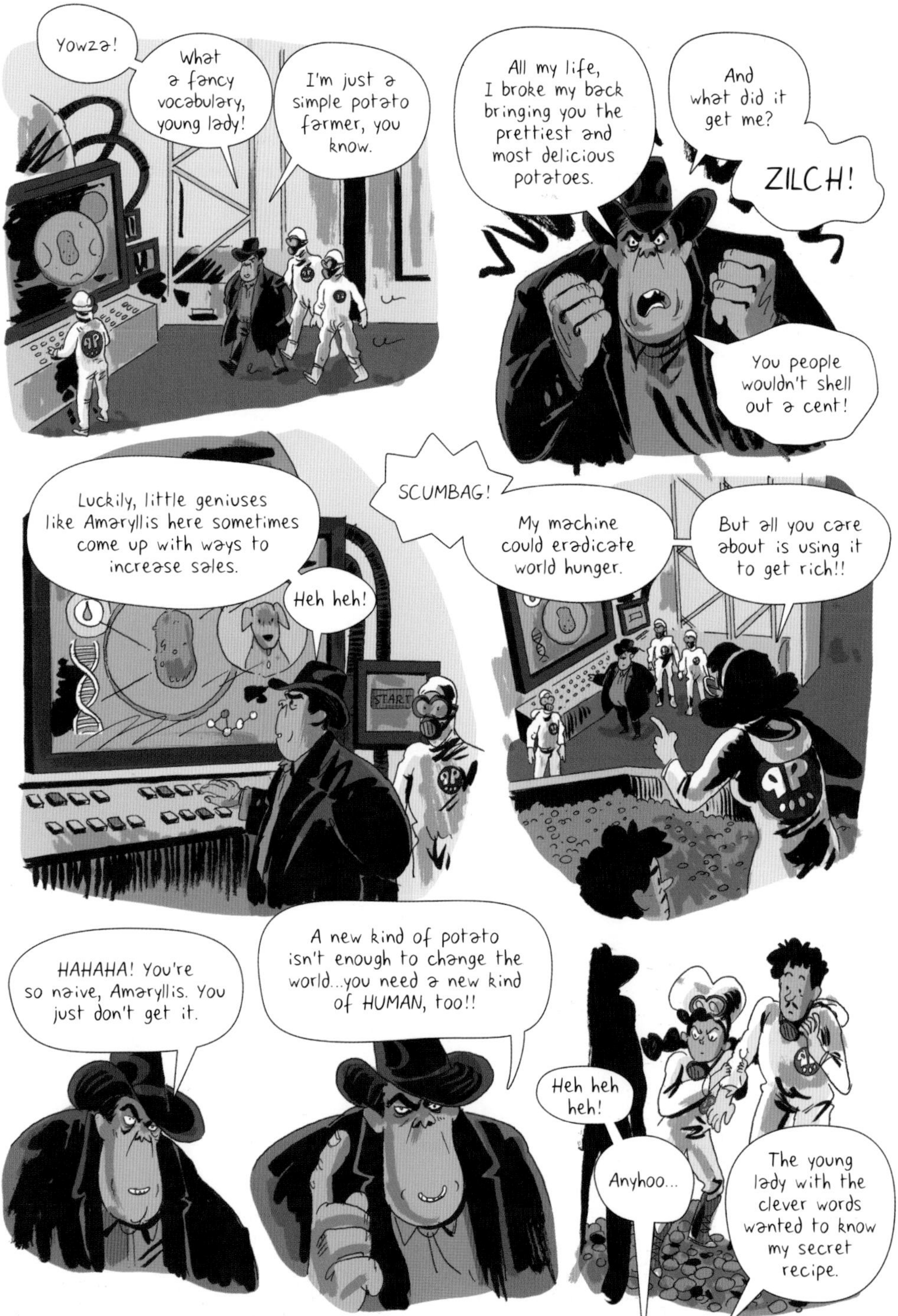

Yowza!
What a fancy vocabulary, young lady!
I'm just a simple potato farmer, you know.
All my life, I broke my back bringing you the prettiest and most delicious potatoes.
And what did it get me?
ZILCH!
You people wouldn't shell out a cent!
Luckily, little geniuses like Amaryllis here sometimes come up with ways to increase sales.
Heh heh!
START
SCUMBAG!
My machine could eradicate world hunger.
But all you care about is using it to get rich!!
HAHAHA! You're so naive, Amaryllis. You just don't get it.
A new kind of potato isn't enough to change the world...you need a new kind of HUMAN, too!!
Heh heh heh!
Anyhoo...
The young lady with the clever words wanted to know my secret recipe.

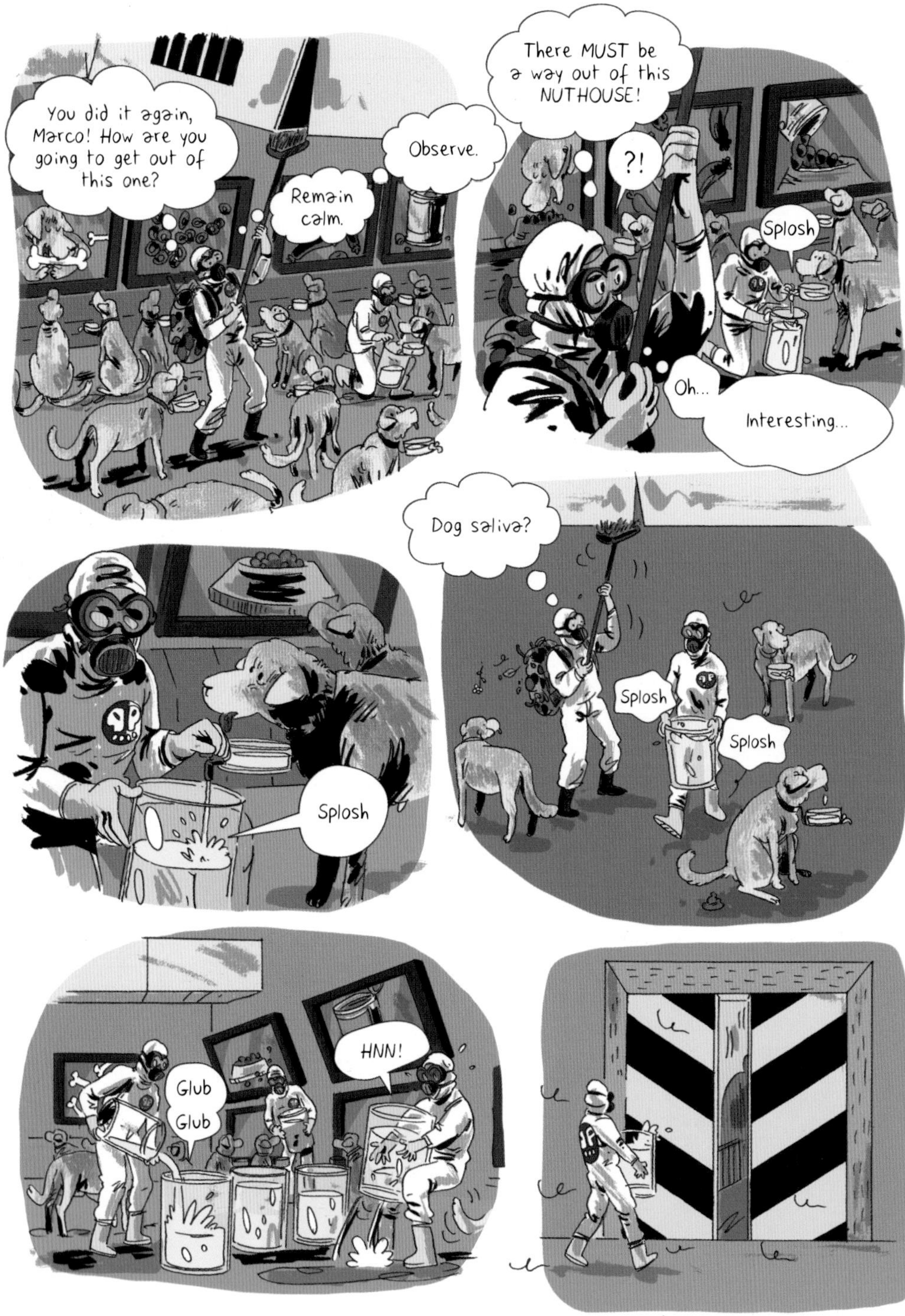

You did it again, Marco! How are you going to get out of this one?
Observe.
Remain calm.
There MUST be a way out of this NUTHOUSE!
?!
Splosh
Oh...
Interesting...
Splosh
Dog saliva?
Splosh
Splosh
Glub
Glub
HNN!

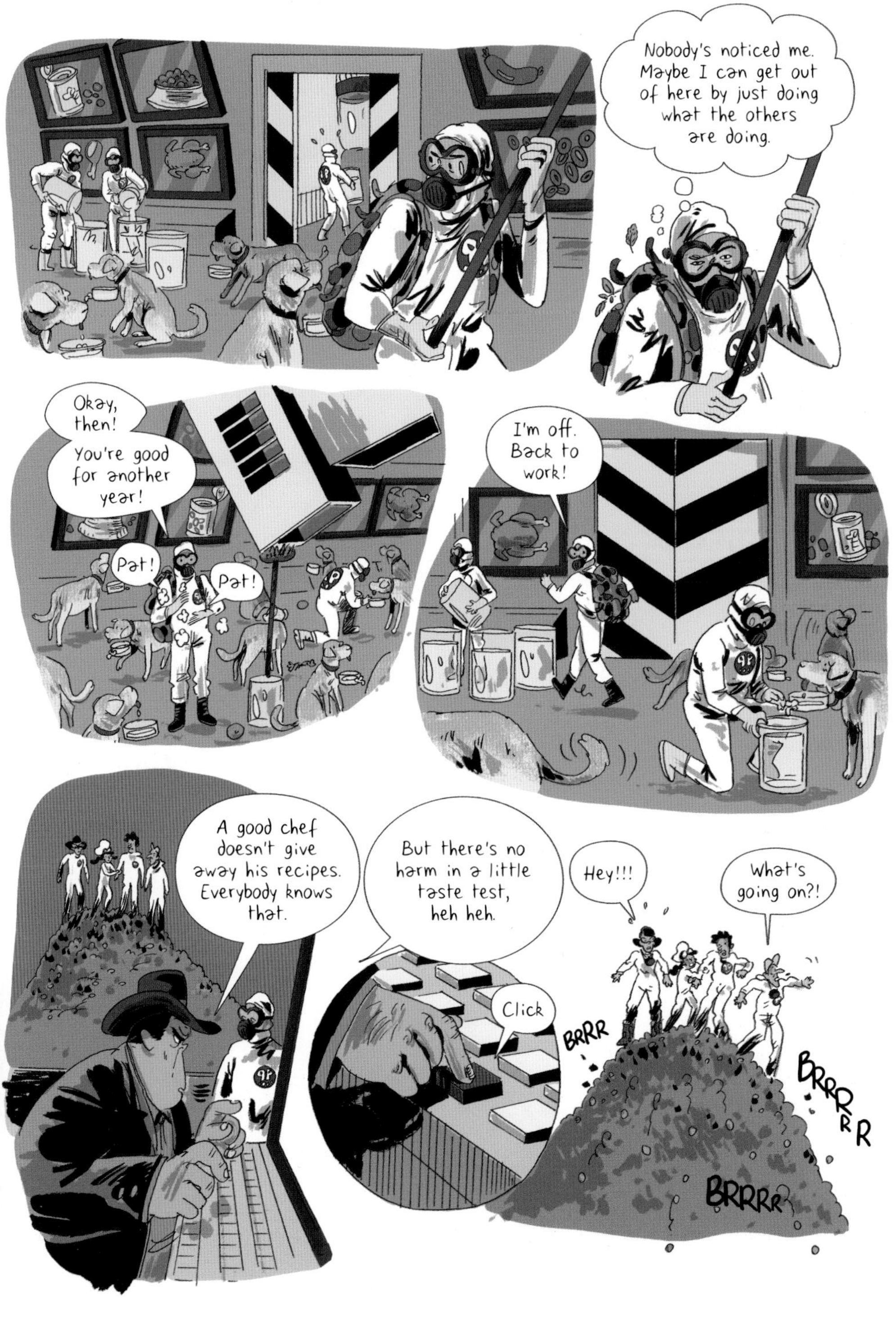
Nobody's noticed me. Maybe I can get out of here by just doing what the others are doing.
Okay, then!
You're good for another year!
Pat!
Pat!
I'm off. Back to work!
A good chef doesn't give away his recipes. Everybody knows that.
But there's no harm in a little taste test, heh heh.
Click
Hey!!!
What's going on?!
BRRR
BRRRRR
BRRRRR

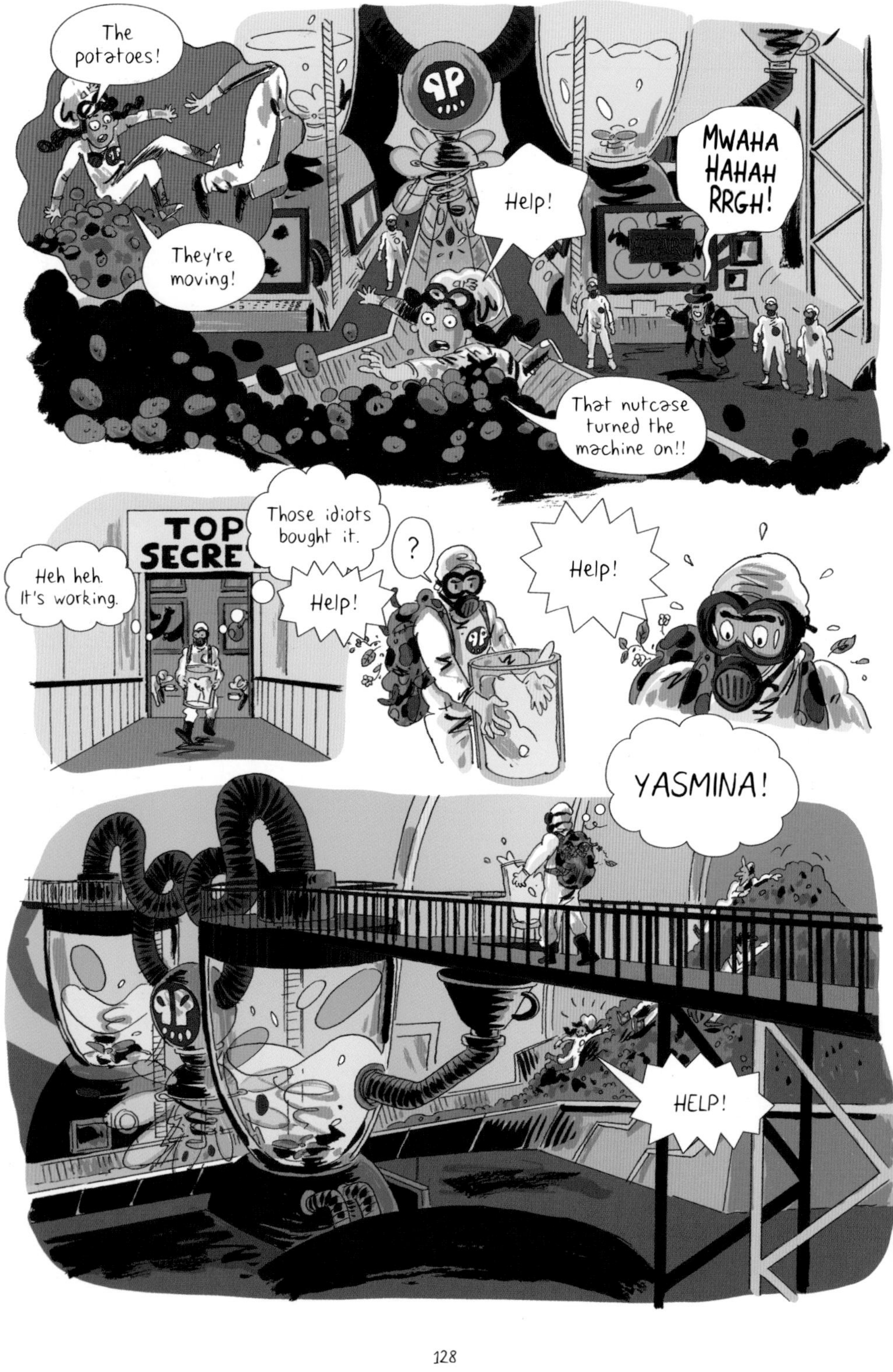
The potatoes!
They're moving!
Help!
MWAHA HAHAH RRGH!
That nutcase turned the machine on!!
Heh heh. It's working.
Those idiots bought it.
Help!
?
Help!
YASMINA!
HELP!

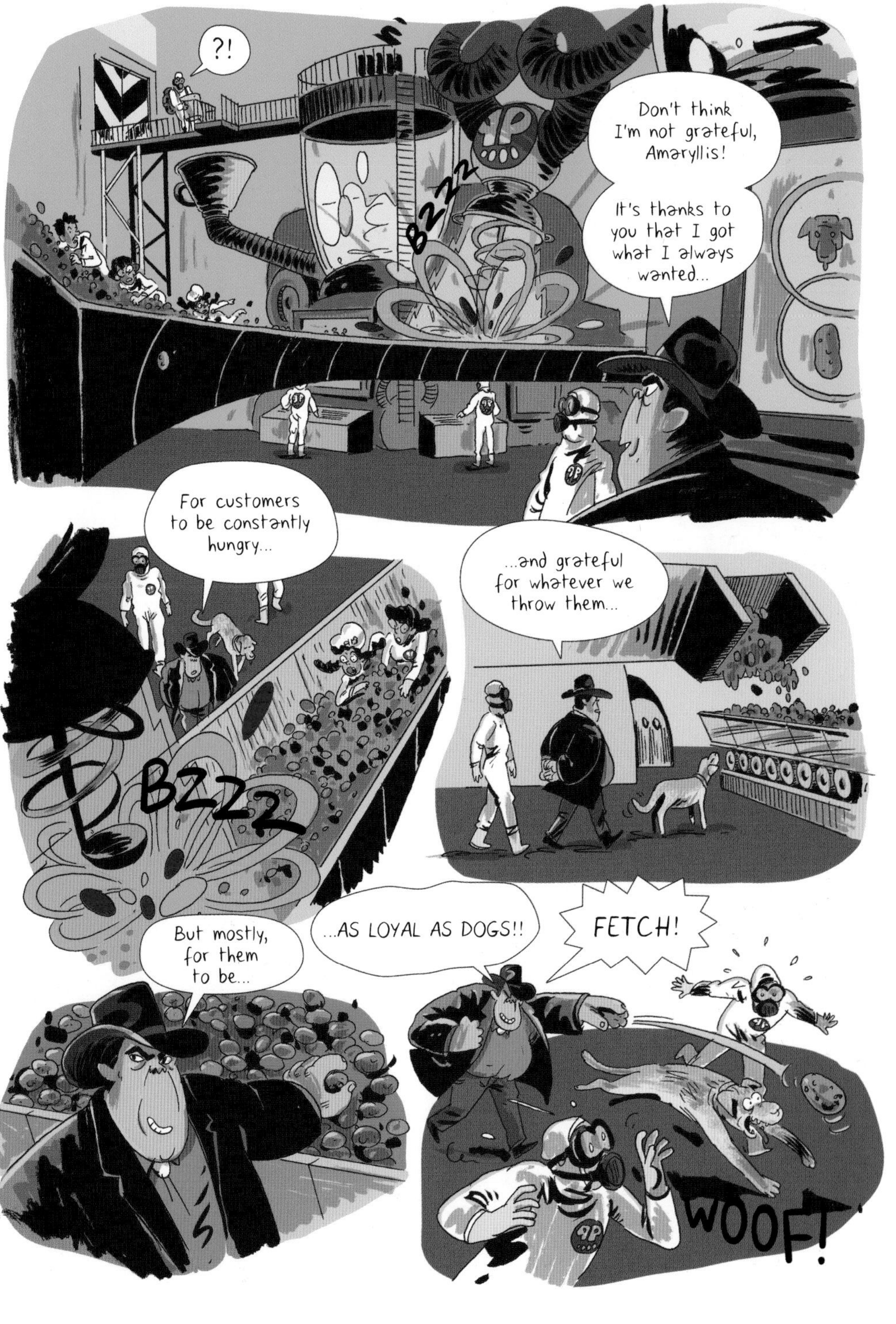
?!
BZZZ
Don't think I'm not grateful, Amaryllis!
It's thanks to you that I got what I always wanted...
For customers to be constantly hungry...
BZZZ
...and grateful for whatever we throw them...
But mostly, for them to be...
...AS LOYAL AS DOGS!!
FETCH!
WOOF!

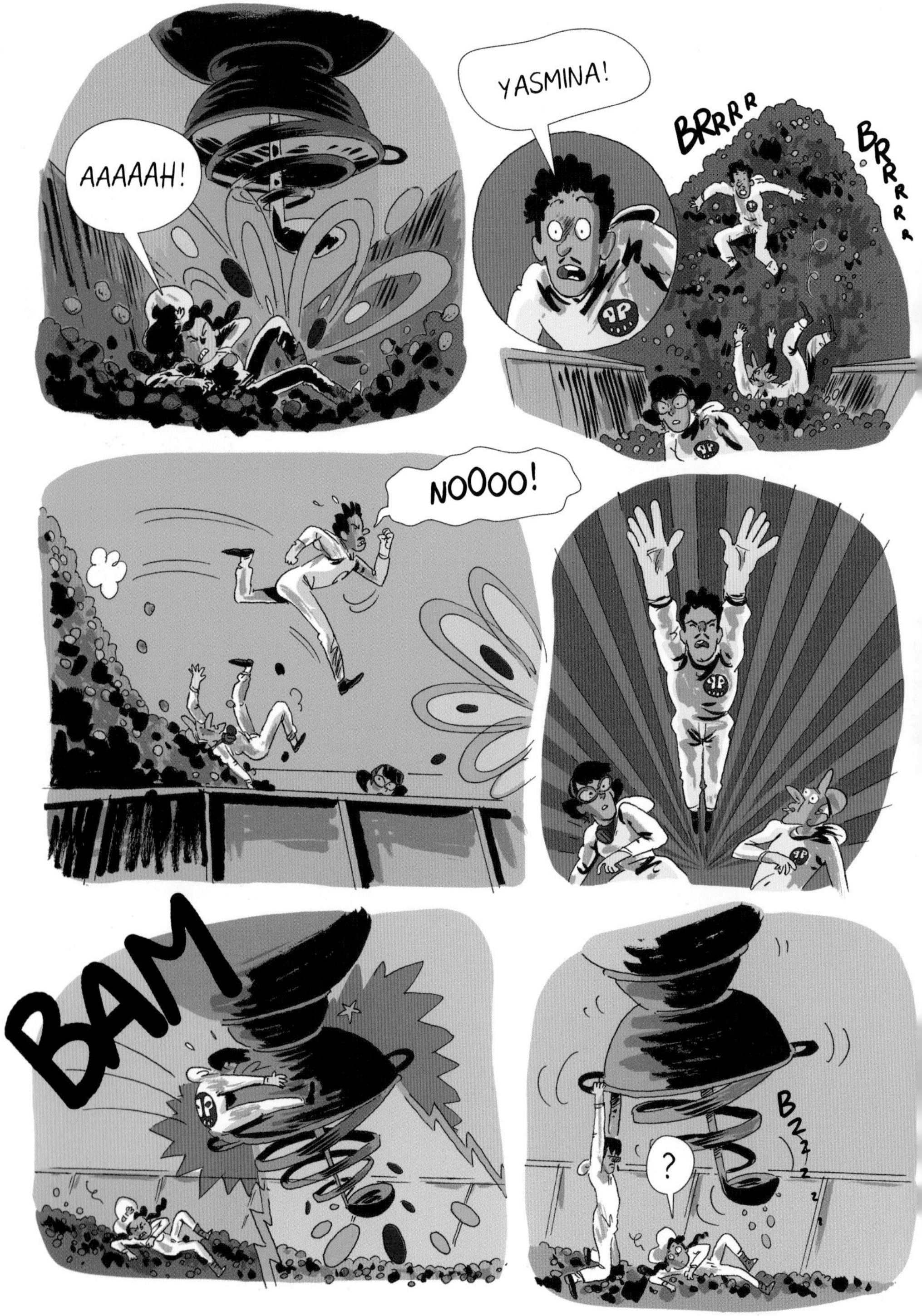
AAAAAH!
YASMINA!
BRRRR
BRRRRRR
NOOOO!
BAM
BZZZ
?

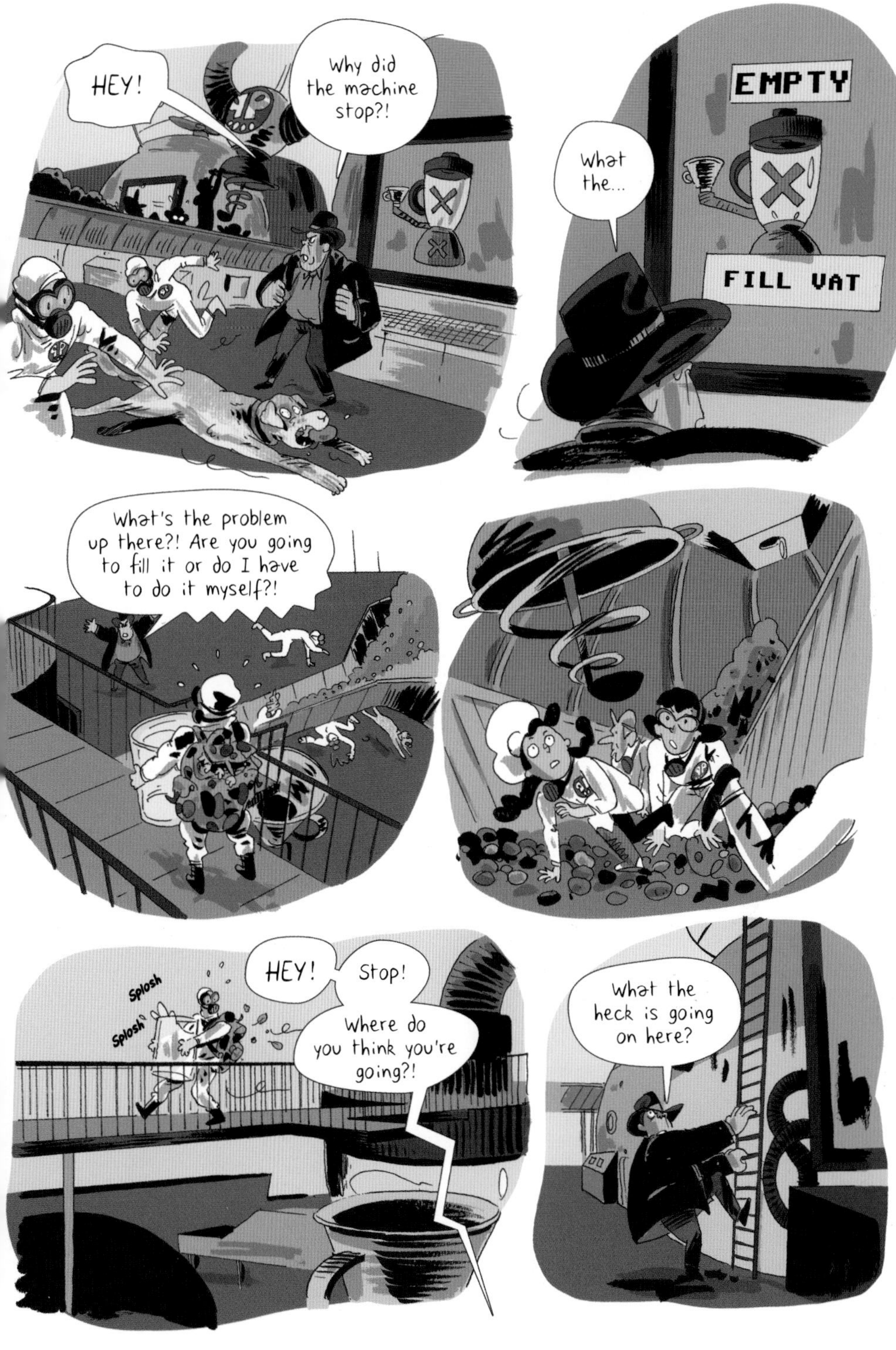
HEY!
Why did the machine stop?!
EMPTY
FILL VAT
What the...
What's the problem up there?! Are you going to fill it or do I have to do it myself?!
Splosh
Splosh
HEY!
Stop!
Where do you think you're going?!
What the heck is going on here?

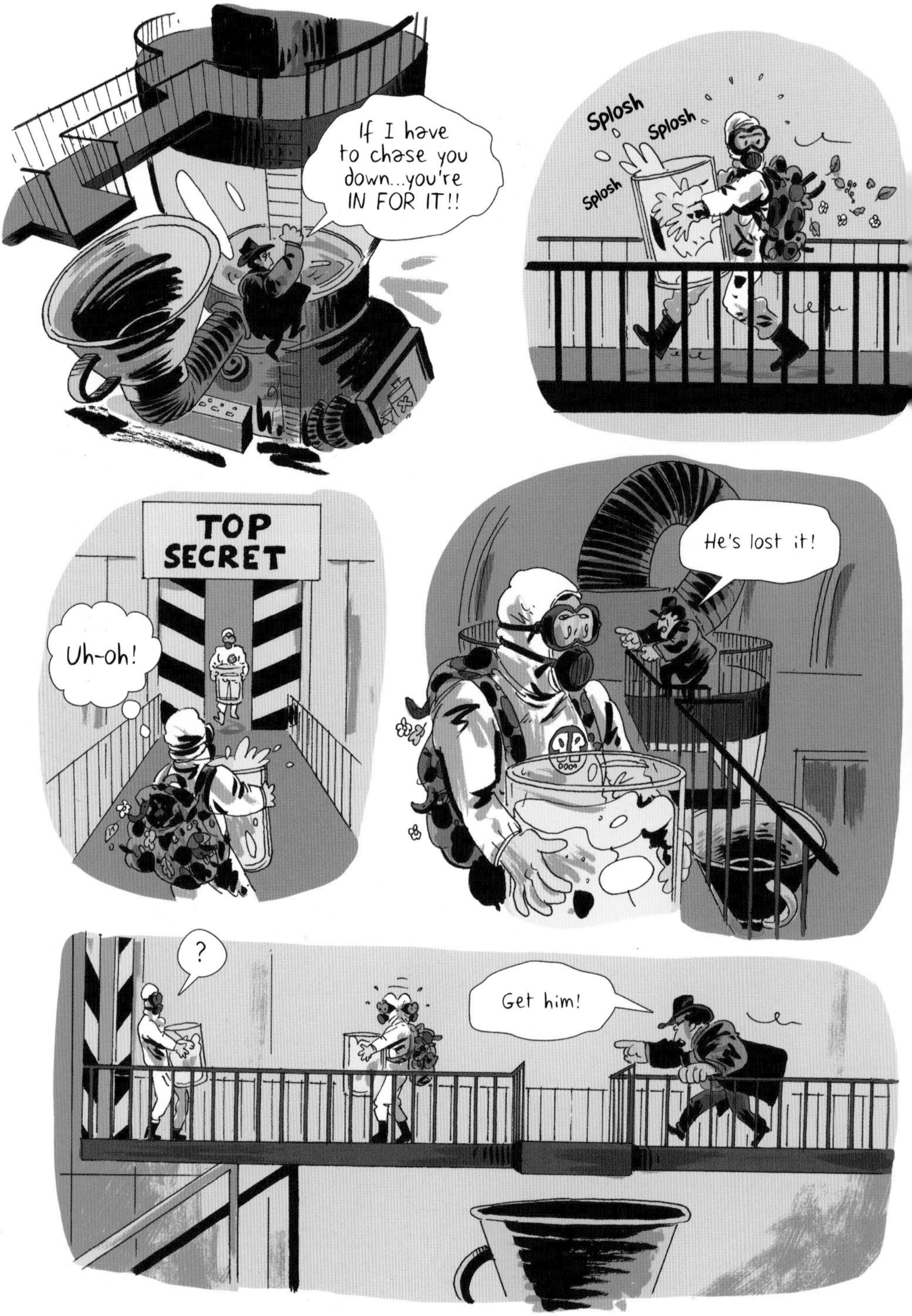
If I have to chase you down...you're IN FOR IT!!
Splosh
Splosh
Splosh
TOP SECRET
Uh-oh!
He's lost it!
?
Get him!

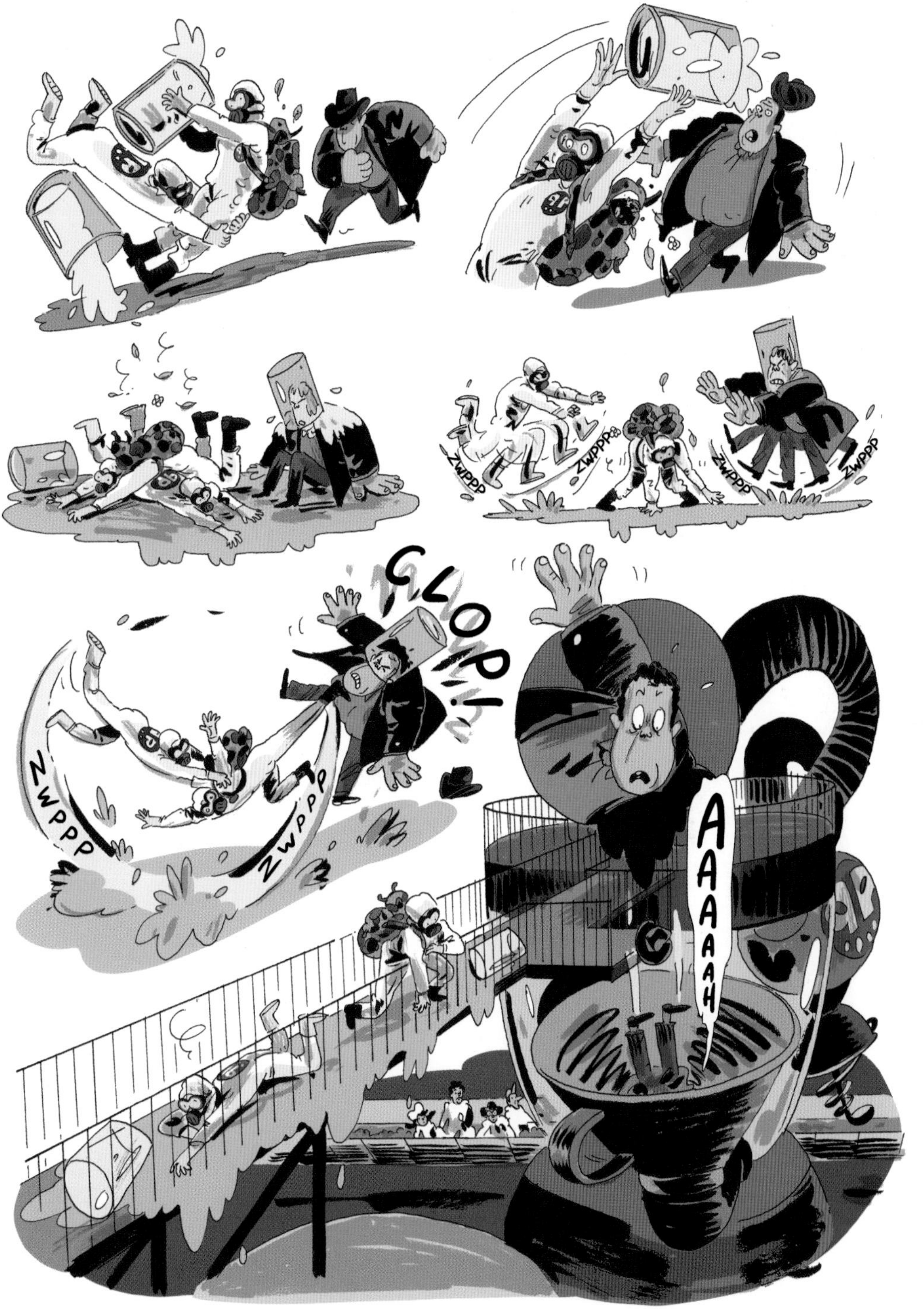
ZWPPP
ZWPPP
ZWPPP
ZWPPP
CLOP!!
ZWPPP
ZWPPP
AAAAAAH

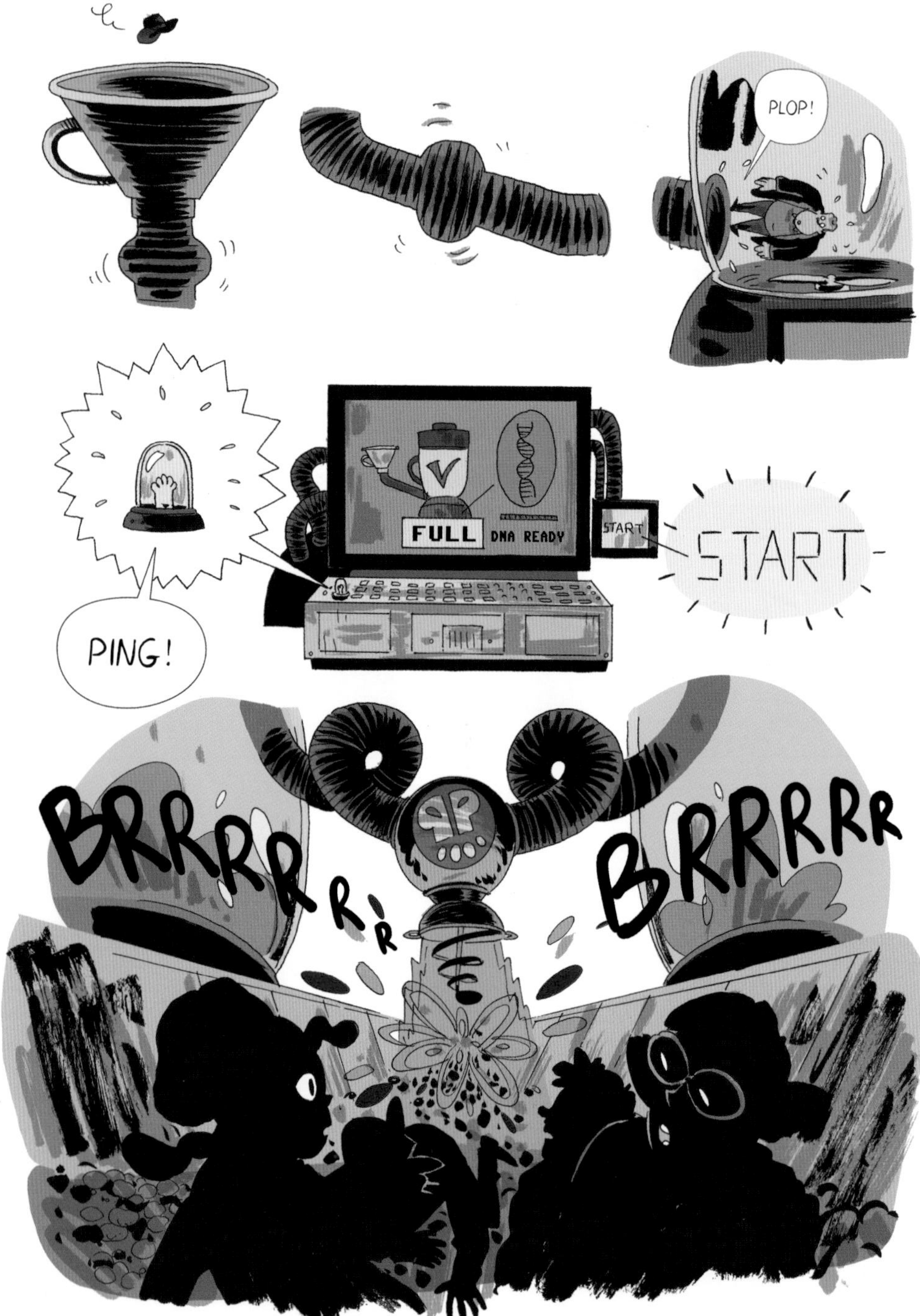
PLOP!
PING!
FULL
DNA READY
START
START
BRRRRRR
BRRRRRR

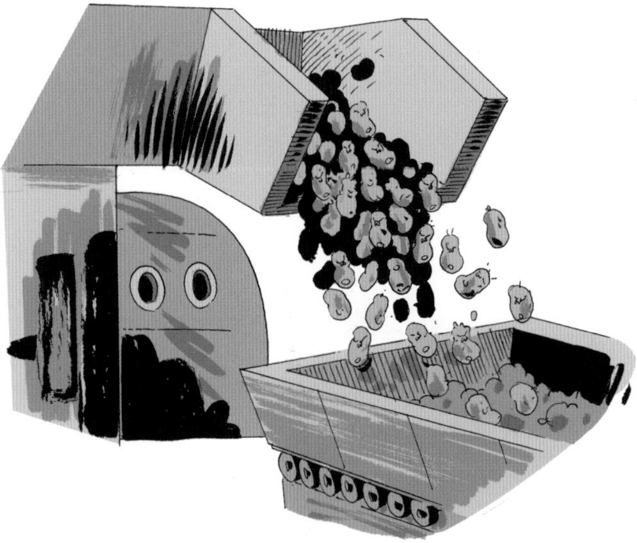
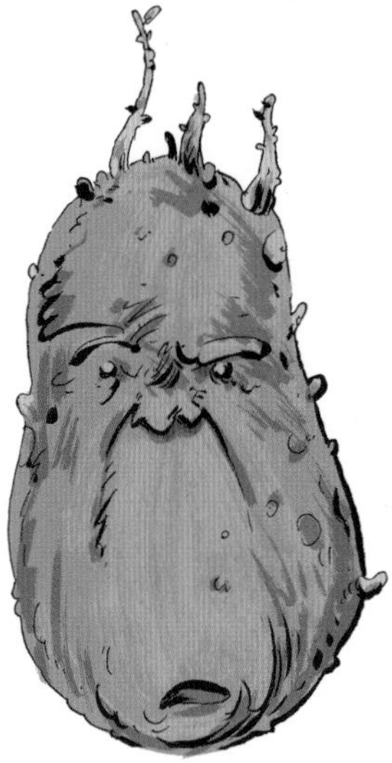

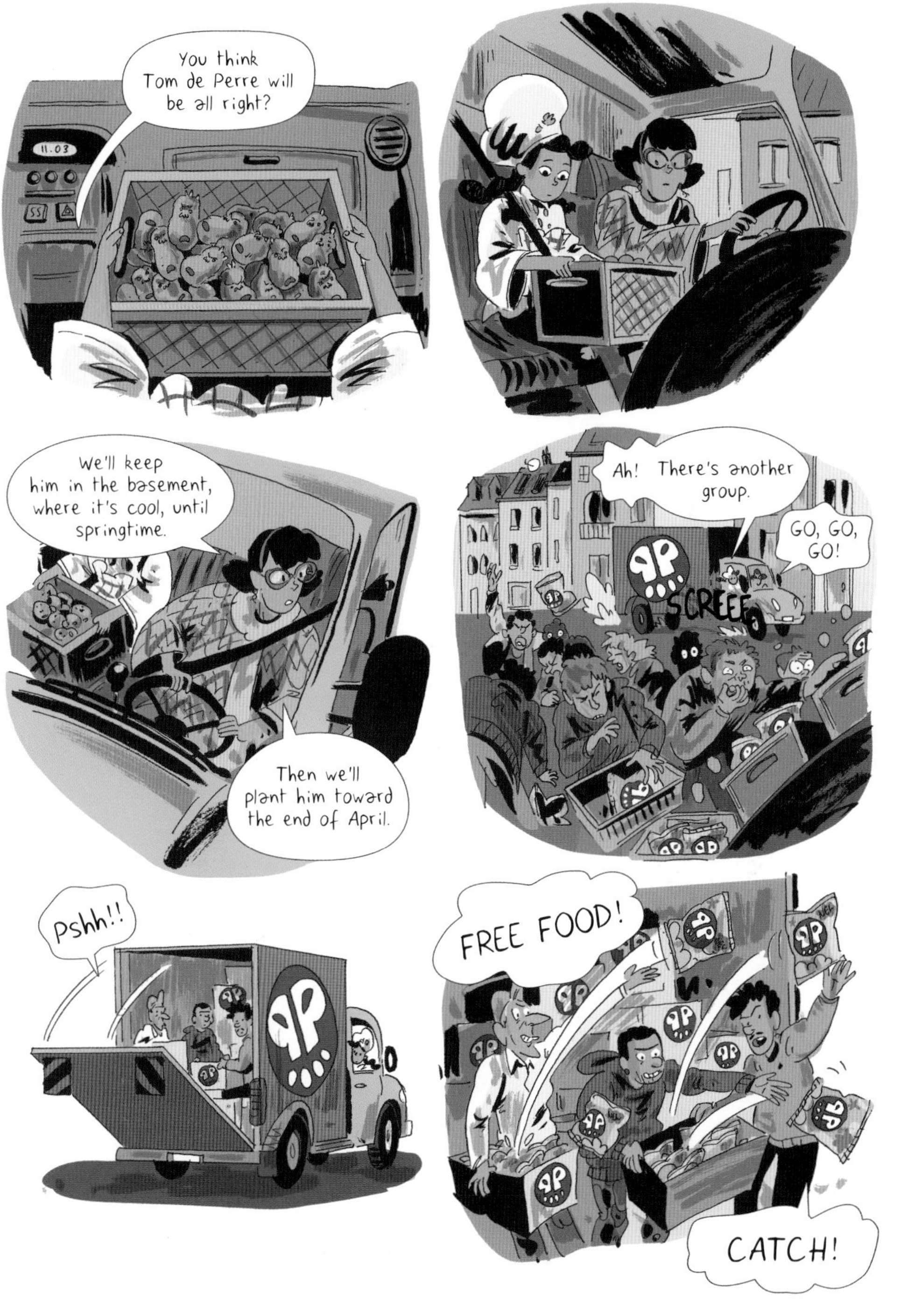
11.03
You think Tom de Perre will be all right?
We'll keep him in the basement, where it's cool, until springtime.
Then we'll plant him toward the end of April.
Ah! There's another group.
GO, GO, GO!
SCREEE
Pshh!!
FREE FOOD!
CATCH!

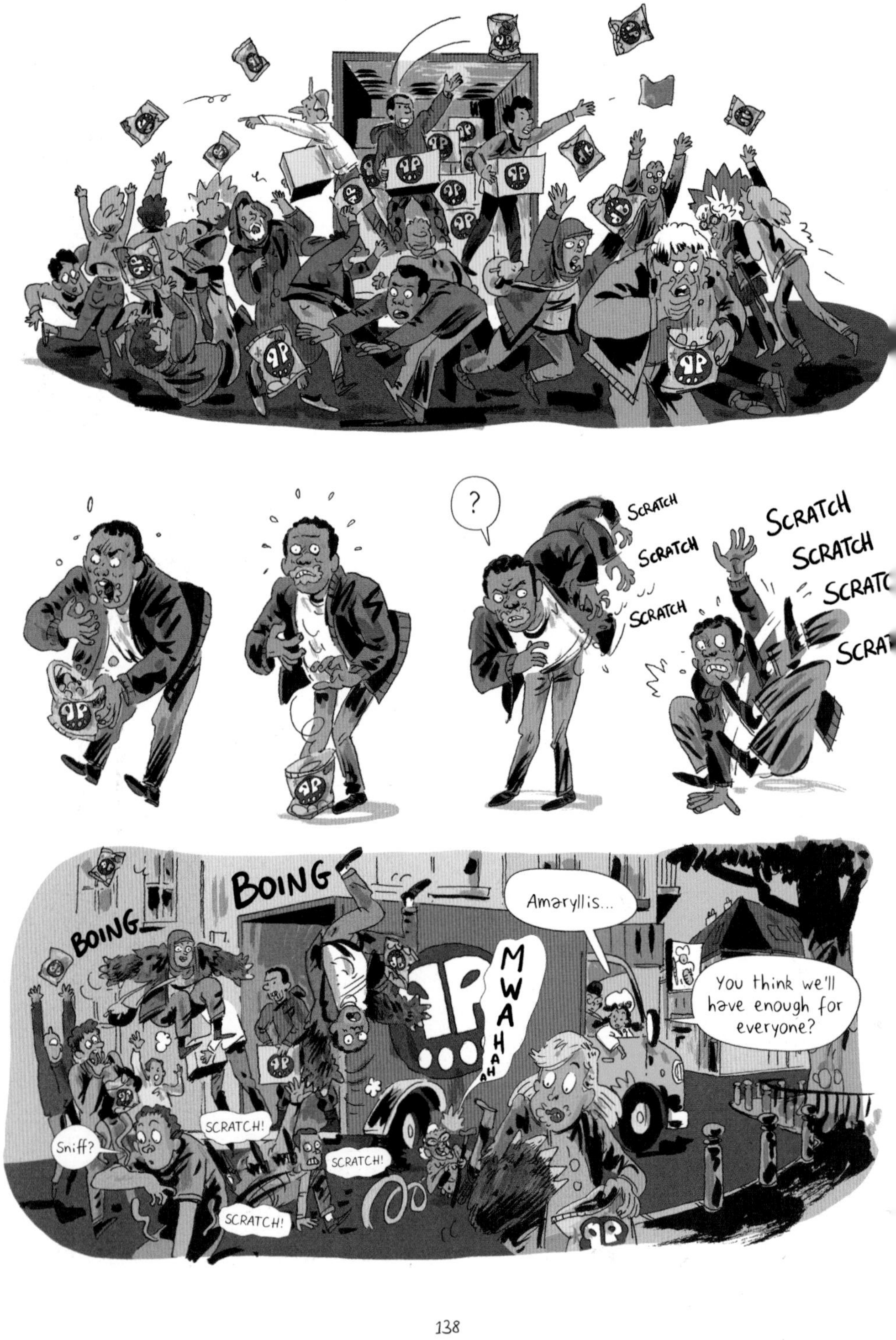
?
SCRATCH
SCRATCH
SCRATCH
SCRATCH
SCRATCH
SCRATC
SCRAT
BOING
BOING
Amaryllis...
MWAHAHAH
You think we'll have enough for everyone?
Sniff?
SCRATCH!
SCRATCH!
SCRATCH!

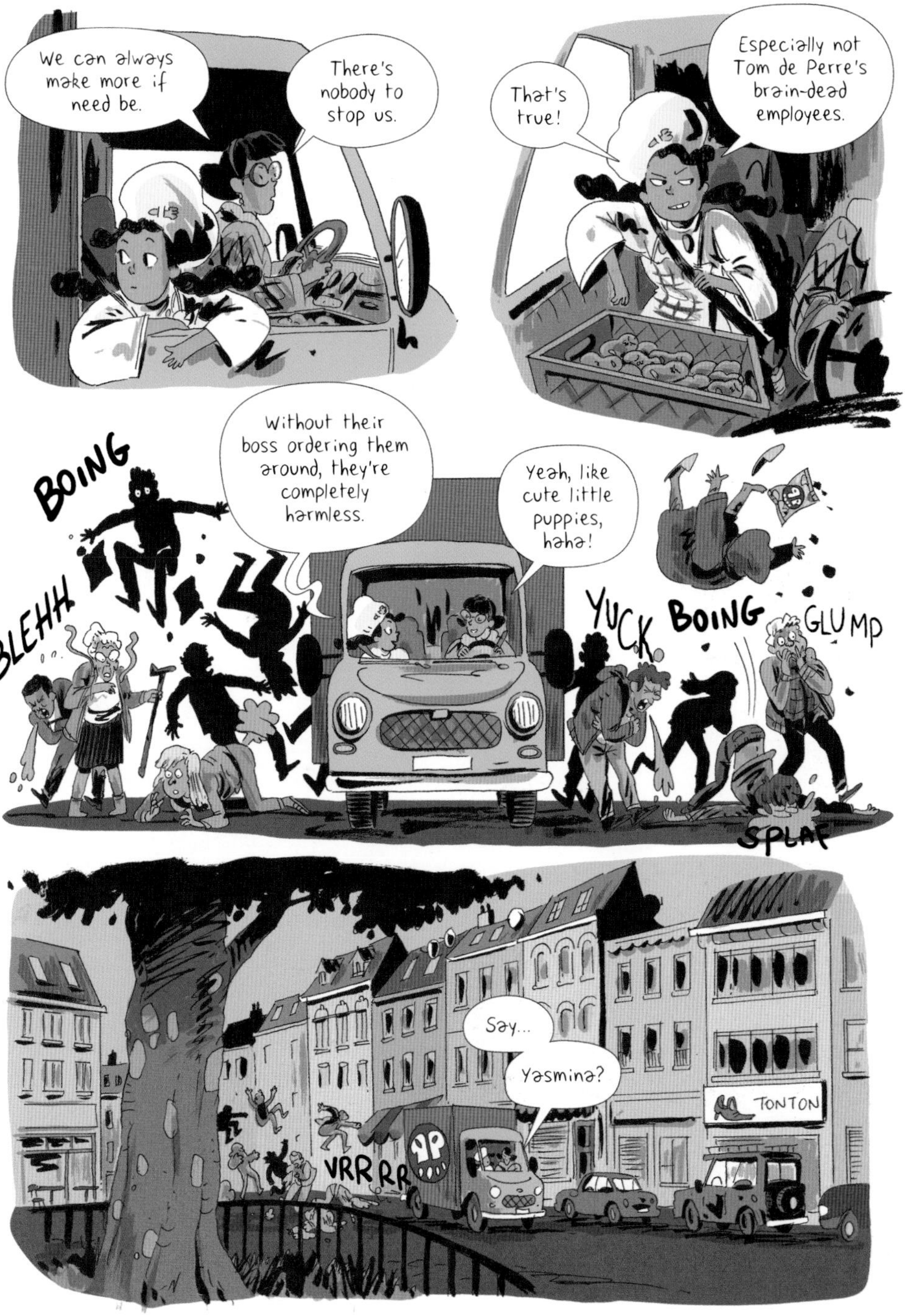
We can always make more if need be.
There's nobody to stop us.
That's true!
Especially not Tom de Perre's brain-dead employees.
Without their boss ordering them around, they're completely harmless.
Yeah, like cute little puppies, haha!
BOING
BLEHH
YUCK
BOING
GLUMP
SPLAF
Say...
Yasmina?
VRRRR
TONTON

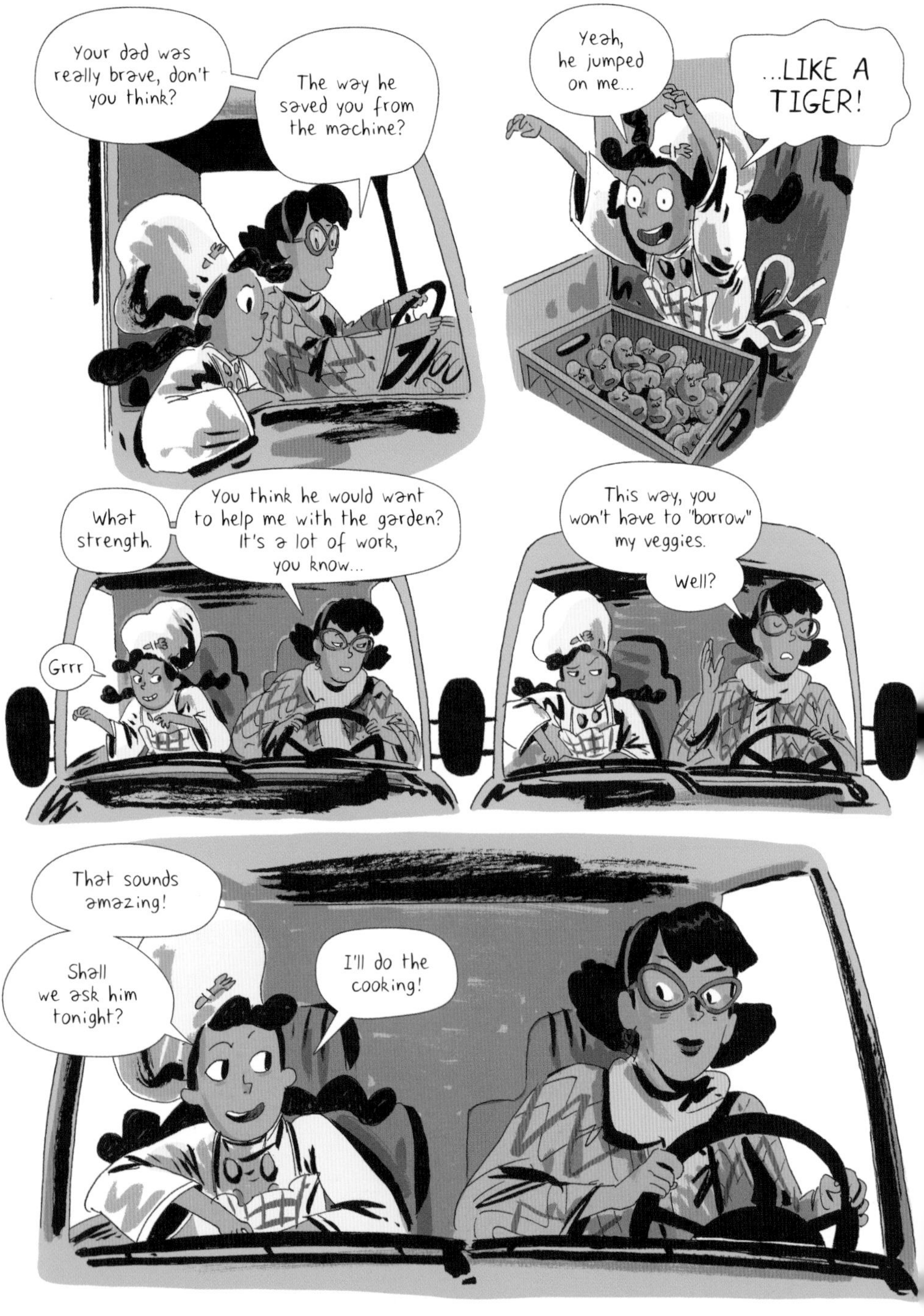
Your dad was really brave, don't you think?
The way he saved you from the machine?
Yeah, he jumped on me...
...LIKE A TIGER!
What strength.
You think he would want to help me with the garden? It's a lot of work, you know...
Grrr
This way, you won't have to "borrow" my veggies.
Well?
That sounds amazing!
Shall we ask him tonight?
I'll do the cooking!

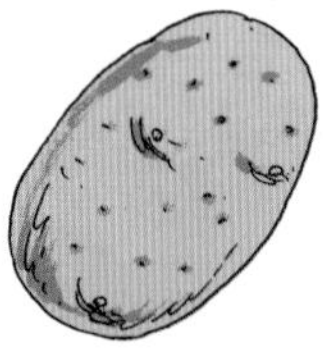

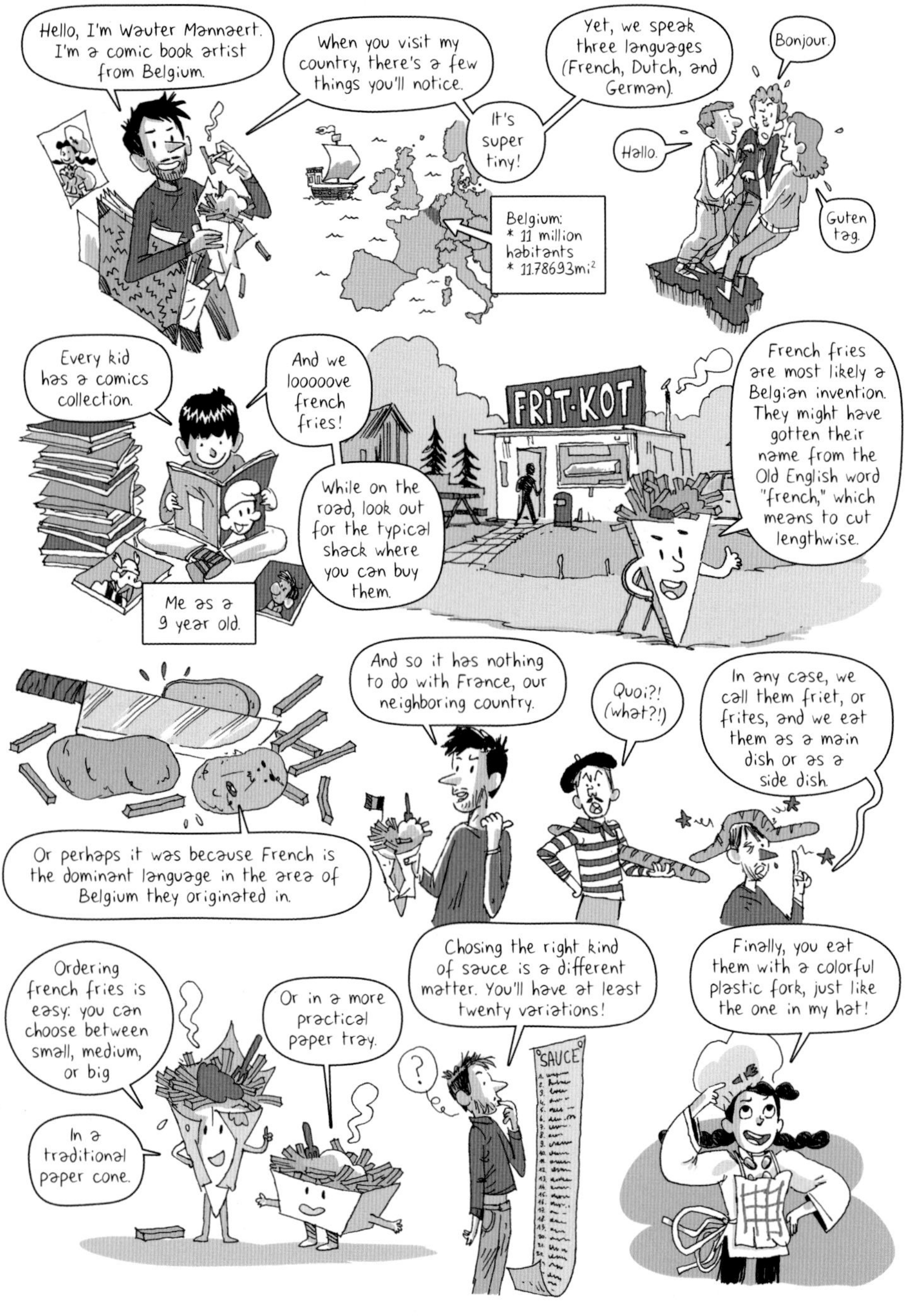
Hello, I'm Wauter Mannaert. I'm a comic book artist from Belgium.
When you visit my country, there's a few things you'll notice.
It's super tiny!
Belgium:
* 11 million habitants
* 11.78693mi²
Yet, we speak three languages (French, Dutch, and German).
Bonjour.
Hallo.
Guten tag.
Every kid has a comics collection.
Me as a 9 year old.
And we looooove french fries!
While on the road, look out for the typical shack where you can buy them.
FRiT-KOT
French fries are most likely a Belgian invention. They might have gotten their name from the Old English word "french," which means to cut lengthwise.
Or perhaps it was because French is the dominant language in the area of Belgium they originated in.
And so it has nothing to do with France, our neighboring country.
Quoi?! (what?!)
In any case, we call them friet, or frites, and we eat them as a main dish or as a side dish.
Ordering french fries is easy: you can choose between small, medium, or big
In a traditional paper cone.
Or in a more practical paper tray.
Chosing the right kind of sauce is a different matter. You'll have at least twenty variations!
?
SAUCE
Finally, you eat them with a colorful plastic fork, just like the one in my hat!

The idea for *Chef Yasmina and the Potato Panic* was born in 2009 while I was working on an art project with children in Brussels, the city in which I live. The goal for the children was to portray their daily lives with photos and videos. My job was to help them as needed.

On one of our walks we wandered over a large piece of fallow land—a real wilderness in the middle of the city. We stumbled upon a small iron gate hidden in the bushes. What we found behind it was a real surprise: a beautiful vegetable garden! With a little imagination, the city disappeared altogether. We might as well have ended up somewhere in the countryside.

The children and I stole some raspberries from the garden and stood in awe before an artfully constructed geodesic dome. Then we were off again, looking for the next treasure.

It was by no means the only vegetable garden I discovered that summer. In fact, it looked like everyone in town was gardening. And not only in the derelict parts of the city: balconies and rooftops were also transformed into vegetable gardens. And if those spaces were not available, people found their own solutions. Plastic bottles hanging in a window or wooden boxes on a sidewalk can also be used to grow beans or tomatoes.

Around the same time, Belgium had what the press called “the potato war of Wetteren.” A group of activists destroyed a field trial of genetically modified potatoes at Ghent University. The activists, who opposed the introduction of genetically modified crops into our agricultural system, stormed the field and destroyed the work of the scientists.

It became clear to me that how and what we eat is an important topic in my community. Two basic questions were at the center of it: Should we trust science to solve the problems that confront the global food supply? Or should we go back to basics and rely on the immense diversity that nature offers?

I don’t have the answers, but the questions kept me busy. And I started to dream along with those city gardeners who not only asked questions, but decided to create their own solutions. I planted some herbs on my balcony, a cherry tree in a pot on the terrace, and a few tomato plants in the living room. After a long wait and a lot of watering I was able to pick my own handful of cherries and three tomatoes. Yum!

But it was not enough. In my imagination it was all much bigger and more exciting. Slowly, a story about vegetable gardens, evil potato farmers, and Yasmina—the best eleven-year-old cook in town—started to take shape.

Now, ten years later, you can finally read the result. And I sure hope it tastes good!

—Wauter Mannaert
February, 2019

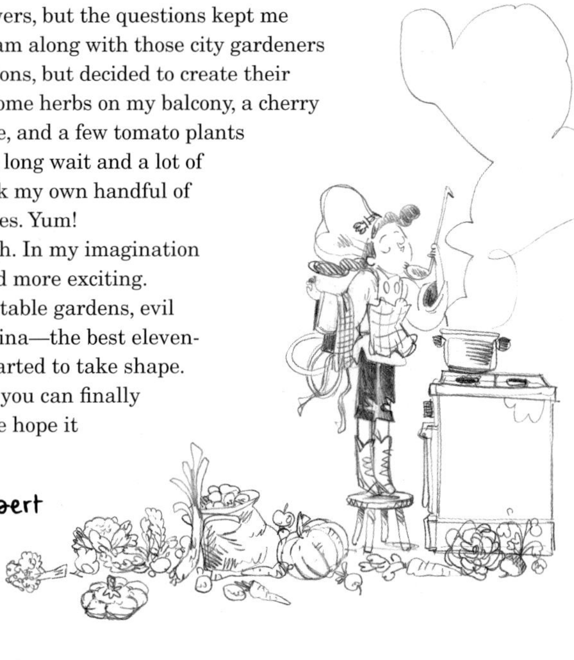

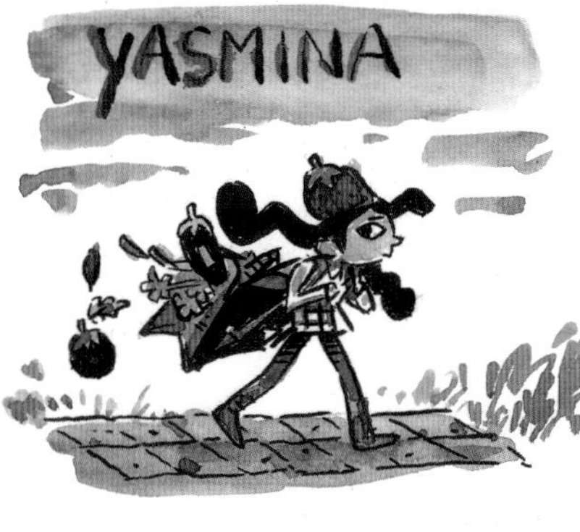
YASMINA

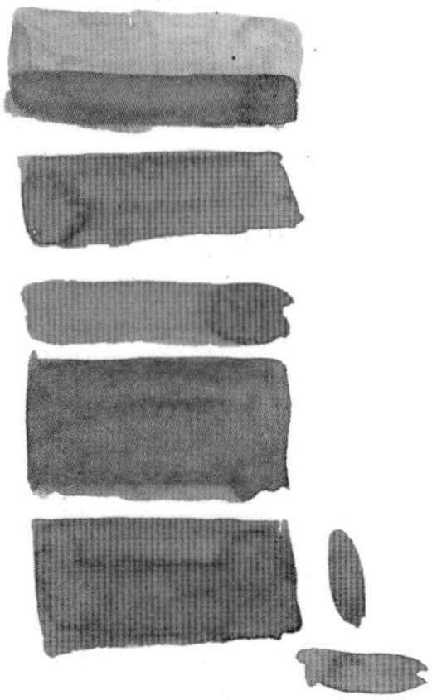

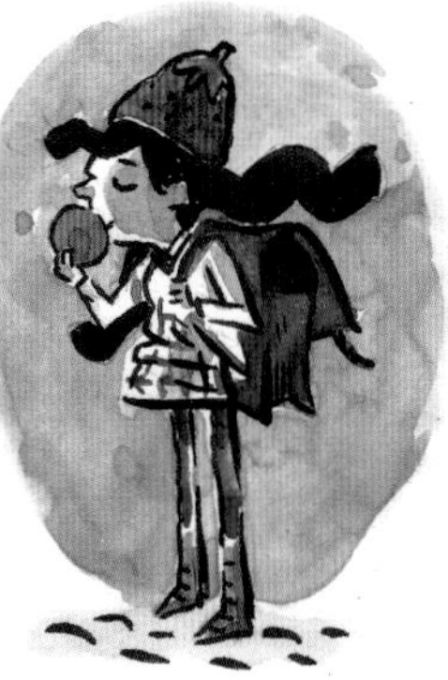

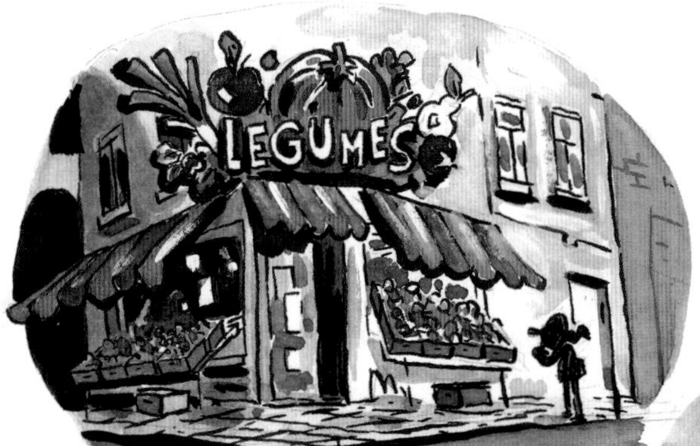
LEGUMES

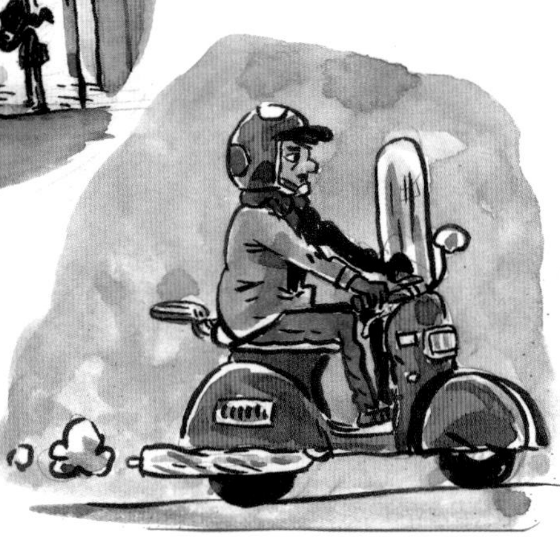

Here are some early concept sketches of Yasmina and her father in watercolor. I first imagined Yasmina much younger and with a strawberry hat. I also had the crazy idea to do the whole book in red and blue. Maybe not the best choice for a book about food and plants!

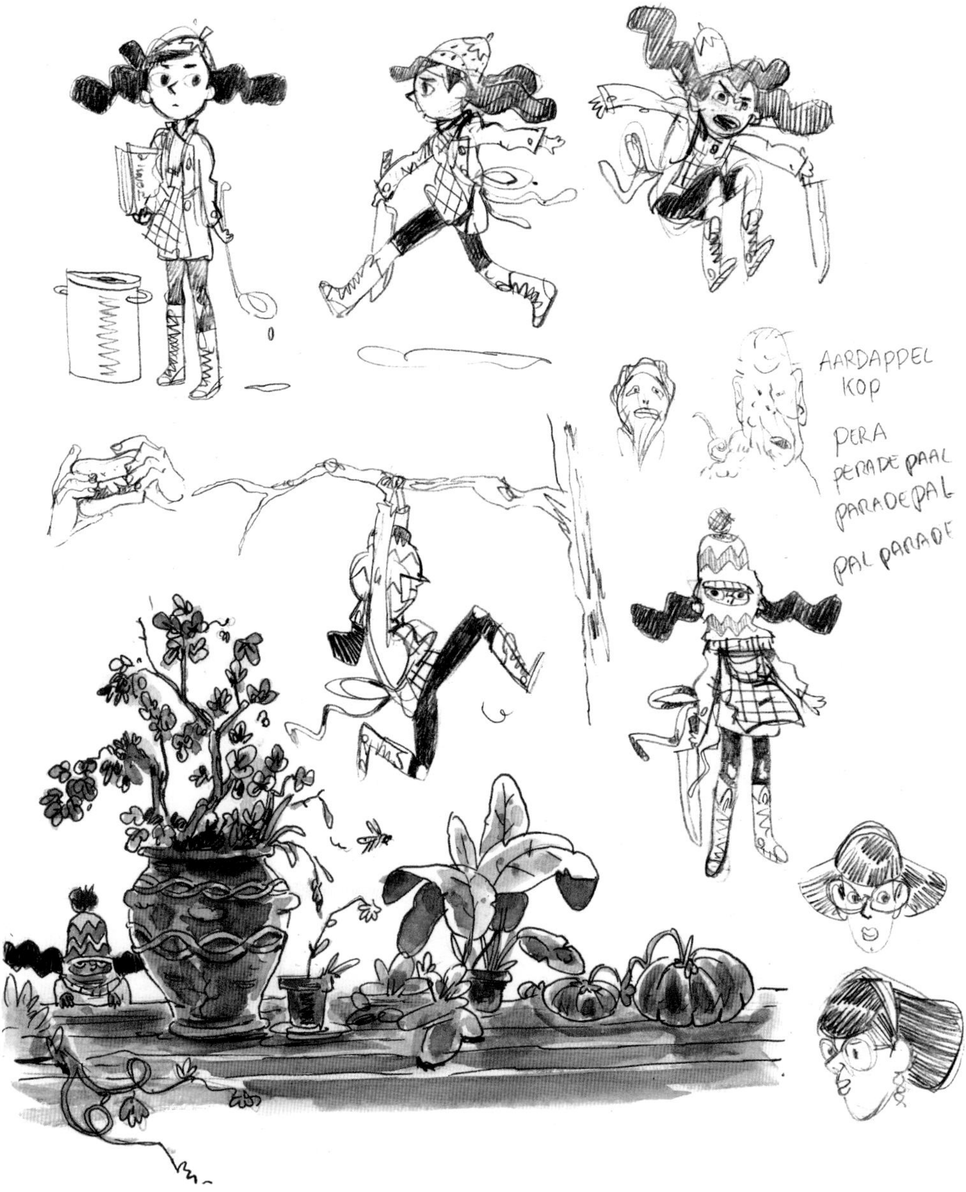
AARDAPPEL
KOP
PERA
PERA DE PAAL
PARADEPAL
PAL PARADE

One of the first scenes I imagined was the one where Yasmina steals vegetables from her mysterious neighbor, Amaryllis. The kitchen knife and the retro ski cap give her something of a ninja look. Also visible: a first attempt to find a name for the bad guy in my story. Pal Parade is an anagram for aardappel (potato in Dutch). In the end I went for Tom de Perre, a variation on pomme de terre (the French word for *potato*).

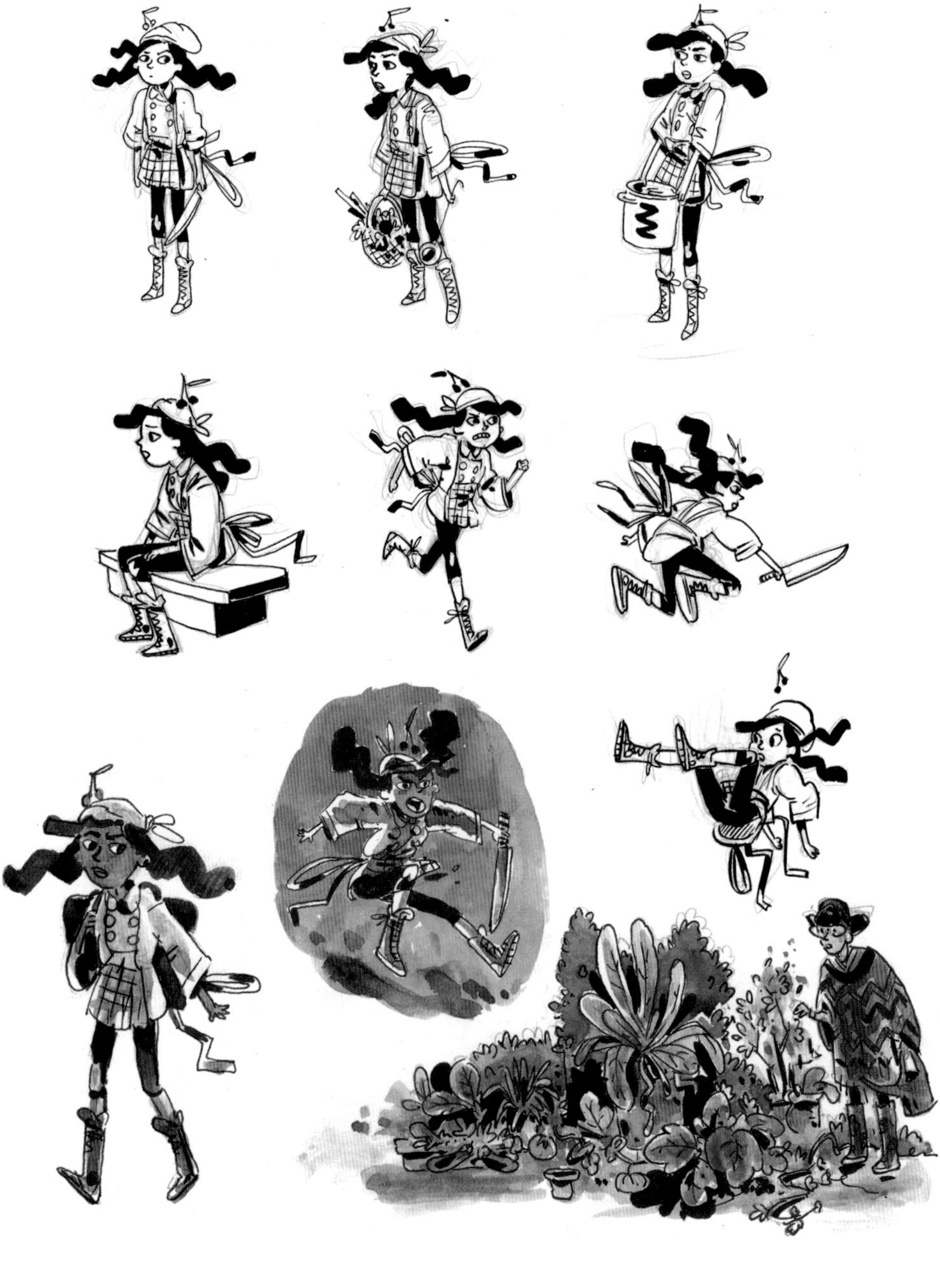

I saw Yasmina as a busy bee—constantly running and cooking.

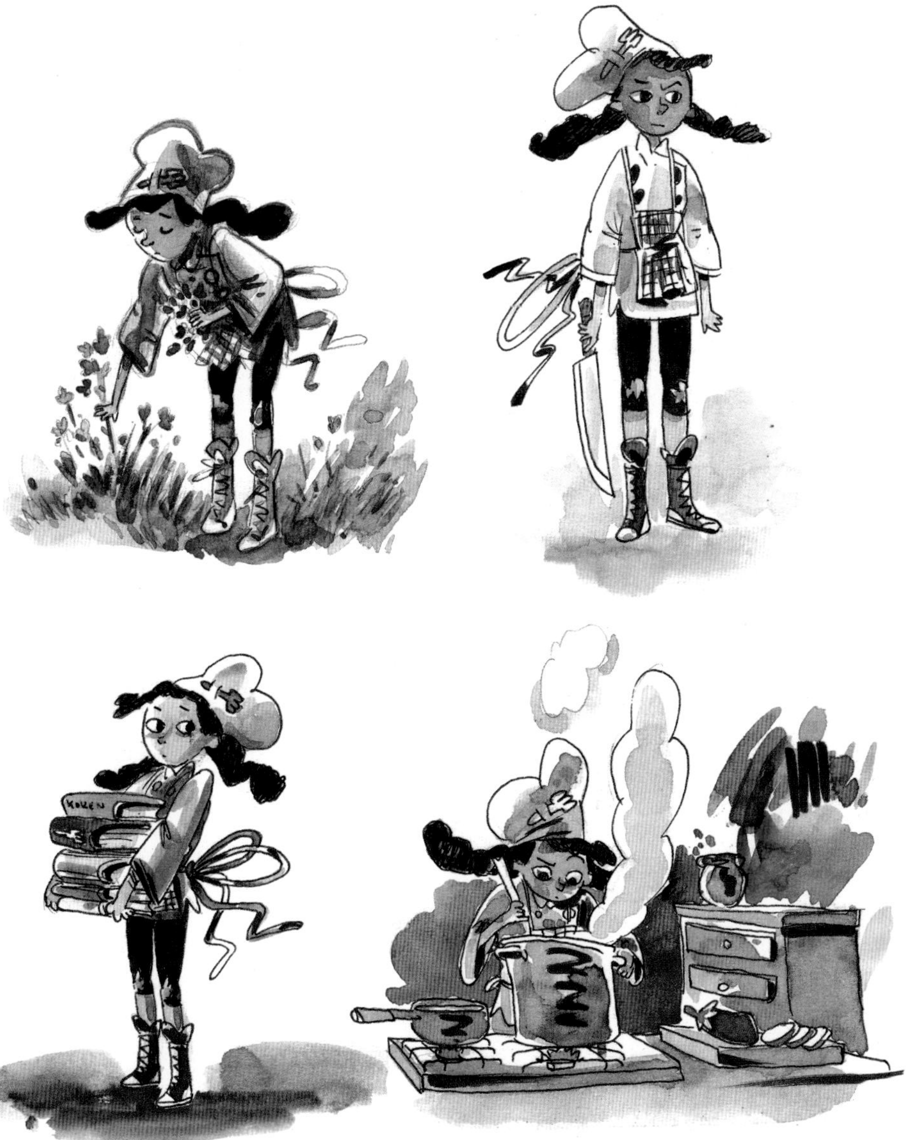
KOKEN

Here Yasmina's appearance gets close to the final version, with her white chef's hat and its little fork. In Belgium, french fries come with a colorful little plastic fork. I thought it was funny to stick one in her hat, like her own personal insignia.

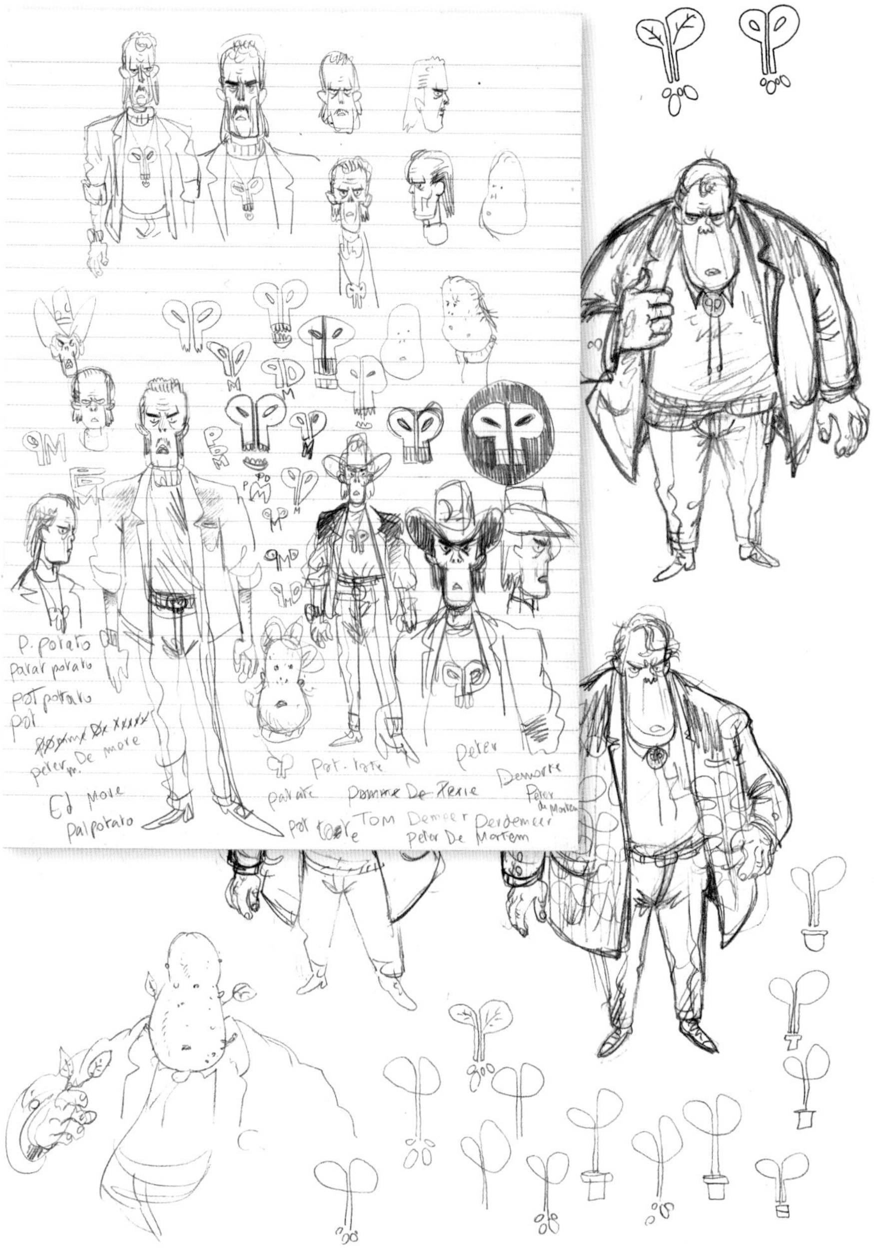
P. potato
pot
peter De more
Ed move
palpotato
Pot-tate
Pomme De Perre
peter
Demorre
Peter de Mortem
TOM Demeer
Perdemeer
peter De Mortem

Tom de Perre went through many transformations before I arrived at his final appearance. Here are just a few of the many sketches I did for this character. You can also see some of my sketches for the logo of his company, Project Potato: a stylized potato plant that transformed into a skull once he got his hands on it.

Before *Chef Yasmina and the Potato Panic*, I made a graphic novel about Weegee, an American photographer who worked in New York in the 1940s. With Yasmina, I wanted to stay away from the archives and find inspiration closer at home. I live in a very culturally diverse neighborhood in Brussels with beautiful houses from the early twentieth century. You can find this building around the corner from where I live. It houses a small Russian grocery store of some kind.

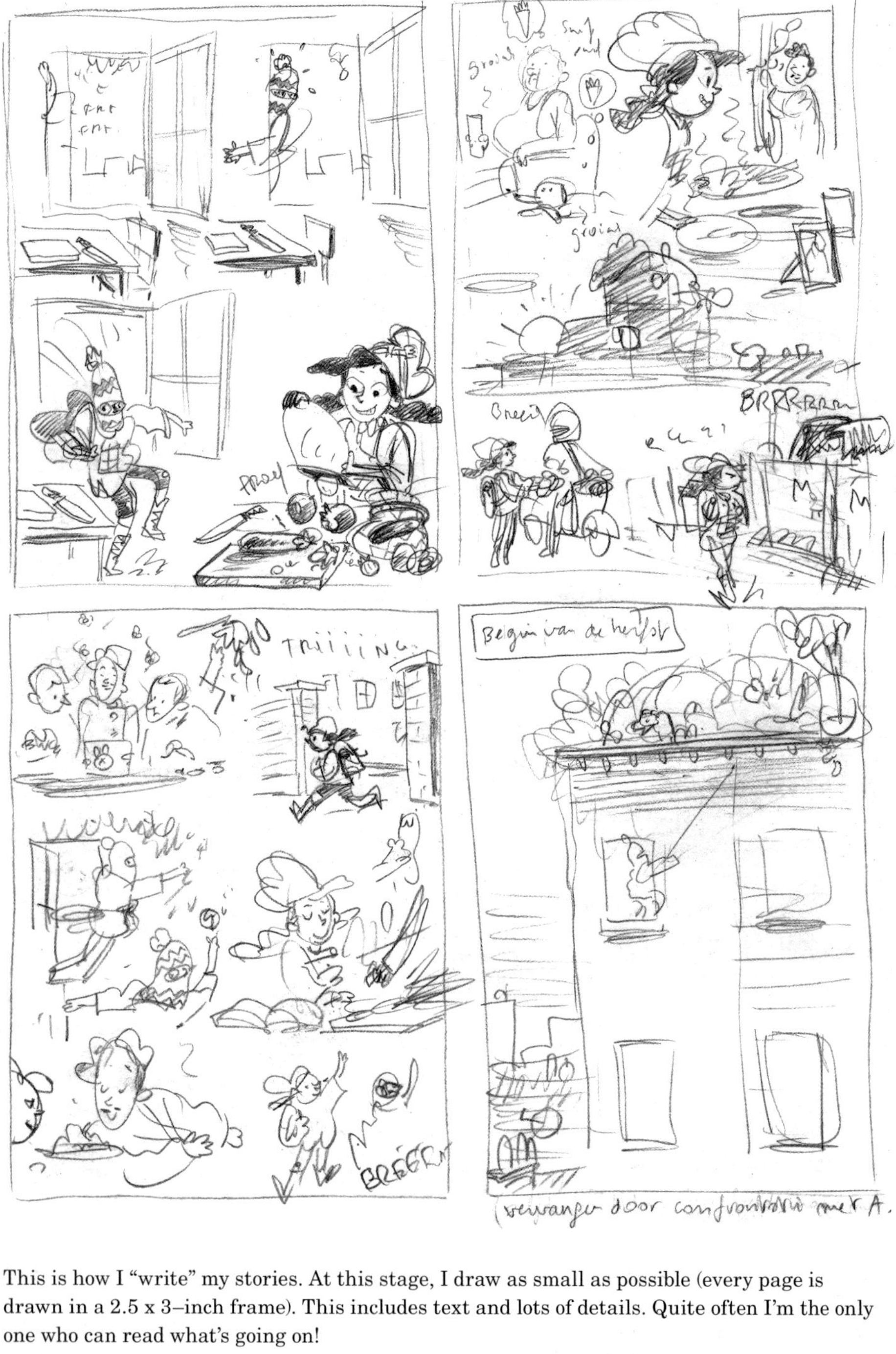
TRIIIING
Begin van de herfst

This is how I "write" my stories. At this stage, I draw as small as possible (every page is drawn in a 2.5 x 3–inch frame). This includes text and lots of details. Quite often I'm the only one who can read what's going on!

Chef Yasmina and the Potato Panic was my first comic in color (up until then I always worked in black and white). It quickly became clear watercolor wasn't the right medium for this book. This is the drawing where I first found a coloring technique I was happy with: a mixture of digital colors and brush pen (the blue shadows are the brush pen). It's fun to do and fits my sketchy drawing style.

First Second

English translation copyright © 2019 by Dargaud Benelux (Dargaud-Lombard S.A.)

Published by First Second
First Second is an imprint of Roaring Brook Press,
a division of Holtzbrinck Publishing Holdings Limited Partnership
120 Broadway, New York, NY 10271

Don't miss your next favorite book from First Second!
For the latest updates go to firstsecondnewsletter.com and sign up for our enewsletter.

Library of Congress Control Number: 2020911190
Paperback ISBN: 978-1-250-62205-1
Hardcover ISBN: 978-1-250-62204-4

Our books may be purchased in bulk for promotional, educational, or business use.
Please contact your local bookseller or the Macmillan Corporate and Premium Sales Department
at (800) 221-7945 ext. 5442 or by email at MacmillanSpecialMarkets@macmillan.com.

American edition edited by Robyn Chapman
English translation by Montana Kane
Cover design by Kirk Benshoff
Interior design by Molly Johanson
Printed in China by Toppan Leefung Printing Ltd., Dongguan City, Guangdong Province

Originally written in Dutch and translated to French by Laurent Bayer
Originally published in 2019 in French by Dargaud as *Yasmina et les mangeurs de patates*
Previously published in 2019 by Europe Comics as two English e-books titled
Yasmina and the Potato Eaters: Part 1 and *Yasmina and the Potato Eaters: Part 2*
Text and illustrations by Wauter Mannaert copyright © 2019 by Dargaud Benelux
(Dargaud-Lombard S.A.)–Mannaert

FIRST
EDITION

First American edition, 2021

Paperback: 10 9 8 7 6 5 4 3 2 1
Hardcover: 10 9 8 7 6 5 4 3 2 1